THE DOLPHINS
OF PERN

THE DRAGONRIDERS OF PERN®

*The author respectfully suggests that books
in the Pern series be read in the order
in which they were published,
which is:*

Dragonflight* Dragonsong
Dragonquest* Dragonsinger
The White Dragon* Dragondrums

Moreta: Dragonlady of Pern*

Nerilka's Story*

Dragonsdawn*

The Renegades of Pern*

The Chronicles of Pern: First Fall*

All the Weyrs of Pern*

The Dolphins of Pern*

The Atlas of Pern by Karen Wynn Fonstadt
and The Dragonlover's Guide to Pern by
Jody Lynn Nye with Anne McCaffrey*
both provide additional interesting information
as companion texts to the main novels.*

*Available from Ballantine Books

THE DOLPHINS OF PERN

ANNE McCAFFREY

A Del Rey® Book

BALLANTINE BOOKS ▶ NEW YORK

A Del Rey® Book
Published by Ballantine Books

Copyright © 1994 by Anne McCaffrey

Library of Congress Cataloging-in-Publication Data
McCaffrey, Anne.
The dolphins of Pern / Anne McCaffrey.
p. cm.
"A Del Rey book."
ISBN 0-345-36894-0
1. Pern (Imaginary place)—Fiction. 2. Dolphins—Fiction. I. Title.
PS3563.A255D65 1994
813'.54—dc20   94-15570
CIP

Map courtesy of Christine Levis

Manufactured in the United States of America

First Edition: October 1994

10 9 8 7 6 5 4 3 2 1

To my granddaughter
ELIZA ORIANA JOHNSON,
a princess-in-waiting

ACKNOWLEDGMENTS

Again I wish to acknowledge the help of Dr. Jack Cohen in keeping me on the straight and not so narrow path of Newtonian physics and common Terran biology, plus inventing whatever Pernese biology has been required.

I would also like to thank Rick Hobson of the Whale Conservation Institute in Lincoln, Mass., for his review of the material dealing with dolphins and delphinic behavior. It was through Rick Hobson that my daughter and I met and swam with Aphrodite and her son, AJ, at the Dolphin Research Center at Grassy Key, Florida. It was an experience that I shall treasure as I will the "visit" we made, to sit on the float and watch Dart, Little Bit, and other dolphins playing in sunset waters and "talking" to us.

Those who have had the privilege of swimming at the Dolphin Research Center will recognize many of the names I have used. Well, why not? I met and valued their acknowledgment of me, a human. They meet many of us, and forget. But I do not forget *them*!

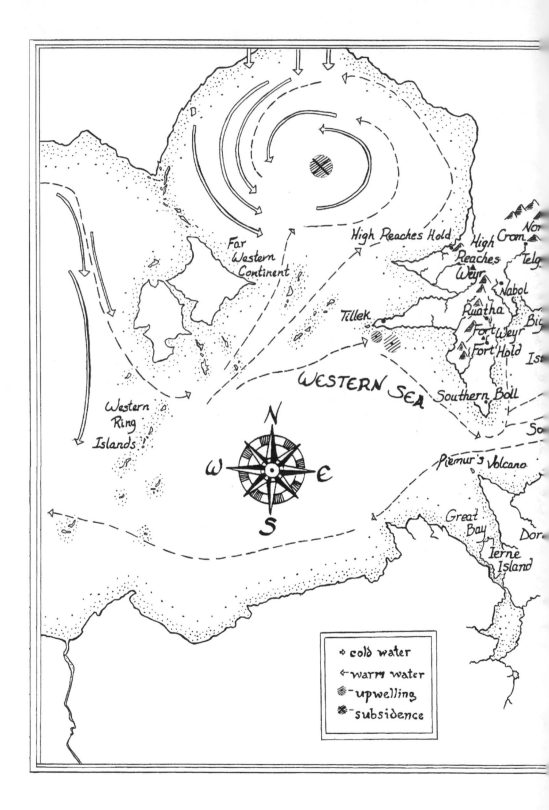

WESTERN SEA

Far
Western
Continent

High Reaches Hold   High   Crom   Nor
                       Reaches   Telg
                       Weyr
                              Nabol
Tillek   Ruatha   Bi
                    Fort Weyr
                    Fort Hold   Ist

                    Southern Boll
Western   So
Ring
Islands   Piemur's Volcano

                              Great
                              Bay   Dor
                                 Ierne
                                 Island

cold water
warm water
-upwelling
-subsidence

NINTH PASS PERN

Range
r Weyr
Lamos · Benden Weyr
· Bitra
an
Weyr · Benden Hold
en · Red Butte
old · Keroon · Half-Circle
old · Nerat

EASTERN
SEA

Eastern
Ring
Islands

SOUTHERN
SEA

thern
Hold

ord R.
hessoly

e's
Cathay
Black Rock
Rubicon R.
Dolphin
Hall
Caspian
Lake
· Xanadu
Barrier Range
Eastern
Range
Paradise
River
Hold
Paradise
Jordan R.
Cove
Paradise
Eastern Weyr
Monaco
Bay
Landing
Cardiff

Christine Levis

THE DOLPHINS
OF PERN

PROLOGUE

▼▼▼▼▼▼▼▼▼▼▼▼▼▼▼▼▼▼▼▼▼▼▼▼▼▼▼

102 YEARS AFTER LANDING

K ibbe gave the bell rope one last pull. He and Corey had been taking turns all morning, but now the sun was descending over the high ground and still no one answered them. Usually someone came out of Man's place on the dock, even if only one of the boat people. But the boats rocked at anchor under the high wharf, and it was obvious that no one had gone out in them, even to bring in fish, for some time.

Corey clicked at him in disgust. The others of their pod had long gone fishing on their own, too bored to see if there might be humans to feed them when there were plenty of small fish to be gleaned at this time of year from the rich northern waters. She "blew" her hunger at him, so annoyed with the lack of human attention that she refused to Speak.

"There has been illness. Ben told us that," Kibbe re-minded her.

"He was not well," Corey replied, reluctantly em-ploying Speech to impart the concept. "Humans can die."

"They do. It is true." Pod Leader, and one of the oldest in their pod, Kibbe had had two dolphineers as partners. He still fondly remembered Amy, his first one. She had been as much fish as he, even if she had to wear the long-feet and had no fins. She had given the best chin scratches and knew exactly where she had to slough off old skin. When he had been injured, she had stayed in the water by his cradle through the days and nights until she knew that he would recover. He would never have survived that long gash if she hadn't sewn it up and given him the hu-man medicines that prevented infection.

Corey had had only one person, and she hadn't seen him in a long time. That accounted for why she was so skeptical. She hadn't had the long association with hu-mans that Kibbe had enjoyed. He missed it. They had worked well together; and there were still many long stretches of coastline to be mapped, and the locations of fishing schools to be determined. The work had seemed more like fun, and there had always been time for games. Lately all he had been able to do to keep the Dolphin Con-tract with men was to follow the ships, to be sure no one fell overboard without a dolphin to assist his rescue. He wasn't even sure if his warnings about imminent storms were heeded: humans sometimes disregarded advice, es-pecially if the fish were running well.

Kibbe was one of those who had been chosen to serve time up near the northwestern subsidence, where lived the Tillek, chosen of all the pods for her wisdom. The name given the pod leader was also traditional. He had been taught, as had other dolphin instructors, why dolphins had followed humans to this world, far from the waters of Earth, where they had evolved: the chance to inhabit clean waters of an unpolluted world and live as dolphins had before tech-nol-ogy (he had learned to pronounce that word very carefully) had spoiled the Old Oceans of humankind. He knew, and taught this despite the astonishment it caused, that dolphins had once walked on land. That was why they were air breathers and were required by Nature to surface to inhale oxygen. He listened to tales so old not even those who had taught the Tillek knew their origins: that dolphins had been special messengers of the gods, escorting those buried at sea to their special "underworld" place. As dolphins considered the seas to be underworld, this caused some confusion. The humankind underworld was where "souls" went—whatever "souls" were.

One of Kibbe's favorite tales was the one the Tillek recounted with great pride: how dolphinkind had once honored those who had died when one of the spaceships had been wrecked in the sea-sky. Since then, the dolphins of Pern had honored those burial rites with their escort. It was a ceremony the humans had not asked the dolphins to include in their traditions, but they always seemed grateful for it.

Learning the names of the dolphins who had slept the Great Sleep and accompanied humankind to these clean new seas of Pern was an important lesson. From these names came the ones chosen for the new calves, to celebrate those first dolphins and those that were born in the Years Before Thread. The names had been set to dolphin music and could be sung on longer journeys in the Great Currents; the name song was always sung before the young dolphins attempted to cross the great whirlpool at the northwestern subsidence, or even the smaller one in the Eastern Sea.

There were some matters taught by the Tillek that had to be learned simply because they mattered as details to the whole story. The Great Sleep, for instance, puzzled even the cleverest calf, male or female, because dolphins did not require sleep. To have slept for fifteen years was an incredible thing. Although they knew to call the sparkling light points in the skies "stars," there seemed to be a very great many of them, and the Tillek could not tell them which had been Old Earth. Humans had had a device that allowed them to see longer, but because stars were in the air, dolphins could not sound them. There were three points of light, at dawn, and again at twilight, which were constant. The Tillek said those points were the spaceships that had brought humankind and dolphinkind to Pern. They must take this on faith, she said, for she had had to learn these facts from the Tillek who had taught *her*. This was fact as well as faith and must be believed, though never experienced. It was History.

And History was another of the Great Gifts humankind had given dolphinkind. History was memory of things past. For the sake of History, dolphinkind had been given the Greatest Gift: the ability to speak. For with the Greatest Gift they could repeat the words of History: words that were sounded as humankind sounded speech, not as dolphins did. And they could speak to humans and to themselves the things that were made of words and not sea sounds.

Kibbe had been very good at learning all the words that humans had used with dolphins, and all their special underwater signals. He was good at singing the words, too, so that the young ones of his pod were familiar with them should they be chosen to go to the waters of the Tillek and complete their training. Kibbe knew the traditions by which humans and dolphins lived in a special relationship: Dolphins would protect humans on or in the water to the best of their abilities, in whatever weather and unsafe conditions, even to the giving up of dolphin life to save the frailer humans; they would apprise humans of bad weather conditions, show them where the schools of preferred fish were running, and warn them off sea hazards. The humans promised, in return for these services, to remove any bloodfish that might attach themselves to dolphin bodies, to float any stranded dolphin, to heal the sick and treat the wounded, to talk to them and to be partners if the dolphin was willing.

In the early days on Pern, humans and dolphins had taken great pleasure in exploring the new seas, and those had been momentous years: the years of the life of the human Tillek whom all had revered. A dolphins' bell had been sited at Monaco Bay, and land and sea beings had promised to answer the bell whenever it was rung. In those days the young dolphins had each had a human partner, to help with the exploration, to explore the seas and the deep abysses and the Great Currents, the Two Subsidences, Greater and Smaller, and the Four Upwellings. There had been courtesy, each to the other, land- and seafaring humans.

The Tillek always spoke respectfully of humans, and severely disciplined any calf who used the term "long-foot" or "finless." When the silly fins complained that humans no longer kept their end of the ancient agreement, the Tillek would tell them, at her sternest, that that did not absolve dolphinkind from practicing theirs. Humankind had had to stop exploring Pern in order to guard the lands against the Thread.

This would set the silliest to clicking nonsense noises of amusement. Why didn't humans eat Thread the way dolphins did?

The Tillek's reply was that humans had to live on land, where Thread did not drown but attacked human flesh like bloodfish, sucking the life out of it. And not over a long period of time but immediately, so that all life was gone from the body in the course of several breaths—indeed, the flesh of the human body was completely consumed.

This was another matter that all dolphins must believe as surely as they believed Thread was good to eat.

Then the Tillek would speak History and tell of the Day Thread Fell on Pern, and how it fed on the flesh of humans. How the humans had battled hard with flame—a source of heat and light that coastal dolphins could recognize but had never felt—to burn Thread in the skies before it could fall on land and eat it, or on humans and humans' animals and eat them. When all the things that humans had brought with them from Old Earth had been used up, the dolphins had helped the humans sail the many ships of the Dunkirk to the north where they could shelter in great caves, forsaking the pleasant warm southern waters. Kibbe had always loved hearing how the dolphins had helped the small ships make the long journey, despite storms and having to cross the Great Currents. There had been a dolphins' bell at Fort, too, and there had been many good years of partnership for dolphins and partners. Until the Sickness.

Kibbe knew that all humans had not died: ships still sailed with human crews, and on land, people could be seen working—when it was not the Time of Thread.

Since Kibbe had had a partner, he knew of humans and their frailties and their skill at relieving the few illnesses to which dolphins were prone. But the young in his pod did not and questioned why dolphins should bother.

"It is tradition. We have always done as we do now. We will always obey the traditions."

"Why do humans *want* to come into water? They cannot surrender themselves to the currents as we can."

"Once humans swam as well as dolphins," Kibbe would reply.

"But then we cannot walk on the land," the calves would say. "Why would we *want* to?"

"We are of different flesh, with different needs: dolphins to the water, humankind to the land. Each to his own ways."

"Why do humans not stay on land and leave the water for us?"

"They need the fish in the seas, as we do," Kibbe would tell them. One had to tell the young the same words many times before they understood. "They need to travel to other land places, and the only way is by water."

"They have dragons who fly."

"Not everyone has dragons to fly."

"Do dragons like us?"

"I believe they do, though lately we have seen few of them. Once, I was told, they would swim in the sea with us."

"How can they swim with those great wings?"

"They fold them to their backs."

"Odd creatures."

"Many creatures of the land look odd to us," Kibbe would say, undulating through the water gracefully and effortlessly beside the calves he was teaching.

Kibbe privately thought that humans were clumsy, awkward creatures, in the water or out. They were, however, slightly more graceful in the water, especially if they swam as dolphins did, by keeping their legs together. The way some of them thrashed about with their limbs moving separately wasted much energy.

Nowadays, humans did not follow the forms laid down by the ancestors of both species. Very few captains leaned over the side of their ship when dolphins appeared to accompany it and asked how the pod was faring and how the schools were running. Very few would give their escort a token fish for the assistance. Of course, it had been many seasons since dolphins had found and brought any drowned human boxes to their attention. As it had been many seasons since dolphineers had swum long distances with their partners. Sad the way tradition declined, Kibbe thought. Like not answering the bell.

He made one last pass in front of the wharf, eyeing the deserted structure. He tolled the bell one last time, thinking it sounded as mournful as he felt for the silence that had once been filled with human noises, the fine work they had done together, and the games they had played.

With a final flip of his tail, he turned and started his long journey to the Great Subsidence in the Northwest Sea to inform the Tillek that, once again, no one had answered the bell. The humans who sailed in the ships would not learn of the latest hazards the dolphins had dutifully come to report. Even the waters of Pern changed the land of Pern, but that was the natural way of things. Or so the Tillek said. The dolphins would keep to their patrols of the coastline, and when, if ever, a human listened to them, at least they could tell him what had changed, and save his ship from being broken on unexpected reefs or rocks; or warn him of where the Currents had altered and might be a hazard to the ships and the humans who sailed on them.

1

When Masterfisher Alemi came by Readis's hold that morning, he found his fishing crony ready and waiting.

"I thought you'd never come, Uncle Alemi," Readis said in a tone that was a thin line away from accusatory.

"He's been on the porch," Aramina told Alemi with a solemn, hiding-a-smile face, "for the last hour. He was up in dawn's dark!" And she rolled her eyes at such eager anticipation.

"Uncle Alemi says the fish bite best at dawn," Readis informed his mother condescendingly as he jumped down the three steps to take a firm hold of the callused hand of his courtesy uncle.

"I don't know which excited him more: fishing with you, or being allowed to attend Swacky's Gather this evening." Then she waggled a finger at her small son. "Remember, you have to take a nap this afternoon."

"I'm all ready to go fishing *now*," Readis said, ignoring the threat. "I got my snack"—he brandished the net sack laden with his water bottle and wrapped sandwich—"and my vest." The last was added somewhat contemptuously.

"You will note that I'm wearing mine, too," Alemi said, giving the trusting little paw a shake.

Aramina chuckled. "That's the only reason he's wearing his."

"I swim good!" Readis announced in a strong, loud voice. "I swim as good as any ship fish!"

"That you do," his mother agreed equably.

"Don't I know that as taught you?" Alemi replied cheerfully. "And *I* can swim that much better and still use a vest in a small boat."

"An' in stormy weather," Readis added to prove that he knew the whole lesson on safety vests. "My mother made mine," he said proudly, puffing out his vested chest and grinning up at her. "With love in every stitch!"

"C'mon, lad, time's a-wasting," Alemi said.

With a farewell wave of his free hand to Aramina, he led his small charge down to the beach and the slab-sided dinghy that would convey them out to where Alemi felt they would likely find the big redfins that were promised for grilling at Swacky's evening's festivities.

Swacky had been part of Readis's life since he could remember. The stocky ex-soldier had joined Jayge and Aramina when Aunt Temma and Uncle Nazer had come from the north. He lived in one of the smaller holds and turned his hand to any one of a number of chores necessary in Paradise River Hold. Swacky had guard stories of all the Holds he'd served in to tell a small and fascinated boy. Readis's father, Jayge, never talked of the renegade problem, which had drawn him and Swacky together. And Swacky, though he was fierce and unforgiving of the renegades for "slaughtering innocent folk and animals just to see their blood run," never mentioned exactly what Jayge had done in those days, except to let on that it had to do with the particular renegades who had attacked the Lilcamp wagon train, which was Jayge's family business.

If Readis had been asked which man he loved best—apart from his father, of course—Swacky or Alemi, he would have been hard-pressed to make a choice.

Both men figured largely in his young life, but for different reasons. Today Readis was going to have the best of both: fishing in the morning with Alemi, and feasting in the evening to honor Swacky's seventy-five Turns of living!

Pushing together, they eased the skiff down the sandy shore and into the gently lapping water. When they had waded out until the water was mid-thigh on Readis, Alemi gestured for him to jump in and take up the paddle. That was the main difference between Readis's two idols: Swacky talked a lot; Alemi used gestures where the other man would have used sentences.

With one mighty last push, Alemi sent the skiff forward over the first of the little combers and jumped in. At another familiar gesture, Readis moved to the stern and sculled his paddle to keep the forward movement while Alemi unfurled the sail and let the boom run out. The inland dawn breeze filled the canvas, and Readis stowed the paddle and reached for the keel board, sending it home into the stern slot and shoving the cotter pin through to lock it firmly in place.

"Hard a-port," Alemi sang out, accompanying his command with appropriate gestures. As the boom swung over he ducked agilely, playing out the lines until he had moved into the seat beside his shipmate. He shortened sail and then put his free arm behind Readis, noting the lad's instinctive handling of the rudder.

Alemi's good wife had given him three fine girl children and was carrying a fourth child, which both devoutly hoped would be a son. But until that time, Alemi "practiced" with Readis. Jayge approved, since it would stand a shoreside holder in good stead to appreciate the moods and bounty of the sea, and Readis would profit by knowing more than one skill.

Alemi sniffed at the offshore breeze, redolent of vegetation and exotic blossoms. He judged that the wind would turn once they got out beyond the Paradise River channel. He didn't intend to sail far from land, but on the landside of the Great Southern Current, they were sure to find the redfins that frequented this part of the sea in great schools. Yesterday, Alemi had sent out the two smaller ships of his little fleet to meet those schools. As soon as the repairs to his bigger yawl had been completed, he and his crew would join them. Alemi was just as pleased to be on shore for Swacky's Gather. He might miss a day's fishing, but until the mains'l had been mended, he was shorebound.

As they hit the rip at the channel mouth, the little skiff bucked and bounced. Readis's merry laugh burbled out of him, as he delighted in the dipping and dumping. Not much phased the lad, and he'd never fed the fishes once. Which was more than could be said for some grown men.

Then Alemi caught the sparkle and shine on the surface and, touching Readis's shoulder, pointed. The boy leaned against him and cast his eye along the extended arm, nodding excitedly as he, too, saw the school: so many fish trying to occupy the same space that they seemed to be flippering on each other's backs.

In a single-minded action, both reached for the rods that had been stowed under the gunnels. These were sturdy rods of the finest bambu, with reels of the stoutest tight-stranded line, and hooks hand-fashioned by the Hold's Smithjourneyman, barbed to hold once sunk in the jaw of the wiliest redfin.

Twelve redfins the length of a grown man's arm were required for the evening's feasting. There would be roast wherry and succulent herdbeast, but redfin was Swacky's favorite. He'd wanted to come along, Swacky had told Readis the night before, but he had to stay about and organize his Gather, or no one would do it the way he wanted.

Alemi let Readis bait his own hook with the innards of the shellfish redfins loved best. The boy's tongue stuck out the side of his mouth as he manipulated the slimy mess securely onto the hook. He looked up at Alemi and saw the nod of approval. Then, with a deft cast for a boy his age, he sent the weighted hook, bait still attached, out across the starboard wake of the skiff. To give the boy a chance to make the first catch of the day, Alemi busied himself furling the sail and performing other chores. Then he, too, hunkered down in the cockpit, bracing his rod on the port side.

They didn't have long to wait for a bite. Readis was first. The rod bent, its tip almost touching the choppy waves as the redfin fought its ensnarement. Readis, biting his lip, his eyes bugged out with determination, set both feet on the seat and hung on to his rod. Grunts came out of him as he struggled to reel in this monster. Alemi had one hand, out of the boy's line of sight, ready to grab the rod should the fish prove too strong.

Readis was panting with effort by the time the equally exhausted redfin was flapping feebly at the starboard side.

With one deft swoop, Alemi netted it and hauled it aboard; Readis whooped with glee as he saw the size of it.

"That's the biggest one yet, isn't it, Uncle Alemi? That's the biggest one I've caught. Isn't it? A real good big 'un!"

"Indeed it is," Alemi replied stoutly. The fish was not as long as his forearm, but it was a good prize for the boy.

Just then his line tugged.

"You gotta bite, too. You gotta bite!"

"That I do. So you'll have to attend to this one yourself."

Alemi was amazed at the pull of his hooked fish. He had to exert considerable force to keep the rod from being pulled out of his hand. For a startled moment, he wondered if he had inadvertently hooked a shipfish, something no fishman in his right mind ever did. He was immensely relieved as he saw the red fins of his captive as the fish writhed above the surface in an attempt to loosen the barb in its mouth.

"That's ginormous!" Readis cried, and looked up in awe at the Masterfishman.

"It's a big 'un all right," Alemi said, jamming his feet under the cockpit seat to get more leverage against the pull.

"And it's dragging the skiff!"

That, too, was obvious to Alemi: it was dragging them toward the edge of the Great Southern Current. He could even discern the difference in color between current and sea.

"And we're right in the middle of the school!" Readis cried, lurching from port to starboard to look down at the darting bodies that surrounded the little ship.

"Best knock your catch on the head before it flips overboard," Alemi said, noting the flapping of the landed fish and not wanting its oil to coat the deck. He managed to reel in a good length, though the tip of his rod went briefly underwater. He hauled mightily and got enough play in the line to reel in again.

"That is the fightingest fish you've ever hooked," Readis said. He'd knocked his redfin smartly on the head and tossed it in the catch tank, remembering to fasten the lid with a deft turn of the fastener.

One eye on the drift toward the Great Current, Alemi hurried the process of reeling the redfin in, Readis cheering him along with reports of the immense size of the fish.

"Get ready with the net, boy!" Alemi called as he maneuvered his catch close to the port side of the skiff.

Readis was ready, but the struggling fish was too much for his young arms, and Alemi flung the rod aside to help. The moment they got the fish aboard, Alemi clouted it on the head, then stepped over it to get to the tiller and alter their course away from the Southern Current. They were close enough for him to see the rapid stream making its inexorable way through waters crowded with fish.

"Wheee, look at that, Unclemi!" Readis cried, pointing a blood-smeared finger at the school of redfin. "Can't we fish here?"

"Not in the Current, boy, not unless you want to take a much longer voyage and miss tonight's Gather."

"I don't want to do tha . . ." Readis's eyes widened and his mouth gaped as he looked astern. "O-oh!"

Alemi craned his head over his shoulder and caught his breath. Boiling up behind them, and far too close for them to reach the safety of the river mouth, was one of the black squalls that this part of the coast was famous for: squalls that defied even his well-honed seaman's instinct for storm. A powerful gust of wind smacked into his face and made his eyes water. Even as he moved to secure the boom, gesturing for Readis to perform the emergency tasks drilled into him for just such a situation, Alemi cursed the freak weather, which gave none of the warnings he was used to noting in the Nerat Bay waters where he had been trained.

His father, Yanus, had often berated the folly of men who insisted on sailing the Great Currents when there were quieter waters that held just as many fish but without the hazards. Alemi, rather liking hazards, had never agreed with his father on that score—among others.

Now he gave a brief tug at the ties of Readis's vest, grinned a reassurance, and then payed out the sea anchor.

"So what do fishmen do in a blow, Readis?" he shouted above the rising wind that whipped the words from his mouth.

"Sail into it! Or run with it!" Readis was grinning with all the impudent confidence of his age. He leaned into the arm Alemi put around him as they braced themselves in the cockpit. "Which do we do now?"

"Run!" Alemi said, adjusting his course to the gusty pressure against the back of his head and keeping the bow in line with the wave pattern.

This dinghy was a frail craft in the high seas that a sudden squall like this could churn up. Devoutly Alemi hoped this would be a short blow. One large roller athwart the dinghy and they'd be swamped.

The shoreline had disappeared in the blackness of the encompassing storm, but that didn't worry Alemi as much as getting caught in the Great Southern Current, which could take them dangerously far from land or ram them, all unseeing, into the headland above Paradise River Cove. Hauling the tiller over as far as he dared, he hoped the wind would blow them to starboard, away from the Current and toward land. But winds were as capricious as these seas. He *had* checked the barometer—one

ANNE McCAFFREY

of the new tools that Aivas had supplied as a weather aid. Knowing himself more attuned to Nerat Bay's more pacific waters, Alemi had availed himself of the device despite the scoffing of other fishmen. He had also studied the weather charts and such information about these waters as the Ancients had amassed in Aivas's seemingly inexhaustible "files." Anything that would aid the crafthold and prevent loss of life and ship was not too bizarre to be tested by Alemi.

But the barometer had been steady on Fair when he had left to collect Readis. Too late to worry about that now, he thought as the skiff was bashed sideways by a white cap. It then dropped down a huge trough, sinking his stomach on the way. Beside him, Readis laughed, even as he tightened his hands on the gunnel beside him. Alemi managed to grin encouragingly down at his brave shipmate.

On the upsurge, the wave seized the small boat and heaved it high on the next crest, then smashed it down again so that water walled them into a dark green pocket, the sea anchor trailing in the air behind them. The skiff lurched, its prow digging into the ascending sea cliff. They took on water and, when Readis would have dutifully reached for the bailing bucket, Alemi tightened his hold on him, shaking his head. The skiff could take on a good deal of water—which would make her somewhat heavier in the seas, all to the good—before she was in danger of sinking. He feared capsizing more. He was glad that he had drilled Readis on how to cope with an overturn. Now he had all he could do to hang on, for a cross rip of surging waves battered the skiff from side to side, as well as up and down. He clung, one hand to the ship and one on Readis, and prayed for the end of the squall. Storms like this one could stop almost as abruptly as they began. That would be their only hope now: a quick end to the blow.

He saw the mast splinter and break, felt Readis's tightened grip, and then abruptly they were upended as the cross waves slammed into the starboard side and decanted them into the roiled sea. His grip on Readis tightened, pulling the boy close in to his chest. Over the scream of the storm he heard the boy's startled, frightened cry. Then they were being milled in the waters, Readis clinging to him like a gray limpet.

Alemi flailed his free arm, trying to reach the surface again. He managed to grab a breath just as another wave pushed them down. Readis struggled in his arms, and all he could do was tighten his grip. He mustn't lose the boy. Then his scooping hand came hard against something. The upturned skiff? He clutched at a roundness that was not wooden, but firm and fleshed.

Shipfish? Shipfish! Through the driving rain and wash of seawater, he could see shapes all around them. How often they were said to rescue fishermen!

The hard edge of a dorsal fin filled his hand, and his body was swung against its long sleek shape just as another wave crashed over him. No, the shipfish was angling its agile body right *through* the wave and out the other side. Readis's small body was on the outside, victim to the pull of the harsh waves. Hanging on, Alemi somehow shoved Readis to his side, against the shipfish. In between the sheets of water that covered them, he saw Readis's hands trying to find some purchase on the sleek, slippery body.

"*Shipfish, Readis!*" he shouted above the tumult of the storm winds. "*They'll save us! Hang on!*"

Then he felt another body nudge into him on the other side, wedging him and Readis even tighter, though how the creatures managed that feat in such rough water he didn't know. But the additional support allowed him some respite; he reset his hand on the dorsal fin and even managed to work one of Readis's small hands onto the sturdy edge.

Then it occurred to Alemi, as they passed through yet another wall of water, that Readis was small enough to *ride* on the shipfish's back. It took three more waves before Alemi had hoisted Readis astride the shipfish. To his immense surprise, the shipfish seemed to be helping by maintaining as straight a line through the plunging seas as it could.

"Hold on! Hold on tight!" Alemi cried, firmly wrapping Readis's small arms around the fin. The boy, his face a scared white but his mouth set in a determined line, nodded and half crouched behind the fin, like the rider of a sea dragon.

A surge of relief caused Alemi to momentarily loosen his grip on the top of the fin, and he floundered about. Almost immediately, a blunt nose bumped him authoritatively, and the next thing he knew a dorsal fin was nudging his right hand. A wave crashed down on him, tumbling him in the water, away from the safety, and he had to fight his panic. But the shipfish was right beside him, pushing him upward with its snout. They both broke the surface together and Alemi thrashed toward the creature, grabbing the dorsal with both hands, only to be thrown sideways against the long body by the next whitecap. This time he managed to retain a grip with one hand. He fought the panic that wanted both hands on this one source of stability offered in the stormy sea and, relaxing into the movement, found the courage to surrender to the shipfish. As they dipped and plunged through the next wave, he saw Readis, crouching over his mount's back. He saw the phalanx of escort on either side and knew that their protection was solid.

Then it seemed as if the squall was lessening, or perhaps they had been conveyed to its fringes where the water was calmer. Either way, their passage improved. Looking in the direction he thought land should be, he saw the smudge of the shoreline and almost cried with relief.

"Wheeeeee!"

Startled by that cry, Alemi turned as he saw a shipfish launch itself above the waves in a graceful arc and reenter the water. Others began the same antic, all wheeing or squeeing.

"Wheee!" cried an unmistakably boyish voice, and Alemi looked over his left shoulder to see Readis, now sitting up straighter on his shipfish, grinning with delight at the exhibition. "That's great!" the boy added. "Aren't they great, Alemi?"

"Grrrreat!" But it was a shipfish who repeated the word, spinning the *r* out.

On all sides, shipfish were crying "Great!" as they continued their leisurely vaultings in and out of the sea. Alemi convulsively tightened his grip on the dorsal fin. He couldn't believe what he was hearing. The stress of the storm, perhaps a blow to his head, or plain fear, had addled his faculties. His companion raised its head and, water shooting up out of the blowhole in the top of its cranium, clearly said, "Thass great!"

"They're talking, Unclemi, they're talking."

"How could they, Readis? They're fish!"

"Not fish! Mam'l." His rescuer got out the three words in a loud and contradictory tone. "Doll-fins," it added clearly, and Alemi shook his head. "Doll-fins speak good." As if to emphasize this, it began to speed forward, hauling the dazed Masterfisher along at a spanking pace.

Readis's doll-fin and the guardian companions altered their course, too, and picked up speed, the flankers still performing their acrobatic above-the-water spins, vaults, and turns.

"Talk some more, will you?" Readis encouraged in his high-pitched young voice. This was going to make some Gather tale. And they'd have to believe what he said because Unclemi was here with him to vouch that what he said was true.

"Talk? You talk. Long tayme no talk," a doll-fin swimming alongside Readis said very clearly. "Men back Landing? Doll-fin ears back?"

"Landing?" Alemi repeated, stunned. The doll-fins *knew* the ancient name? Wonder upon wonder.

"Men *are* back at Landing," Readis said quite proudly, as if he had been instrumental in their return.

"Good!" cried one doll-fin as it executed a twist in mid-air, knifing back into the water without splashing.

"Squeeeeee!" another cried as it vaulted upward.

In the water all around him, Alemi heard excited clickings and clatterings. The area seemed so full of shipfish bodies that he wondered how they could move without injuring each other.

"Look, Unclemi, we're nearly back!" Readis said, jabbing his finger at the fast-approaching land.

They had been conveyed so rapidly and smoothly that Alemi struggled between relief that they were so close to dry land and regret that this incredible journey was ending. The forward motion of the shipfish slowed as they came to the first of the sandbanks. Some leaped over it, others followed Readis's and Alemi's mounts to the channel, while the majority altered their direction seaward again.

Moments later the smooth transport came to a complete halt and, tentatively lowering his feet, Alemi felt the firmness of the seabed, gradually sloping up to the shore. He released the dorsal fin and slapped the side of his mount, which turned and rubbed its nose against him, as if inviting a caress. Bemused, Alemi scratched as he would his dog or the small felines who were beginning to invade the Hold. Readis's mount continued past him.

"Thanks, my friend. You saved our lives and we are grateful," Alemi said formally.

"Wielcame. Uur duty," the shipfish said clearly, and then, with a swirl, it propelled its body sinuously back out to the break in the sandbar, its fin traveling at ever-increasing speed as it rejoined its fellows.

"Hey!" Readis cried on a note of alarm. His mount had unceremoniously dumped him in shallows where, if he stood on tiptoe, he could just keep his chin out of water.

"Thank the doll-fin," Alemi called, wading as fast as he could toward the boy. "Scratch its chin."

"Oh? You like that, huh?" Readis, treading water, managed to use both hands to scratch the face presented him. "Thank you very much indeed for saving my life and giving me that great swim ashore."

"Wielcame, bhoy!" Then the doll-fin executed an incredible leap over Readis's head and followed its podmate out to sea again.

"Come back. Come back soon," Readis called after it, raising himself up out of the water to project his invitation. A faint squeee answered him. "D'you think he heard me?" Readis asked Alemi plaintively.

"They seem to have very good hearing," Alemi remarked dryly. Then he gave Readis as inconspicuous an assist up out of the water as he could. The boy had been magnificent throughout. He must tell Jayge that. A father sometimes didn't see his son in the same light as an interested observer.

Tired as they were from the experience, the exhilaration

of their rescue provided enough energy for them both to reach the dry sand of the beach before they had to sit and rest.

"They won't believe us, will they, Unclemi?" Readis said with a weary sigh as he stretched full length on the warm beach.

"I'm not sure I believe us," Alemi said, mustering a smile as he collapsed beside the boy. "But the shipfish unquestionably rescued us. No mistake about that!"

"And the shipfish—whadidhe call himself—mam'l? He did talk to us. You heard him. Wielcame! Uur duty." And Readis made his voice squeakier in mimicry of the dollfin. "They even got manners."

"Remember that, Readis," Alemi said with a weak chuckle.

He knew he should get to his feet and go reassure Aramina that they'd survived the storm. Though, as he turned his head to look down the shoreline, he couldn't see a soul. Was it possible that no one on shore had noticed the sudden squall? That no one had even known they were in danger? Just as well not to unnecessarily mar what would still be a happy occasion in Swacky's nameday Gather.

"Unclemi?" There was a disturbed wail in Readis's voice. "We lost our redfins." Then the boy added hastily, to show he was aware of the priorities, "And the skiff, too."

"We have our lives, Readis, and we've a story to tell. Now, just get your breath a few more minutes."

A few more minutes became an hour before either stirred, for the warm sand had taken the last of the squall's chill from their bones, and the sea sounds and the light winds had combined with the fatigue of their recent labors to send them to sleep.

Except for the fact that Alemi was not given to fanciful tales, the rest of Paradise River Hold might not have believed the astounding tale the two of them told. By the next morning tide, however, pieces of the skiff were deposited on the beach.

By then everyone in Paradise River Hold knew the bare bones of their near-fatal fishing trip. No one on shore had noticed the squall, busy with their chores and getting ready for the evening Gather. Aramina had been in Temma's cothold, baking. She nearly fainted when Alemi informed her, as gently as possible, of the recent ordeal her son had come through so magnificently. Then she fussed so over Readis, who was trying to eat lunch because his had been lost at sea, that she looked hurt when he shrugged her attentions off so he could get on with filling his very empty stomach. She reprimanded him severely when he told her that shipfish talk.

"How can *fish* talk?" She glared at Alemi as if he had filled the boy's head with nonsense.

Before Alemi could support him, Readis gave his mother a very fierce scowl. "Dragons talk," he insisted.

"Dragons talk to their *riders*, not small boys."

"And you heard dragons, Mother," he protested boldly even though he knew she didn't like to be reminded. That made her pause so long that he wished the words back in his throat and chewed more slowly.

"Yes, I heard dragons, but I certainly have never heard shipfish!"

"Even when they rescued you and Da?"

"In the middle of a storm?" she asked skeptically.

"Mine didn't start talking until *after* the storm."

His mother glanced again at Alemi for confirmation.

"It is true, Aramina. They spoke."

"Their noises may have just *sounded* like words, Alemi," she tried to insist.

"Not when they said 'wielcame' after I said 'thank you,' " Readis went on hotly, and Alemi nodded vigorously under Aramina's outraged eyes. "And they know that the Ancients called the place Landing and they're mam'ls, not fish!"

"Of course they're fish!" Aramina blurted out. "They swim in the sea!"

"So do we and we're not fish!" Readis retorted in disgust with her disbelief, and stormed out of the room, refusing to return when she called him.

"Now see what you've done!" Aramina said to Alemi, and then she, too, left Temma's kitchen.

Alemi regarded the older woman blankly.

"If you say they spoke, 'Lemi, they spoke," the former trader said with a definitive nod of her head. Then she grinned at his confused expression. "Don't worry about Ara. She'll calm down, but you gotta admit you frightened the life out of her. And none of us here even knowing there'd been a bad squall. Here!" She handed him a cup of freshly brewed klah, to which she added a dollop of the special brew she kept for emergencies.

"Ha!" Alemi said, smacking his lips after a long swig. "I needed that!" He handed back the cup, with a quizzical expression.

"You don't need any more or you won't be able to regale the Gather tonight with your adventure," Temma said with a wink.

The pod swam back into their customary waters full of elation that they had once again saved landfolk. This was worth relay-

ing to the Tillek now, instead of waiting until the year turned and pods gathered at the Great Subsidence to watch the young males attempt the whirlpool and exchange the news each pod gathered in its waters. The southern pods did not have as many occasions as the northern ones did to perform traditional duties. So the sounds went out and were broadcast that Afo and Kib had played with mans lost at sea. It had been a great moment. For they had spoken to mans in Words and mans had spoken to them, using the ancient Words of Courtesy. So Kib rehearsed the tale, murmuring into the waters as he swam the Words of his Reporrit. He sent the sounds out to be repeated from pod to pod until they came to the hearing of the Tillek. Maybe this was the time that the Tilleks had promised would come: when mans once more remembered to speak to seafolk and became partners again.

The sounds traveled to the Tillek, who had them repeated from one end of the seas to the other, to all the pods in all the waters of Pern. There was envy at such good luck, and some even wished to join the fortunate pod. Afo, Kib, Mel, Temp, and Mul swam fast and proud, with great leaps. And Mel wondered if mans would still know how to get rid of bloodfish, for he had one sucking him that he could not seem to scrape off, no matter how he tried.

2
▼▼▼▼▼▼▼▼▼▼

Readis fell asleep that night some time after his third repetition of their adventure.

"He's got it down as pat as any harper," his father said with some chagrin.

"Just so long as you've made it *plain*," Aramina said, emphasizing the word "that he isn't to swim out or go sailing—"

"Skiff's gone, remember?" Jayge put in reassuringly.

"—to try and find those shipfish again," she finished, glaring at him.

"You heard him promise, 'Mina, that he wouldn't go too near the water without a companion. He's a child of his word, you know."

"Hmmm," Aramina said ominously.

But, as she kept strict track of her son's whereabouts for the next two days, he did not disobey, though she saw him often shielding his eyes from the sun, gazing out across the restless waters of the Southern Sea. Perversely now she worried that he had taken a fear of the sea. When she hesitantly mentioned this to her mate, Jayge stoutly denied there was a fearful bone in Readis's body.

"He's obeying—isn't that what you wanted of him?" Jayge demanded. "You can't have it both ways."

Aramina sighed and then was summoned out of her preoccupation over Readis by a loud cry of frustration from Aranya, who was having trouble with a toy cart that kept losing its wheel.

The next afternoon, while holders were taking their midday rest, avoiding the heat of the sun, Aramina received a polite message from Ruth that he and Lord Jaxom were visiting Paradise River. She told her husband. She was halfway to the kitchen to prepare the fruit juices that she knew Jaxom liked when she turned back, puzzled.

"They're already here at Paradise," she said. Then she went to the edge of the wide veranda that shaded their house and peered up into skies empty of the recognizable form of a dragon. "But where? Isn't that just like Jaxom? Although why he would tell me he was coming when he's already nearby . . . Oh, maybe I misheard Ruth. I do that now and then." She sighed in exasperation, shrugged, and went back inside.

Jayge seated himself where he could command a good view of the approaches to the house and propped his feet up on the railing. The days when Aramina had heard every single dragon conversation were long past—to her infinite relief. Now the dragons had to think specifically *at* her to convey a message. Jayge couldn't imagine what could have delayed Ruth, who was generally very prompt to follow any announcement of his coming. Lord Jaxom of Ruatha Hold was always welcome, but Jayge smiled at the surprise Readis would have to see the white dragon when he woke from his afternoon nap.

"Not that that would rate as high now as swimming with a dolphin," Jayge murmured aloud. As well it was Ruth and Jaxom who were the first dragon pair to land at Paradise River after Readis's adventure. The very ones to answer candid questions.

Just then Ruth glided with deft backwinging to land in front of the house. Jayge rose to his feet and went to greet them, a broad grin on his face. "Ara started squeezing juice the moment Ruth told her you were coming. You've confused her. She said you were already here, but we couldn't see the white hide anywhere. And I'm glad you've come, because something's come up!"

Jaxom grinned and Jayge frowned because he suddenly realized that Jaxom was carrying his riding jacket and had sweated through his light shirt. His face also bore sweat marks. Considering that *between* was beyond measure cold, Jayge was confused. Then Ruth turned and, in a hop-glide gait, made for the shore while happily chirping fire-lizards converged above him.

"Off for a scrub, is he?" Jayge gestured his human guest up to the coolness of the porch. "How could you work up such a sweat in *between*, Jaxom?"

"Stealing sand." The young Lord Holder grinned with mischief. "We've been examining the quality of your local stuff."

"Indeed? Now what would you need Paradise River sand for? As I'm sure you're going to tell me anyway." He motioned for Jaxom to take the hammock, strategically placed at the corner of the house where it caught any breeze, seaward or landward. He leaned against the banister, arms folded across his chest, awaiting an explanation.

"The settlers had a sandpit back in that scrubland of yours. They thought highly of Paradise River sands—for glass making."

"There's certainly enough. Did Piemur and Jancis find those whatchamacallums . . ."

"Chips?" With a grin, Jaxom supplied the proper term for all the odd bits that had been stored in the Hold's barn by the Ancients. It was only in recent days that anyone had understood their purpose: parts for computers, of which the Artificial Intelligence Voice-Address System recently discovered at a Landing building was the most complex. Aivas, as it was known, was the receptacle in which all the Ancients' vast knowledge had been stored. Jayge had had a brief glimpse of the incredible machine, in its special room at Landing, and heard what miracles of information it had.

"Chips, then . . . useful, after all?"

"Well, we managed to salvage the usable transistors and capacitors, but they haven't actually been installed yet."

Jayge gave him a long suspicious look for the way the strange words came so easily from his mouth. "As you say," he said with a grin.

Just then young Readis, clad only in a clout, came out on the porch, rubbing sleep out of his eyes. He peered at Jaxom, swinging lazily in the hammock, then swiveled his head around to the front of the house. "Ruth?"

Jaxom pointed to where the white dragon, surrounded by industrious fire-lizards, wallowed in the shallow water.

"He's enough of a guardian, isn't he?" Readis asked, tilting his head back in a stance that mirrored one of his father's postures.

Jayge nodded, glad that Readis was so conscious of his promise not to go in the water unattended. "But Ruth's bathing right now, and besides, I'd like you to tell Jaxom what happened to you and Alemi the other day."

"Did you come just to hear?" Readis asked, though he knew that Lord Jaxom had a lot of other things to do, since he was aware of how hard his own Holder father worked. On the other hand, he was certain that even a busy man like Lord Jaxom would find his adventure interesting: because it was a *real* adventure.

"Well, that *was* one reason," Jaxom said, smiling. "So what did happen to you and Alemi the other day?"

Aramina emerged from the house, carrying her squirming daughter under one arm and a tray in her free hand. Jayge quickly sprang to relieve her of the tray, but she gave him Aranya instead, and served Jaxom a tall cool drink and some freshly baked sweet biscuits. It took a few more minutes until Readis was settled on his stool, with two biscuits and a small glass. When his mother was seated, Readis looked to his father for his cue to begin.

He took a deep breath and launched into the well-rehearsed tale. He kept his eyes on Lord Jaxom's face to be sure he was listening properly—and he was—almost from the start.

"Shipfish?" Lord Jaxom exclaimed when Readis got to that part of his recital. He glanced at Jayge and Aramina then, and Readis saw their solemn confirmation of his claim.

"A whole pod of 'em," Readis said proudly. "Unclemi said there must have been twenty or thirty. They pulled us far enough in for us to reach the beach safely on our own. *And*," he added, pausing to give emphasis to his final words, "the next morning the skiff was found beached up by the fishhold, like they knew exactly where it belonged."

"That is some tale, young Readis. You're a harper born. An amazing rescue. Truly amazing."

Readis caught the genuine feeling in the Lord Holder's tone.

"The redfins weren't by any chance returned with the skiff?" Jaxom asked.

"Nah." Readis dismissed that with a flick of his wrist, despite his own disappointment at the failure of the lockbox to reappear on shore, as well. "They drowned. So we had to eat ol' stringy wherry 'stead of good juicy redfin steaks. And you know something else?"

"No, what?" Jaxom responded.

"It wasn't just that they rescued us—they talked to us, too!"

"What did they say?"

The expression on Lord Jaxom's face was suddenly alert, and his eyes bored into Readis as if he'd caught him out in a lie. Readis stiffened his back and threw out his chest.

"They said 'wielcame' when we thanked 'em. And they called themselves 'mam'ls,' not fish. Unclemi will tell you!"

Readis caught Jaxom glancing at his father, as if doubting him. His father gave a slow nod to Jaxom, then turned to him. "Readis, why don't you run down and see if the fire-lizards are giving Ruth a proper scrubbing?"

Having said his piece, Readis was delighted to be released to help bathe Ruth, who was his favorite dragon of all the ones he'd met so far.

"Can I? Really?" And he looked up at Lord Jaxom.

"Really, you can," Jaxom said.

Readis let out a loud yell as he jumped off the porch and pelted down to the shore where Ruth was afloat.

When the boy was out of earshot, Jaxom turned to his

parents. "I know for a fact that dolphins—what we've been calling shipfish all these centuries—came with the original settlers. And they speak? Amazing." He glanced towards Ruth.

"They'll never be competition for dragons," Jayge said quickly, flashing Jaxom a look.

"No," Jaxom replied with an easy grin, "nothing could be, but you seaside holders might want to encourage a renewal of the old friendship. Especially with the squalls you have."

"Hmmm . . ." Jayge was clearly taken with that idea.

"You are *not*—" Aramina paused to emphasize the negative. "—to give my son any more ideas than he already has."

"Why not?" Jayge said, blinking at her. "Catch 'em while they're young and train 'em up in the way they're to go."

"Readis will follow you as Holder of Paradise River," she began hotly.

"And, as he is Holder of Paradise River right on the coast, I think it'd be smart if he is aware of all the possibilities available," Jayge said, sweeping his arm out to include the sparkling waters beyond. "Of course, only when he's old enough to appreciate the advantages," he added as her expression turned slightly mutinous.

"Can't start 'em too young, you know," Jaxom told Aramina.

"You're as bad as he is. Don't tell me that Sharra would allow Jarrol to go careening about the coastline?"

"We don't have much of a one at Ruatha," Jaxom said with immense good humor. "And speaking of my wife, I'd best get back to her. Surprise her with my early return. So I have your permission, Lord Holder, to use Paradise River sands . . ." He turned to Jayge.

Jayge raised both hands in broad assent. "However much you need."

"Thanks." Jaxom drank the last of the juice, made a satisfied smack of his lips. "That hit the spot. Now, to entice my dragon away from all his admirers."

Jayge, circling Aramina's shoulders with one arm, waved a farewell. Then he looked down at his wife, always somewhat amazed that she had chosen to live her life with him.

"Some people have affinities for the sea, others for runnerbeasts or dragons." He gave her an encouraging squeeze when her face clouded, hearing that preamble. "Readis has had a great adventure for a young lad. Let's bend with it for the time being. I would like to hear what Aivas has to say about the shipfish. After all, love, we, too, owe our lives to them—and all that they brought us to. We ought, for the sake of our son, to listen to what is known about them."

She leaned into him, borrowing his strength once again. "He is just a little boy."

"Who will grow, I hope, into a fine sturdy man. Who will probably be as stubborn as his mother." He grinned down at her.

"Ha! And not just his mother by any means," she replied tartly. "Just don't force the issue, Jayge."

"I hadn't intended to, but I must admit to being curious as to what Aivas will say about talking fish."

"Yes," Aramina said, moving away from his side to take a sand-covered biscuit out of her daughter's hand. "People can imagine such odd things in moments of stress."

"Didn't we though!" Jayge's grin was for their own rarely mentioned rescue. "We never thought to thank them, either."

Aramina gave him a long and indignant stare. "Consid-

ering we barely made it to shore, and never really thought
the shipfish were *speaking* to us, why would we have?"

*The dolphins kept patrolling the waters off Pardisriv, hoping to
ask mans to remove bloodfish. Most of them had the annoying
things. Sometimes one could bite it off a podmember, but the
parasites could take a hold that only a man's sharp knife could
remove. It had been one of the great things about having a partner: he or she would keep the dolphins' flesh free of the parasites.
So when they found the broken pieces of the mans' boat, they
pushed it to where the tide would bring it ashore, since the waters were not deep enough for them to swim all the way in to the
sands. Maybe, seeing that the dolphins were remembering the
tasks tradition had told them to perform, mans would perform
the tasks dolphins could not do for themselves. They kept watch
until they saw mans finding the wreckage. Kib called and called,
asking when the bloodfish could be taken off, and where should
they go for that healing. The mans were so happy to find the
ship pieces that they walked away without answering.*

*If there was only a bell, Kib thought. There should be a bell.
Then they could ring it as their ancestors had, and mans would
answer. The dolphins at Moncobay had a bell that they could
ring, but they had not yet had the blood fish scraped off. Had
mans forgotten their duty to dolphins?*

*The Tillek had said that, one day, when the dolphin bells were
rung again, mans would remember what mans should do to help
dolphins.*

3

$\blacktriangledown\blacktriangledown\blacktriangledown\blacktriangledown\blacktriangledown\blacktriangledown\blacktriangledown\blacktriangledown$

I f Aramina secretly hoped that Lord Jaxom would forget so trivial a matter as speaking to Aivas about her
son's adventure, she was mistaken. However, it was
Masterfishman Alemi who was asked to come and recount the event to the Artificial Intelligence Voice-Address
System.

Jayge was somewhat irritated that Readis would miss
an opportunity to meet this astounding artifact of the original colonists, but Aramina thought it was much the best
thing.

"He's only just settled down, Jayge. Seeing this Aivas
thing would upset him. And how much would a boy of
his age understand? I mean, it's not as if he were meeting
a living person he could relate to, is it?"

"I could insist that Readis accompany me," Alemi said,
not wishing to cause bad feelings between holder and

lady. His initial elation had been much dampened by realizing that his young friend was being excluded from the interview. He had been to the Admin with other Fishmasters, and had been awed by the vast amount of still-relevant information the facility had on ocean currents and deeps. The boy would be so proud of having been granted such a privilege.

"No!" Aramina said with some force. "It's enough he had the adventure. He tends to magnify things out of proportion, and I don't want him thinking of swimming with those shipfish again. You go. Find out what this Aivas knows. We can decide then if Readis is to be told. Right now, I'd rather the whole affair was forgotten."

"Forget that we owe the doll-fins our son's life?"

"We owe them ours, too!" she snapped at him. "But I'm not out looking at the sea to see fins all day. Readis has to learn to deal with life on the land, not the sea." She gave Alemi a quick glance and added in a gentler tone, "I mean, for a boy his age, he already knows a good deal about the fishman's Craft, and I'm grateful you wanted to teach him." Then she let out a gush of held breath and said in a fierce tone, "He's only seven Turns old! He's got a lot more to do with dragons than with doll-fins."

The two men exchanged glances and a silent understanding was reached.

"I'll go to Landing then," Alemi said calmly. "See what Aivas has to say about these creatures. I must admit, I'm some fascinated with them myself. And," he added with a wry grin, "I saved some fish to feed them with on this latest sail. You know, I hadn't realized just how often they *have* escorted my ship. And how often they've saved lives. Each of my older hands had some tale to tell: in their family or from other crews they've sailed with. Oly said that once he was certain doll-fins had kept his skiff afloat until he was close enough to land to swim. The boat sank the moment he left it."

"Do me a favor, Alemi?" Aramina asked, her expression severe.

"What?"

"Don't tell Readis any of those tales."

"Ara . . ." Jayge began in protest.

She wheeled on him. "I know all too well, Jayge Lilcamp, what can happen to a child who gets its head full of *notions*!"

Jayge pulled back and gave her a sheepish expression. "All right, Ara, I take the point. Alemi?"

"Oh, aye, I'll keep my mouth shut."

There was an awkward pause and then Aramina relented. "If he asks, tell him the truth. I won't have him lied to or put off."

"You want it both ways?" Jayge asked.

She gave him a scowl, then relaxed a bit with a rueful smile on her lips. "I guess I do. But he's only seven and the least said the best as far as I can see."

They were all of one mind before Alemi left the house that evening. He arranged for his first mate to take the sloop out the next day to trawl for redfins, which were still running. What he couldn't sell fresh, they'd smoke, so he didn't want to lose the day because he was asked to go to Landing.

Kitrin didn't wish him to be away from her at all.

"I'm longer gone on the ship fishing, dear," he gently reminded his wife. She was well gone in her pregnancy and apt to fret. He took her hand and pulled her into his embrace, stroking her fine dark hair. "And I promise I shan't even look at those forward girls who work at Landing."

They both felt the baby kicking at her belly and smiled at each other.

"You've only to send Bitty after me," he assured her, nodding at the little bronze fire-lizard curled up in a sunny patch on their veranda. "Returning from Landing is much easier done than from the sea."

"I know, I know," she said, and settled against the curve of him.

If Alemi were truthful—and this was not the time to be with Kitrin so uneasy in herself—he would have admitted that being asked to visit Landing, to speak to Aivas itself, was an excitement he didn't wish to miss, and one he would have preferred to share with no qualifications. He could, indeed, understand and appreciate Aramina's anxieties about Readis. The boy was adventurous enough and sufficiently self-confident, perhaps, to undertake more than he was truly able to. Alemi had planned to tell him all that he had observed on this latest sail of the doll-fins: how he had taken up a position on the prow of the ship to hail the shipfish, to see if others would talk to him, to feed them the fish he had saved as thank-you. He had done this every morning and evening. To his own amazement he had begun to notice differences in the colors, even in the scars on their muzzles, so that they were distinguishable one from another. It occurred to him that doll-fins, like dragons, could be identified once one knew what to look for: like differences in shade and scar tissue.

Alemi was also delighted at the opportunity to ride a dragon. He hadn't had that many chances. His initial ride *between* had been at his sister Menolly's request. She'd heard from her Master, Harper Robinton, of the settlement at Paradise River and thought Alemi might well consider sailing south and founding his own Hold. How well his sister had read his circumstances, had seen him chafing at his father's conservatism. So he'd been conveyed a-dragonback for the initial meeting with the recently confirmed Holder, Jayge Lilcamp, and they had liked each other enough to take hold on it. He'd been conveyed twice since then to various Fishcraft meetings in the Tillek Masterfishmen Hall. Although Menolly had repeatedly told him that, as a Mastercraftsman, he had the right to call for a dragon to convey him whenever that was needful, he did not abuse the privilege.

He had often sailed to what was now called Monaco Bay, with tithes for the Weyr and supplies for the growing population at Landing. Excavations were still going on, and he had acquired a thing or two of use from the Catherine Caves when those were being shared out.

For this appearance at Landing, he dressed in his new formal tunic, embroidered with his Master's emblem, and in the Paradise River Hold colors, and newly braided Master's shoulder knots. Kitrin had a deft needle and did much of the special handwork for the entire Hold.

He had asked the dragonrider to collect him on the sea side of his holding, where Readis would not be likely to see him leave. Alemi was somewhat surprised by the youth of the bronze rider, who appeared exactly on the time set.

"I'm T'lion, Masterfishman, to collect you," the boy said from his high perch on the bronze's neck. "This is Gadareth, my dragon." His voice was vibrant with deep affection and pride. "Do you need help mounting, Master Alemi?"

"I think not," Alemi said, keeping his features composed even as he wondered if this was the first time the lad had been sent to convey a passenger. "If Gadareth will oblige me by a knee up," he added. The bronze had not achieved his full growth yet, so mounting was not the problem it would soon become.

"Oh, yes, sorry about that, Master." The boy's features set as he "spoke" to his dragon.

Gadareth had his head turned toward Alemi, his eyes whirling a trifle faster than the speed Alemi thought of as normal to these huge beasts. Then he raised his left foreleg slightly.

"If you'd lean your hand down?" Alemi suggested.

"Oh, that's right," young T'lion said, flushing.

He leaned so far over that he had to clutch at the neck ridge to keep from tipping himself out of his perch. So Alemi sprang to the offered knee, touched the hand only enough to give him an upward surge, and swung himself in the slot between the two neck ridges aft of the rider.

"Nothing to it, really," Alemi said, settling himself.

"No, Master, there isn't, is there?"

When they had sat there a few moments longer, Alemi cleared his throat. "I'm all set. Whenever you're ready?" he asked in a gentle prompt.

"Oh, yes, well, fine. We're just going. Gadareth!" Now he spoke with more conviction and no hesitation.

As Gadareth sprang from the ground, Alemi had a moment's doubt about the boy's expertise and devoutly hoped they wouldn't end up somewhere unknown, far from familiar coordinates. He had heard tales . . .

Abruptly they were in the cold of *between*, and Alemi caught his breath . . . one . . . two . . . three . . . fo. . . . They were high above water—at least that was right—and then Gadareth veered, pivoting on his right wing tip, and the magnificent crescent strand of Monaco Bay appeared in front of them. The young bronze swooped down, gliding straight for the ground in a maneuver that made Alemi hold his breath and sit as hard into the neck ridge as he could, jamming his feet down and his knees against the neck of the dragon as hard as he could.

The landing was achieved with great ease, however, and Alemi wasn't even bumped about as the dragon backwinged and settled to the firm surface in front of the Admin Building, which housed Aivas.

Alemi knew the story of its discovery—it had been a harper's tale at many a gather. It had been one of the last of the Ancients' buildings to be excavated, a task undertaken by Mastersmith Jancis, Journeyman Harper Piemur, and Lord Jaxom—on a whim, it was said. And Ruth had helped. Then they had found the curiously reinforced end of the building, which had suggested that something special had been carefully protected . . . and discovered the Artificial Intelligence Voice-Address System left by the first settlers on Pern: an intelligence that could tell them much of the first years of human habitation on this planet, and much about Thread. Aivas, as the intelligence preferred to be called, had also promised to help destroy the menace of Thread forever.

Of course, the building had been extended, since Aivas was teaching so much of the lost knowledge of every craft. Alemi wasn't sure how this Aivas could teach so much and to so many. He was more than pleased that he would have a special interview with the intelligence.

Dismounting from the young bronze, Alemi remembered to thank them both for the conveyance.

"We're to wait and take you back, Master Alemi," T'lion said. Then, glancing over his shoulder to see other dragons spiraling down to land, he hastily added, "We'll be up on the ridge where the others are waiting." He pointed in the right direction. "Give us a wave."

The bronze was already lifting himself out of the way of those wanting to land, and the boy's words were carried away in the breeze. Alemi waved his hand to show that he'd heard. Then he turned to the entrance of the Admin Building. Just inside the door was a desk at which sat no lesser a personage than Robinton, the Masterharper of Pern. Alemi gawked a bit, but Robinton smiled a warm welcome, rising from his table to hold out his hand to the young Masterfishman.

"Ah, Master Alemi, how good to see you. And on such an errand. You and young Readis were so fortunate to be rescued in that extraordinary fashion."

"You know about it?" Alemi was amazed. But then, the Masterharper, even if he was now retired from active duty, had a way of "knowing" a great deal that went on all around Pern.

"Of course I do," Robinton said emphatically. "Lord Jaxom himself told me. But, why isn't young Readis with you?"

"Oh, yes, well, his mother decided that she doesn't want him involved just yet. He's only a few months over seven Turns. She feels that's just too young . . ." Alemi heard his own disagreement with that decision in his tone and wished he was better able at dissembling.

"I see. Well, Aramina might have reservations about associating with just a mere dolphin." The Harper smiled sympathetically about maternal misgivings. "In any event, you're here. Aivas has much to tell you, too, about the shipfish. He was delighted to know that they have prospered so and have remembered how to speak. If you'll just come this way—" The Harper gestured to the lefthand corridor. "Have you been here before, Alemi? Yes, well, then you'll see how much we've expanded," he continued as they made their way past rooms occupied by small groups intent on screens to a smaller room at the end. "Here." He stepped aside to let Alemi enter.

"Aivas is in here, too?" the Masterfishman said, rotating on one heel as he looked about a room that held only chairs of the same ancients' design as the two Alemi had acquired for his hold. Then his eyes stopped at the blank screen centered in the long outside wall. A little red light blinked in its corner.

"Good morning. Masterfishman Alemi. It is good to see you again," said a deep bass voice.

"He remembered me? I never even spoke to him the first time."

Master Robinton chuckled. "He remembers everyone and everything." And he left.

The screen brightened, and an active scene of shipfish plunging and diving filled the space.

"Were there not to be two attending this meeting? Yourself and your young companion during the incident?"

"Yes, well," Alemi said, and explained Aramina's hesitations. They sounded even weaker than ever in the presence of such an august audience.

"Mothers are reputed to know what is best for their offspring," Aivas said and Alemi did not suspect a "machine" of irony. "The young are able to learn language skills much more quickly, having fewer inhibitions. It would have been useful to have a younger student. To the discussion at hand: It was good to learn that the dolphins have not forgotten their duties during the long years— Turns—that have passed. Please be seated, Master Alemi. The input of your experience with the dolphins would help update that apparently overlooked segment of the original colonizing team."

Struggling to absorb the concept that the dolphins, too, had been original colonists on this world, Alemi stumbled into the nearest chair and seated himself, eyes glued to the scene. There was something . . . not quite . . . right about the scene he was viewing. The dolphins were correct but—and then the concept of seeing moving pictures of living creatures staggered him.

"How do you do that?" he asked. In the previous meeting the screen had only shown maps, or what Aivas had called "sonar" readings, not these glimpses of dolphins, doing what he had observed them doing, disporting in the seas, most of his life.

"This is but one of the many tapes available to this facility," the Aivas said. "Moving pictures were an integral part of the information services of your ancestors' culture."

"Oh!" Alemi was fascinated by dolphin antics. "I've seen them do that! That's—that's exactly what the shipfish do!" he said excitedly as the scene shifted to the creatures escorting a ship, diving along its forward wake.

"This tape was taken more than twenty-five hundred of your Turns in the past," Aivas said in a gently instructive tone.

"But— but they haven't changed!"

"Evolutionary changes take much longer than twenty-five hundred Turns, Master Alemi, and zoologists are of the opinion that this species has gone through several changes in the developmental path to this present form."

"Including speaking?" Alemi blurted out.

"The dolphins which accompanied the colonists to Pern had been treated with mentasynth to enhance their empathic abilities and to assist them in learning human speech. It was reported that you heard them speak understandable words?"

"Readis and I both heard them speak." Alemi chuckled. "Readis was far more credulous than I," he admitted ruefully.

"The boy was considered too young to attend."

"Yes," Alemi agreed with a sigh. "I'll tell him you asked."

There was a brief pause. "As you wish. It is reassuring to know that dolphins have not forgotten either speech or their duties."

"Duties?"

"One of their prime functions was to perform sea rescue operations."

"Well, they not only saved Readis and me, but since then, every crewman in my hold has some tale to relate about doll-fins rescuing folks."

"Elucidate, please."

"You mean, explain?"

"Yes, if you please."

"For a machine, you're very polite," Alemi said, trying to master his awe for this amazing creation of the ancients.

"Courtesy is essential in all dealings with humans."

"Especially between humans," Alemi added drolly.

"Would you be kind enough to detail your recent personal experience with the dolphins?"

"Of course, although really you should have had Readis tell you. He's got it all down pat."

"So Lord Jaxom said."

"You've a sense of humor?"

"Not as you know it. Relate your experience."

"I'm not harper trained . . ."

"You *were* there. Your firsthand account will be greatly appreciated."

Though there was no hint of censure or impatience in Aivas's tone, Alemi obeyed. To his own amusement, he found himself repeating phrases that Readis had used in describing the adventure. The boy did have a gift for the dramatic. He must remind Jayge to apply for a harper at Paradise River Hold. Fleetingly he regretted Aramina's decision for Readis.

"They called themselves 'mam'ls,' " Alemi added as he concluded the actual events. "Not fish."

"They are," Aivas said in an uncontradictable tone, "mammals." He emphasized the correct pronunciation.

"What, then, are mammals?"

"Mammals—m-a-m-m-a-l-s—are life-forms that bear live young and suckle them."

"In the seas?" Alemi demanded incredulously.

The picture on the screen altered to one of swirling waters and tails, and suddenly Alemi was conscious that he was watching the birth of a shipfish. He gasped as the tiny creature emerged from its mother's body and then was assisted by two other shipfish to the surface.

"As you see, oxygen is important and essential to the dolphins as to all sea-living mammals," Aivas remarked.

The next scene showed the little creature suckling from its mother's teat.

"On Earth," Aivas continued, "there were many mammalian life-forms living in the sea, but only the dolphins, of the family Delphinidae, the bottle-nosed variation, the *tursiops tursio*, were transported from Earth to Pern. By the time this facility was put on hold, they had already multiplied and prospered well in the Pernese waters. The volume of sea available on this planet was the reason for including the dolphins in the colonial roster. It is good to know that they have survived and seem to be in great numbers now. A census is being taken of pod sightings. Estimates of populations have not been completed, since they seem to have developed a migratory culture."

Through this brief synopsis, the screen showed the wondering seaman more dolphins with young calves.

"That's nowhere on Pern," Alemi said, pointing to the screen, suddenly realizing what was "wrong" with the pictures, "at least that I've ever seen," he added.

"A keen observation, Master Alemi, for this footage was taken on Earth in an area called the Florida Keys. These are the ancestors of your dolphins in their natural habitat. I shall now play scenes of how those dolphins worked with their human partners, called dolphineers."

"Doll-fin ears?" Alemi exclaimed, slapping his knee with one hand as he saw men and women working with the dolphins, both undersea and being propelled across the surface of the water alongside their unlikely mounts. "Like dragons and their riders?"

"Not as close a bond as I am told that is. There is no ceremony similar to Impression as dragons and riders undergo. The association between humans and dolphins was of mutual convenience and consent, not lifelong, though congenial and effective.

"Certain groups of dolphins—there were more than twenty varieties of the species known on Earth—agreed to the mentasynth treatment in order to form a close working partnership with humans. Those that came on the spaceships with the colonists, twenty-four in number, were experienced in such matters and undertook to explore the oceans and provide certain services to the humans. Up until the eruption of Mounts Picchu and Garben, a high standard of communication was possible between humans and dolphins."

"If they like to work with humans, then as a sea captain I'd like to work with them, if I could," Alemi said. "I owe them my life—and others have. Readis was highly amused that the . . . d-dol . . . phins"—he made an effort to say those syllables as one word—"had such good manners."

"Courtesy has been observed in the interactions of many species and not necessarily in vocal expression. Other abstract concepts, however, require semantics and suitable attitudes and postures adapted to convey cultural differences."

"What would I have to learn to talk to dolphins?" Alemi was pleased to hear how firmly the word came out.

"There has been a linguistic shift over the centuries," Aivas began, "but both species can adapt to the changes. Here is an example of humans interacting with dolphins."

A scene unrolled in which a human and a dolphin were checking fish traps of some kind. The human wore some sort of apparatus on his back and a short-sleeved, short-legged black garment with brilliant yellow stripes. The picture was as fresh as if Alemi were at a window looking out onto the lagoon. He leaned forward, not wishing to miss a single detail.

Alemi watched, fascinated, murmuring to himself phrases exchanged between the pair. The dolphin towed the man, who gripped the dorsal fin, among the traps, inspecting the line. Briefly he wondered what his reactionary father would say to the idea that shipfish could talk.

"How do you get them to talk to you, Aivas?"

"It is frequently a matter of record, mentioned by numerous dolphineers, that getting the mammals to stop talking was considered more of a problem."

"Really?" Alemi was delighted.

"Dolphins apparently have an unusual ability to delay 'work' in favor of 'games.' "

The screen shifted to a new picture and Aivas recognized Monaco Bay—but the bay as he had never seen it: populated with sailing craft of many sizes and types, with vehicles zooming about in the sky like squat, rigid, ungraceful dragons. A huge wharf dominated the farther tip of the Monaco Bay crescent, and then he was looking at a solid plinth, a large bell atop it.

"I've seen that," Alemi exclaimed, pointing to the bell. "It was hauled up from the seafloor."

"Yes. It is being scaled of the encrustations. This bell was rung by dolphins to summon humans when they had messages to deliver, and by humans to summon the dolphins."

"The dolphins summoned humans?" Alemi was delighted by the notion. "D'you think they would respond to a bell now?"

"It is recommended that you use that means of convening them," said Aivas. "It would be interesting to see if current dolphins would recognize old imperatives. The printed sheets are summaries of files on the subject of dolphins and dolphineers. They also contain the hand signals which the dolphineers used to communicate underwater—which you might find useful—as well as a vocabulary list in the dolphin lexicon."

Suddenly thin sheets of the new writing material that the Masterwoodsman Bendarek had been making began to extrude from a slot at the base of the screen.

"Instructions on how to conduct yourself in reestablishing a meaningful contact with the dolphins, Master Alemi. A report on your progress would be appreciated."

Alemi gathered the sheets with careful hands, awed by the responsibility he somehow found himself eager to accept. He had always half envied riders their dragons, though, unlike many of his boyhood friends, he had never aspired to *be* a dragonrider: the sea was already in his blood. He found his sister Menolly's fair of fire-lizards engaging, as well as useful creatures, but the thought that he could have contact with an intelligent sea creature was irresistible: creatures as awesome in the medium of water as dragons were in the air.

As he left the Admin Building, absently responding to the Harper's farewell, he wondered where he could find a bell that would call dolphins.

Young T'lion had been watching from his vantage point on the hill behind the Admin Building, so he and Gadareth were landing before Alemi could signal them.

"How did you know I was here?" Alemi asked, surprised and gratified.

The boy flushed. "Well, sir, I saw you leave Admin. You walk different. You sort of roll."

Alemi laughed. "Look, are you required to be back at the Weyr right away?"

"No, sir, I'm on duty for you today."

"Good. Could we go down to the bay?" Alemi pointed in the general direction of the distant unseen crescent of Monaco Bay. He wanted to see how big the dolphin bell was.

"Certainly." T'lion reached his hand down as Alemi neatly jumped to Gadareth's raised forearm and settled himself between the neck ridges.

"Do we have to go *between*?" Alemi asked. "Would it be too long to fly straight?"

"No, not at all," T'lion replied.

So, when Gadareth reached a cruising height, he began to glide toward the sea, now visible as a sparkle on the horizon. Alemi had never had a chance to see much of the Landing area, where so many marvels from the early days of Pern's settlement had been unearthed over the last Turns. Now he had a panoramic view of the excavated buildings, the old "landing field" and its crumpled tower, even the ship meadow where the three ancient aircraft had been unearthed. They continued over thick forestry that no longer could be destroyed by Thread, protected as it was by the grubs that had spread in the Southern Continent to neutralize the deadly organism.

T'lion turned his head occasionally to be sure his passenger was riding comfortably; Alemi gave him a thumbs-up signal that he was, and a big grin. This was the longest he had ever flown on a dragon, and he was enjoying it immensely, not even feeling slightly guilty about monopolizing the services of a dragon and his rider for personal reasons. But there was a purpose to the trip, Alemi reminded himself, and felt for the sheaf of instructions he had tucked into his jacket pocket.

Then the superb vista of the almost perfect crescent of Monaco Bay came into view and what was left of the pier jutting out on its easterly tip. It must have been built of that almost indestructible material the ancients had used. At that, Alemi had heard from Masterfisherman Idarolan that half of its original length had been sheered off. Pictures from Aivas's archives had shown a substantial building at the sea end, floating docks and machinery of some kind. Alemi sighed. There were fisherman out on the deeper waters offshore, plying their ancient trade, which Master Idarolan had said had been conducted in the first days of Pern much as it was now. Some basic skills did not change. Still, so many others had benefited by processes and ideas that had become lost, or disused, during the darker Turns.

Then, from his lofty perspective, Alemi saw on the beach the long column and what had to be the bell. He touched T'lion's shoulder and pointed down at it. T'lion nodded his understanding. A moment later, Gadareth angled downward, veering to the right and swinging around so that he landed neatly a few lengths from the flotsam.

Despite himself, and hoping he wasn't hurting the dragon, Alemi tightened his grip on the neck ridge.

A thick coating of barnacles on the long plinth distorted its actual shape, Alemi noted as he walked its length. The bell, which rested on a stand, was of a generous size—fully four of his hand spans across its mouth. A good deal of the encrustations had been chipped off, and someone was polishing the metal. The clapper was missing. He pinged the bell with an irreverent snap of his index finger and thumb and was mildly surprised to hear a muted tolling, slightly distorted.

"Here, use this," T'lion suggested, handing Alemi a fist-sized rock.

Alemi got a much better sound with that, a mellow rich sound that rolled resonantly out across the bay.

T'lion grinned. "Nice sound!" So, picking up a larger rock, he clouted the bell, getting a more forceful peal. Grunting, Alemi bent over and peered up inside the bell, trying to figure out how large the original clapper must have been.

"Mine was louder," T'lion said, offering his rock to Alemi.

Alemi hefted both rocks in his hands and then clattered first one, then the other, against the bell, turning his ear to catch the echoes of the lovely sound. Suddenly T'lion exclaimed, looking up at his bronze dragon, whose eyes were beginning to whirl with excitement. T'lion swung his torso halfway toward the water and then stood bolt upright, staring at the bay.

"Shards! Gadareth's right! Look!" he cried, urgently pointing.

Alemi, his back to the water, craned his neck and saw a phalanx of dolphins racing toward the shore, leaping and vaulting out of the water. The waters beyond seemed to be full of dorsal fins and leaping shipfish. The Masterfish-man rose to his feet, gawping at the noises that drifted to him.

"Bellill! Squee! Bellill! Bellill rings! Squeee! Bellill! Bellill!"

Alarmed by their headlong charge straight to the strand, Alemi raced to the edge of the water, waving his hands. "No, be careful! You'll beach yourselves! Careful!"

He doubted his words could be heard over their bab-bling of "bell" and their squeeing. So he waded out into the water, hoping to turn them aside. Instead, he was butted and knocked off his feet by the many bodies that roiled the waters about him. Then he was uplifted by one dolphin body, nose-prodded by half a dozen more, and seemed to be flipped from one to another of the exultant creatures.

"Easy! Take it easy! You'll drown me," Alemi yelled, half laughing, half sputtering at these exuberant antics.

A huge shadow compressed the air above him, and he saw bronze Gadareth hovering, his claws extended as if he intended to pluck Alemi bodily from the attentions of the dolphins.

"I'm all right, T'lion, I'm all right. Call Gadareth off!"

"They'll drown you," T'lion shrieked, jumping up and down on the beach in his concern.

Simultaneously, Alemi tried to reassure the dolphins, fend off Gadareth, who still saw the human endangered, and reassure the young rider.

"Belay this!" Alemi roared.

Abruptly the commotion about him ceased and bottle-nosed faces were turned up at him in a tight circle, an even larger ring just beyond them and more dorsal fins and leaping bodies homing in on him from farther out in the bay.

"I am Alemi, fishman. Who are you?" He pointed to a dolphin whose nose brushed his thigh.

"Naym Dar." The dolphin squeed happily.

Two words, then, Alemi realized, hearing the first word as a distorted "name." He was delighted that his question had been understood. "Who leads this pod?"

A second dolphin did a wiggle and came closer. "Naym Flo. Long . . ." And the creature used a word that Alemi didn't recognize.

"I do not speak good dolphin," Alemi said. "Say again, please?"

A ripple of squeeing and clicking greeted that admission.

"We titch. You lis-ten," Flo said, turning one eye on him so that he could see the happy curve of its mouth. "Bellill ring? Trub-bul? Do blufisss?"

"No, no trub-bul," Alemi said with a laugh. "I didn't mean to ring the bell to *call* you," he added. And then shrugged because he didn't understand their last question.

"Good call. Long lis-ten. No call. We . . . [a word Alemi didn't catch] . . . bell. Pul-lease?" She cocked her head— Alemi didn't know why, all at once, he decided she was a female, but something about her seemed to give that clue to her gender. He was also peripherally aware of how much he had actually absorbed from the pictures that Aivas had shown and the explanations of these . . . mammals. That was going to shock the conservative fishmen. His father especially. "Fish" had no right to be intelligent, much less answer humans.

"That bell"—Alemi pointed back to the shore—"is . . . not working. I will get a bell that works. I will put it at Paradise River Hold. I will call you from there. Can you hear me anywhere?"

There were squeeings and clickings and noisy blowings out of their airholes as they seemed to be trying to understand him.

Suddenly Flo reared up out of the water, holding herself aloft by what Alemi decided could only be sheer determination. She tilted her head, her left eye regarding him. "Lemi ring bellill. Flo come. You oo-ait? 'Mis you oo-ait? Flo come!" She emphasized the last word with a flick of her tail before she sank into the water.

" 'Mis you wait?" Alemi repeated.

"I tell you I come. I come," Flo said with a burble and a whoosh from her blowhole. Everyone about her clicked and squee'ed in tones so emphatic that Alemi grinned broadly at their insistence. "Ooo skraaaabb blufiss?" Flo sounded hopeful.

The last thing he had expected was the eager participation of the dolphins in reestablishing contact with humans. He tried repeating her last query just as he'd heard it. "Ooo" meant "you" but what "skraaaabb" or "blufiss" were sounds for, he couldn't even guess. Beside him, Flo turned over and over in the water. He had to laugh at her antics: they were childlike, almost. Then he became aware of being uncomfortably hot, in water now up to his chest, and weighed down by the sodden heavy jacket.

"Let me go ashore, will you?" he asked, indicating that he needed to pass by the dolphin bodies pressing about him. He put out his arms to swim and found himself crowded by helpful sleek forms. "I can swim. Let me."

"Suwim, mans suwim, mans suwim . . ." Suddenly the ring about him parted, dolphins flipping up and overhead, out of his way.

Dragon and rider were at the water's edge, dubiously surveying the incredible scene.

" 'Member! 'Member! Oooo ring. Oo-ee come!" a dolphin shouted as Alemi waded out of the bay. "Oooo do blufiss."

He nodded enthusiastically as he turned, waving at the dolphins crisscrossing each other as they made for deeper water. There seemed to be an incredible number occupying the bay waters. Then, as the chorus was picked up by other voices, he cupped his hands. "I ring. You come. I wait."

T'lion looked at him in blank amazement. "They were talking? Speaking to you?"

Alemi nodded, slipping out of his soaking jacket while he worked his sodden boots off his feet. "That's what I saw Aivas about—the dolphins. I never thought we'd get that sort of response, just *tapping* a bell."

T'lion shook his head slowly from side to side. "Me neither!" He let his breath out with a sigh and took Alemi's coat from him, draping it on the bell, as Alemi now stripped off his shirt and began wringing it out. "I better go get you some dry clothes. Even in the midday sun, it's going to take time to dry 'em, and you can't go *between* in wet clothes."

"No, I can't, and I would appreciate dry things. Is that a problem?"

T'lion sized him up for a moment and shook his head. "No. It'll only take a few minutes," he said as he vaulted to his dragon's back. "I'll borrow some from a rider your size. We always have spares."

Sand briefly showered Alemi as the young bronze leaped from the beach.

"Shards!" Alemi said, diving for the Aivas papers in his jacket.

With shaking hands he opened the wet sheath, but the writing appeared not to have suffered. Carefully, using pebbles to hold them down, he spread the sheets out on the sand to dry in the hot sun.

Now it was the turn of Flo, pod leader at Moncobay, to sound the news far and wide that the bell had been rung. Not exactly as it should be rung, but it had been rung and they had swarmed to answer, to prove to mans that they would reply when they heard the bell. It had been so long since that sound had been heard upon the waters or under them. No member of the pod, even Teres, who was the oldest and had to be accompanied when she fed in the schools of fish, had ever heard the bell. But they had remembered to remember. Those at Pardisriv were not the only ones to talk to mans and use the Words.

The mans had been two and they had sent happy feelings to the pod. There had been scratches and pats that had long been denied the dolphins. The entire pod had been made glad to answer the bell. They had shown their appreciation with great leaps and tail walks and flips and deep divings. Mans had said they would scrape off the bloodfish, which was the best news of all. That evening as they rested in the Great Current, Teres repeated the old tales that she had learned from the Tillek in her time at the Great Subsidence, before she had swum cleanly through the whirlpool and been considered worthy of bearing dolphin calves. When mans had swum alongside dolphins, above and below the surface, and they had accomplished many wonderful things together. And now there would be mans to heal the wounded and keep the stranded from dying on the sands. There would be good Work to be done. The sea had changed the land in the time since humankind and dolphinkind had come to these waters. Humankind should know. Dolphins could show mans where the shore had changed, and the Currents, and where the biggest schools of fish were. And there might even be games to play.

4

▼▼▼▼▼▼▼▼▼

When Alemi returned to Paradise Hold, he was
bursting with his tidings and tracked Jayge down
to make his report.

Perhaps what Jayge was doing—chopping down the
verdant undergrowth that relentlessly encroached on the
clearings about the holds, a sweaty, difficult job but one
best done to inhibit growth during the coming hot
season—made him sour. In any event, the Holder's enthusiasm for Alemi's new adventure with dolphins was less
than appreciative.

Jayge paused in his labors, wiping the sweat that was
overflowing the band on his forehead.

"That's all very well and good, Alemi. I suppose—"
Jayge hesitated. "—it's good. We've got fire-lizards and
dragons, why not intelligent life in the seas? The Ancients
apparently knew what would combine to make a perfect

world, so these doll-fins had their role to play . . ." He hesitated again.

"But you're worried about Readis?"

Jayge let out an explosive sigh. "Yes, I am. He's still talking about his mam'l . . ."

"They are," Alemi said, regaining his perspective on the matter, "mam-mals." He repeated the word carefully, not glottalizing it into one syllable. "Creatures who give birth to live offspring and suckle them."

Jayge gave him a long incredulous stare. "Underwater?"

Alemi grinned, appreciating his amazement. "Saw moving-picture records of a birth as well as the suckling so I can't doubt it."

"Aivas wastes time on such things?"

"I wouldn't call it wasting time," Alemi said wryly, "if the result is dolphins ready to rescue the shipwrecked."

Jayge had the grace to flush and concentrated on honing the edge of his wide blade.

"Look, I'll keep my findings to myself then. You didn't mention my interview with Aivas to Readis, did you? No. All right. I certainly won't, but I'd like your permission, as my Holder, to discreetly pursue a closer association with these creatures. With squalls like the one Readis and I were caught in, those at sea in these waters need all the help available."

"And these doll-fins would *always* help?"

"According to what I saw and what Aivas said, water rescues are a dolphin's responsibility and duty."

"Humph. What does Master Idarolan say to this?"

"I'm only just back, Jayge. Haven't told him yet, but I certainly shall. Most ships carry bells. If masters know what sequence summons dolphins to their assistance, we'd have just that much more of a chance in the water. You can't deny that, can you?"

"No." Jayge had been vividly recalling the storm that had tossed himself and Aramina overboard, and the shipfish who had rescued them. "I can't. Ah, very well. Just be sure, Alemi, that Readis doesn't get wind of all this. He's much too young."

Alemi nodded, perversely pleased that he could try to establish himself with the dolphins without having to share the experience. After all, they had that jetty now on the sheltered cove just around the headland. He could rig a bell there, and a float like the one he'd seen in the pictures, where he could meet the dolphins on the same level.

"I'll take some of this heavier bambu away for you, Jayge," Alemi offered, noting the size of the stalks the Holder was cutting.

"Your doll-fins eat vegetation?"

"No, but I've uses for this," Alemi said, gathering up the lengths that were suitable for his purpose. With air bladders to increase their flotation, he'd have a platform similar to the one that used to ride the water at Monaco Bay—smaller, but adequate for one man. "Have you had any further word from the Benden Weyrleaders as to when we can expect the new settlers?"

"I should hear by the end of this sevenday." Jayge paused to wipe his brow. "So they'll probably be grateful for fish to lay in as supplies."

"No problem there," Alemi said, grinning. The delicious whitefish were running—and plentiful. They could be salted, pickled, or smoked and retain their flavor.

He knew that Jayge was looking forward to having a new hold farther down the river. He was, too. Jayge's boundaries were confirmed; Alemi, Swacky, Temma, and Nazer had helped the dragonriders survey the new hold that would start on the eastern side of the river, below the bend that marked the end of his Paradise River Hold, and continue down to the origin of the river. The best site would be in the foothills, as the new arrivals were farmercraftsmen; they would round up and protect the wild runner- and herdbeasts, and grow the grain crops in the higher lands that did not grow along the coast.

Alemi had met the Keroon leaders, a large family complete with aunties and uncles, who had applied for the holding. Good solid men and women. He looked forward to having them as neighbors. And there was talk of another group interested in settling the southwestern bank of the Paradise.

Alemi didn't have as much time for his new enthusiasm as he would have liked. He'd have to assign sailors to help ship the settlers' belongings down the Paradise to the Bend, so his fishing crews would be shorthanded. With the whitefish running, he wanted to net as much as possible. He and his crews were out all the hours of the lengthening days, trawling and long-lining. Alemi was extra mindful of some of the precautions Aivas had mentioned—precautions Fishmen always observed but without knowing why: taking care for the size of the nets, as well as the old warnings of the "sin" of netting a shipfish. Even his father, who hadn't the imagination to be superstitious, followed those precepts. Now Alemi knew the reason behind those practices, but he doubted his father would ever admit to it—much less admit that dolphins could talk and were intelligent. One more of the many gulfs between them.

Armed with Aivas's confirmation of the intelligence of shipfish/dolphins, Alemi did inform Master Idarolan of his investigations and his plan to renew the partnership to mutual benefit—though he wasn't sure what benefit the dolphins might derive. As he respected the Masterfishman and did not wish to lower himself in his Craftmaster's estimation, he qualified his interest by virtue of his and Readis's escape and the turbulence and unpredictability of these tropical waters. He sent that message off by Tork, his bronze fire-lizard. The creature's speedy return pleased him: proof of his success at using Menolly's sensible suggestions to train the fire-lizard. Alemi felt that if he had handled a fire-lizard's instruction so well, he could certainly deal with the more intelligent dolphins.

Aware that water magnified sound, Alemi nonetheless felt he would need a larger bell than the one on his ship— which he was borrowing whenever she was at anchor. He wondered if the alarm triangle that Jayge had put up outside his hold after Thella's invasion would also call the dolphins but quickly discarded that notion. A triangle just didn't produce the same resonances.

So he needed a bell. He sent Tork on a second journey that day, to the Smithcrafthall in Telgar Hold, asking them to cast a bell for him, similar to the one at Monaco Bay.

The Mastersmith Fandarel sent back a message to Masterfishman Alemi that he would be happy to cast a bell of that splendid size, but that the commission would have to wait its turn, what with all the other work that the Halls were currently undertaking to the purpose of eliminating Thread. Alemi had to be content with the promise. In the meantime, Masterharper Robinton found him a small handbell, then later sent him a message by his fire-lizard Zair that the harper at Fort Hold thought he'd seen a big bell in the extensive storage area of the Hold's lower levels.

Every evening Alemi studied the notes Aivas had given him until he had memorized the hand signals and the basic commands that he hoped had survived in shipfish memories. As he studied, he was occasionally given to fits of incredulous head shaking.

"Why does reading those sheets make you shake your head, Alemi?" Kitrin asked him with a sigh of exasperation.

"Wonder," Alemi answered, leaning back in his chair. "Wonder that we missed every single clue the dolphins gave us that they wanted to be friends. Shards, they tried to *tell* us and we humans didn't *listen!*" Kitrin made such a grimace that he laughed. He often knew her thoughts before she spoke them aloud. "Yes, indeed, I can just picture my good father, Yanus, listening to a shipfish!" He snorted.

"Exactly," Kitrin said with some heat, for a moment abandoning the little wrapper she was hemming for their expected child. "I mean no disrespect—well, maybe I do," she added with a rueful expression, "but he is sometimes . . ."

"*Always*," Alemi amended firmly with a smile.

"So set in his ways. You know, neither he nor your mother have *ever* mentioned Menolly. Though your mother often remarks on ingratitude in my presence." She sighed. "It's as if Menolly never existed."

"I think she prefers it that way," Alemi said with a wry and slightly bitter grin, knowing all too well the treatment given his talented sister during her adolescence at Half Circle Sea Hold. "Both of them—mother and daughter."

"Menolly's never been back? Ever?"

"Not to the Sea Hold. Why should she?"

Kitrin shrugged. "It seems so . . . so awful . . . that they cannot accept her accomplishments." Then she added shyly, "Sebell always remembers to send us copies of her latest songs. Alemi, *when* are we going to have a harper?"

He grinned, for he knew that had been the main reason for this trend of their conversation.

"Hmmm. I've asked Jayge and Aramina. Readis is growing old enough to learn his ballads and so are enough other youngsters, including our own, for the hold to have its own harper. Enough for a journeyman surely, and we can offer many benefits here: decent weather and property to develop."

"Ask if *they've* asked," Kitrin said with unusual force. "I'm not going to have the girls, or our *son*"—and she said this defensively, one hand on her gravid belly—"grow up ignorant of what they owe Hold, Hall, and Weyr."

Alemi laughed. "Stoutly said."

He did bring up the matter of a harper for the Hold the very next afternoon when he delivered the Holder's best of the day's catch: three grand big redfins.

"I could almost *wish*," Jayge said with some acrimony, "that Aivas hadn't been discovered! Everything depends on what he needs first!"

"But surely harpers . . ."

"Every harper who's done his journeyman's walk wants to have some part in transcribing Aivas's information, which seems to be inexhaustible on every subject imaginable and *all* of it seemingly has to be done *now*!" The Holder rubbed an agitated hand across the stubble of his close-cropped black hair. He scowled. "I've *asked* and asked."

"Master Robinton?" Alemi suggested hopefully.

Jayge dismissed that hope. "He's worse than anyone else, stuck up there at the Admin." Then he gave a snort of amusement. "Still has his finger in most pies! But I no more want Readis ignoring his duties—even if those, too, are apt to change with all these new gadgets and information—than you want your girls growing up untrained. Push comes to shove, the farmcrafters have an elderly harper who might be persuaded to travel up to us now and again, but . . ."

"If you don't mind me doing so, I'll drop a word to my sister," Alemi offered.

A look of intense relief passed over Jayge's tanned features. "I didn't want to impose . . ."

"Why not?" Alemi grinned. "I haven't fished for many favors from my well-placed Master of a sister. She's got a child, too, you know. And another one on the way."

Jayge gave him a stare and then winked. "Seems she does more than craft all the songs anyone sings these days."

"It's one way of being *able* to do just that, according to her, what with everything else harpers seem to be required to do right now."

While it was the hot season on the Southern Continent, it was bitter cold in the North, and there were few who would turn down the opportunity to come south. So it came as no surprise that Alemi's plea to Menolly for a harper to teach the children of Paradise River Hold resulted in the message that one was coming as soon as transport could be arranged. What no one at Paradise River expected was to see Menolly herself and her young son, Robse, carried by the sturdy, loyal, lack-witted Camo, stepping out of Master Idarolan's longboat onto the beach.

On learning that a harper was being sent, Jayge had organized a work party to put up a neat three-room hold near the old storage shed. The shed could be used as the schoolroom, and the little hold was far enough away from other dwellings to give a harper privacy. When he discovered that the Masterharper Menolly had arrived, he was all set to oust one of the younger settler couples and give her better accommodations.

"Nonsense. It's not as if I can make Paradise River a permanent home," Menolly said to an embarrassed Jayge. "I can only stay until the babe is born. And that is solely," she added wrinkling her nose in disgruntlement, "because even Sebell's got tired of my complaining about being too cold to compose, much less play. See?" She held out her long fingers. "Chilblains!" She brushed past a dithering Jayge and onto the wide veranda, which had a hammock slung on its "breeze" corner. "Besides, down here you spend more time outside than in. There's enough space for a small cot for Robse in my room and a room for Camo; he's so good with Robse, who adores him, since he's not much more than an overgrown baby himself. You've made a very nice kitchen, and I can always use the store shed, can't I? If I need space to work in?"

"No problem. Or I can settle Camo in space in the store shed. That way, he's near but not underfoot all the time."

"Well, then, we move in here," she said, turning on the ball of one foot to circle back to the house, hugging herself before she threw her arms out in an expansive gesture. "Oh, it's so grand to be warm."

Jayge gave her a cynical smile. "Wait till the hot weather really starts."

"Whenever," Menolly responded, tossing her thick mop of hair behind her, "but at least my blood is thawing." She gave a convulsive shudder. "It's *never* been so cold."

Camo arrived then, pushing the barrow with the household effects she had brought with her, Robse perched on the top, hugging a lap harp case. A good third of the baggage consisted of musical instruments and an enormous supply of writing materials. Later Aramina told Jayge that Menolly had brought only two changes of clothing for herself and one long, elegantly embroidered "harpering" gown.

The gown was worn by Menolly the first evening, when Aramina and Jayge hosted her at a quickly organized Gather. Everyone living in or near Paradise River Hold wanted to meet Master Menolly. Only the new settlers at South Bend Holding were unable to attend—they were too busy raising a big stone beasthold—but two of their aunties came to help with the cooking. Jayge could be proud to host such a large crowd that night, for the inhabitants had increased over the past Turns, each new arrival bringing needed skills or crafts. Jayge had been able to be selective, though there was only one couple he had actually dismissed. So forty-seven Hold residents, adults and children, gathered that night along with the crew of the *Dawn Sisters*, anchored in the bay.

With a Gather to attend, Masterfishman Idarolan was quite willing to stop over a day to see these "doll-fins" of Alemi's.

"Catch two fish on the one hook," he said drolly to his craftsman, his eyes surveying the neat fishhold that Alemi and his two journeymen had constructed.

Alemi had had to sternly keep under control his eagerness to prove dolphins' intelligence to Master Idarolan because, of course, Menolly's arrival had to be celebrated. It had never once occurred to Alemi that his *sister* would appear to harper at Paradise River. It had certainly thrown everyone into intense and exciting surprise. Keenly aware of the prestige of her husband's sister, Kitrin had been all for giving up her beloved house, but Alemi had laughed.

"Menolly'd refuse to accept the offer, dear heart," he told his wife, "especially with you further along in pregnancy than she is."

"But she's the Masterharper!"

"She's also Menolly, my sister, and hasn't really let her exalted position go to her head."

So Kitrin launched into a full-scale baking and cooking operation to prepare for the evening's eating. "After all, we can't be lacking in any courtesy to a *Master*harper, especially your *sister* Masterharper."

Alemi laughed and left her organizing the other fishmen's wives to produce the specialties that abounded in Paradise River Hold at this time of the year.

It was a very late evening, but tremendously enjoyed by all the Paradise River holders, hungry for new songs and new faces. Menolly had sung and sung, request after request, as well as the newest songs. Without, Alemi noticed, mentioning which she had herself composed, though somehow he knew which those were. Her style was inimitable. She'd made him harmonize with her on some of the sea songs they had both learned from Harper Petiron as children. Alemi was genuinely glad that they'd have a long-delayed chance to enjoy each other's company—in ways they had not when living at Half Circle Sea Hold.

As Alemi, done with duets and back in the audience with Kitrin, listened to his sister's lovely, rich deep voice lilting up and down octaves, he was more amazed than ever that no one at Half Circle Sea Hold—with the exceptions of old Petiron and himself—had recognized her talents and encouraged her. He had been furious with his parents' vindictive attitude when she'd cut her hand on a venomous packtail fish and it looked as if the injury might prevent her ever playing again. They had been so *pleased*!

"Why are you grimacing like that, 'Lemi?" Kitrin asked in a low voice during a brief pause in the singing while Menolly had a sip of juice and chatted with her audience.

"What you said about my parents," he replied cryptically.

"What? When?" she asked, surprised.

"Oh, their lack of appreciation of our Menolly."

"Oh, that!" Her tone was scoffing. "What they miss, we can enjoy the more. You two sounded well together. You ought to sing more often at Gathers. And that was such a lovely ballad about Landing. Imagine! People just like us made that incredible journey across skies to begin a new life here. Just as we have at Paradise River, in a way. And we didn't have to sleep fifteen Turns to get here."

Alemi patted her shoulder and chose not to remind Kitrin of how difficult she had found settling into their new hold. Menolly's song was doing its job, he thought, and his grin broadened. He had always respected his sister's abilities as a singer; now he respected the song for its subtleties. Still, that was what harpering was all about, wasn't it? Getting people to think and feel and, most of all, learn. The Fishercraft fed bodies, but the Harpercraft fed souls.

Having had Master Menolly for a spell, would Paradise River be able to cope with whatever journeyman was willing to come to such an isolated place? Well, he'd still be singing the good songs she introduced.

Maybe—and here Alemi allowed his mind to spiral upward with aspiration as Menolly struck a rousing chord on her gitar—maybe the dolphins would make Paradise River that much more attractive. He must give that notion more thought. First, he reminded himself, he had to convince the Masterfishman that the dolphins could become more than acrobatic . . . mammals . . . that liked to outswim ships.

Though Alemi hadn't had much time, he had used his ship's bell one evening—sort of tentatively, almost afraid to ring it loudly for fear no dolphin would answer the summons. He waited and, when nothing happened, he gave the bell one final ring in the Report sequence mentioned in the instructions Aivas had printed out for him. It probably wasn't loud enough to attract dolphins.

"Bellilll! Bellilll!"

He had to listen hard to be sure he wasn't imagining the cry, ringing across the evening waters. The setting sun was in his eyes and dancing across the water, obscuring his view. He heard the unmistakable cry again and saw the leaping bodies of half a dozen dolphins, speeding shoreward. He nearly sank to his knees on the float in relief. He genuinely hadn't thought he'd get a response.

"Bellill! Squeeeeee!" "Bellilll! Reeeeppppporrreett!"

The gladness in the cry repaid Alemi's efforts.

As the instructions had indicated, the dolphineer should reward respondents, and so he had provided himself with a pail of small fishes that weren't worth the effort of salting or smoking. Since dolphins were quite capable of catching as much as they needed for themselves, he wondered about the custom. Still, it was a hospitable gesture. Humans offered klah or fruit juice to every visitor, when everyone had the same commodities in their own homes. It was the principle of the offer.

"Who's here?" he asked. "I'm Alemi."

One dolphin, his gray skin colored pinkish by the setting sun, wriggled up out of the water. "Know you! Sayve you 'n' caff!"

Alemi tossed him a fish. "Thank you again."

"Sayve mans me, too!" squeaked a second dolphin, winding itself out of the water on its tail.

"And a fish for you! A fish for all you who answered the bell!"

"Bellill!" Bellill." The dolphins seemed to put another vowel in the word, and Alemi laughed as he threw fish to them.

"Reporit?" one of them asked. Alemi thought it was the first one that had spoken to him, but he couldn't be sure: they all seemed to look the same in the dusky light. But by the time he had emptied the pail, he had noticed distinguishing scars on several head domes—he thought some were similar to ones he'd noticed at sea in the dolphin vanguards—and that they were actually different sizes and somewhat different shapes.

"I just wondered if you'd come if I rang the bell."

"Bellill bring pod. Aw-ways! Heyar bellill, come."

While Alemi understood the words they were saying to him, he could see what Aivas had meant about language shifts. Did they really understand what he said to them? Should he correct their pronunciation? Aivas hadn't said anything on that account. Well, he could only try, and it was better for him to speak as he normally would and maybe improve their speech as he went along. "Good! Please come always when you hear the bell. I'm getting a bigger one made."

"OO-we ring? Oo-we ring bell. Mans answer?"

Alemi burst out laughing at that cocky query and was bold enough to reach out and rub the nose of the dolphin who had spoken.

"Gooddee. Gooddee. Skraaaabb blufisss now? . . ." There were those odd words again, which apparently were very important to the dolphins.

"Blufisss?" he repeated. "What are blufisss?"

"Deese ..." Kib rolled half over so that his lighter-colored belly was visible. There, stuck to his side, was a nasty-looking patch that Alemi, when he peered more closely at it, recognized as a bloated sucker fish, a creature every seaman knew would cling to an open wound.

"Bloodfish ... Of course, blufisss!" Alemi said, mimicking the dolphin's higher-pitched tone. "How could I have been so dense!" He slapped his hand to his forehead. He grabbed the bloodfish by its head and tried to dislodge it, but it seemed glued to the dolphin's side. "Well and truly sucking, isn't it? I don't have a fire out here ..." Sailors usually touched the head with an ember or a brand.

Kib turned faceup and raised his upper body out of the water. "Nifff."

"Won't a knife just make the wound worse?"

"Ooooold fisss. Small hole."

"It'll hurt," Alemi replied, wincing.

"No eeeeert more good gone."

"If you say so ..."

"Ooo-ee ssay so. Good good good. Mans do good good good for dolphins." And Kib heeled over so that Alemi could attack the parasite.

His knife blade was sharp enough to shave the bloodfish off. He had to dig slightly to remove the sucker, but that left only a small hole in the longer-healed gash.

Two more ecstatic dolphins had him remove bloodfish, one very close to the dolphin's genitalia. When he had excised the parasites, each dolphin did happy aerial rotations and dove and jumped about. He also got to notice them as individuals. Kib had a healed slash along his lower jaw and was the largest male. Mul had blotchy coloring and had had the parasite near her tail. Mel had the longest nose, while Afo was the smallest female. Jim seemed the most acrobatic—certainly he displayed it by walking a long distance on his tail when Alemi had rid his belly of the pests—and Temp was definitely fatter than the others. Aivas's notes had remarked that dolphins had a thick layer of blubber just under their skin, which kept them warm in cooler waters and generally provided temperature controls.

When the quick tropical dusk deepened into full dark, with the tree whistlers beginning to sound off, he bade them good night.

"Good night," he called as he climbed up the short ladder to the pier head.

"T'anks for blufisssing cullings. T'anks good good good. Nigh . . . nigh . . . su-leap tigh . . ."

He heard, more than saw, the shapes leaping easily in and out of the water and heading back out to the Currents.

Once again Afo's pod had good news to sound to all quarters, to tell that the mans had taken off troublesome bloodfish. Mans had not forgotten their duty to dolphins. They heard other good newses on the sonar echo, for now several ships would feed the dolphins who escorted them out to fish. Sometimes, though, the ships did not follow the dolphins once they were far offshore so that the places of the best fishing went untouched. The Tillek was asked how to teach mans to do the right. Dolphins remembered. Why did not mans?

Afo could say with pride that her mans remembered. He had had to be reminded and shown but he had taken out his steel and done the service. A few more needed to be freed of the parasites but he was one mans and there were many in the pod which already had had good good good luck. They had a bell at Pardisriv and they had had one removal. Alta and Dar sounded that the bell was not yet up where the Moncobay pod could ring it. Soon. The Tillek sounded back that they must be patient. When the bell was up, she would come to see mans now they were back to their First Place. Perhaps there would be a Tillek among the mans who would remind mans of their part of the Bargain.

Although Master Idarolan had imbibed as deeply as everyone else at the Gather, he rowed himself ashore from the *Dawn Sisters* as the sun lifted above the horizon. A gentle following sea made the journey easy. Alemi was there to meet him, a cup of hot steaming klah in his hand. Turns of early mornings had made it almost impossible for Alemi to sleep past daybreak.

"Thanks, lad. Ah, that's a grand cup," Idarolan said, smacking his lips after his first judicious sip of the hot liquid.

Alemi offered him a basket of fruit and some of the leftover Gather breads.

"Didn't think there'd be a morsel after my crew took their haul from the tables," he said, helping himself to pastry. Unobtrusively he was peering into the wide windows of the hold. "Nice place you've made here. As neat as the yard! Shipshape. I like to see that, not that a son of your father would be anything else."

"Ah, mention of Master Yanus, ah ... I trust, Master Idarolan, that ... ah, you would be ..."

"Not mention your doll-fins to your sire?" Idarolan laughed, his eyes crinkling into well-established wrinkles, carved by wind and sun. "Not likely, though I like to see a man accept something new and different—now and then. Someone who latches on to just any newfangled—"

"The association of humans and dolphins is not newfangled . . ." Alemi said firmly.

"Certainly not if you got your information from Aivas itself!" And now Idarolan did chuckle, deep in his chest. "Masterholder Yanus is a fine seaman, trains up a good apprentice, has a good feel for Nerat Bay weather and a solid knowledge of his own coastline . . ." Idarolan paused, then glanced sideways at Alemi, his eyes twinkling. "But, as a man to accept a new idea . . . oh, no. Doesn't trim sail that way." He leaned closer to Alemi, at the same time dipping his hand into the bread basket again. "Between you and me, lad, he doesn't believe there *could* be such a . . . creature, a device, like Aivas. No, there can't be such a *thing* as this Aivas."

Alemi rubbed the back of his head, grinning. "Doesn't surprise me a bit."

"Surprises me that Yanus and Mavi could produce children like you and Master Menolly."

"*She's* the real surprise."

Idarolan shot his craftsman a quick look. "At least *you're* proud of her."

"Very!"

"You're why she came, you know. Told me one night she'd never had a chance to get to know you but you were the best of the lot."

Alemi stared back at his Master. "She said that? About me?" He felt his throat get tight with pride and love of her.

"Not that ship journeys don't get people saying things they'd never admit to on solid ground," Idarolan added slyly. "Come, lad, pour me another cup of klah and then show me these doll-fins of yours."

"Dolphins." Alemi absently corrected the pronunciation

as he refilled both cups. He reached for the second pail—
with the half-eaten breads and cakes. He hadn't any fish
left over from yesterday's catch to give and didn't know if
the dolphins would accept human food. Then he led the
way, taking the track that crossed directly from his house
to the jetty.

Idarolan scrambled down the ladder to the float as
neatly as Alemi did. Feeling a trifle self-conscious, Alemi
grabbed up the small handbell and vigorously sent the
peals of the Report sequence out across the gently lapping
tide.

Both he and Idarolan flinched when two dolphins,
crossing each other's paths, leaped out of the water,
finger-widths from the edge of the float.

"That's jumping to with a vengeance, boy!" Idarolan
said.

"Lemi, ring bellill! Reporrrit! Afo reporit!" The words
came distinctly to both men.

"Kib reporrrit!" came from the second dolphin.

"As I live and breathe!" Idarolan gasped in a low, awed
tone. Kneeling at the very edge of the float, he tried to follow the motion of the now submerged dolphins. He
lurched back as one surfaced right in front of him, its rostrum nearly touching his chin. "My very word!" He stared
at Alemi for a long moment.

"OOO rang?"

"Kib?" Alemi said, holding out an offering of bread.
"You eat mans food?"

"No fish?"

"Not this morning."

"He distinctly said 'No fish?' Interrogatory tone!" Master Idarolan exclaimed softly, rocking back on his heels.

Alemi grinned.

"No fish?" the second dolphin queried, bobbing up in front of Alemi, who put out his hand to scratch under the chin.

"Will scratching do? Or do you need bloodfish taken off?" He grinned as he explained to Idarolan about the parasites.

"Well, I never! And they let you scrape 'em off with your knife?"

"They seemed very pleased to get them off. I think I've done five in this pod. And they like to be scratched. Sometimes their skin sloughed off, but that's normal. Skritching?" he asked again. "Or does someone have another bloodfish?"

"Skritch. Bloodfish." The dolphin enunciated carefully as he raised his head. "Gooddee. Again!" The dolphin twisted his head so that the exact spot was under Alemi's fingers.

"What do they feel like?" Master Idarolan asked, his hands twitching.

"Find out yourself. Give Afo a caress. Don't touch the blowhole, but just about anywhere on the head—the melon—and the nose will please them."

"They're rubbery, but firm. Not at all slimy. Like a fish."

"Not fish. Mammal!" was Afo's instant response.

"Stars!" Idarolan lost his balance in surprise and sat down so heavily on the float that it bounced in the water and they got soaked by the backwave. "It knows what it is!"

Alemi chuckled. "Just like we do. Do you doubt their intelligence now?"

"No, I can't," Idarolan admitted. "I'm just gobsmacked, is what I am. All these Turns I've admired 'em and never thought to pass the time of day with 'em. Never thought the sounds they were making *could* be words so I didn't *listen*! Oh, I've heard others who got rescued tell me what they *thought* ..." He put a gnarled finger to his temple and twisted it in the old gesture of mental instability. "But a course, they'd have been under stress being nearly drowned and all—and the wind and storm so bad anyone could easily mistake the matter. But I've heard 'em now and no mistake." He gave his head a decisive jerk. "So, what do we do now, young Alemi?"

"Reporrrit?" Kib asked, one eye on Alemi, mouth parted in a dolphin smile.

Both men laughed aloud at that, and the two dolphins tailed it, squeeing and clicking.

"Belllill? Belllill?" The cry sounded across the sea, and Alemi and Idarolan saw more dolphins heading toward them. "Bellill rrrring! Bellill ring!"

Idarolan shook his head from side to side. "They're making 'bell' into two syllables."

"And 'oo' is you. 'Blufisss' are the parasites." Alemi grinned at the stupidity of not having understood such a common marine hazard. "A couple of other oddities, but I think if I just use the correct pronunciations, we'll have them talking the way we do. What I'd like to do now, Master Idarolan, is consolidate this start. Aivas gave me instructions on how to proceed. You could use your ship's bell at sea . . . use the sequence I rang, and ask them to report. Aivas said they know where fish are schooling, where rocks and reefs form, what the weather's likely to be. We know they rescue the shipwrecked. But there were lots of other tasks that humans and dolphins did together."

"Hmmm . . . check a ship for barnacles and holings. Check the current for speed . . . Aivas gave me the logs kept by a Captain James Tillek . . ."

"Tillek! Tillek! T'ere is a Tillek?" the dolphins cried with such passion and surprise that Alemi and Master Idarolan were startled.

"No, no Tillek here," Alemi said. *"James"*—Alemi stressed the first name—"Tillek is dead. Long dead. Gone." The dolphins nosed each other and a sad sort of sound came up from the group.

"Any rate, the captain"—Alemi grinned at Idarolan's choice of words to forestall another violent delphinic reaction—"was one of the first settlers to chart our Pernese waters. I've been reading about how the dolphins helped people get safely to the North after the volcanoes erupted. Amazing journey. Lots of small boats, and the dolphins saving everyone from drowning in one of those squalls you whip up down in these latitudes." He gave Alemi a dour glance for such squalls. "Hmmm, smart as they are, maybe they could take messages now and then. Maybe not as fast as fire-lizards, but some of those distract easily—not smart enough to keep their minds on one thing at a time."

The other dolphins had reached the float by then and were crowding about to be recognized, to speak their name and find out what Idarolan's was.

"How do they tell us apart?" Idarolan wondered.

"Ezee. Mans color," Kib said, gargling.

Alemi was positive the dolphin was laughing at them.

"These are clothes, Kib, clothes," Alemi said, holding out the fabric of the light vest he wore with one hand and the sturdy sailcloth short pants.

"Dolphins . . . not . . ." Kib enunciated clearly, "dressssssss." Then he rolled over and over in the water as if convulsed with mirth.

"Iddie" was what they could say of the Masterfishman's name, but the man didn't feel at all insulted.

"I'm honored, you know. I've talked to an animal and it

has understood my name," Idarolan said, puffing out his broad chest a bit in pride. Then he went on more confidentially: "Never would I tell of this morning to Yanus of Half Circle Sea Hold! Never! But I shall enlist the assistance of those Masters I know would appreciate the connection." He was nearly butted off his feet by an impetuous prod of a rostrum. "Excuse me, where was I?"

"Ski-ritch Temp," he was told in a very firm request. "Ski-ritch Temp."

Idarolan complied.

"This's one thing I never thought I'd find myself doing," he remarked in an undertone to Alemi.

"Nor me!"

5
▼▼▼▼▼▼▼▼▼

Alemi was not the only one wanting to have a closer understanding of the dolphins.

After T'lion and Gadareth returned Alemi to his Sea Hold, and collected the clothes that T'lion had hastily borrowed from a sleepy brown rider, the boy and the bronze did not immediately return to the Eastern Weyr.

"They're not as good as you, Gaddie," T'lion told his dragon as the bronze leaped skyward. "But don't you think talking sea animals are *great*?"

Would they talk to me, too?

"Ah, Gaddie, don't for a moment think I'd trade you for a dolphin!" T'lion laughed at the very notion, scratching the bronze neck as hard as he could with gloved fingers. He had yet to grow into all his flying gear, and the glove fingers were a joint too long, so scratching was difficult. "You and me are different . . ."

You are my rider and I am your dragon and that is a good difference, Gadareth said stoutly. *I chose you of all who were there the day I hatched* . . .

"And I wasn't even supposed to *be* a Candidate," T'lion said, grinning, vividly remembering that most exciting of all days in his life.

His brother, Kanadin, had been the official Candidate and, even though he had Impressed a brown, Kanadin had never quite forgiven his younger brother for making such a show of himself and Impressing when he hadn't even been *presented* as a possible rider. Impressing a bronze was an even more unforgivable injury.

"You're too young!" K'din had yelled at his brother when the weyrlings were led to their quarters. "You were only brought along because Ma and Pa didn't dare leave you home. How could you do this to me?"

It had never done any good for T'lion to tell K'din that he hadn't *meant* to Impress a dragon, much less a bronze, but K'din saw it as a personal offense. Not that he would have swapped his Bulith for Gadareth even ten minutes after the Impression was made. It was the fact that what should have been a momentous day for the eldest son of a journeyman resident at Landing had been trivialized by a much younger brother who had been barely the acceptable age at the time of his Impression.

T'lion had tried to explain that perhaps if this had been a Weyr like the northern ones, an interior cavern with tiers of seats set up high for the witnesses, instead of an open space around the Hatching Ground, Gadareth wouldn't have found it so easy to reach him. But the little bronze had flopped and crawled, keening with anguish, from the Hatching Sands and right up to T'lion where the boy had been standing with his parents and sister. It wasn't as if T'lion had *tried*, in any way, to attract the hatchling's attention. He hadn't so much as moved a muscle. Of course, he had been so flabbergasted to find a little dragon butting him that he had had to be urged by T'gellan—the Weyrleader—and the Weyrlingmaster to accept the Impression. Not that he could have resisted much longer, not with Gadareth so upset that he wasn't immediately accepted by his choice of partner.

Even three years on, at fifteen, T'lion stayed out of K'din's way as much as possible. Which was easier now that K'din was with a fighting wing and could sneer that T'lion had Turns yet before he, as a bronze rider, would be *useful* to the Weyr that housed and nurtured him.

T'lion was very grateful to T'gellan, the Weyrleader, and his weyrmate, Mirrim, green Path's rider, because they never once made the youngster feel unacceptable.

"The dragon chooses," T'gellan had said at the time, and often at other Impressions, shaking his head ruefully at dragon choice. Then he'd congratulated the stunned family on having *two* such worthy sons.

Since T'lion could not be included in a fighting Weyr until he was sixteen, T'gellan used the bronze pair as messengers, giving them plenty of practice in finding coordinates all over what was settled of the Southern Continent as well as the major and minor Holds and Halls in the North. T'lion took pride in being a conscientious messenger and was infallibly courteous to his passengers, never once mentioning the behavior of some of them who found going *between* frightening or unnerving. Or those who tried to order him about as if he were a drudge. No dragon *ever* chose a drudge personality. Of course, his being so young made some adults feel as if they had to patronize him . . . *him*! A dragonrider!

There are some of the fins, Gadareth said, adroitly interrupting T'lion's less than amiable thoughts. And, knowing his rider's wish before T'lion could even think it, the bronze glided down toward the pod.

Being up high gave T'lion a superb view of the pod, of their sinuous bodies leaping and plunging in the water. It was sort of like the formation of fighting wings going against Thread, T'lion thought. Only he'd heard that shipfish—no, dolphins—*liked* Thread. They'd been seen by dragonriders, swarming with other types of marine life, actually following the leading edge of Thread across the ocean.

"Less for us to flame, boy," bronze rider V'line had remarked.

However, being airborne made it a little difficult for T'lion to speak to the dolphins, even though Gadareth was agreeable to flying just above the surface, being careful not to plunge a wing into the water and off-balance himself.

Then a dolphin heaved itself up out of the water, momentarily on a level with dragon and rider, eyeing them as it reached the top of its jump before sliding gracefully back into the water.

The surprise was enough to make Gadareth veer, catching his wing tip in the water. He struggled to recover his balance, tipping T'lion dangerously against his riding straps.

"Squeeeeceh! Squeeeh! Carrrrrrerfullllll!"

There was no doubting the shout from several dolphins as Gadareth righted himself and kept a reasonable distance above the waves. Two more dolphins launched themselves up, each eyeing dragon and rider.

Recovering from the fright, T'lion responded to their scrutiny with an enthusiastic wave, trying to keep his eyes on them as they cued up and down. Then Gadareth caught the rhythm of the dolphins' maneuver: dipping down as he saw a dolphin nose appear, he arched up and over with the acrobat.

This is fun! the dragon said, his eyes whirling with green and blue.

"Funnnhn! Funnnhnn! Gaym! Pullay gaym!" the dolphins cried as they leaped up and over.

Did they hear me? Gadareth asked his astonished rider.

Getting any dolphin to answer that question was beyond the physical constraints of their present maneuvering, though T'lion shouted as loud as he could at each dolphin arching past him.

"I'll have to ask Master Alemi, Gaddie," T'lion told his dragon. "Maybe he'll know. He said Aivas told him a lot about dolphins. That's what they really are, not ship-fish, you know."

I know now. Dolphins, not shipfishes. And they can talk.

"I think we'd better go back to the Weyr," T'lion said, checking the slant of the westering sun. "And, Gaddie, let's keep this adventure to ourselves, shall we?"

It's fun to know something other people don't, the bronze replied, just as he had on several other occasions when he and his rider had spent some private time investigating on their own. There was so much to explore! Of course, if T'lion had not been conscientious about his *duties,* Gadareth would not have been so willing to take free time, but T'lion was very good about doing fun things only when he had finished his assigned chores.

Sounds were sent that the dragons which mans had made still liked dolphins. Dolphins had seen dragons in the skies since mans went to the New Place North. Dolphins had sung to dragons but had not been answered. Dragons talked to their riders in a fashion that dolphins did not quite understand. They felt the speech and saw the results—the dragon doing what the rider asked. Dragons provided many new games. They liked having their undersides ski-ritched and mans were always inspecting them so they did not have any more blufiss. They did not mind being jumped and providing sport for dolphins. They had very big and colored eyes, not like dolphins. Dolphins had jumped to see. Dragon had been pleased to see them play.

Back at Eastern Weyr, T'lion was sent off to help in the kitchen, which he never minded because it gave him a chance to see what dinner would be and he always managed to sneak a few bites. When his brother twitted him about having to do drudge chores because he wasn't big enough or old enough for anything else, T'lion invariably gave K'din the reaction he expected and never admitted that he *liked* doing the tasks set him. The best part was that he never knew from one day to the next what he'd be doing.

Before appearing at the main Weyr Hall, T'lion saw Gadareth comfortable in his own sandy wallow, a clearing in the thick jungle that T'lion had prepared for his dragon when they were considered old enough to leave the weyrling barracks. T'lion lived in a single-roomed accommodation that looked out onto the clearing. He even had a covered porch where, on the hottest nights, he slept in the hammock slung between wall and porch support. Having lived, up until his Impression, in a hold too small for all the brothers and sisters he shared it with, T'lion treasured his privacy. He felt very lucky indeed, because he could just remember the cold winters and the harsh winds of his birthhold in Benden Hold. Living south was much better. Even in Benden Weyr riders had to live in cold caves high up on the Weyrside. Here, he could live right in the forest, with fruit to be picked from branches whenever he wanted.

Over the next few weeks, T'lion and Gadareth spent a good deal of time conveying Master Menolly about, usually by direct flight, since she was too pregnant to go *between*—sometimes to Landing, but most often to Cove Hold to see Master Robinton, old Lytol, and D'ram. Neither were long flights if the winds were right, as they often were at this time of year. While he was waiting to return Master Menolly, he and Gadareth had plenty of time to bathe in the lovely waters of the cove. Then, when he and Gadareth went exploring one day, they found a second cove to the west, with deep waters, where dolphins swam.

That was quite a boon for T'lion and Gadareth, for dolphins seemed as eager to talk to them as they were to improve their relationship. Neither rider nor dragon realized that dolphins swam in groups called pods, patrolling certain areas as their home waters, just as dragons had certain areas they patrolled to keep Threadfree. T'lion didn't have a bell, couldn't find one at the Weyr Hall, but Gadareth's melodic bugle seemed to work just as well. Gadareth got brave enough, too, to settle on the water, wings spread wide to aid flotation. This provided the dolphins with yet another entertainment—leaping across the wings or coming up between Gadareth's forelegs. The dolphins also enjoyed tickling the bronze dragon by caressing their bodies on his ticklish underside, a "game" that caused T'lion to be submerged on several occasions until he learned to unfasten his riding straps before the dolphins could "attack" Gadareth.

It was Menolly's custom to send her gold fire-lizard,

Beauty, or one of the bronzes, Rocky, Diver, or Poll, to summon him back to Cove Hold. The fire-lizards were fascinated by the dolphins, perching on one of Gadareth's outstretched wings and learning just where dolphins like to be scratched with the excellent talons that were fire-lizard equipment.

Gadareth would know the gist of what the fire-lizards wished to express, and he'd tell his rider, who then informed the dolphins. It was a three-cornered conversation, but T'lion thought it helped develop more usable words and terms. Sometimes, teaching dolphins proper pronunciations, he felt like a harper. They were using words more properly now: like "we" instead of "oo-we" and "report" instead of "reporit" and "bell" instead of "bellill."

Sometimes he'd come away from these sessions feeling bigger than T'gellan!

What with all these flights and despite being in and out of Paradise River often, it was nearly six sevendays before T'lion saw Master Alemi again.

"T'lion, Gadareth, how are you?" Master Alemi said, arriving with a creel of fresh fish for Menolly.

"I'm fine, Master Alemi. How are your dolphins?"

Surprised, Alemi grinned at the boy's proper pronunciation; he was still having trouble getting others to say the word properly.

"You remembered?"

"Yes, Master, I'm not likely to forget a day like that. And ..." Then T'lion hesitated.

Alemi took him by the shoulder and looked down at him kindly. "And you've been talking to dolphins since, have you, lad?" He looked up then at Gadareth, who turned calmly spinning eyes on the fishman. "And Gadareth? What does he think of them?"

"He likes them, Master Alemi, he really does. You know

the cove west of Cove Hold? Well, the water's really deep there and the dolphins love it, too, and we've sort of had a chance to get to know some of them."

"Good!" Alemi was delighted. "Which ones? I'm trying to make a list of dolphin names. They're rather proud of them, you know."

T'lion grinned mischievously. "Don't they just get stroppy when you miscall them! Well, the ones I've met are Rom, Alta—she's pod leader—and Fessi, Gar, Tom, Dik, and Boojie, that's Alta's latest calf. And—"

"Steady on, lad," Alemi said, laughing at the torrent of names he had unleashed as he fumbled in his belt pouch for pencil and pad. "Give me that list more slowly, will you?"

T'lion complied. "Have you met any of them, Master?"

"No, but *I've* met Dar and Alta from Monaco, Kib, Afo, Mel, Jim, Mul, and Temp. You ask yours if they know mine and I'll do the same. We can compare notes later, shall we? I see you now and again, flying in, to collect Menolly, but it's usually when I'm making out to sea and can't turn back. How do you call them? D'you use a bell?"

"Gadareth bugles and they come. They like him!"

"I'd be surprised if they didn't."

"Well, we're sort of on the opposite side from the dolphins, though, aren't we?" T'lion remarked, looking up at the tall fishman. "They eat what we char."

"Point. Dolphins and dragons are both intelligent creatures. I'd say they'd respect each other's ways."

"Yes, yes, they do," T'lion said excitedly.

"What do you talk about? Does Gadareth understand them, too?"

"That's what I wanted to ask you," T'lion said, turning solemn. "*Could* they hear what he thinks?"

Alemi considered that. "Well, now, I've never heard a

dragon—not in my head as you riders do. I understand dragons can make themselves heard to people they want to talk to but, well, I haven't been so complimented."

I will speak to you, Masterfishman, Gadareth said immediately—and to T'lion's surprise.

A stunned expression came over Alemi's tanned face. "Ooosh." He put a hand to his temple, rolling widened eyes. "The words *do* just come into your head." Then he bowed formally to Gadareth. "Thank you, Gadareth. That was very kind of you."

My pleasure, Master.

"Yes, well, to answer your questions, Aivas didn't say anything about any telepathic ability in dolphins, just that they had had mentasynth enhancement."

"What's that?"

Alemi chuckled. "I'm not at all sure I understand, but it was a treatment the Ancients used and it allowed dolphins to use human speech."

"The reason I wanted to know is, well, sometimes they say something just after Gaddie and I have been talking, and it just seems as if they're answering us. Only I'm not talking out loud."

"Really? That could be merely coincidence, you know. Great minds thinking along the same lines."

T'lion absently hauled off his riding helmet, scratching at his sweaty scalp. "I suppose it could be. But you'd know, since you talked to Aivas."

Alemi gave a chuckle. "Aivas only told me what he knew, and what he got from the records. I doubt he's enjoyed our personal contact with the dolphins, or yours with your dragon."

T'lion cocked his head at Alemi. "Are yours speaking more? I mean like, telling you more things?"

Alemi thought a moment. "I believe they are. I don't

know about yours, but I've been trying to teach mine the correct pronunciation—or, rather, how *we* say words."

"It's better if they speak more like us, isn't it?"

"If we want them to be understood by people here and now, it is. But I do believe they are remembering more words." He grinned drolly. "Do try not to use words that sound alike and have different meanings. Like 'whole' and 'hole.' Dolphins know of only one hole." Alemi tapped the top of his head.

"Then it's all right for me to correct them?" T'lion asked, grinning. "I've got mine to say 'bell' and 'report' and other words properly. How come they got so . . . twisted?"

"Ah . . ." Alemi held up one hand. "We don't speak the way our ancestors did."

"We don't?" T'lion exclaimed, his eyes widening. "But the harpers are forever saying that they've helped keep the language pure, just as it's always been spoken."

Alemi laughed. "Not according to Aivas. He had to make adjustments to allow for—" Alemi hesitated briefly, trying to get the next words right. "—lingual shifts. But let's not rub harper noses in the fact. I certainly want to keep on the good side of my sister the Masterharper. I've only to mention her name and here she is! Good day to you, Master Menolly."

"Good day, Master Alemi brother. T'lion. Gadareth. How good you are to fly me so patiently," Menolly said, putting her arms through the straps of the pack she carried. "D'you mind if we hurry on, Alemi? It's so hot in riding gear. And fish for me? Thank you, 'Lemi. I'm being spoiled rotten. Camo?"

The big man came, carrying a chortling Robse pickaback.

"Here, dear, put these in the cooler, will you? What are you to do with the fish, Camo?" she said, tweaking his sleeve arm so that he looked right in her face.

"Fish?" Camo said, his expression blank as his mind tried hard to recall what she had just told him.

"Put in cooler."

"That's right." She turned him around and gave him a gentle push toward the door. "In the cooler now, Camo. Then you take Robse to 'Mina."

"Fish in cooler, Robse to 'Mina," Camo said under his breath, and he could be heard repeating his instructions as he obeyed them, Robse's happy laughter as counterpoint to his litany.

"There, now, thanks again, 'Lemi, and have a good day. Let's go, T'lion, before I sweat off my breakfast."

As they walked to the waiting bronze dragon, Menolly asked him what he and Alemi had been talking about so earnestly.

"Oh, this and that," T'lion said in a noncommittal tone, unwilling to mention what Alemi had said about the "linguistic" shift and harpers.

"You've conveyed Alemi a time or two?" she asked casually.

"That's what I'm good at," T'lion said. "You can still get up all right, Master Menolly?"

"Of course I can," she said with a trilling laugh, and proceeded to prove it. Though, in fact, it took an effort to hoist her gravid body into position between Gadareth's firm neck ridges. "Good thing you've a bronze. I'd never fit now on a blue or a brown." Then, just before T'lion urged his bronze into the sky, she added ruefully, "And very soon I fear I shan't be able to fit on Gadareth. Guess I'll have to get that brother of mine to sail me around to Cove Hold."

"Or I could bring to you the people you need to see," T'lion offered, shouting over his shoulder at her.

"That, too, if push comes to shove," she yelled back, and then the difficulty of speaking against the wind of flight kept them both silent.

T'lion was just as glad, because he wasn't sure if he should mention all his visits with the dolphins to anyone. Not even Master Menolly, who was so nice that it was easy to forget she was one of the most important Masters on Pern.

One of the archivists who thronged Cove Hold these days was on the porch and hurried down to them when they arrived.

"Master Menolly, Master Robinton would like you to go up to Landing today. Aivas has had time to release more music." The journeywoman's eyes shone with eagerness. "I hear it's simply splendid."

"Oh, it must be the sonatas we've been after him to copy to us," Menolly said, shifting herself a bit from the long ride. "Well, let's go, T'lion. I can see how Sharra's doing, too. She came south on the *Dawn Sisters* with me."

All the way up to Landing, T'lion wondered what he'd do if she started to have the baby while he was conveying her. His mother was always having babies at night, at which times he and his brothers were shoved out of the hold. He'd never be forgiven if anything happened to Master Menolly while she was in his care. He'd ask Mirrim.

That distracted him from the fact that he would have to forgo his day's idling with the dolphins. Well, he was lucky to have as much free time as he did, he told himself sternly. And the kitchens up at Landing *did* produce much better food than he generally got at noontime at Cove

Hold, where everyone usually grabbed a meatroll or cold food and continued working.

Landing was really less fun than Cove Hold. Gadareth took himself up to the heights and sunbathed, or exchanged draconic comments with whoever else had arrived from the various Weyrs.

Gadareth told him that most of the dragonriders were in some sort of conference. There were Mastersmiths, too, and half the Harper Hall, trying to construct something called a "printing press."

When T'lion sidled hopefully into the kitchen, he was immediately pounced on by the headwoman.

"Another pair of hands. T'lion, isn't it? Yes, here, make yourself useful. Take this tray—and be careful not to spill it—to the large conference room. I've all that lot to make a nooning for and not enough hands to do it." She added several more sweet rolls to the tray and winked at him. "Something for you, too, lad."

T'lion hurried off before she also thought to order him to come back so he could help her more in the kitchen.

He managed to deliver the tray and remove both his rolls and himself from the conference room before anyone questioned his presence. Hearing voices and the tread of booted feet, he ducked into the small empty room next door so he could eat his rolls in peace.

"Yes? Identify?" a deep voice requested.

Struggling not to choke on the generous bite he had just taken out of a sweet roll, T'lion looked guiltily about the room. There was no one else in it, and the door was still shut. He swallowed.

"Who's speaking?"

"Aivas. I did not realize there was a meeting scheduled here."

"Where *are* you?"'

"Please address the screen," T'lion was told.

"Huh?" But he turned toward the screen and saw the blinking red light in the lower right-hand corner.

"Identify, please?"

"You can see me?"

"Identify! Please!"

"Oh, excuse me. I'm T'lion."

"The rider of bronze Gadareth?"

T'lion gawped. "Y-y-y-y-y-yess. How'd you know?"

"A listing of all current riders in the Weyrs, their names, and the names and colors of their dragons has been input. You are welcome, T'lion. How may I help you?"

"Oh, I'm not supposed to be here. I mean, I didn't think anyone was in here and I needed a place ..." T'lion trailed off, shaking his head at his own words and stupidity. He was embarrassed to be caught where he had no business being, and amazed to be *known* by someone—something?—everyone else in his Weyr respected so highly. He didn't know what to do and felt foolish, standing there with sweet rolls in his hand. "I certainly shouldn't take up your time, Aivas."

"You have nothing of interest to report? All input is valuable."

"You mean about the dolphins?" T'lion could think of nothing else he'd been doing that would be of interest to Aivas.

"You have been in contact with the dolphins? Your report would be appreciated."

"It would?"

"Yes, it would."

"Well, I haven't done much more than correct them when they use words wrong, but Master Alemi told me that it's us who're using the wrong words." T'lion found himself grinning. It was surely all right to tell Aivas that, since Alemi had heard it from Aivas.

"Yes, that is true. Are the dolphins adapting to the correction?"

"Well, the ones I've been talking to have been very quick to correct what they say," T'lion said with a tinge of pride in his voice. " 'Gave' instead of 'gayve' and 'we' instead of 'oo-we.' They're using *more* words than they did when we first started talking."

"A fuller account is awaited."

"You really want to know? I haven't told anyone else," T'lion began, still reluctant to admit to his pastime.

"All input is useful. No one will be informed of your association if that is your wish, but your account will provide further insight into the renewal of contact."

"In that case . . ." T'lion settled himself on a chair and related his experiences, as concisely as he could since Weyrlingmaster H'mar had always insisted on detailed reports. Aivas did not interrupt him, but when he had finished speaking, he was asked to repeat all the dolphin names he had been told.

"Interesting that the names have been handed down."

"What?"

"The present dolphins seem to have shortened names from those given the original complement of *tursiops tursio.*"

"Really?"

"Kib is a short form of Kibbe, Afo possibly derived from Aphrodite, Alta from Atlanta, Dar from Dart. It is gratifying to see that they perpetuated many traditions. Please continue with your independent contact and report further discussions of any significance. Thank you, T'lion of

Eastern Weyr, bronze Gadareth's rider." The light on the screen darkened and the pule of the red corner light became much slower.

"Oh, you're welcome," T'lion replied, somewhat bemused.

His stomach put in a strong rumble, and he looked down at the sweet rolls he hadn't had a chance to eat. He mulled over the conversation with Aivas as he consumed them.

Menolly is looking for you, T'lion, Gadareth told him suddenly.

Licking his fingers clean, T'lion hurried down the hall and out the door to collect his passenger.

Master Idarolan did inform many members of his Craft of dolphin intelligence and his personal experience of it. He did not inform *all* his Craft, since he knew that some of the hidebound ones, like Yanus of Half Circle Sea Hold, would simply deny the facts. The replies he got indicated that many of his Masters and journeymen had had experiences with dolphins, or knew of them from reliable sources. Some mentioned relief at vindication of what they thought they had just imagined: shipfish talking to them. Idarolan had supplied the report peal sequence, annotated by his Hall harper, so that even the most nonmusical could ring a proper summons. He recommended that requests for assistance be rendered in simple language; he suggested asking about local fish runs, weather, or depth reports in dangerous waters.

Perusing records kept of ship sinkings, he found that most of them occurred either during storms or by sailing too close to unknown reefs, shoals, and sand banks. On some occasions the captains reported seeing dolphins veering suddenly to the port or starboard.

Now it was obvious to Master Idarolan that the dolphins had been trying to urge the helmsman to change course. Invariably the presence of shipfish was reported when a ship was storm-tossed. Not all gave credit to the saving of life by the shipfish, but it was often implied that help had been received from an external agency, most seamen being honest in what they logged.

Two incidents had been faithfully reported of small vessels that had been caught in one of the Great Currents being pushed vigorously out of the current by the efforts of shipfish.

Idarolan asked for, and received, an interview with Aivas to report his findings and to request additional advice on how to promote the association to the benefit of both parties.

He learned that pods were autonomous, following their chosen leader—usually an older female. Young males and old ones were apt to go off on their own for most of the year. He was also given a copy of the same instructions that Aivas had printed out for Alemi: the basic vocabulary of words that the dolphins had been trained to understand and the hand signals that were used underwater.

Both men were somewhat disappointed, though, to find that the news of intelligent shipfish was overshadowed by the growing industry aimed at a final battle with Thread. That was the top priority and everything else subject to that goal. Even Idarolan, after his initial fierce interest, found little time to pursue a meaningful relationship with the dolphins. He did, however, keep available on deck a pail of the small fish that Aivas said the creatures preferred. Whenever the *Dawn Sisters* had an escort, he himself offered them the reward. He also ordered his helmsmen to watch the directions the dolphins were taking and to follow their lead to the fishing grounds. In that way his hauls improved, and twice *Dawn Sisters* avoided unexpected reefs by following dolphin directions.

It was Kitrin who alerted Menolly to her brother's evening-time occupation. When the sea winds began to cool the day, Menolly gave herself such exercise as her condition permitted. Mostly she swam, delighted to have the weight of her unborn child buoyed by the sea. Aramina often joined her, with Aranya in tow. Menolly also used these evening swims as an opportunity to get to know her brother's wife better. She couldn't get Kitrin to join Aramina and herself in doing laps, but at least the woman would sit in waist-high water and benefit from the cooling circulation of water about her gravid body. Alemi had taught his older daughters how to swim, and they were quite adept, though they obeyed their mother the instant she called them to stay closer to the beach. Readis, on the other hand, needed careful observation, for he was utterly at home in the water, or under it, and had a tendency to swim farther out than his mother liked. Camo would come, too, wading out to no more than knee depth and following the fearless toddling Robse about in the shallows.

After Menolly had done what she considered sufficient laps, she would join Kitrin in the shallows to dote over the antics of their children and Readis. On one evening, Menolly asked if they could inveigle Alemi to join them. She hadn't actually had as much of Alemi's company as she had hoped, though certainly more than in previous Turns. They were very comfortable with each other in a way that would never have been possible at Half Circle Sea Hold, and she would have liked to spend more time with him.

"Oh, he's off on some Craft project most evenings," Kitrin said with a dismissive wave of her hand and a grin for male enthusiasms. "I never interfere with Hall matters and whatever it is, he comes back well pleased from the time spent on it."

Menolly frowned. She had explored most of the area in her daily walks, with and without her pupils, and she couldn't remember seeing any evidence of a project. "Building a new skiff, is he?"

It was Kitrin's turn to frown in concentration. "I don't think so, because I believe he sent an order to the crafters at Ista—about the one Hall that isn't overinvolved with Aivas commissions." She straightened abruptly, one hand going to her belly. "Oh, I do so hope this one's a boy. They say that if you've morning sickness, you're carrying a boy?" She cocked her head to Menolly for confirmation.

Menolly shrugged, grinning in Robse's direction. He was having an argument with the little ripples that flowed in as he tried to dig something out of the sand at his feet. Imperiously he held up one hand to the next wave and shrieked with indignation when it, too, splashed him. Camo came bounding over to see if the toddler was in any danger.

"I'm not the one to ask. I didn't have morning sickness with Robse and certainly none with this one. What about Aramina?"

Kitrin sighed. "She never has problems."

"Don't fret, Kitrin," Menolly said gently, laying a soothing hand on the other woman's forearm. Kitrin was a dainty person, with fine features and long black hair now braided and coiled about her well-shaped head. Her brown eyes were clouded with anxiety. "Alemi adores you and will continue to do so whether you ever give him a son or not." Then she wrinkled her face. "I remember that most Seahold women wanted daughters so they wouldn't have to face losing them to storms at sea."

"Oh?" Then Kitrin looked about, although they were alone in the water. Touching Menolly's arm to indicate a confidence, she leaned closer. "Have *you* heard that shipfish—Alemi insists on calling them doll-fins now—are intelligent? And speak?"

"Yes, I have heard that rumor. From Readis," she added with a smile, "who told me in great detail the first day I held class that he had been rescued by 'mam'ls.' Quite a harper tale it was, too."

Kitrin heaved another of her sighs. "Well, it was *true*. Alemi says so. He was even sent for by Aivas to come to Landing and give a report on the incident." She leaned ever closer. "*I* think that it's the doll-fins he talks to in the evenings. If the wind is right I can hear a bell. He put in an order, I know, to the Smithcrafthall for a big bell, but with all they're doing for Aivas and the Benden Weyrleaders, it'll be ages before they get around to casting it. So he got a small one from Master Robinton. I think he uses it to summon the doll-fins. He's got it on the pier around on the headland so he won't upset Aramina, or let Readis know what he's doing."

"Readis?" Menolly's gaze went to the intrepid boy, who was diving in and out of the water, in much the same way she had observed shipfish disporting themselves.

"Yes, well, she does not want Readis getting keen to talk to shipfish. Just see how he's swimming right now. Readis!" she called. "Swim back into shore now!" She turned back to Menolly. "That's what I mean and what worries her. Why, he'd swim right out to sea to meet a dolphin. No fear on him."

"Well, I can help distract him from that," Menolly said. "At his age, they don't have a long concentration span." She gave a sigh. "You have to keep one step ahead of them, with something new to do, a game or a challenge. Your girls are a great help with him, by the way. Such biddable children."

Kitrin sat a bit straighter, delighted at such praise of her Kitral, Nika, and Kami, and neatly diverted away from the previous topic.

Curious, Menolly took the next opportunity she had to follow the well-used lane through the trees and shrubs that flourished on the headland to the pier. On that quiet evening, the three fishing ships were at anchor in the small bay on the eastern side of the head, their skiffs tied to the rings on the pier. At first she didn't see Alemi, though she could hear voices—some of them pitched at a very odd level and emitting some very odd sounds. She saw the splashing first, and realized that half a dozen shipfish heads were protruding from the water. And it was they who were making the odd sounds: squees and clicks and watery noises. Only when she had walked to the end of the pier did she see her brother, below the pier deck, sitting cross-legged on a fragile raft that was nearly flooded by the vigorous wavelets splashed on it by the shipfish.

She nearly fell off the side of the pier when a shipfish suddenly jumped into the air, one black eye fixed on her before it fell back into the water, squeeing.

"Squeee! New game coming, 'Lemi?" it asked plainly.

Alemi's head appeared above the deck of the pier. "Menolly?"

"None other, brother," she said at her drollest, peering

down at his surprised face. "Is this a secret?" she asked, gesturing at the attentive faces, now turned in her direction.

"This is Menolly, my pod sister," Alemi said to the dolphins. Menolly suppressed a burst of laughter as he went on. "Menolly, starting on the port side, here are Kib, Afo, Mel, Temp, Biz, and Rom. Jim and Mul are missing this evening."

"I am pleased to make your acquaintance," Menolly said in slow formal tones, nodding her head at each smiling shipfish face in the circle.

"G'day, Nolly," several chorused at her. She was unable to suppress laughter any longer. "Nolly has babbee inside."

"My word! I know I'm big with child but how would they know?" she exclaimed, pausing in her attempt to get her awkward pregnant body arranged in a sitting position on the edge of the pier.

"They know or, as they put it, 'member' rather a lot about humans. Nolly! That's a fair nickname."

"The dolphins may, but *you* may not," she said sternly. "What're you discussing?"

"I'm getting tomorrow's weather and a fish report," he told his sister.

"Really?"

"The dolphins have been very helpful over the past few weeks. We've never had better hauls. They know exactly where schools are feeding and lead us right to them. My men are delighted, since it means less time at sea as well as sufficient warning on squalls."

"Oh, yes, that would be helpful, wouldn't it?" Menolly made herself as comfortable on the hard planking as she could. "Readis told me all about your dramatic rescue."

Alemi grinned. "I don't think he's embroidered it much

from the last time I heard him tell it. And it really happened, sister. Only," he added, waving his hand at the raft and dolphins, "Aramina would rather Readis forgot that adventure."

"So Kitrin told me, and now I know, I can divert him. 'Mina should have told me."

Alemi shrugged. "She's still recovering from the shock of your appearance, Masterharper sister dear."

"Oh? She seems pleased."

"Of course she is. Who wouldn't want a harper of your talent to teach their children?"

"Teach? Teach?" asked two shipfish.

"Oh, sorry, fellas," Alemi said, turning back to the bottlenoses. "Where were we? I teach them new words—or, rather, get them to remember them."

"You? Teaching?"

"C'mon, Menolly, I was Petiron's pet student until you came along."

"Oh, and you've sung to your new friends?"

"No."—Alemi refused to rise to her bait.—"You're the singer in the family. And the teacher!"

Menolly shot her brother a close look. Alemi had a teasing streak in him, but he was quite sincere.

"Go on," he said. "You sang to the fire-lizards, why not to dolphins? I'll do the tenor line, if you'll sing something I know."

"Very well." She launched into one of the sea songs she had composed not long after she had walked the tables as a journeywoman. Alemi's well-placed voice joined immediately in harmony. After the first startled squees and clickings, her audience was silent. Beauty, Rocky, and Diver appeared suddenly in the air, settling on pilings, eyes whirling fast with curiosity as they saw her audience.

"Zea zong," one of the shipfish said when the last notes

died away. "Nolly zing zea zong." The sibilants were drawn out.

"Zeee, squeeee zong," another added, and Menolly laughed.

"Sea song, you silly creatures. Sea, not *zee.*"

Then abruptly the shipfish began an intricate maneuver in and over the sea's surface, all the time squeeing "Ssseee song, seee song" and on several tones so that it was almost a chord to what she and Alemi had sung. Delighted at their antics and the apparent compliment, Menolly clapped her hands. Two shipfish splashed water with their flippers as if imitating her action.

"They *are* intelligent, 'Lemi. Do they mean to be funny?"

"Just look at their smiling faces. They're right rascals when they want to be," Alemi said, hauling himself up off the float to sit beside her.

"Sing song, Nolly? Sing two song, Nolly?"

"All right, but settle down. You can't hear me when you're splashing around like that."

Beauty assumed her usual perch on Menolly's shoulder, wrapping her tail about her neck but being careful how she placed her talons on the fabric of the light top Menolly was wearing. Menolly put up a caressing hand as she began one of the Traditional ballads. Menolly was accustomed to respectful listeners, but the attentiveness of these sea creatures was the most intense she had ever encountered. They listened with eye, body, and whole being. They didn't even seem to breathe. Softly, in her ear, she heard Beauty begin her usual soft descant. The shipfish heard it, too, for their eyes turned slightly to her left and their grins, if anything, seemed to widen. Menolly had had many rare musical experiences with audiences, but this surely was unique. She would have to tell Sebell all about it. She would never forget this evening! From the expression on his face, she doubted Alemi would either.

Darkness came with the usual tropical immediacy, and suddenly they were enclosed in the dark of full night, the attentive dolphin heads gleaming silvery in the light of Timor just rising over the sea.

"Thank you one and all," Menolly said in a voice vibrant with gratitude. "I shall never forget meeting you."

"Thank you, Nolly. Love man song."

"In this case it is a woman song," Alemi said in wry correction.

"Nolly song. Nolly song!" was the rejoinder.

"Diff'rent, better, best," Afo added, ducking her head and flipping a spray at them with her nose in farewell.

Menolly and Alemi watched as the six plunged seaward, leaping and diving gracefully until they could no longer be seen.

"Well, that was much more than I could ever have anticipated," Menolly said as they walked slowly back toward the Hold, Alemi holding the glowbasket that he had learned to bring for the dark return walk. "It's almost a shame, really."

"What?"

"That there's all this fuss and industry over Thread when Aivas has so much more to offer us."

"What could be more important than getting rid of Thread forever?" Alemi asked, surprised by her comment. "Interest in the dolphins is likely to be limited to my Hall and totally ignored by land dwellers. No, I'm as glad to keep them as useful allies, like dragons or fire-lizards. They're far more intelligent than runner beasts, or even the canines, and are far more use to us than fire-lizards. Especially since they can communicate verbally, rather than mentally the way dragons—or even fire-lizards, with their limited range—do."

"No, let's not belittle fire-lizards, not to she who has ten and uses all her fair. Does Master Idarolan know of these—" She laughed. "—sea dragons of yours?"

"Of course. He was the first person—besides Aivas—I talked to. I send him regular reports on my progress with this pod."

"Pod?"

"Yes, that's the name for individual units. Pods. Each one has waters it prefers to fish and play in. They're great ones for games, dolphins are." Alemi laughed indulgently. "As far as they're concerned, I'm just a new game they're playing."

"But you said that they gave you information about fishing and squalls?"

"Oh, they do, but reporting's more like a game to them."

"Oh, I see."

"Don't discount the usefulness of such a game, Menolly," he added earnestly.

"No, I won't, but I do see that their appeal would be—should be—limited. They're certainly not as easy to take home as fire-lizards."

"True," Alemi said, chuckling. "But they are endlessly interesting with their observations. They're much more their own selves than fire-lizards or even dragons. If they're not interested, they go off." Alemi shrugged.

"Like children . . ."

"Yes, very much like children at times."

"Well, fire-lizards have proved useful," Menolly said with a tinge of irritation in her tone. Some people discounted the many ways in which fire-lizards *were* useful.

"Easy, Nolly," Alemi said, and his tone made her look up at him to see his white teeth showing in his grinning face. "And it was your method of teaching a fire-lizard manners that has helped me make meaningful contact with the dolphins."

"Sorry, brother," Menolly said sheepishly.

"We have much to be thankful to the Ancients for," Alemi said in an expansive tone.

"Though I wonder," Menolly replied thoughtfully, "if we will say the same in a few Turns' time when Aivas unleashes all the wonders stored up."

"I thought Harpers were applauding all the—what is it Aivas calls it—input?"

"Knowledge is sometimes two-edged, Alemi. You learn about all the marvels that used to be and they set the standard for what can be, and maybe shouldn't be."

"Are you worried?"

"Oh," she said and shook herself, "put my fancies down to pregnancy. There's so much we don't know, don't remember, have lost. Like shipfish—excuse me, doll-fins—being able to speak intelligently. Every time I visit Cove Hold, D'ram or Lytol or Master Robinton have something newly remarkable to recount. The mind can only absorb so much."

"Isn't it up to the Harper Hall and the Benden Weyrleaders to see that we learn only the best of what there is?" He was half-teasing, half-serious.

"Indeed it is." She was very solemn. "A great responsibility, I assure you."

"You must find it dull living here in such a backwater."

"Not at all, 'Lemi." She paused, catching his arm and giving him a little shake. "Frankly, living here and teaching your lovely children has given me a much-needed respite and a chance to gain some perspective on all that's happening to our way of life."

"It's improved, that's what's happened."

"Ah, but is it really *improvement*?"

"You're in an odd mood, Menolly."

"I think of more things than the next song to write."

"I never said you didn't."

"No, you never did. Sorry, 'Lemi. Nighttime confessions and doubts generally are regretted in daylight."

Alemi put his arm about her shoulders in reassurance. "Don't ever doubt yourself, Menolly. You've come such a long way."

She chuckled. "Yes, I have, haven't I?" She clasped his hand on her shoulder, suffused with warm feelings for this favorite brother.

"But you can see, as a Harper and a sea-bred holder, how helpful the relationship with dolphins can be."

"Yes, indeed I can, above and beyond my gratitude for their rescue of you and Readis."

"Mind you," he put in, his fingers squeezing her shoulders in warning, "don't mention this evening to Readis or Aramina, will you?"

"No, of course not. But I'd like to tell Sebell and Master Robinton."

"Them, of course."

She declined his invitation to join him and Kitrin for an evening cup of klah or wine. He saw her safely to her holding despite her protests that she was able to see her way clear to her own door. She had every intention of sitting down and writing to Sebell of the evening's surprise, but the sight of the hammock swinging lightly in the night breeze was irresistible, and she sank into it—only for a moment, she thought—and fell instantly asleep.

Afo ecstatically reported the Nolly singing to them. Dolphins had songs of their own, which all the Tilleks had taught so well they were embedded in their memories, which they sang remembering the waters they had come from. Sometimes the songs were sad—from the times when many dolphins died in nets that entangled them. Sometimes the sadness came from missing the mans, the great work that had been done and the happy partnerships. The happy songs were from the things dolphins had learned to do with mans, the Dunkirk, the Crossing of the Great Currents, the Swimming of the Whirlpool, or the finding of man things that got into the water and shouldn't stay there; the saving of mans in storms. There were many songs dolphins would sound. Sometimes every pod would join in, weaving the sounds back and forth across the sea of Pern.

That darktime many songs floated on the Great Currents.

That they disturbed the sleep of two women and one small boy at Paradise River Hold was something that ended on the morning tide. But the song remained, a faint and pleasant memory, not a sad one as it had been at other times.

6

Although Aramina suspected that Alemi spent a great deal of time talking to the doll-fins, he never mentioned it to anyone in her hearing. Gradually, Readis's adventure with the shipfish faded as other experiences—such as learning his Traditional ballads under the guidance of Master Menolly and the births of her second son, Olos, and Kitrin's long-awaited son, Aleki—superseded that occasion. She began to relax again.

Readis was a very strong young swimmer, but she had no wish to see his strength overtaxed by further direct association with the sea creatures—mammals or whatever they were—luring him out beyond his depth. Readis was to succeed his father as Holder of Paradise River, though she secretly harbored the thought that he might be Searched for a dragonrider to the Eastern Weyr: He might be what she hadn't had the courage to pursue. He certainly enjoyed the company of the many dragons that came to Paradise River Hold; he'd scrubbed many a hide in the warm waters, and most often Lord Jaxom's white Ruth, who appeared to have a special affinity for her son. It wasn't beyond the realm of possibility, really, she thought, that Readis might have the same extraordinary option of being both rider and Holder that Lord Jaxom had enjoyed. Although, with all the plans to rid Pern of Thread forever, there'd be less objection to his dual role. From time to time, she wondered—as many did on Pern—if Weyrs would be disbanded after Thread no longer plagued them.

Of course, *if* Readis became a dragonrider, he would still be quite young—in his early thirties—when this Pass ended: more reason for him to be both rider and holder. After all, Jayge was a vigorous man and likely to last well past the end of Thread. So Readis *could* ride and hold.

Then, too, dragons *would* speak to him, a momentous concession even if he didn't realize it yet in his youthful innocence. He wouldn't know how much their willingness to do so gladdened her heart. Maybe that would weigh in their accepting him as a Candidate on the Hatching Sands. She wasn't at all sure how Jayge would view her ambitions for her son. But that didn't mean she couldn't have them. Readis's case was entirely different from hers in every respect. There was no reason *not* to consider that tantalizing future for her son.

The new harper came, appointed by Menolly herself to succeed her: a journeyman named Boskoney, in his early twenties and bred in a fishing hold on Ista, so he was accustomed to the climate and occupations of Paradise

River. She'd done the Paradise River holders the courtesy of presenting several candidates.

"I'm not going to let those lovely children be saddled by some journeyman who only wants to warm his bones in this climate," she told them. "They have to have someone as alert, eager, and," she added with a smile, "as adventurous and understanding of this environment as possible. We do have a lovely girl finishing her apprenticeship, if you wouldn't mind a woman harper ..." Menolly had cocked her head at her friends with a sly grin and a twinkle in her eye.

"Of course we wouldn't mind," Jayge and Alemi said in unison, then smiled at each other.

"As well, but Hally won't walk the tables for another nine or ten months and it's not good to start the teaching process and then interrupt it for such a long time. The children of this Hold are *eager* to learn, and I don't like to put them off."

She went on to point out the strengths and failings of each of the other young men. Perschar, the best artist in the Harper Hall, had sent along portrait sketches of Boskoney, Tomol, and Lesselam, several poses of each, including a full-length drawing in color.

"I never expected we'd have a choice," Aramina said, scrutinizing the drawings.

Menolly grinned at her. "What? And deprive my nieces, and nephews, of the best education there is? Of course, whoever comes here will have to spend some time helping the archivists with the music Aivas has been churning out for us. Tagetarl's in charge of the actual printing, but the Paradise River Hold harper is close enough to assist the work. That won't be a problem, will it?"

"Not at all," Jayge said. "We're quiet here and there are not that many children . . ."

"Yet," Aramina added with a wink. When the excitement of that admission had abated, she asked if any of the men were married.

"Not yet." Menolly grinned. "You've several lovely girls here among your holders. We have to give *them* some choice, too, and not limit it to smelly seamen." She grinned at her brother.

"I like him," Aramina said, pointing to Boskoney. "He has a kind eye." Boskoney was not the handsomest of the three, nor the tallest. His curly hair was sun-bleached, and there were laugh wrinkles at the corners of his eyes. She felt comfortable looking at his portrait, whereas the other two faces didn't seem as . . . candid. "Ista bred, did you say? Then he won't mind the heat so much as the other two. And we won't have to explain about firehead and the other *dis*advantages of living in a tropical climate."

"Very well," Menolly said briskly, pushing the sketch of Boskoney over to her. "Sebell will inform Boskoney of his posting and I'll ask T'gellan to send a rider to collect him. I'd like to discuss the various children with him so he'll know what aspects to concentrate on. They're such a lovely handful. I've quite enjoyed my time. Ooops, there's the baby awake again."

Boskoney arrived, was duly briefed by Menolly on his students' abilities, and settled in the harper's hold as if he'd always been there. Menolly promised to visit Paradise River Hold again, especially when Camo volunteered the information that he would like to stay warm here. He didn't like winter, but then, as Menolly explained, he had trouble remembering to put on his jacket as the year progressed into winter, and he would forget to take it off as the year wound into spring and summer.

Boskoney elected to do his Harper Hall duty at Landing in the evenings, and T'lion and Gadareth were usually assigned to convey him. That suited T'lion, Gadareth, and Alemi, for they continued to improve their relations with the dolphins, and now there were many pods that would respond to the bells. In the biggest tree bordering the strand nearest Eastern Weyr, T'lion had cobbled a sort of belfry arrangement—using a smaller bell than Alemi used at Paradise Head.

It wasn't that he was *trying* to be secretive about his activity. It was more that he was relishing the association so much—as was Gadareth—that he didn't want his efforts ridiculed or demeaned. After all, it wasn't as if Weyrleader T'gellan didn't *know* that dolphins rescued the sea-stranded. It was only that he, T'lion, hadn't exactly explained the relationship he was improving all the time.

A summons to the Weyrleader's quarters that morning in no way alarmed T'lion, since T'gellan often sent for him to assign the day's chores. But he did not expect to see his brother there, and he was not at all reassured by the smug expression on K'din's face and the stern ones T'gellan and Mirrim wore.

I don't know why you're upset, Monarth, T'lion heard his dragon say quite loudly in his head. *They are dolphins that the ancients brought here. They save lives. They can speak to anyone.*

That gave T'lion the clue he needed: K'din had been spying on his evening sessions with the dolphins.

"I believe you have some explaining to do, T'lion,"

T'gellan said sternly, cocking an eyebrow at his young rider. Mirrim also looked repressive.

"About the dolphins?" T'lion hoped he sounded more relaxed then he actually was.

"Dolphins?"

"Yes, dolphins is what Aivas called them." He saw the Weyrleaders exchange glances as he casually dropped in that authority. "They came with the Ancients, you know. They had been given mentasynth enhancement so they could speak with their human partners, the dolphineers." He got all the big words out without tripping over them.

T'gellan frowned. "You've been to Aivas with this?"

"Well, no, *he* interviewed *me*. Master Alemi at Paradise River Hold is working very closely with the dolphins, since they give him weather reports, news about what fish are running and where. Saves the fishmen a lot of trouble. And better yet, they warn about squalls."

"They do!" T'gellan said, more statement than question, digesting T'lion's cheerfully rendered explanation.

"And just how did you get involved, T'lion?" Mirrim wanted to know.

"Oh, you know how these things happen, Mirrim. Like the time you impressed your fire-lizards."

She frowned, giving him a don't-you-be-cocky-with-me stare. "You Impressed these creatures?"

"No, nothing like that." T'lion dismissed the suggestion with a flick of his hand. "Nothing like dragons." His tone also relegated the association to a less significant interface. "They are useful, though." He decided not to add "like fire-lizards." "You summon them with a bell peal. If they feel like it, they answer. Mostly they do because we're sort of a new game for them."

"New game?" T'gellan leaned forward.

"That's what Master Alemi said. The pod that lives in

these waters is different from the one he's in contact with. Aivas wants us to find out how many there are and try to improve their language skills."

"Language skills?" Mirrim said, blinking at him.

T'lion gave a shrug. "That's the term Aivas used. They speak badly—they say 'mans' for 'men' and 'gayve' instead of 'gave,' messing up words something fearful. I have to sort of teach them how to speak correctly."

K'din gave a scornful guffaw. "You, a teacher?"

"I do know more words than the dolphins do," T'lion replied serenely.

"Just when do you teach them, T'lion?"

The young bronze rider could see he wasn't out of the fire yet as far as his Weyrleader was concerned. "Oh, when I have time. Like when I'm bathing Gadareth. He rather likes the dolphins. They swim under him and tickle his belly. And when I'm scrubbing his wings, they vault over them."

"Do they so?" The Weyrleader's tone was rhetorical, and T'lion remained silent, trying to act nonchalant.

Had K'din actually suggested that he was depriving or neglecting Gadareth in favor of dolphins? Not that he could be drummed out of the Weyr or anything! However, he could be disciplined and kept from associating with the dolphins. Had he mentioned Aivas enough so that T'gellan would be satisfied? Or had he made too much of that association for a Weyrleader's unease?

"I think we'd better meet these . . ."

"Dolphins, Weyrleader. They'd be pleased to make your acquaintance, too." T'lion sounded as cheerful as he could, but he hoped the dolphins would display their positive talents instead of their love of play and games. "Can my brother come? So he can get a good square look at the dolphins?"

T'gellan regarded the older brown rider with a speculative look. "I do believe that might be salutary."

"Yes, very," Mirrim added with a sour look in K'din's direction.

Monarth and Path are interested. I told them everything we do. But we should have told the Weyrleaders sooner. That is one thing wrong. I don't understand the other.

Not the most reassuring remark Gadareth could have made.

As T'lion turned to follow the Weyrleaders out to their waiting dragons, he realized that Gadareth was correct about not informing his Weyrleaders sooner. But, with conveying Menolly and others about, he hadn't been much in the Weyr these days.

But much on the seaside talking to dolphins, Gadareth reminded him conscientiously.

That brother of mine, T'lion thought back to his bronze. *He'd love nothing better than to get me in trouble with the Weyrleaders.*

Buleth doesn't like it.

Good on Buleth, then.

Fortunately for T'lion's purpose of demonstration, Tana and Natua appeared as soon as the bell peal had echoed across waters slightly roughened by a sea breeze and the incoming tide. T'lion walked in to waist depth to meet the two, while the others stood on the shore, dragons, riders, and Mirrim's fire-lizards.

"Just you two?" T'lion asked, having hoped to have more of the pod to show off. Then he raised his voice so those on the beach could hear what he said as he made introductions. "Tana, Natua, that's my pod leader, T'gellan,

and his mate, Mirrim. And K'din." He was *not* going to
introduce him as his brother.

"G'day, Gellin, Mirm," Natua said politely while Tana
splashed water in their direction.

"G'day, Natua," Mirrim said, and waded out to stand
by T'lion. She had a grin on her face. Her fire-lizards
swirled above her head protectively. She patted the
bottlenose that Natua pushed at her. Tana did a swim-by,
observing Mirrim with first one eye and then the other on
the return trip. Then she reared up in the water so that she
and Mirrim were at eye level. "G'day, Tana. Water good?"

"Fine. Fish fine, too. Pod eating. Good eating."

It was clear that Tana wanted to know what game
they'd be playing, so T'lion hastily intervened. "Sorry to
call you from feeding, Tana."

"Bell ring. We answer. We promise. We here."

He was also pleased that their speech was so clear—
he'd finally broken their habit of saying "oo-ee" for "we."

"It's very good of you to be so prompt because my pod
leaders wanted to meet you."

Natua did a backward flip, showering water on Mirrim
and T'lion. Mirrim's expression went blank as water
dripped from her head and shoulders. T'lion winced. He
was so accustomed to such antics, that he hadn't thought
to warn her. Mirrim flicked water off her arms and gave
a deep sigh.

"You didn't need to soak Mirrim," T'lion said, shaking
a finger at Natua. The dolphin squee'ed and cut a circle
about the two humans.

"Water warm. Good," Natua said, his lower jaw dropping in a smile as he came to a halt by the young rider.

Mirrim began to laugh. "What's a soaking to sea creatures? And I did enter his water." She used both hands to
shake water out of her hair. "You like soaking humans."

"You woman, not oomans," Natua said.

Mirrim made an O with her mouth, amazed that he recognized the difference. "Thank you, Natua! C'mon in, T'gellan, you're missing half the fun and the water's . . . warm!"

Then, to everyone's shock, Tana delivered a surprise. "You have a baby inside."

"*What?*" Mirrim cried, arching her body toward the dolphin.

"Tana sees baby."

"What did you say? Now, wait a minute, you, you *fish!*" Mirrim said, shock briefly draining color out of her face before indignation brought on a deep flush under her tanned skin.

"What'd that critter just say?" T'gellan demanded, wading out to his weyrmate and putting a protective arm about her.

T'lion was aghast. He didn't know what to do. He gulped and stammered, until he caught his brother's smug expression.

"It said I'm pregnant," Mirrim replied. "This is not a joking matter, doll-fin!"

"Not joking," Tana said. "I know. Always we know. Sonar tells truth about wo-man body."

"Sonar? What's that?" T'gellan demanded of his young rider. "Just what is going on here?"

"I don't know," T'lion said in a wail.

"I right. You ask medic. Squeee! Good time is baby time. I have baby, too. Like it."

"Medic?" T'gellan echoed, ignoring the rest of the comment.

"That's what the Ancients called healers," Mirrim murmured, her head bent to watch the hand she put on her belly, just below the watery surface.

"I'm sorry, Mirrim. I don't know ..." T'lion said, appalled by the incident and Tana's declaration. How could she queer this meeting? He'd thought they were his *friends*! He might just as well plead to be transferred to another Weyr before his disgrace became planetwide—and he had no doubt at all that K'din would see that everyone knew! He'd truly shamed his family now. And he'd been so proud to speak to shipfish! To his growing horror, Tana didn't stop chattering and Natua was nodding violently as if he, too, concurred!

"I know. Woman is preg-nant," Tana repeated, excitedly weaving about in front of the three humans. Then, before anyone guessed her intent, she dropped back into the water and, with the greatest care and lightest touch, put her nose over Mirrim's hand. "Have baby. Not soon. Small."

T'gellan exchanged glances with his weyrmate and began to smile tenderly at Mirrim.

"Not that I don't wish you were, Mir," he said so softly that T'lion wasn't sure he'd heard properly.

"But nothing's happened yet—I mean, it's much too soon to be sure," Mirrim murmured back, looking up at the tall bronze rider, her expression equally tender. Then she gave herself a shake and started to wade to the shore. "First thing, we find out from Aivas if that silly sea creature could possibly know what it's talking about." She swiveled back toward T'lion. "You come, too, T'lion, and we'll just settle the matter for once and all. Can't have a rider your age dealing with erratic creatures like these."

I love you, T'lion, Gadareth said in such a vehement tone that T'lion was a little comforted. Until he saw the triumphant expression on K'din's face. He closed his eyes, trying to close his ears against the joyous sounds of squeeing and clicking the two dolphins were making as he waded out of the water. *I like the dolphins,* Gadareth said. *They have such fun and make things fun for us, too.*

Don't talk to me about doll-fins right now, Gaddie. You don't know what they've just done.

I know. Path knows. Path is glad if her rider is to have a baby.

T'lion groaned as he obeyed T'gellan's hand signal to mount the young bronze.

"You'll come, too, K'din," T'gellan said, and his expression was suddenly severe. "I want you where I can see you. We're flying straight."

Mirrim had mounted Path, water dripping from her wet legs and clothing and running down the green's sides.

"Keep it a low flight," she said. "We'll dry out as we go, but I don't want it fast either." She did not so much as look in T'lion's direction, which depressed him even further.

Schools of fish and warnings of shoals and squalls were well within a dolphin's abilities, but this? T'lion allowed his body to move with Gadareth's upward leap, but he felt wooden, and scared, and totally miserable. How could Natua and Tana treat him so? Just when he needed them to show at their very best. He'd never even had a chance to ask them about weather bearing down on them, or schools in the sea off Eastern Weyr . . .

The straight flight, though it wasn't actually that far, seemed to take ages. His clothes were dry and his nose burned enough to hurt by the time they reached Landing. K'din's smugness became slightly tinged with awe as he followed his leaders into the Admin and right up to the table where D'ram was currently serving as visit monitor.

"T'gellan, Mirrim, how very good to see you! Monarth and Path are well? And here's T'lion again, and this is your older brother, isn't it, T'lion? A noticeable family resemblance."

"Good day, D'ram, Tiroth looks fat and fine up there in the sun," T'gellan said pleasantly but with an unmistakable urgency in his tone.

"A problem?"

"Yes, and one which only Aivas can solve for us. Is there any free time to query him?"

"Yes, certainly. Try the small conference room. T'lion knows the way."

T'lion would have given anything right now not to be so well known to D'ram. As the ex-Istan Weyrleader gave him a smiling permission to proceed, T'lion shrank in on himself.

"Lead on, T'lion," T'gellan ordered, an indefinable expression on his face as he followed.

T'lion trudged disconsolately toward the conference room and utter humiliation, a short walk that seemed as long as the flight straight.

Monarth said they would like to have a baby, Gadareth told him in a cheerful tone. *Path agrees.*

But what if Tana can't know? What if she's wrong? I'll die!

No, Gadareth said, his tone chiding him for rashness, *because you would not like me to die, too, would you?*

No, of course not! T'lion gave himself a shake. Whatever happened now, he still had Gadareth. No one could part him from his dragon.

He pushed open the door.

"Aivas, it's T'lion here with Weyrleader T'gellan and green Path's rider, Mirrim," he announced to the screen. Only when he had caught a reproving glance from T'gellan did he mutter K'din's name.

"What is the topic of your discussion today? The dolphins?"

"How did he know?" Mirrim asked in an undertone.

"Because T'lion usually reports on the progress of his meetings with the dolphins, Mirrim," Aivas said, and Mirrim winced, having forgotten the acuteness of the facility's "hearing."

Mirrim came straight to the point. "One of the dolphins, Tana, said I was pregnant."

"If the dolphin noticed an alteration in your womb, she is likely to be accurate."

A profound silence fell on the small conference room.

"Well, now, how? I didn't even know myself, Aivas," Mirrim said, easing herself onto a chair. "I mean . . ."

"Dolphin sonar—"

"That was the word she used!" T'gellan exclaimed. "Sonar . . . What is that?"

"Dolphin sonar is the means by which they navigate across the oceans of Pern, sending out signals and reading the sound waves that return to them. Sonar also informs the dolphin of minute changes in body mass. Dolphins accurately diagnose not only pregnancy but bodily tumors and growths and often other illnesses in their early stages. Medics—healers in your current parlance—relied on dolphin diagnostics as unique and correct."

"You mean, Mirrim *is* pregnant?" T'gellan asked.

"If a dolphin has pronounced it, indubitably she is with child."

T'lion looked from the radiant smile that suffused Mirrim's face to T'gellan's proud posture. Out of the corner of his eye he caught the grimace on his brother's face, but he was careful not to exhibit his elation at Aivas's verdict. He didn't want to prod K'din into further acts of retaliation. It was enough that he, T'lion, was right, and he mentally kicked himself for doubting the dolphins. But he hadn't had any idea they could "see" into human bodies!

"Perhaps this facet of dolphin abilities has been over-looked?" Aivas asked after T'gellan and Mirrim had shared a happy embrace.

T'gellan looked at T'lion, who shrugged.

"I think we should ask the Weyr healer to look into the matter," T'gellan said. "Would the dolphins see infections that lie under the skin and then erupt?"

"The records so indicate. Do you refer to a puncture wound?"

"Yes, I do. M'sur nearly lost his leg because it wasn't until he saw the red lines of blood poisoning that he real-ized he had a severe injury. Persellan had a time saving his life and his leg!" Then T'gellan turned to T'lion. "I think we'd best inform the Healer Hall at Fort about this."

"D'you think they'll believe you?" Mirrim said with a laugh. Her left hand hovered on her belt, fingers spread over her belly as if she still couldn't credit the diagnosis.

T'gellan shrugged, grinning. "They can or cannot as they so choose but I've a duty to inform them."

"There's a healer here at Landing, isn't there?" Mirrim asked. "Oh, thank you, Aivas, for your time."

"You are welcome, dragonrider Mirrim."

"My gratitude, Aivas, on several counts." T'gellan gave T'lion a reassuring grin. "That meeting with your dolphin friends took a most unexpected turn, lad. We thank you. Mirrim's lost two babes because she didn't know she was pregnant. We don't want to lose another. Come." He put one hand on Mirrim's waist, guiding her out the door. "We'll inform D'ram of this. He'll see that the Healer Hall is informed."

"Yes, best coming from him," Mirrim agreed, but she beckoned for T'lion to walk beside her on their way out.

It took a moment or two for D'ram to absorb the astonishing news; then he rose from his chair and heartily shook T'gellan's hand, beaming at Mirrim.

"It's always been a problem for Weyrwomen to know when they have conceived . . . and stay out of *between* in the first few months. You'll have women flocking to the shores to speak to dolphins."

"I'm not sure that's what we want," T'gellan said, somewhat alarmed.

"Oh, well, yes, but I shall inform the Healer Hall and they can make what arrangements they find useful."

"If they believe the story," Mirrim said.

"Oh, I know a few who are open-minded enough to investigate—especially if Aivas has verified the matter. First I shall ask Aivas to give me what information he has on the diagnostic abilities of the dolphin. Nothing like the printed word to reassure." Then the old Weyrleader turned to T'gellan. "You were wise to confirm this with Aivas instead of dismissing the matter."

"It was certainly worth the trouble of flying here straight," T'gellan agreed, smiling fondly down at his weyrmate. "Though I won't deny I found it hard to credit. Sorry about that, T'lion."

"Oh, that's all right, T'gellan." T'lion could honestly say now that his friends were vindicated. "I didn't believe it myself, you know."

If T'lion found himself appointed as dolphin liaison—a word Kib suggested to him from his revived vocabulary of Ancient terms—for the skeptical medics who did come, sometimes with patients, more often not, he had no objections. It kept him out of K'din's way and made it less likely that any tale K'din might concoct would discredit him in the Weyrleader's eyes. Persellan, the Weyr's healer, a journeyman from the southernmost tip of South Boll, was nearly scornful as he announced that it was impossible to detect a pregnancy so soon after conception. But Tana neatly demolished his disbelief when she pinpointed yet another festering puncture wound in the arm of a weyrchild who kept complaining that his arm hurt. The headwoman had been sure it was an attempt to avoid his chores. Not only was Tana correct about the infection, but she touched her nose on exactly the point that the skeptical Persellan was to poultice. The next morning the infection had come to a head, and in it could clearly be seen the needle-fine thorn that had caused the problem.

Thorns from a variety of vegetation on the Southern Continent were a constant problem to the healers. Most people wore little in the hot summers, so there was more bare flesh that could be invaded by a casual brush against leaves and plants. Even tough dragon hide was not impervious, though the protective layer just under the skin was rarely penetrated. More often it was the rider, scrubbing his dragon, who found a thorn embedding itself in a water-soaked hand.

Not by any means thoroughly convinced of this method of diagnosing pregnancy, Persellan did bring women in various stages of *known* pregnancy to test Tana and other members of her pod, who seemed eager to prove their abilities.

It was, however, a broken bone that persuaded Persellan. A broken bone, moreover, that had healed badly just below the elbow, inhibiting the free use of the woman's right arm. She had come to discover if she was pregnant again, a condition she didn't wish to continue since she considered that three children were more than enough to saddle the Weyr with.

"Bone broke. Healed wrong," Tana told Persellan. "Here."

"What about a baby, fish?" the woman, Durras, demanded even as Persellan seized her arm, his trained hands finding the thickened joint. "I've had no bleeding in two months."

"How long ago did that happen?"

Durras jerked her arm out of his grip, scowling at the healer. "I didn't come about the arm. I was a child when it broke. Fish, what about the baby?"

"No babbee, but full womb. Not good. Needs cleaning out."

"*What?*" The woman backed out of the water and ran up the sands and away from the dolphin.

"What do you mean? Full womb? Needs cleaning out?" Persellan asked. He had been startled by Durras's reaction but, in his long apprenticeship, there had been not infrequent occasions of interrupted flows where the patient had later had severe and constant abdominal pains, and several instances where the woman had died—and where his only recourse had been heavy doses of numbweed to ease the pain.

"Growwwwsse," Tana said, trying to enunciate a difficult word. "Bad things."

"Growths?" Persellan asked. Intrusive surgeries were not a facet of healing, though he knew that some specially trained healers were actually cutting into a human body to relieve some conditions. Aivas had had much to tell the Healer Hall, but very few had actually undertaken operations. He'd heard that the Hall had authorized after-death examinations. Even thinking about such intrusions made him shudder, but valuable information had resulted. "Did the Ancients cut into a body to remove growths?"

"No need. Opening is there. Clean out. Then have babbee."

"How? What opening?"

"Main one down below. Way babbee comes."

Persellan shuddered again. The very idea of entering by that passage was repugnant. Still, a healer was often required to perform measures unpleasant, and even hurtful to the patient, to restore health.

The next surprise Persellan had came later that eventful morning when T'lion came to summon him to the bay.

"They're bringing in an injured dolphin. Natua and Tana say you'll need to sew him up."

"Sew up a dolphin?" Persellan halted in the act of reaching for his healer's bag. "Really, T'lion! That's enough!"

"Why?" T'lion demanded. "You do dragons when they're cut."

"But . . . fish?"

"They are not fish, Healer, they're mammals, same as humans, and Boojie won't heal properly unless you stitch the wound."

"Have you seen it?"

"No, but Tana asked. She's helped you, now you help her."

Persellan could not fault that argument, but he muttered under his breath all the way down to the beach about having to extend his practice to heal sea creatures. The moment he saw the long deep gash he was set to turn right about and return to his Weyr.

"There's no way I could close that. Why, the—creature would bite me . . . or something. The pain would be intense."

"Numbweed," T'lion said, stubbornly blocking Persellan's path and sending Gadareth an urgent plea to come help.

"How do I know numbweed would help? It might even be dangerous!"

"Tana told me. She said Boojie's too young to die, but he will if that wound is not closed."

"How'd he gouge himself like that?" Persellan continued to argue even as T'lion pulled him toward the water and the swarm of dolphins clumped together in the shallower water. "I don't even know if stitching's the answer."

"Sew Boojie," Tana said. Then, daring water almost too shallow for her to swim in, she pushed the healer with her nose toward the injured dolphin, being kept afloat by podmates.

"Come *on*, Persellan," T'lion said, up to his chest in the water.

"How can I possibly . . . It's so absurd!" the healer cried, but a stiff nose in his crotch pushed him forward. "Stop that!" And he batted his free hand at Tana's importunate melon. "I simply don't know how to go about . . . Shock from such a wound, not to mention suturing . . . I mean, I've never *done* anything like this in my life."

"Didn't they tell you life in a Weyr would never be boring?" T'lion said, silly with relief that the healer was complying.

He almost gagged when he saw the depth of the wound, the flesh laid bare to several levels. The moment of nausea passed as he became fascinated that any creature so badly injured had survived the journey here. Boojie was barely breathing, too exhausted to make so much as a soft squee. Only the gleam in the visible left eye was evidence that the bottlenose lived. T'lion placed a hand close to the lung, far enough away from the ghastly slice not to cause any additional pain, and felt the rumble of activity within the dolphin's body.

"If you're going to do something, you better do it now, Persellan," T'lion murmured. "Boojie's just hanging on."

"How on earth am I going to do any suturing in the ocean?"

Seeing the problem, for the dolphin nurses had to prop the patient and that made it difficult for Persellan to reach the wound, T'lion called Gadareth.

"Dragon claws were made useful," he told Persellan. "Gaddie will cradle Boojie, just enough in the water, but with his side turned to you."

There was a flurry as the bronze dragon, perceiving from his rider's mind what had to be accomplished, entered the water and approached the group.

"Gaddie'll help, Tana. Tell the others to let him take Boojie. He won't harm him. You know dragons wouldn't harm a dolphin."

Tana clicked, squee'ed, and spouted water so urgently that the maneuver was deftly accomplished, though it took a bit to get Boojie angled just right for the repair.

"By the first shell, will you look at this?" Persellan exclaimed, and pointed to the thick layer of blubber lying just under the dolphin's rubbery skin. "I suppose it's normal? Would she know? Come to think of it, a very fat herdbeast has a fatty layer. I suppose it's all right. Oh, well, it can only bite me." Keeping up a running monologue—which T'lion rightly had the sense not to answer—and muttering darkly about a most unusual healing, Persellan began to smear numbweed on the lips of the wound. "Don't know if the stuff will penetrate enough to do any good, but the Masterfarmer always uses it on injured animals, so I don't see why I can't use it on a sea creature." His dabbings were tentative at first, but his motions became more confident when his patient did not twitch or move during the procedure.

T'lion helped when he saw what to do, and his smaller fingers managed to ease the paste all along the edges of the wound.

"I've never done anything so bizarre in my life," Persellan muttered as he paused, the long thin needle he used for dragon flesh poised for the first stitch. "I've never heard of anything so weird as suturing a fish . . . "

"Boojie's not a fish," T'lion corrected, but he was grinning. "He's a mammal."

"Put your hands on either side, would you, and see if you can't push the lips together?"

It was not an easy job Persellan asked of T'lion, and toward the end, though the healer worked swiftly, the young rider's muscles began to spasm in protest. But together the humans finished closing the gash.

"Three hands long . . ." Persellan said, measuring and shaking his head. "I doubt he'll live. Shock alone . . . Although saltwater wounds do heal well . . ." He shook his head again as he scrubbed the remaining blood from his hands before passing the brush to his equally gory assistant. He washed the needle and replaced it in its leather, then put it and what was left of the fine strong thread he had used back in his now-soaked healer's bag.

"So what do we do with this Boojie now, T'lion? Nurse him here, in the shallows? I'm water-pocked from the waist down."

"Afo, what now?" T'lion asked, seeing her in the circle of observant dolphins grouped on either side of Gadareth, who still held Boojie in his talons.

"You do good. Tell dragon to let Boojie go. We care him." With a sharp series of whistles, she organized her helpers, Gar, Jim, and Tana among them, as Gadareth obediently and very carefully lowered his forearms into the water until Boojie's body floated free. T'lion was relieved to notice a slight motion of fins as Boojie wearily responded to his freedom. Then his podmates renewed their support and pointed him seaward.

"T'ank you! T'ank you! T'ank you!" came the unexpected chorus as the group headed slowly out to sea.

"Will he be all right, Natua?"

She gave a little leap in answer, which he took to be affirmative. Both he and Persellan watched in silence until the dorsal fins of patient and nurses were no longer easily visible.

"Never done anything like that before in my life," Persellan muttered as he strode out of the water. He took no more than a few steps up on the sand before he collapsed, to spread out his length on the warm sand. "And I don't even know if it will be enough. But I tried."

"You did indeed, Healer, and I'm very grateful you did," T'lion said. *Gaddie, you were great!*

I know it. I've never done anything like that either. But the dolphin lives. We all did well. Tell the healer.

"Gadareth, too, says you did well, Persellan," T'lion murmured, with a weary grin. A snore answered him. A nap seemed like a good idea, but he had enough common sense remaining to collect two of the wide leaves they often used to shield the harsh sun rays. He put one on Persellan's head and face, and draped the second over himself.

Gadareth, wings carefully tight against his back, rolled this way and that in the warm sands before he, too, settled his head on his front legs and relaxed in the sun.

7
▼▼▼▼▼▼▼▼▼

Early the next morning Persellan joined T'lion and Gadareth on the strand when the young dragonrider rang the Report peal. He had spent an anxious night, worrying about Boojie, and was rather pleased to see that Persellan was also concerned.

No sooner had the last note of the ring echoed across the waters than two dolphins leaped above the surface, a distant squeeing audible.

"Hope that's a happy sound," T'lion murmured.

"Hmmmm" was Persellan's reply as he shielded his eyes and peered across the dawn-lightened waters.

"They feed at dawn, you know," T'lion informed him conversationally. "Best time to get them."

"Am I likely to be on call to dolphins, too, now?"

T'lion looked up to check the healer's mood. He didn't know the man well enough to judge whether or not his gruffness was genuine. Most people tended to be grumpy in the early hours of a day. Healers certainly had the right, called up at the most inconvenient of times.

"Would that bother you?" T'lion asked apprehensively.

"Hmmmm. Depends. I could see that the creature had to have that gash sutured. Are they often injured? How did that happen to it?"

"I don't know about injuries in general. Most of the dolphins have scars here and there. I haven't asked how they get them, though. We haven't reached that sort of thing. Most of our conversations have been pretty basic. Maybe Master Alemi knows. I can ask him."

"Who's Master Alemi?" Persellan asked, his gaze still on the incoming dolphins' progress.

"Master Fishman at Paradise River Hold. He got me interested in the dolphins. Aivas asked me to continue."

"Did he?" Persellan shot a glance down at his young companion.

"Yes, yesterday wasn't my first visit to report to Aivas," T'lion said in a tone he hoped wasn't boastful.

"Indeed! Hmmm, well."

The squeeing was louder now and T'lion thought it sounded happy. Maybe because he wanted it to. He let out a sigh. Then, as the two dolphins neared the shore, he couldn't wait any longer and ran out into the water until he was waist deep.

"Is Boojie okay?" he shouted through cupped hands.

"Squeeee yes. Squee yes!"

"Yes?"

"Yessssssss, squeee yessssss!" The two dolphins made it a chorus and seemed to speed up. Their final leap splashed T'lion thoroughly but he didn't care. Natua pushed his face right up into the dragonrider's, and his ever-grinning smile was deeper than ever. He dropped his jaw and squee'ed again.

"Boojie best grateful. Ate well."

"Swims little, is better."

"Tell them," Persellan called from where he stood at the water's edge, "Boojie must have the sutures removed—are dolphins aware of time? I mean I don't want to leave those stitches in forever. They could tear the flesh."

"When d'you want Boojie back?" T'lion asked.

"In a sevenday. Would they understand that?"

T'lion nodded vigorously even as he repeated the instructions to the two dolphins. "In seven"—T'lion held up sufficient fingers, tapping them in turn on Natua's nose—"dawns, Boojie is to come back to the healer. Understood?"

"Squeeee! Understand. Seven dawns."

"We tell!" Tana added, clicking affirmatively.

"Thanks for coming," T'lion added.

"You ring. We come. We promise. Thank medic." And Tana did her half stand, nodding her head vigorously before she gave a final tail swish and leaped sideways, over and under the water, and swam off, Natua squeeing after her.

"Did you hear, Persellan?" T'lion asked as he waded back out. "Boojie's very grateful. He ate and they understand to bring him back in a sevenday."

"I must say, I'm gratified, since I hadn't a notion if I was doing the creature any good at all."

"Oh, you did, Persellan, you did!"

"Amazing incident, actually. I must report . . . Now, who would I report to? Not the Masterfarmer, certainly, for the sea is not his province."

"Master Alemi says that the Masterfishman, Idarolan, is interested in the dolphins."

"Well, then, I shall report to him, and to T'gellan, as well as to Master Oldive. At least *he* will find this case interesting. Many wouldn't, but Oldive will." That seemed to please Persellan even more as they made their way back to the Weyr.

T'lion hoped he'd have a chance to tell Master Alemi all about yesterday and dolphin sonar. Well, maybe he shouldn't talk about Mirrim's baby yet, but he could tell about Persellan's sewing up Boojie.

It was several days before T'lion had a chance to stop off at Paradise River Hold. He was on his way back from conveying Master Fandarel to Telgar Smithcrafthall and saw no harm in stopping off that evening to see Alemi. The big yawl, the *Fair Winds*, was not at anchor, nor was the other sloop, or the ketch that fished from Paradise River. T'lion was about to tell Gadareth to go on to the Weyr when he saw a ship sailing into the next cove. The northern coast of the Southern Continent had many inlets. He thought it very odd that the ship didn't put into the Paradise River anchorage. Could they have mistaken their port of call? That cove also had a river, but a small one, feeding into the sea. Could the captain have mistaken this one for the true Hold? Puzzled, he asked Gadareth to glide over that way. What he saw on the beach did nothing to reassure him. For people were hurriedly unloading small boats: quite a mound of crates and stuff already on the beach. Was Paradise River opening new holdings on its land? He'd heard remarks at dinner in the Weyr that more and more people were heading to the Southern Continent after what had been an extremely cold winter.

Gaddie, let's just check with Holder Jayge, T'lion said, and his dragon obliged, winking into *between*—before, it was he hoped, those on the beach had seen him. They'd had the sun at their backs and wouldn't have been all that visible. There had been something furtive about the beaching.

"Holder Jayge, were you expecting more new settlers?" T'lion asked, presenting himself and apologizing for interrupting their supper.

"No." Jayge frowned, rising. "Why?"

"Well, there's a ship anchored next cove over and stuff's all over the beach. I thought you should know."

"Indeed I should, T'lion." Angry sparks lit his eyes. "Did you happen to see the *Fair Winds* on her way in?"

"No, sir, we came out of *between* above the pier and no sign of any of your ships."

"I know that dragonriders are not supposed to intervene in Hold matters," Jayge said, beckoning T'lion to follow him to the front porch, "but if Alemi knew about this . . . intrusion, he could assist us." He glanced west where the tip of the setting sun was just visible. "Could you estimate how many are on that beach?"

T'lion shook his head. "They were unloading two small boats, coming and going."

"Did they see you?"

"No, I was coming in from the west. Sun behind me."

"Good." Jayge emphasized that by gripping T'lion's arm in approval. "Possibly eight, ten men, if they had two boats. Well, if we start now, we should reach the cove by moonrise! But I'd want Alemi's reinforcement." He waited for T'lion's response.

"I'd never find Alemi at sea," T'lion began, half of him wanting to help Jayge and the other half most loath to get into further trouble with T'gellan. Which he would if he interfered even in a minor way. Someone would drop the word that a dragonrider had told Alemi.

Dolphins find Alemi faster, Gadareth said slyly from the shadow where he waited.

"Dolphins! They could find Alemi and tell him to come," T'lion cried.

"Good lad!" Jayge clapped him on the back now. "Those critters really are good for something."

While T'lion knew that this was not the moment to mention the dolphins' latest skill, he had no reservations about using them.

"I'll just go ring the bell on the pier," T'lion said, running back to his dragon.

"My gratitude, dragonrider," Jayge called after him.

As Gadareth lifted into the night and angled himself toward the head of the bay, T'lion heard Jayge hammering on the alarm triangle.

The pier was long enough to accommodate the bronze dragon, so Gadareth set T'lion down right by the bell tower. He clanged it as vigorously as Jayge had been plying the iron. Dusk was always a good time to get a quick response from dolphins, who would be looking for a game to play. In his head, T'lion sorted out the words to use to convey the message to Alemi.

Kib, Temp, and Afo answered the summons.

"You must find Alemi, Kib," T'lion said, holding the dolphin's head at an angle so the eye was on him.

"Can do easy. Not far now."

"Then tell him Jayge needs his help immediately at the next cove. Over there." T'lion jabbed his hand in the appropriate direction.

"Where ship is?"

"You saw them?"

"Northern ship smelly. In wrong place?"

"You bet your safety straps they are," T'lion said. "They are invading Paradise River Hold."

"Invade no good?"

"That's right. Those men do no good to Alemi, Jayge, and Readis."

T'lion was amazed by the hostile notes in the clicking and squeeing, which came out in a deeper, almost menacing, tone and tempo.

"Go. Find Alemi. Tell him trouble comes here. Be at next cove by moonrise to help Jayge and his men."

Kib wriggled himself on his tail, waving his flippers. "Find Alemi. Tell him trouble. Moonrise. We know where! We go!"

In one of their incredible maneuvers, the three dolphins simultaneously launched themselves high above the water and, turning their agile bodies, dove back. T'lion saw them emerge briefly, traveling at great speed out to sea, as if they knew exactly where they were going.

They probably do *know exactly where they're going,* T'lion told Gadareth. "Well, we'd better get back home as fast as we can or someone might wonder how long it took us to get Master Fandarel home."

You were given food when you arrived, Gadareth remarked as T'lion settled himself again between his neck ridges.

T'lion chortled as he slapped the dragon's neck. "That's right, and a good meal it was. I had seconds! Let's go home!"

Several days later at dinner in the Weyr Hall, T'lion heard that a group of northerners had been forcefully expelled from Paradise River Hold. The master of the ship that had brought them would be severely disciplined by Master Idarolan and deprived of his command. Ingenuously T'lion asked for details.

"You know, I used to go there a lot," T'lion remarked. "Nice folk."

He was told about the clever way in which Holder Jayge and his small force of men had emerged from the forest, caught the intruders asleep in their hastily set-up camp, and tied them up. The Paradise River Fishmaster Alemi and his fishmen had boarded their transport ship and, with a crew from his own fishhold, had sailed it and the unwelcome immigrants into Ista Harbor, where the vessel was impounded and its crew and passengers transported back to their point of departure in Igen. Lord Holder Laudey of Igen was not best pleased by this escapade, and the men and women were sentenced to work in the mines. The episode was well spread by harpers, with the moral that those who wished to settle on the Southern Continent had to obtain permission.

"There'll be more of such occurrences," V'line remarked. "Paradise River Hold's already had a couple of problems along that line."

"You mean when that self-styled Lady Holdless Thella attacked the hold a couple of Turns back?" one of the Wingleaders asked.

"That was the worst," V'line replied.

"The Weyrs can't involve themselves in hold matters," the brown rider M'sur said, frowning. "It's enough that we have to convey people in and out of Landing all the time." He nodded at T'lion. "Not to mention having to survey every inch of this continent to prepare for the day Threadfall stops forever."

T'lion shrugged and grinned when several other riders glanced in his direction. No one had even noticed his return after full dark on the night in question. And after all, he hadn't really been involved. The dolphins had! And who would know that?

Lord Toric heard about the attempted intrusion and smiled. So long as they kept away from his zealously guarded holding, it amused him that more people were illegally attempting to invade the South and ignoring the Benden Weyrleaders' edict that immigration must be to sites they had approved. That only verified Toric's suspicions that the Weyrleaders were indeed keeping the best sites for the dragonriders. He was hoping that some of the tries would succeed, if only to prove that people could survive very well, thank you, wherever they were willing to work hard enough to "hold." It didn't matter to Toric that these would-be settlers could die from sampling exotic-looking and sweet-smelling tree fruits, that there were hungry and feral beasts quite able to take down a full-grown adult, that there were the most insidious dangers from thorn-poisoning and fevers. Toric's notion was that the strong survived—and if the unfit died, they merited no mourning. What irked him most was that the Benden Weyrleaders felt they had the right to apportion the South where they wished to bestow it. Just because they'd found some document that told how the Ancients had dealt with settling? Land was held by those strong enough to hang on to it and improve it.

And then there was that infamous meeting of Weyrleaders and Lord Holders—which he had been unable to attend while he was involved with ousting the renegade Denol from Ierne Island. That's when all those old-womanish Lords had actually established that the dragonriders had the right to control the Southern Continent land grabbings. "Out of respect for the services dragonriders have given Hold and Hall over the centuries of Threadfall." As if tithing to support the indolent riders hadn't been reward enough for dragons doing what they had been bred to do. Much less the gratuities that had always been lavished on dragonriders.

When Toric had heard of that decision, he had been infuriated, especially as it had been voted on behind his back. He'd have stopped the whole notion right then if he'd been able to come. The first insult to him had been that the northern Lords hadn't waited until he could come to a meeting that, when all was said and deplorably done, affected him more than any of them, since he *was* the only confirmed Lord Holder in the South. And lord of a Hold so much larger than anything in the North, including Telgar, that it had been ludicrous to *hold* such a meeting without him. Of course, the Weyrleaders had planned it that way, knowing he would protest. Knowing he would have been able to sway some of the indecisive idiots who had their titles by default and certainly wouldn't have been able to survive a season in the South. He'd've seen that the Southern Continent would be wide open for those with the guts to *work* to hold any land—and apply for confirmation to a *full* Council of Lord Holders and no Weyrleaders present, for it *wasn't* up to dragonriders who held and where! Not in Toric's lexicon.

On his bedroom and office walls were outsized maps of the Southern Continent: several aspects, including one that had cost him a sack of marks, a spatial view of the south, its terrain stretching out and out to the curve of the horizon. That view caused him the most irritation, since it was proof positive that he had been cheated. The Weyrwoman had shown him only a small section of the continent when she and Flar had tricked him into settling for only the land between the two rivers. He had been deceived into settling for a tiny portion when he could have had more, much more. And those two Weyrleaders had known it. Although his wife had tried to convince him that they couldn't have known the extent of Southern: not until Master Idarolan and Master Rampesi had sailed, one west and one east, until they had met, was the size of the Southern Continent truly discovered. Toric could not be convinced otherwise. He had wanted *more*, and since the Weyrleaders had thwarted him in that devious meeting, he would have more. Especially when the dragonriders had not helped him regain the big island from Denol's clutches. He was especially bitter about that.

Right now, of course, with everyone scurrying about following the orders of that machine, Aivas, he had to bide his time. It was as essential to his future plans as everyone else's that Thread be stopped from ever falling on Pern again. He had even allowed his brother Hamian, the Hold's Mastersmith, to spend full time experimenting and contriving the new machines and equipment needed to end the airborne menace. He had informants in place so that anything of any significance occurring at Landing was reported to him. He appeared when vital decisions were being discussed. He also tagged those who would be of use to him later on. *If*, and Toric entertained some doubts, Aivas managed to do as it had promised: rid the planet of Thread.

He had already started to make his plans—spurred by his animosity for the Benden Weyrleaders. He still had the notes that young Piemur had made of his explorations along the coast. He himself had taken short trips—no absences long enough to arouse suspicion, and never where dragonriders might inconveniently overfly him. He would personally select those he placed where he wanted them, and sufficient numbers on large enough holdings so that, after Threadfall, there would be enough Lord Holders grateful to him, Toric, to vote a majority over the northern idiots. When the time was ripe . . . And he smiled again. The domination of the Weyrs over the Southern Continent would suffer a major curtailment. He had no doubt he would find support among the Lord Holders, especially since he could use that Ancient document to justify the actions. Ah, yes, when the time was ripe . . .

The next morning was the seventh day, when Boojie was supposed to report to Persellan. Healer and dragonrider arrived at first light on the beach and saw dolphins cavorting in the water on a shoreward course.

"I do hope Boojie isn't one of those leapers," Persellan said in a grouchy tone. "He'll pull his stitches and I won't sew him up again."

T'lion gave the bell a few pulls to be sure their presence was noticed. Then he and Persellan, who was dressed in short-legged pants and had put what he needed out of his healer's bag in a small pouch slung over one shoulder, waded out to meet the incoming sea creatures.

The one who glided in across their path stopped right in front of them and eased over onto his back. The long gash was visible, just under the water.

"Gaddie, we may need you again . . ." T'lion began.

"No, I don't think we need trouble, Gadareth," Persellan said. The dolphin was holding steady, presenting the injury well enough for the purpose of removing the sutures. "Here, hold this for me." He had removed a blunt-ended pair of scissors from his pack and now pushed them at T'lion.

Running skilled fingers along the injury, Persellan gave one of his meditative hums, his expression registering approval and satisfaction. "It's well closed, not a single suture torn or pulled. Really, if I'd known they heal so quickly, I could have removed the stitches earlier. Remarkable recovery."

"The salt water?"

"Could be, and the excellent state of health these wild creatures enjoy. Now, tell him not to move. I don't want to inadvertently puncture him at this stage of his recovery."

T'lion bent close to Boojie's head, noticed the brightness of the eye regarding him, and patted the melon. "Hold as still as you can, Boojie. Won't hurt."

Boojie dropped his jaw in token of understanding. T'lion nearly fell backward, though, as the tip of another dolphin snout protruded from the water just beyond Boojie's head. He hadn't been aware that another dolphin lurked that close—Tana probably.

"Hold your hand out, please, T'lion. I need to be sure I've removed *all* the stitches."

T'lion obeyed, and the procedure was very quickly accomplished. Persellan bent his head to peer at the closed wound.

"Hmmmm. Yes, remarkable. I really should encourage patients to swim. Or at least to immerse themselves in the water here for its curative powers. Good fellow, Boojie. You've been a grand patient. Where do I scratch?"

"Not there," T'lion said hastily and grabbed Persellan's hand away from what was indecently close to dolphin privates. "Here, under the chin. They love it."

Persellan caressed Boojie. "You've been a good patient.

I could wish humans were as well behaved. But then I didn't have to oversee you in your watery ward, did I?" Persellan's hum turned into a chuckle. "Dragonriders do not take kindly to having to remain in bed. Shards!" The healer backed away in surprise as Boojie suddenly loomed up out of the water until he was on eye level with him.

"Thank you, Peerrrssss-lan," Boojie said with an enthusiastic squee to emphasize his statement.

"You are very welcome, Boojie. Very welcome indeed," Persellan said, executing a few short bows at the dolphin. "Hmmm. I don't always get thanked by my human patients either. You know, T'lion, I don't think I'd mind being healer to the dolphins after all. D'you think I should see what other information Aivas has on sea-mammal ailments and cures?"

T'lion grinned as he handed the healer back his pouch and they both waded out of the sea.

"I don't see why not. The more we learn from Aivas the better. Have you heard anything from Master Oldive?" T'lion asked.

"Yes, I have. Most gratifying. Oddly enough, it was the Harper Hall—Master Menolly, in particular—which supported my suggestion." Persellan glanced quizzically at T'lion.

"She was at Paradise River Hold and Alemi is her brother. He might have told her what he was doing with the dolphins."

"Which is?"

"Much what I'm doing, getting to know them and teach them our words."

"But they know them . . ."

"No, they know the words people used to use," T'lion said, mastering an urge to grin at the healer's confusion.

"Our language has shifted slightly from what the dolphins learned long ago from us."

"Language shifted?" Persellan was indignant.

"Aivas told me."

"For a rider who hasn't even flown Thread yet, you seem to be remarkably well connected."

"Me? Shards, no, Persellan, I just have to convey a lot of people here and there," T'lion said in an earnestly self-deprecating tone. He didn't wish to give Persellan the impression that he was boasting or anything. "I was conveying Master Alemi when *he* rang that old bell they dredged up from Monaco Bay and summoned the dolphins. That's how I got involved."

"But you've put up a bell here."

"Aivas asked me to. I'm supposed to help count how many dolphins there are these days."

"Doing well, I see. Hmmm. What does Gadareth think about all this?"

"You saw for yourself, Healer. He was quite ready to help with Boojie."

"So he was." They had entered the clearing around the Weyr Hall. "Well, let me know if they need any more stitching or something. Like dragons, they are appreciative!" He sniffed once disparagingly and made for his quarters.

At Fort Hold, Menolly, Sebell, Master Oldive, and two of his journeymen had made their way to the Fort harbor.

"I find it most fascinating that no one—" Master Oldive paused to emphasize the negative. "—ever bothered to ask why that bell was known as the 'doll-fins' bell.' "

Menolly laughed, enjoying this outing from the Healer Hall now that the weather was more clement with an early spring warming. It was good to be on runnerback and especially to have something that could pry Sebell loose from his increasingly heavy duties as Masterharper. They scarcely seemed to have any time together these days with all the activity and industry connected with Aivas's plan to rid Pern of Threadfall. "Surely you've come across enigmas in your Healer Hall records."

"Oh, indeed," Master Oldive said with a laugh. "Even the most legible entries contain references to procedures the authors were familiar with but which we lost over the centuries. Thankfully, Aivas is explaining more and more." He sighed, his expression thoughtful. Then he shook off whatever reflection troubled him and spoke more briskly. "And you'll be able to communicate with the dolphins? If any come in response."

"My brother assures me that they assured him that all dolphins have maintained their traditions. And we know that there are dolphins in these waters. So we shall ring the peal and see what happens."

"I do so hope they come," Oldive said, sighing heavily. "If they can, as Weyr Healer Persellan said, pinpoint irregularities in a human body with this sonar ability of theirs, I might just be able to treat three puzzling cases that have worried me excessively."

Menolly lowered her voice so it would not carry to the journeymen riding behind them. "You're having trouble convincing your Craft of the 'surgical' treatments the old records recommend."

"Indeed!" Oldive's comment was heartfelt. "The cesarian to release a womb-held baby is permitted, and the one to remove the pendicks, but not the lengthy repairs or deep delving that Aivas reports were last measures even then. But we don't have the medicines that the Ancients did that would dissolve or shrink other conditions to which occasionally people are subject."

They had reached the pier and were welcomed by Masterfishman Curran, who delegated men to take the runnerbeasts from their riders. Menolly noticed that all five vessels of the Fort fishing fleet were in port. She grimaced. She hadn't anticipated an audience, but they had had to inform Curran of their intentions for the day's excursion.

Master Idarolan had, of course, informed him of dolphin intelligence. Sebell, also spreading such news, had met with considerable skepticism, especially from those inland who had never seen dolphins escorting ships.

"A long cold ride, you will need at least a cup of klah before you ring any bells," Curran said jovially, gesturing them to enter his hold, situated on the height above the sea. There was another, smaller cot built on the T-bar of the pier itself for the harbormaster.

Menolly, always conscious of being away from her children, would have preferred not to dally, but courtesy required the grateful acceptance of hospitality. And hot klah would be welcome. She was somewhat stiff after the long ride, having had little occasion to exercise of late. She almost resented the ease with which Sebell, who was constantly riding both runners and dragons, dismounted.

More than klah was offered, which was very nice of Curran and his wife, Robina, and actually very welcome: small fish rolls that were delectably spiced, the cold roe of fish spread on tiny bread rounds, hot spiced klah, and a cup of a chowder that was also highly seasoned. Masters and journeymen alike, as hungry as any ever born, tucked into the food with a good will. Even Master Oldive made a good meal.

Finally, they were able to go to the long pier, accompanied by a throng of interested fishers and cotholders. Menolly should have known that this would become an occasion, especially after a long and sequestering winter. Everyone took what excuses for diversion they could find. This would certainly be a more interesting one. No sooner had she stepped out of the hold than Beauty, Diver, and Rocky launched themselves from the roof, Beauty settling to her shoulder while Diver and Rocky swanned about in the air above. Other fire-lizards joined them, uttering glad cries, though Menolly knew they could hardly appreciate the reason for the day's activities.

The dolphins' bell had been given a new housing, the wood preservative still rank enough to catch a person in the back of the throat despite the light breeze. The bell itself had been shined to a high polish.

"We added a new clapper," Curran said proudly. "Made Master Fandarel hold up some other work to get it done in time."

"I could wish to know how you did that, Master Curran," Oldive said with a wry smile.

"How long has the bell been without a clapper then?" Sebell asked in that quiet way of his that was so good at extracting information.

Curran threw up arms thick from years of hauling nets and sails. "Oh, it had none when I became Master here."

"Did *your* Master not notice?" Sebell asked, his eyes twinkling.

"I suppose he did, but he must have taken it on in that condition." Curran looked a trifle embarrassed.

"The Monaco Bell had no clapper either," Sebell said to pacify the man, but Menolly noticed her mate did not mention that the Monaco Bell had been at the bottom of the sea for centuries. "But it has one now and can be put to its original use again. Will you do the honors, Menolly?"

"Delighted," she said, and seized the rope by the end. "I think, Curran, the purpose of the dolphins' bell is for them to be able to ring it, too, to summon men to hear their reports."

"I didn't know *that*," Curran said, surprised. "But what would I do if they should ring it?"

Menolly smiled reassuringly at him. "Ask why they rang it, of course. This is to let them know the bell's back in service." She gave the pull a hefty yank, and then settled into the Report sequence that Alemi had taught her. She sincerely hoped it would be effective, or Curran would think he had wasted time and effort—not to mention badgering the Mastersmith for no purpose. So, pretending that the sequence was longer than it actually was, she pealed off the Report a second time. "Alemi's had very good fishing since he's listened to the dolphin reports. He's also been able to avoid some of those appalling squalls the southern waters spawn."

"*Look!*" cried one of the fishmen who had followed them to the pier. On her shoulder, Beauty let out a piercing cry. Rocky and Diver swooped off to investigate.

Distance viewers appeared from pockets to aid the naked eye.

"Fins!" cried Curran's first mate. "Half a dozen—no, more than that. Coming from all directions. Heading here!"

Curran reached for the distance viewer from his mate and peered out to sea. Beauty spread her wings, tangling them in Menolly's winter cap so that she had to grab it before it fell into the sea.

"Easy there, now, Beauty. You've seen dolphins before."

Beauty chittered, but obediently folded her wings and blinked bright blue eyes.

"Quite a display they're making," Curran remarked, and politely passed the viewer to Menolly. She grinned and gestured for him to give it to Sebell, who had not yet had a chance to see a dolphin pod arriving in answer to the age-old summons.

How had the creatures remembered for such a long time? Maybe there were dolphin equivalents to harpers? The pod leaders?

Sebell sucked in his breath as he watched. "They are moving at an incredible rate and doing all those leaps and ah . . . one just somersaulted midair."

"I'd say they were delighted to hear the bell rung again," Menolly said with a nostalgic little smile and a catch in her chest. To be ignored, to have one's abilities neglected must have been hard, and yet the dolphins had continued to do what they could to aid humans all these long centuries. She must write a special song for them. A very special song of loyalty and joy.

The squeeing was soon audible to the watchers on the dock.

"How can they speak?" Curran asked.

"They do," Menolly said, "if you listen." She glanced up at Sebell, standing straight and tall beside her, and grinned impishly. "Despite all we harpers did, the language shifted, but the dolphins are adapting to the new words."

Sebell gave her a jaundiced stare for that familiar tease, and she chuckled at harper discomfiture over the "purity of speech" that the Craft had *tried* so hard to preserve.

"But I thought . . ." Curran began, and then stopped, clearing his throat.

ANNE MCCAFFREY

The vanguard was now closing the gap, and the watchers were unable to count the number of dolphin bodies in their leaping and plunging.

"Where's the boat we need to be close to them?" Menolly asked. Curran pointed to a ladder at the side, and peering over the edge, Menolly saw the long boat bobbing at its painter. Curran led the way and carefully guided her feet to the rungs and safely into the tossing boat. It was one of the offshore fishers and accommodated a fair number of folk; an orderly descent was made by those whom Curran had apparently chosen as audience to this momentous occasion.

They were barely settled when the first dolphin raised its head above the waters.

"Bellill ring. Oo-ee come! Bellill not ring long long." The creature squeeed, and was joined by other importunate heads, all of them jostling for a view of those in the boat.

"Your name? I'm Nolly," Menolly said, leaning over the side of the boat and extending a hand to scratch a bottlenose chin.

Almost ecstatically the dolphin allowed the caress; the jaw dropped into the water in its excess of delight.

"Inka! Inka! Pod leader. Inka!"

"By the first Egg," Curran cried, and there was excited muttering from the other fishmen.

"Here is Curran," Menolly said. "Fishmaster."

"Oo-ee know," Inka said.

"Flip me," another dolphin said, raising itself well above the water to reach an eye level that startled the Fishmaster.

"Flipme?" Curran asked.

"Flip! Flip! 'On-ra-bul naym."

"On-ra-bul?" Curran repeated, amazed.

"Maybe he means honorable?" Sebell suggested, and

held out a hand, hoping to entice a dolphin to him. One immediately raised up and offered fins in his direction. "Your name?" he asked.

"Ajay, Ajay. Man's name?" The interrogatory lift to the word was unmistakable.

"Sebell. Sebell, Ajay!"

"Sebell." "Sebell, Nolly, Cur-ran," chorused dolphins in their high funny voices.

"Oldive," Menolly said, putting her arm about the Masterhealer. "Healer. Medic," she added.

"Me-dick! Meddick!" The dolphins passed this information back and forth among themselves; the gray bodies thronged the waters above the boat and great pier bollards that rose above the surface and supported the T-shaped facility. "Oll-deeve, medick!" Excited squees and clicks followed this introduction, and the immediate waters seethed with dolphins changing position as so many attempted to inspect the healer simultaneously. "Ooooo heal? Oooo skraabbb blufisss?"

"How remarkable!" Oldive said, surprised to be the focus of such attention from so many cheerful faces. "Oooo heal?" he asked, turning to Menolly for a translation. "Skraaabbb blufiss?"

"Bloodfish. It's a parasite and has to be cut off," Menolly said. "Alemi did it for his pod. Something they are unable to do for themselves."

"I shouldn't wonder with just flippers and no fingers. How would I . . ."

"Who has blufiss?" Menolly asked, and four dolphins squee'ed and pushed in toward her. She had a chance to study Aivas's tapes on the dolphins and now gave the signal for them to lie on their sides.

"Oh I say," Oldive remarked with great sympathy.

"They must be very painful. One would have to use a sharp knife."

"Niggghhhff, nigghhhfff" was repeated back to him from those nearest with exposed bellies. They waggled themselves from side to side. "Skraaabbb blufiss."

"Well, I suppose they'd know . . ." Oldive said. He took out his belt knife and tested its edge. "Sharp enough, I'll hope."

He leaned over the side of the boat. Before any of the seamen could warn them, the harpers and healers leaned over to watch the operation. The boat, of course, rocked and spilled Master Oldive and Menolly into the water.

"No, no, leave me, I'm fine. I swim quite competently," Oldive said, batting at the hands stretched out to retrieve him.

"Ooooo, it's cold," Menolly said, but she also declined offers to drag her back into the boat. She did, however, slip off her boots and pass them up to Sebell. Then she took out her belt knife. "Ah, is that how you do it?" she commented as Oldive deftly sliced the head off the fish, removed the clinging body, and then pried out the head's sucker, leaving only a tiny hole. The sucker was of remarkable length, since it had had to penetrate through the layers of blubber to tap a vein.

Just as Oldive dealt with his first patient, another dolphin nosed through its fellows, clicking in such an authoritative tone that the others parted for it.

"You really should wait your turn," Oldive said in a gently chiding tone.

The dolphin smiled and turned its head this way and that as the bright black eyes fixed themselves on the healer.

"Bad back!" the creature said quite plainly.

There was a brief, appalled silence. "My goodness!" Oldive held out his hand to the creature's nose as if absolving it from mentioning what few did. "How could you know?" he asked. Despite his wetting, the hump was not that apparent under his carefully contrived shirt, and the creature had only observed him from the front.

"Seeee. Seee. I Bit, Oll-deeeve medick."

"I don't really believe what I'm hearing," Curran murmured to Menolly. "And it knew about . . ." He closed his lips. *"How* could it *see?"*

"Perhaps what Persellan said about the creatures'—" Oldive looked at Menolly for the word.

"Sonar," she supplied.

"—Is very true. Proof positive!" Because Oldive appeared cheerful about the matter, everyone began to relax. "What is it, this sonar?"

Menolly recollected the exact phrasing she'd had from Alemi. "Sonar. Dolphins can emit high-frequency sounds and register the vibrations coming back to their ears. That's how they navigate in the sea and send messages long distance to other dolphins. Somehow they can use it on human bodies as well."

"If this Bit could see my hump through all my clothes, I'm willing to believe. Bit, do you wish me to skraabbb your blufisss?"

"Now, see here, Master Oldive," began one of the medics who had been upset to see his master in the water, "there are more and more coming. You had better come out of the water. There are too many for you to do them."

"I've counted forty so far," Sebell said.

"Pleeesss, Ol-deeve. Many many blufiss."

"Skraabbb blufisss," the cry went up from the crowding dolphins.

"I can really only do one more today," Oldive said. "The water is very cold." His teeth were beginning to chatter, and the others kept begging him to come back into the boat and be dried off.

Menolly's teeth began to chatter, too. "Look, we are humans, not dolphins. But there are enough in this boat to remove any more parasites those dolphins have. Those we don't do today, we can do tomorrow. All right?"

"Rigggh. Rigggh" was the enthusiastic delphinic response. The humans were not quite as pleased by her offer. But when she insisted that Oldive reenter the boat with her, and blankets were brought for them, she found willing enough hands to assist.

Over the next few hours, most of the humans in the boat had gotten wet—but still they were unable to attend to all the dolphins who asked to have bloodfish removed. When Sebell remarked that I Bit and Inka, who had a dark splotch like a cap on her head, seemed to have some authority over the pods, he, Menolly, and Oldive managed to explain to the newcomers that they should return the next day.

"When the sun comes up," Menolly said, using the hand signals for "next day." "More blufiss cull. Understand?"

Squeeings and clickings, as well as some happy acrobatics, answered her, and the press of dolphin bodies about the boat eased. They were later to learn that I Bit was one of the oldest dolphins in the nearby seas. Certainly she seemed to understand more and certainly appeared to be the most respected member of the pod. I Bit taught the young calves and sent the smartest ones to the Great Whirlpool to the Tillek. At first the use of that name confused the two harpers. Gradually they realized that the

Tillek meant the oldest and wisest dolphin, who was evidently the repository of all marine knowledge, the way harpers preserved knowledge for humans.

When Sebell and Menolly asked if they would ever meet the Tillek, I Bit said she would ask. The Tillek was known to be very pleased with the mans.

"The Tillek is wo-mans," I Bit said, giving them a long stare with her very bright and intelligent eyes. "Best, biggest, wisest."

"I'm sure she is," Menolly said, and proceeded to ask I Bit detailed questions of what dolphins learned from the Tillek.

"T'e Tillek sing too," I Bit remarked, her lower jaw dropped in what was the most expansive dolphin grin they had yet seen.

"I guess that settles me," Menolly told Sebell, grinning. About then she noticed that most of the people on the boat were holding what looked like two-way conversations with individual dolphins.

The cold of twilight, augmented by a sharp southern wind, finally forced the humans out of the boat—but with many promises to continue the contact the next day, and every day.

"Oooo ring bell. Oo-ee come. Oo-ee promise. 'Member! Oooo 'member! Next sun more blufisss skraaabss." Though, by the fall of night, the dolphin numbers had shrunk from the nearly one hundred that had swum into the pier in response to the Report peal to twenty, those last were as loath to leave as the humans.

Curran urged all back into the warmth of his hold, where the hot mulled wine that was passed around was very welcome indeed. The first mate, Texur, and three of the other skippers then took folks back to their cotholds where they could dry their clothing. Robina clucked about, handing out fur rugs and fussing over Master Oldive.

"You'll be treating yourself if you don't have more of a care for your own health, Master," she said, scowling fiercely. "And then where will the rest of us be?"

"Ringing the dolphin bell," Oldive murmured in a whisper that only Menolly and Sebell heard. "There is so much, so much more than we could have ever anticipated," he went on in a slightly louder but still reflective tone of voice, "and we *must* learn all we can. All we can." His voice fell again and his hand nearly let go of the cup of mulled wine. Menolly rescued it with a smile, which he returned. "Goodness, I don't think I've had this much outdoor activity in decades."

"We should have had you conveyed a-dragonback," Menolly said anxiously.

"No, no, my dear," Oldive said, sitting up straighter. "I'm always after my patients to exercise and get fresh air and I never listen to my own advice. This has been a truly remarkable day."

"As soon as you're dried out enough, I'll send Beauty to Fort Weyr and we'll get you home safe, sound, and un-wet," Menolly said firmly, and gave him a stern look.

"Oh, no, not today. I must wait over and speak with I Bit again. But let us send back Worlain and Fabry. I have a particular patient in the Hall at the moment. I Bit might just be able to see what ails her, for without some help, I fear she will die. There is so much we don't know," he added, shaking his head.

"Now, Master," Fabry said, for he evidently had an ear cocked in his Master's direction, "Mislue's the last person to expose to a dolphin. In the first place, she'll be terrified . . ."

"She's also terrified of dying," Oldive said crisply.

"But how will you transport her here? The jolting of a Gather wagon would be too painful . . ."

"A dragon will oblige."

Fabry snorted. "She'd be even more afraid of riding a dragon—if we could get her astride one—than even the doll-fin."

"Dolphin," Sebell said in absent correction.

"Whatever," Fabry said, glancing at the Masterharper with all the arrogance some of the healers often displayed for other Crafts.

"If that holder woman intends to live to see the grandchild she hopes her daughter-in-law carries, then she'll obey my orders," Oldive said with a tinge of impatience in his usually serene voice. He laid a sensitive, thin-fingered hand on Fabry's arm, and the stocky journeyman assumed an attentive stance. "You will make the arrangements on your return to the Hall, Fabry. I know I can count on you but you are not to forewarn her . . ."

"She'll want details. She always wants details," Fabry said with a much-put-upon sigh.

"The sea, Fabry. It is possible that a sea cure will help her," Oldive said, one of his irresistible smiles lighting his gentle face and kind eyes.

"A sea cure?" Fabry barked a laugh.

"A sea cure," Oldive repeated, smiling back.

So Menolly dispatched Beauty to Fort Weyr with a request for N'ton to provide dragons for those returning that evening. Though she received a warm invitation from Robina to stay overnight, too, she declined, anxious to return to her children. Sebell elected to remain with Oldive for a further meeting the next day with the dolphins. That left the question of the runnerbeasts they had ridden down to the Hold, but Curran said he'd have one of his holders lead them back, laden with fish, in a few days.

Sebell gave Menolly a quick embrace when the dragons arrived. "Now, don't spend all night composing, will you?"

"Much as I'd like to," she said, hugging him fiercely, "the fresh air's got me yawning, too. I'm so glad that it all worked."

"Were you worried?" Sebell asked, looking down into her face with searching eyes.

"Well, not exactly worried, but I certainly didn't expect the turnout! I'll have to tell Alemi. He'll be thrilled. It is too bad, though," Menolly added, uxoriously smoothing the wrinkles of a jacket only just dried from the afternoon's soaking.

"What?"

"That so much else is happening to detract from the dolphins."

"Hmmm. Yes, but we'll have the dolphins with us for the rest of our lives on Pern. Right now it is imperative that we follow Aivas's timetable and rid us of Thread."

"You're right, of course, Sebell. The dolphins will be with us as they have been with us all along. I do hope Lessa doesn't mind."

"Why should she mind?" Sebell asked. She could come out with the most astonishing observations.

"Well, you know how she was about fire-lizards!"

"Not yours, my love. Just the undisciplined mob. I'll brief Master Robinton and he'll break it to her."

8

"Doll-fins?" Lessa demanded, her eyebrows rising in black arcs of astonishment. She stared at Alemi, glaring fiercely until Masterharper Robinton laughed at her.

"Dolphins, Lessa." Adroitly he corrected her pronunciation. "They have been mentioned. They came with the original settlers and have been happily plying the seas, saving lives when they could, and waiting until humans remembered them. Aivas is very interested in reestablishing the association."

She blinked at the Harper. "Well, I suppose I do remember some mention of the sea creatures, but there's been so much else going on . . ." Her tone chided him for bringing up a subject that she plainly considered irrelevant and immaterial.

"They've been around longer than dragons," he said teasingly. "And they're proving far more useful than, say, the fire-lizards." He shot her a wicked glance for her well-known disgruntlement with fire-lizards pestering her gold dragon, Ramoth.

Lessa awarded him a very sour look until she caught sight of her golden dragon, Ramoth, splashing in the waters of Cove Hold, her bathing assisted by wild and tame fire-lizards alike.

"The dragons that have met them seem to like them, Lessa," Alemi said, taking his cue from the Harper and not letting himself be intimidated by the diminutive but forceful Weyrwoman of Benden.

"Which ones?"

"First, Gadareth, the bronze of young T'lion from Eastern Weyr. He was conveying me the day I inadvertently summoned the Monaco Bay pod." She accepted that with a flick of her fingers, so Alemi went on. "Master Oldive had a very puzzling patient, which the dolphins at Fort Sea Hold diagnosed as having an internal growth in the belly."

"And that caused enough problems with his Hall," she said dryly. "I really don't like the idea of cutting into human bodies." She gave a little shudder.

"No more than when a child is hard to birth," Alemi said, knowing that Lessa had had to have that surgery. Probably why she disliked intrusive operations. "The woman's recovering and most grateful. However," he went on briskly, "the dolphins are certainly proving invaluable assets to my Craft."

"I did hear Master Idarolan on the subject but now is *not* the time to go off half-cocked," she said. "We must not let anything interfere with Aivas's program."

"No more will the dolphins," Robinton said soothingly.

"I've met one or two and they are charming. It's so nice to see creatures smiling all the time."

Lessa's glare intensified and then, abruptly, she burst out laughing. "I have been a grouch, haven't I?"

"Indeed you have," Robinton said as cheerfully as any dolphin. "You should meet a few. They all have names."

"Sea creatures with names?" Lessa exclaimed and her frown returned. That the dragons knew their own names at birth was an indisputable mark of their self-awareness and intelligence. To hear that the dolphins also had names smacked of heresy to the Weyrwoman.

"Each calf is named as it's born, I'm told," Alemi hastily explained. "Aivas said those names are variations on the names of the original dolphins. They have traditions, too, you see."

"I suppose the next thing will be the formation of yet another crafthall to take care of dolphins."

"They seem to take very good care of themselves, my dear," Robinton said, "if they've survived on their own in our seas all this while."

"Hmmm, yes, well. I don't want anything to detract from the priorities Aivas has set us."

"This won't," Alemi said with such conviction that he won a smile from her.

She rose then. "If that's all today?" she asked Master Robinton.

He rose, too, and his stiff movement gave Lessa a pang of concern for her valued friend. He'd never been quite as vigorous—though he protested constantly that he was well—since the heart attack he'd suffered at Ista Weyr. All this fuss with Aivas and the discoveries at Landing were not at all the sort of stimulation he needed. And yet . . .

"There're several very engaging fellows out in the

cove," Robinton said, gesturing toward the beautifully colored waters of his bay.

She made a disgruntled noise, dismissing the notion. "I've more than enough to do as it is. And far more 'visitors' to meet and sort out than I can comfortably deal with." She saw the disappointment on the Masterharper's face and laid a kind hand on his arm. "Once we've finished Aivas's grand scheme, I promise you I'll make time to meet these doll—dolphins of yours."

"Grand! You'll love the games they play."

"Games?" Once more Lessa's frown returned.

"Games can be as necessary as work, Lessa," Robinton said gently. "You don't take enough time for yourself."

"I don't *have* enough time for what I *have* to do, much less myself," she said, but she gave him an encouraging smile and left the cool, shady comfort of Cove Hold for the midday heat.

Ramoth waded out of the water to meet her. *The sea creatures know where to scratch my belly just where it itches,* she told her rider.

"They do?" Lessa looked out at the cove waters, where these dolphins were leaping and diving about her dragon as easily as tumblers did at a Gather. They did have smiles on their faces. "They were born that way," she told herself. "C'mon, Ramoth, we have to see if another holding is feasible below the others on the Jordan River," she said as she stepped up to Ramoth's neck. The dragon had not completely immersed herself, since she knew they'd have to go *between* and Lessa would not like sitting on damp hide.

She'd been trying to find time to make this inspection for some weeks, but something more urgent always came up. Not that allocating lands to properly trained northerners from overcrowded Holds wasn't also urgent. It was a matter of priorities. Since the Jordan River—flanked by all those fascinating ruins of the Ancients' stakeholds—was so close to Landing, they had been able to explore it sufficiently to release holdings: none as large as the original but respectable properties. Still, sometimes one had to wait until there were sufficient representatives of each of the crafthalls to provide self-sufficiency within each new holding, and at least one journeyman or journeywoman healer who could tend the needs of several holds. Taking one last look at the lovely cove, Lessa reminded herself how deceptive the beauty and lushness of the Southern continent could be. It was just as well not to allow the settling of the new holds to be rushed. People had to be trained to recognize the dangers in this wilderness.

Back in Cove Hold, Alemi was berating himself for not mentioning the newest job that Jayge had suggested for the dolphins. The Paradise River Holder had been furious over the recent invasion of his holding. He was not the least bit mollified to know that he wasn't the only one of the dozen confirmed Holds along the coast to suffer such depredations. He didn't want any more! So he asked Alemi to find out if the dolphins could patrol the waters off his holding and warn of any more unauthorized landings.

"For a pail of fish, they'd be delighted to," Alemi had reported to the Holder after he had explained this new work to the pod.

"Good ships and bad ships," Afo had told him.

"The bad ships never have fish for dolphins?" Alemi asked, grinning.

"You right! Bad ships smell, leak 'n' leave badness in

our water. Not nice." She squirted from her blowhole to emphasize her distaste.

Alemi decided that was a fair enough measure of identification since invariably those masters willing to transport unauthorized passengers were those operating at the very fringes of their craft. Men like that would do anything for a few marks—well, a good heavy sack of marks, Alemi amended. The men who had tried to land on Paradise holding had paid a substantial amount to the captain to sail them south. The ship had not been in very seaworthy condition, its holds wet and dank, sails and hull patched, its bilges spewing wastes into the sea.

"As bad as the Igen caves," one man had said in disgust. "With all this land down here, why can't we have some?" he had demanded bitterly.

"You can if you do it in the proper fashion," Jayge had told him.

"Ha! Dragonriders're keeping the best parts for themselves." But there was a wistful envy in his eyes as he looked over the fine situation of Paradise River.

"I'm no dragonrider and I hold this proper, with neighbors farther down the river who've proved up their lands."

"And paid a great sack of marks to get it, like as not."

"No, they did not," Jayge snapped back. "They applied, and with the required number of crafthalls among 'em. That's what's required and if you lived here, you'd know that this Southern Continent's not easy just because it's warm."

Jayge had walked off then, scowling deeply, Alemi following him. Although Alemi knew that Jayge and Aramina had been shipwrecked, they had proved the Hold long before they had been found by Piemur. He also knew that he'd been very lucky to be asked to start a fishman's hold at Paradise River, and he certainly knew the dreadful conditions of the holdless, crammed into the caves at Igen and other, even less salubrious places in the North. He was also now aware that settlements were being established where ruins indicated that the Ancients had had holdings.

Lord Toric had accepted quite a large number of those wishing to immigrate south—even before the Council of Lord Holders and the Benden Weyrleaders had formalized the ways such settlements could be allowed. Toric had been choosy, preferring men and women who were proven hard workers and preferably at least of journeyman status in their Craft. The iron-handed Lord of Southern did not suffer fools and had already had one incident with renegades trying to settle the big island that happened to be part of his holding. He had tried to get dragonriders to help him flush the squatters out but had had no luck there. The policy of noninterference from the Weyrs had been reinforced a few Turns back by the Benden Weyrleaders. Alemi had approved. The dragonriders must be above partisan leanings, no matter what Hold or Hall they had been born in. But, even as he helped Jayge flush the intruders out, he had thought how much easier it would have been with dragons aloft to "encourage" the men to surrender without bloodshed.

Alemi was one of the few people to know for a fact that the dragonriders intended to have first choice of the lands in the Southern Continent. A stray remark by Master Idarolan had set his thinking in that direction, and nothing had happened to disabuse him of the notion. It stood to reason that, once Thread no longer fell on Pern, the dragonriders ought to have some reward for their long service to Hall and Hold—and what better one than their own Holds where *they* wanted to live?

As a Craftmaster, Alemi undoubtedly entertained a slightly different opinion to that held by the Lord Holders who could well feel that they should have the disposition of land, no matter where it was. Master Idarolan had remarked that there was far too much open land to bring folks to blows over who had what and how much. As he'd circumnavigated the Southern Continent, the Masterfishman certainly had a good idea of what vast expanses of land were available.

On the other hand, fishmen needed only enough land to tie up their ships in a safe harbor and sell their catches. More would be greedy. Alemi did not approve of being greedy.

"Well," murmured the Masterharper, bringing Alemi back to the present, "that went off better than I expected. I adore Lessa of Benden Weyr but she tends to be . . . say, a bit too obsessed with draconic prestige."

"Shouldn't she be?" Alemi asked, startled.

"Yes, of course she should," Master Robinton said quickly. "And she behaves as a Weyrwoman should. But occasionally, she does not consider other matters in quite the light you and I would. Now, tell me about this dolphin sea watch you wanted to set up to guard against more intruders?"

"I should have told the Weyrwoman about that . . ."

"Oh, no, I don't think that was necessary or even a sound idea," Robinton said, smiling slyly. "Let her get accustomed to the idea of dolphin intelligence first. Then spring this further evidence of their ingenuity on her. Don't you think?"

"If you say so," Alemi replied, not totally convinced.

"The Paradise River pod is organized now to repel intruders?"

"Yes, and I believe that T'gellan at Eastern Weyr has

had young T'lion initiate a similar watch along that coast-line. Although," Alemi added with a grin, "I think the Weyr healer is doing as much work with the dolphins as T'lion."

"Yes, tell me about that," Robinton said, pouring wine for both of them and gesturing Alemi to sit beside him in the cool shade of the wide porch that surrounded Cove Hold. "They actually come to be treated by a human?"

Inside, other residents were preparing a light midday meal. Cove Hold had a changing population made up of the archivists and harpers who were organizing the vast amount of information that Aivas was constantly produc-ing. It was unusual for there to be so few people demand-ing Master Robinton's attention. D'ram and Lytol, who were his companions in the lovely Hold, were busy at Landing.

"Yes, they do," Alemi said. "A bell can summon hu-mans as well as dolphins." He had put a good long sturdy chain on the bell at Paradise Head; the loose end hung well down into the water by the float, making it easy for the dolphins to pull it to summon him. Though it was usually one of the children who ran to answer the dol-phins' peal. And Alemi was as often approached by "his" podmembers while he was at sea.

"And they ring the bell in this Report sequence you mentioned?" Robinton was clearly fascinated.

"And keep ringing until someone comes," Alemi said, with a twisty grin. He'd been roused out of his bed a time or two. Still, those occasions had been emergencies: Once, would-be settlers from the North being overturned in their totally inadequate skiff; the other time a dolphin with a nasty gash. Temma had sewn it up as neatly as a healer could have, and the dolphins had been very grateful.

"Aivas very kindly printed out medical information for any healers who encounter dolphins," Alemi went on. Then he paused. "I remember once, finding six dolphins dead in a cove up Nerat way. We never did know what had affected them because there weren't any visible marks. Dolphins can get just as sick as humans, and with the same sorts of problems, with digestion and lungs and hearts and kidneys and livers."

"Really?" The Harper regarded Alemi with surprise. "One never thinks of fish—excuse me," he corrected himself before Alemi dared to, "mammals . . . as being subject to the frailties that beset human flesh. What on earth would cause a heart attack in a dolphin?"

Alemi shrugged. "Stress, physical exertion, even birth defect, according to the report." Then he remembered that stress and physical exertion had retired Master Robinton well before the man had been ready to step down. He stole a nervous look at the Harper, who was apparently considering the information he'd been given.

"Six heart attacks at the same time?" Robinton asked, surprised.

"No, that incident had to be caused by something else. Aivas's report mentioned that 'beachings' were not uncommon on old Earth and were thought to have been caused by polluted waters that poisoned the dolphins. But our waters are clean and clear."

"And they will stay that way!" Master Robinton said with unexpected vigor. "With Aivas to guide us we shall not repeat the mistakes our forebears made on their world." He paused a beat and then went on with a wry grin. "At least not the same ones and for the same reason. We can—perhaps—be grateful that what the Ancients had, Pern's resources will not provide. That will be our saving."

"Oh?" Alemi wasn't above a little prompting.

Master Robinton's mobile face lit with a knowing smile. "Despite all we have endured since the Dawn Sisters took their orbit above us, this world has stayed remarkably well in the parameters set out by the colony founders. Of course, we couldn't know that we were abiding by those precepts"—he grinned roguishly at Alemi—"but the fact of the matter is that we did keep to just the technology needed to survive. Once the threat of Thread is abolished, we can improve the quality of our lives and still remain within these precepts: a world that does not require as much of the sophisticated doodads and technology that so obsessed our ancestors. We'll be the better for it."

"And the Weyrs?" Alemi was burning to ask that.

Robinton's smile abated but his expression was more pensive than anxious. "They will, of course, find a new level for themselves, but I sincerely doubt that dragons will disappear because Thread does."

His smile returned, slightly mysterious as if he had information he would not impart to Alemi—which was fair enough, the Masterfishman thought. It was sufficiently comforting to be reassured by the Masterharper, however circumspectly.

Alemi was loath to leave the porch and the easy companionship of Master Robinton, but he was also aware that he couldn't justify monopolizing the man's attention for much longer that morning. There were so many other demands on the Harper's time and his reserves of energy. Alemi felt much pride at being awarded as much of an interview as he had.

T'lion was, perhaps, a little indignant about being constantly warned by Weyrlingmaster H'mar not to neglect his dragon for his new enthusiasm, the dolphins. But he kept his tongue in his mouth, especially when Gadareth protested vehemently to him, and more importantly to bronze Janereth, that he was *not* for a moment being neglected and the dolphins were even helping keep 'him clean.'

Most evenings, T'lion was the rider assigned to collect the Paradise River harper, Boskoney, and bring him to his work at Admin. He liked Boskoney, so the task was no burden. It also meant he could arrive a little early and spend a few moments getting to know the Paradise River pod, Kib, Afo, and exchange greetings from Natua, Tana, and Boojie. Sometimes he encountered Alemi, thanking the pod for good fishing or warnings on weather.

"The pod's also sweep-swimming," Alemi said, grinning at the alteration of the Weyr term, "along the Paradise holding to prevent any more intrusions. That way we won't compromise you, T'lion, though I assure you we were very grateful to you for your help two months back."

T'lion shrugged and grinned. "Just so long as my Weyrleaders don't hear about it."

"Of course not."

Then T'lion frowned a bit. "But that only protects you." He waved to the east. "There's an awful lot of unpatrolled coast from here to Southern Hold."

It was Alemi's turn to shrug. "Well, that's not my problem. Not that I won't mention—where it will matter—if in my sailing I happen to see other incursions."

"There's such a lot of land here," T'lion said, shaking his head slowly.

"Lad, you can't worry about everything, though it's a credit to you that you take additional responsibility. Now, help me feed these fish faces."

"Sssh . . ." T'lion made an exaggerated gesture of dismay at the word. "They don't like being called . . ." He mouthed the terrible word.

Alemi laughed. "I have dispensation. I'm a fishman." And he formally introduced T'lion.

"No need," Kib told him, raising his head up out of the water. "Tana 'n' Natua tell. Good man, dragonrider."

"Thanks," T'lion said, rather pleased to be acknowledged so warmly.

"Stitch Boojie." Kib ducked his nose in the water and flicked it at T'lion.

"I'll get my death of a cold talking to dolphins," T'lion said, wringing the front of his sopping shirt. "Oh, well, I've learned to carry a spare and he didn't get my jacket."

"I've learned to not wear a thing," Alemi remarked with an understanding grin, his tanned body bare to the folded clout so many wore in the hot season. "So where's tomorrow's fish, Afo?"

Afo gave the information, which included sonar "readings."

"They know where the school is, but the only way they can express that to me is to give me the return time of their sonar responses," Alemi said. "I'm getting good at figuring distances that way."

"That's—that's amazing," T'lion said, awed.

"Not as much as you getting Boojie stitched." Alemi grinned at T'lion's surprise. "Oh, we heard all about it. They can pass quite a bit of information around—if they feel like it."

"Dragons are still the most responsible," T'lion said, proudly glancing up at his splendid bronze.

"Don't deny that for a moment, lad. Each to his own purpose on Pern."

"Which reminds me, I'll be late collecting Harper

Boskoney." T'lion clambered back up the ladder to the pier, tugging free his wet shirt as he made his way to his dragon. He finished changing to the dry one from his pack as Gadareth flew the short distance.

When he and Gadareth glided in to land in front of Boskoney's cothold, the harper peered around the door at them.

"Be a moment," he called.

T'lion knew these harper "moments" and laid his shirt out on the nearby bush to dry, then hunkered down to lean back against Gadareth's haunch to wait.

A darkly tanned youngster came out and, grinning at the sight of a dragon, came confidently up to him.

"You must be T'lion and this is Gadareth." The boy reached a hand up to the dragon's muzzle. Gadareth touched it in polite greeting. "Boskoney said you'd come to collect him so I could run along now."

"And you are?" T'lion asked, amused at the boy's poise. He couldn't be more than seven Turns.

"I'm Readis, son of Holders Jayge and Aramina. I wash Ruth, Lord Jaxom's dragon, whenever he comes to visit. Can I wash Gadareth sometime too?" Then he eyed the bulk of the bronze, who had not yet reached his full stature. "There's a lot more of him than Ruth, but I could help."

T'lion laughed. "You can, if we ever have a chance to stay long enough. Generally, though, the dolphins help me wash Gadareth."

The boy's ogle-eyed reaction made T'lion laugh.

"You're speaking to dolphins?"

It was T'lion's turn to be surprised: the boy not only knew that the dolphins spoke but he pronounced their name correctly.

"Have *you* spoken to dolphins?" T'lion asked. Maybe

the boy answered the dolphin bell for Alemi. It would be a good task for a young lad and a Holder's son.

"Only the day they saved my life. But Unclemi said they ask him how I'm doing."

"They saved your life? Tell me how." Sometimes T'lion missed the youngest of his brothers, Tikini, who had much the same ingenuousness about him as this Holder's son. He and Tikini had been very close.

Just then Boskoney came out of his cothold, sweat breaking out on his forehead from the heavy flying jacket he was wearing. "You scoot on home now, Readis," he said to the boy, "and let's get above this heat, can we, T'lion?"

"I'll see you around, Readis," T'lion called as he speedily mounted Gadareth and then helped Boskoney aboard. Circling upward away from the sultry air of the steaming hold, T'lion saw the boy waving as long as he could be seen.

Over the next several weeks, in the course of T'lion's collecting the harper, T'lion and Readis met again. Readis invariably asked what was new with *his* pod, and who was sick, and who had been cured, and T'lion was only too glad to talk to someone who avidly soaked up his tales. He hadn't realized how much he had bottled up his interest in the dolphins until he began to talk to Readis, who responded enthusiastically, his eyes sparkling, his whole body almost vibrating in his intensity.

"Look, you can speak to the dolphins again, if you want to," T'lion told Readis one day.

"I'm not 'sposed to be near water alone," Readis said. "I promised."

"Well, if you're with me and Gadareth, you're scarcely alone."

Readis considered this, thoughtfully and wistfully, digging at the sand with his bare toe. "Yes, a dragonrider and a dragon would keep me my promise." He gave T'lion a radiant grin. "But where?" His arm swept to the wide expanse of the river mouth.

"Oh, that's the easy part and very safe," T'lion said. "D'you know where Master Alemi anchors? Are you allowed to go that far?"

Readis nodded vigorously, the dark curls on his head bouncing, his eyes solemn and his expression so eager it was hungry.

"You meet me there tomorrow afternoon, say, at the fourth hour, so we'd have a whole one before I'm due to collect Master Boskoney."

"Oh, I will, I will, I will. Thank you!"

Begun innocently enough, the afternoon sessions with the dolphins became a happy routine for them both. If his mother asked Readis "Where have you been?" or "Who was with you?," he could honestly reply that he was with T'lion and Gadareth. The fact that he was also swimming with the dolphins off Alemi's float simply was not mentioned.

T'lion was delighted not only with the boy's fearlessness in the water and with the dolphins, but in how quickly Readis seemed to understand their odd speech. They, in turn, liked his high-pitched young voice and, having been warned by T'lion that the "calf" was young and must be carefully handled, never swamped him or roughed him up, even when Readis dove under the water to swim with them.

"You've got lungs like a dragon to stay under so long," T'lion said one afternoon when he had almost feared the boy had gone too deep, only to have him and Afo's latest calf, Vina, burst out a good two dragonlengths from the float. "Don't do that to me again, Ready," he shouted. "Now, come on in. Take a breather!"

Laughing, Readis allowed Vina to tow him in to the float. He climbed up, grinning and thoroughly pleased with himself. "We got way far down but not to the bottom. Vina clicked it too far for us. So we surfaced. She's great to swim with."

"I can see why your folks want someone with you when you do swim," T'lion said, still recovering from that long moment of fright. "You can promise me that you won't stay under so long again."

"Sure, I promise. But it was great fun. You try it. You can get ever so much deeper with a dolphin!"

"I'm sure, but next time, we'll do it together! Promise?"

Then Readis looked irritably down at Afo, who was pushing her nose at his foot.

"T'orn. Bad t'orn," she said, and squee'ed urgently up at T'lion.

"Your foot hurting you?"

Readis looked blankly at his friend, then down at the foot. "Oh, now and then. I stepped on somethin' but it doesn't hurt when I swim."

"Lemme see."

Readis swiveled on the float so he could obey. Though T'lion prodded the strong, callused foot, he didn't strike a sore spot.

"Bad t'orn," Afo insisted.

"Nothin's there, Afo," Readis insisted, and twisted so

his face was on a level with hers. He reached out one hand and scratched her chin just where she liked it. "Nothin' hurts."

Afo ducked her head vigorously, scooping water at them with her nose.

"Maybe, Readis, you better show your foot to your mother, or your aunt Temma. She's Hold healer, isn't she?"

"Ah, it's nothin'. Let's swim again . . ."

"No," T'lion said so firmly that Readis knew better than to coax him. "I've got to collect Boskoney."

"He's always late," Readis said with good-humored scorn.

"That doesn't mean I shouldn't be on time. C'mon now."

It so happened that that day either they were later than they should have been or Boskoney was actually on time. T'lion deposited Readis on the ground and helped Boskoney up, so he had no time to remind the boy to get the foot seen to.

The next day he had to attend the Fall, delivering fire-stone sacks to the fighting wings far out over the huge inland lake. Then he was sent to collect Mastersmiths attending one of the endless discussions now held daily at Admin, so it was three days before he resumed conveying Boskoney. He arrived at Alemi's float, eager to see Readis, but the boy didn't come. When T'lion and Gadareth landed to collect Boskoney, he asked the harper if he'd seen the boy.

"No, he's ill. Quite ill, I understand."

T'lion experienced a pang of fear. Shard it! Readis had promised to see his aunt Temma.

"Got one of those swift high fevers that kids his age so often have," Boskoney added, settling himself between the bronze's neck ridges. "He'll be fine in a day or two. Bright child."

"Yes, he is," T'lion replied, his anxiety only partially abated. One of his sisters had died of one of those swift high fevers, but she'd been younger than Readis and not nearly as sturdy as the Holder boy.

"Maybe a dolphin should look at him. They're good at diagnosing."

Boskoney laughed, giving the young rider's shoulder a comforting pat. "Oh, I don't think it's anywhere near critical enough for *your* friends, T'lion, but it's nice of you to be concerned."

"I am. He's like a brother to me."

"I'll tell him you were asking for him."

"Do. Please."

The next day, T'lion went to the float and rang the bell, asking for Afo when the first dolphin reported in.

"What kind of thorn was it in Ready's foot, Afo?" he asked urgently.

"Swim w'us," Afo squeed, clicking in excitement. "You not ring bell three suns now."

"No, Readis is sick."

"Bad t'orn. Told him."

"A thorn could cause him to have a fever?"

"Bad t'orn. Sea t'orn, not land. Badder."

"I'd better tell his mother, then," T'lion said, and promptly had Gadareth fly him to the Holder's cottage.

There, he found not only the boy's parents and Aunt Temma but the Masterhealer from Landing as well. All looked anxious, the mother was drawn and haggard from sleeplessness. Even Jayge showed the strain of anxiety.

"I heard Readis was ill," T'lion began, nervously clutching his flying cap. "Anything I can do? The dolphins are good at telling what's wrong with people, you know."

"Dolphins!" Aramina spat the word out. "He's delirious about dolphins." She turned her face up to Jayge. "He can't possibly be reliving that rescue, can he?"

She's afraid of dolphins, T'lion, Gadareth said.

Why should she be?

She's just afraid of them for Readis.

That was when T'lion had his first inkling that he had perhaps done wrong in taking the boy to Alemi's float. But he'd been very careful with him, and the boy hadn't broken the promise he must have made his fearful mother.

The Masterhealer gave T'lion a keen glance. "You're the bronze rider who's helped Persellan at Eastern Weyr?"

"Yes, Master, T'lion, Gadareth's rider."

"You're kind to offer, dragonrider, but this is a child's fever. More tenacious than they usually are, it's true, but nothing within the problems which the dolphins can solve."

T'lion hesitated. "Isn't he always running about the place, barefooted? I don't mean that as a criticism, Holder Aramina," he added hastily when he saw that she was bridling at his comment. "I wish I could." he gestured to the heavy boots, in which his feet were perspiring. "But I know how nasty thorns are and it would be so easy . . ."

"His limbs are swollen," the healer said slowly.

"Both legs," Aramina said with such an irritated glance in T'lion's direction that he shrugged as if he regretted making the suggestion.

"But the right foot is unusually swollen . . ." The healer spoke on his way down the wide corridor that led to the sleeping rooms, and Aramina and Temma hurried after him.

"I'd better go," T'lion said to Jayge now that he'd done what he could. "I'll come in again. I collect Boskoney every day." He looked anxiously at Temma and Jayge.

"You're good to be concerned, dragonrider," Jayge said kindly, though it was obvious to T'lion that the Holder's ears were pricked toward the sickroom.

"Not at all. Not at all. He's such a friendly lad, like my brother . . ." T'lion made a hasty retreat, more concerned than ever. *We didn't do anything* bad, *did we, Gadareth? He* wanted *to speak to the dolphins. He already* had *spoken to the dolphins. But his mother was sure upset.*

She heard dragons too much. We are careful not to speak too loud. It upsets her. Maybe dolphins upset her, too.

T'lion walked quickly across to Boskoney's cothold. If he asked just the right questions, maybe he'd find out what he needed to know. But if he *had* done wrong, then he'd have to admit it. Or he'd be in real trouble with T'gellan. Being a dragonrider didn't save him from making stupid mistakes sometimes. But how could he have known?

"Yes, there was no way you *would* have known," Boskoney said with a heavy sigh when T'lion stumbled through his recital of events. "And I don't think you've done *wrong*, exactly. It's just unfortunate it's turned out so badly. You say, one of the dolphins 'saw' a sea thorn in his foot four days ago?" He sighed. They were both aware, having been raised in the tropics, how treacherous thorns could be in human flesh. The harper laid a reassuring hand on the young rider's shoulder. "I'll do what I can, lad. And I've canceled tonight's meeting. They need me here right now. You go on. Speak to your Weyrleader. That's the best thing to do now. I'll find Alemi and tell him what you've told me."

The upshot of the matter was that T'lion and Gadareth were assigned other duties, and a blue weyrling and his rider conveyed Harper Boskoney to and from Paradise River Hold. A sevenday later Boskoney appeared at Eastern Weyr on his way to Landing to tell the guilt-tormented bronze rider that Readis's fever had broken and he would recover. Out of respect for T'lion's feelings, the harper did not mention that the poison had affected the boy's right leg, knotting the tendons so that he might never have full use of the limb.

"Alemi managed to insist that they take the boy to the dolphins, and Afo accurately identified the site of the thorn, and the poison which had traveled up to the knee by then. It could have traveled all the way to his heart, I'm told, and killed him."

T'lion sank to the hammock on his porch, head in hands. "I should have told them *then!*"

"Now, lad, don't take it so to heart. You told me and I told them."

"Could . . . I go see him?"

Kindly the harper shook his head. "He's too weak to see anyone, though he asked Alemi to tell you why he hadn't been around."

T'lion groaned again. "I—I—should have taken him right then to the Hold healer, right when Afo told us there was a bad thorn, but I was late to collect you . . ."

"And I was annoyed and rushed you off that day. It's by no means all your fault, T'lion, and you mustn't take it so hard. And"—the harper's tone lightened and T'lion saw he was smiling wryly—"all the healers insist that Readis must swim every day to regain tone in the leg muscles."

"They did?" Some of the heavy pressure in T'lion's chest lightened.

"It's the best chance he has to recover."

"What does his mother say to that?"

Boskoney's grin was even more ironic. "She has had to agree to the treatment. It *is* the only way he'll walk again."

"Ohhhhh!" T'lion buried his head in his hands again, shaking it from side to side. "He was like my brother . . ."

"Now, T'lion, enough of this guilt. It was an unfortunate concatenation of circumstances. However, I may say unreservedly that Readis is delighted. He finds it no chore to have to associate with dolphins daily. I heard him tell his mother that he walks in water better than he can on land!"

T'lion gave a rueful laugh. "He would, wouldn't he? He's such a brave lad."

"He'll be fine. You will be, too."

9

▼▼▼▼▼▼▼▼▼▼

Over the next four Turns, while Readis earnestly exercised his legs in the warm waters of Paradise Head, momentous events unfolded at Landing, Benden Weyr, Cove Hold, and Fort Hold. With advice and counsel from Aivas, Weyrs, Halls, and Holds combined their efforts with the technology available from Aivas and altered the orbit of the Red Star so that it would never again come close enough to Pern to threaten the planet with Threadfall. On the day that the explosion of the antimatter engines of the three colony ships was viewed through distance lenses, everyone on Pern celebrated the end of Thread tyranny. Only Thread did not stop falling, a demonstrable fact that confused many, including Readis.

"Then why did you celebrate?" he asked his father four days later, when Thread fell across Paradise River Hold.

"Because Thread *will* end—this is the last Pass."

"It is? Harper says that we've had it for centuries and every time we think it's going to stop—in a long Interval—it comes back anyhow."

Jayge grinned at his son, tall for his eleven Turns, and tried not to glance down at the wasted right leg, which cocked on tiptoe beside the uninjured left foot. He ruffled Readis's curly hair and thought instead that it was unfair for the boys in the family to have the curls while the two girls had straight hair.

"The dragonriders have gone to the Red Star and steered it away from getting close enough to bring Thread to Pern ever again."

"How could they move a star?" Readis demanded. "It's too big, even for dragons."

"They used the engines from the Dawn Sisters. They pulled the Star out of an orbit that brings it too close to Pern. Do you understand what I mean?"

"Sure. Harper's told us all about our star system. He put a coconut down for the sun and then walked all the way to the edge of the river to put down a tiny pebble for Pern." Readis giggled. "He said that's the re-la-tive distances involved." Patently Readis could only repeat what he had been told and did not quite comprehend the subtleties of the explanation. "Pern isn't as small as that pebble. I know that!"

"You'll understand better as you grow up."

"Everyone's always saying that," Readis replied disgustedly.

"You'll find it's true," Jayge said, hearing an echo of his own boyish voice. "However, Boskoney has advised us to enroll you in the Landing school."

"Huh? And leave Paradise?" Readis was appalled at the very thought.

"Daytimes, six of a sevenday, with a break during the hot season."

"Daaad!"

"You, Kami, and Pardure are enrolled. At that, Paradise River is exceedingly lucky to gain three places out of the twenty-five available to special students . . ."

"You mean, because of my leg I have to go away?"

"There's not a thing wrong with Kami and Pardure, my young lad!" his father said sternly.

Readis was not completely mollified. He hated anyone making concessions for him. He rode the small runner Lord Jaxom had trained especially for him only because Ruth had said that he, the white dragon, had selected the beast for Readis, who had been so good about scrubbing his hide all these Turns. The little creature had made it possible for Readis to go wherever the other youngsters of the Hold roamed: the boy was as good a rider as he was a swimmer. Aramina preferred him to use Delky, the runner—anything to keep him out of the water and away from the dolphins. She could not be convinced that the dolphins were not responsible for his illness and subsequent crippling. It was Aramina who had heard about the proposed special classes to be held in the Admin Building, using the information machines that were the legacy of Aivas. Menolly had told Alemi, who had requested the concession not only for his own eldest daughter, but for Readis as well.

"How'll I get there?" Readis demanded of his father, sticking his chin out almost impertinently.

"A-dragonback. I trust you won't mind that." Jayge knew that the transport might be the final persuader.

"Every day?" Readis brightened considerably. "We'd have to ride a dragon every morning and every evening?"

He hoped that T'lion and Gadareth would do the conveying. He'd never been able to convince his mother that T'lion wasn't in some way responsible for his illness. He'd told her time and again that the dragonrider had told him, twice, to go see Temma for the thorn and he'd forgotten. So his illness, and his bad leg, were *not* T'lion's fault, but his own. He heard what his father was saying then.

"This is a special dispensation for the three of you, until a dormitory can be set up for the pupils."

"A-dragonback twice a day?" Readis did not hear the qualifier, his eyes shining with the prospect of riding dragons on a regular basis.

"Only as long as you study hard enough to deserve the honor," his father said sternly.

Boskoney's report listed Readis as his top student over Kami and the studious Pardure, Journeyman Weaver Parren's eldest. While Pardure studied hard for his knowledge, everything seemed to come easily to Readis, who would benefit from the challenge of a more structured learning climate. Competition for the few places available had been intense, but Master Robinton, whose scheme this was, had insisted that the students be harper-recommended and that they be proportionately drawn from Weyr, Hall, and Hold.

Master Robinton wanted to be sure this current generation of young people grew up trained from an early age to absorb and utilize the vast amount of knowledge available through Aivas. He had started special classes with just a few suitable pupils from the Landing residents, and each Turn, had increased the size of the classes. Aivas had agreed, remarking that it would be easier to train youngsters—since they would have no misinformation to be corrected—than to retrain men and women who would have to alter lifelong habits of thinking and learning. Now that the main push of everyone's efforts—the Red Star project—was accomplished, the Halls could concentrate on spreading new devices that would raise living standards all across Pern. Once power could be generated in Holds, Halls, and Weyrs, the special equipment Aivas had taught people how to use could be extended throughout the planet, instead of centralized at Landing.

Wind and tide generators were being studied by Jayge and his crafthall residents to see which would suit their needs best. Using a powered loom, Journeyman Parren could produce in quantity the coveted fabrics he made from the local fiber plants. Better lights would be a tremendous help in every household, and fans would make life more bearable during the hot season. Other applications of power generation were being studied, especially the manufacture of ice so the fish catches would remain fresher longer. Alemi was very keen for that amenity.

Jayge found some of the concepts difficult to understand, so he was delighted that Readis would have the opportunity to start off absorbing the new wonders at a better "learning" age. Such training would also make the boy more acceptable to the Council of Holders when it came time for him to be confirmed in his holding. In the meantime, Jayge was determined to improve the Hold and its resources. The basics of figuring, reading, and scripting taught by harpers along with Traditional ballads and songs were well enough for those who would be apprenticed to a Craft, but a Holder needed a broader, overall view. Jayge had learned how to hold through trial and error back when he and Aramina had been shipwrecked on this coast, but he wanted more for his sons and daughters.

Readis was all set for his first session at school the following morning—his knapsack was packed and a flying jacket and cap on to protect him *between*—when a fire-lizard came screaming in to land on the porch. He heard its distressed cry at the same time as his family and reached the porch just as his father was unfastening the message tube the fire-lizard wore. As soon as he released it, the little creature, still desperately keening, flitted out and was gone, followed by the resident fair, who picked up its tormented cry.

"No, no, nonono," Jayge said, shaking his head in denial as he scanned the message. "No. He can't be!"

"What's the matter, Dad?" Readis asked. He'd never seen such a look of anguish on his father's face.

Jayge bowed his head to his chest and slumped against the railing, covering his eyes with one hand while the other held the message, a narrow strip of paper.

"Dad?" Readis felt the first twinge of panic. Something terrible had happened. "Dad?" Readis needed to be reassured.

"Readis, go tell Boskoney to come. Take Delky." He gestured toward the little runner, standing hipshot in the shade at the corner of the house.

As Readis vaulted to her back, he looked over his shoulder and saw his father, sagging and motionless. He dug his heels into the willing little beast's ribs and she was away in a flash. Readis really liked having Delky to ride on land, but it wasn't a patch on swimming with Kib or Afo. For all she was patient and willing, Delky couldn't talk to him, not as the dolphins and the dragons did, so he found her distinctly lacking. Even fire-lizards gave one some sort of reaction. Delky only did what she was asked to do. Still, she was useful. He sat back on her rump and, as she'd been trained, she came to a complete halt, showering sand into the harper's open doorway.

"What's the rush, now, m'lad?" Boskoney asked, coming to the door.

"Dad wants you. Urgent. Fire-lizard brought a message and it's upset him."

"It has?"

Readis gestured for Boskoney to mount behind him, though the harper's legs would catch any bushes on the way back. Obedient and uncomplaining, Delky swiveled neatly on her hindquarters and cantered back as easily with her double burden as she had with only Readis's light body.

"What sort of message?" Boskoney demanded, reaching through Readis's arms to clutch Delky's mane.

"He didn't say. Just told me to get you. He hasn't moved a muscle since I left," Readis muttered to Boskoney as the harper dismounted at the porch steps. Readis was really worried now. Bad news didn't often trouble Paradise River. When something did go wrong, his father was more apt to curse and pace and wave his arms about, but he was never silent and all drawn in on himself like now.

Hearing the harper's step, Jayge reached the message strip in his direction. Boskoney scanned it. Then, in the act of stepping up, the harper halted, foot held midair a long moment before he sort of turned and sank to the top step, head in his hands and his shoulders shaking. Readis kneed Delky around the house to the door of the kitchen, where his mother was preparing their supper.

"Mother," Readis said, edging into the house and touching her arm, "I think you better go see what's wrong with Father."

"What could be wrong with your father, dear?" she asked in a voice that suddenly seemed too loud to Readis.

"He got some bad news and sent me for Boskoney. Now *he's* sitting on the porch and—what would make a harper cry, Mother?"

Aramina shot her son a startled look before she took the heavy pan off the fire and half ran to the front of the house. Readis moved after her in the touch-toe/step gait he had adopted to get him places almost as quickly as anyone else on two good feet. Before he could reach the porch, he heard his mother crying, not loudly as she had when she learned of Granddad's death but softly, as if the pain inside her was unbearable. She had her arms about Jayge and was comforting him even as she wept.

The scene was too much for Readis, and he retraced his steps, vaulted up on Delky's back again, and raced her toward the cluster of cotholds down the riverbank.

"I think you better get up to the hold, Aunt Temma, Uncle Nazer. You, too, Uncle Swacky," he added when the burly figure of the grizzled old soldier appeared in the doorway. "I don't know what's happened but it's made Dad, Mother, *and* Boskoney cry." He didn't wait to see if they followed but turned Delky around again and had her galloping past the tableau on his porch and on to Alemi's hold. He brought Alemi back with him on Delky, leaving Kitrin and the other fishmen to follow on foot.

When Alemi arrived, Temma, Nazer, Swacky, Parren, and his wife and oldest daughter were standing about, weeping, too. The strip of paper was passed to Alemi, who began to breathe deeply and swallow while tears crept down his cheeks. Seeing his chance, Readis turned Unclemi's hand toward him so he could read this awful message.

" 'Master Robinton and Zair have died. Aivas, too.' " The stark words did not immediately make sense to him. Master Robinton couldn't die. Everyone needed him. Readis knew that. And how could a machine die? He

knew that Aivas was a machine, a very intelligent machine who knew a great deal—but still a machine. Machines didn't die, they just . . . just ran down? Wore out?

Suddenly the air was full of fire-lizards, all of them uttering the most incredible keening noise, sort of edgy and
hurting the ears: sounds he'd never heard them make ever
before in his life. They went diving about the air, swoop-
ing down to the roof of the hold, and then up again, unable to settle, all the time making that dreadful noise.

"What's the matter? My fire-lizard is terribly upset,"
cried Lur, one of the landsmen, who came running up to
the main hold.

Behind him on the path, Readis could see other holders
and crafters making their way here, attracted by the fire-
lizards' unusual behavior. Alemi had slipped off Delky
and joined those mourning on the porch, so Readis kneed
his runner to meet Lur, showing him the message. Lur's
face went very pale under his tan and he collapsed against
the nearest tree, bawling in great sobs. So Readis pointed
Delky on down the path, showing everyone the message
as he reached them. Soon everyone had congregated
around the porch, weeping and immersed in this grief.
Their children, not quite understanding the terrible loss,
assembled a little away from the adults, confused by the
atmosphere and the sight of their grieving parents.

It was the strangest evening Readis ever lived through.
He watched as his father took a long time to coax Tork, his
fire-lizard, to come to him so he could send off a message.
Some of the women followed his mother into the house
and they came back with wine. Another group went back
to their houses and brought food, not that anyone other
than the hungriest of the little kids ate much.

When the sun set, no one seemed inclined to go home.
The harper was still on the steps, turning a half-empty

wineglass—Aramina or Jayge kept filling it—in his hands. Readis noticed that tears kept dripping off his jaw and Boskoney made no move to dry them. Well, he was a harper and he would have been taught by Master Robinton, so one could understand his grieving for the death of his Master. Readis thought it even sadder that the Masterharper's fire-lizard had died at the same time. That sort of loyalty brought a lump to his throat—even thinking that Delky, Kib, or Afo might die along with him, should he die soon. He nearly had, the time he'd been so sick with the thorn poison in his foot. He knew that dragons died when their riders did, but no one who had a fire-lizard had died in Paradise River, so he wasn't sure about their reaction. Then he realized that the grown-ups on the lawn were talking softly among themselves. Kami thought they should get some glowbaskets. So Readis led her and Pardure, who had offered to help, to where they kept them and set enough out so that this remarkable scene was lit.

Many Turns later, Readis remembered that night and the shadows cast on familiar faces all saddened by their loss. He remembered that, although there had been many skins of wine opened, and everyone was drinking, no one got merry from the wine. There was no singing, which was most unusual for any group with a harper in the center of it. Readis wondered as the night got later and later why no one was chasing him and the other youngsters off to their beds. The littlest ones fell asleep where they were, in a parent's lap or on the ground beside their parents. Eventually he got up and collected covers for Aranya, Kami, and her sisters and himself and Pardure and Anskono: his baby brother was sleeping in the hammock on the porch with their mother.

He tried to stay awake, to see what staying up all night

was like, but the soft murmur of sad voices lulled him to sleep.

When he woke the next morning, he was in his own bed. Checking outside, he saw that a fair number of people had slept the night on the grass. Boskoney occupied the hammock, Aramina's prized rug covering him. This was the day Readis was supposed to start school, but he knew it wouldn't start today. The school had been Master Robinton's idea. Maybe it wouldn't happen now he was dead. Somehow Readis didn't like being deprived of that opportunity, especially when it meant he'd be going journeying to school a-dragonback.

His stomach was rumbling, since he hadn't eaten much last night out of deference to the occasion, so Readis went to the larder to see what he could find to eat. Evidently alerted by the small noises he was making, Aranya entered the kitchen, little Almie tagging beside her.

"Hungry," Almie said clearly, pouting. Although Aranya was in a clean coverall, Almie was still in the rumpled things she'd worn yesterday. "I'm empty in my middle."

"I'll feed you, so be quiet," Readis said in a low voice. He sort of figured his parents wouldn't want to be awakened. His baby brother would sleep until someone, or some loud noise, woke him. Readis didn't want the loud noise to be Almie.

He set out bowls, filled them with the fruit that was always sliced and ready in the cooler, and toasted bread for his sisters so they'd keep quiet. He spread Almie's bread with the sweetener she loved because he knew if he didn't, she'd demand it and loudly, too. Aranya was much easier to deal with than Almie. Then he got the grain for the poultry and took care of them, and Delky, who patiently waited out the back door for her morning handful of corn. The canines were just getting restless when he deposited their bowls in the run. They could howl loud enough to wake the dead, as his mother often said. Back in the kitchen, he heated water and ground more klah bark because the jar was empty. One thing he knew for sure would be needed was plenty of klah.

He got Aranya to take Almie into their room and wash her and dress her. Aranya loved playing "mother" to their sister. He was just sitting down to his own toast when Kami slipped in the back door, her blue eyes wide with the tidings and her expression solemn.

"It's awful, isn't it?" she whispered at him.

"They're still asleep," Readis said, speaking in a low voice. He gestured with the toasting fork and she shook her head. She did, however, look wistfully at the pitcher of fruit juice on the table, so he poured her a glass of it.

"Father got messages this morning," she said. "We're all to sail to Monaco to escort the Harper to sea."

Readis felt his throat close over. Boskoney had sung a very moving song about an honorable sea burial, for another old harper, Aunt Menolly's first master. It would be like that.

"All of us?" Readis asked after swallowing the lump. "All of us in Paradise?" He meant children as well as grown-ups.

Kami nodded. "Father says we'll use all three ships so just about everyone can be there to honor our Masterharper. Father said we should never forget what we owe Master Robinton."

"Then we will be able to go to school?" Readis asked.

"Oh, how can you think of something like school when the whole world mourns?" Kami's voice rose in her disgust of his innocent query.

"It's a fair question," Jayge said from the doorway. "Ah, klah! That was thoughtful of someone," he added, and cocked his head toward Readis. "Good lad. Your sisters are fed and occupied? Thank you." He poured three cups, adding sweetener in two, and placed them on a tray. "I'll be back. Toast me some bread, would you, Readis? I don't think any of us ate anything last night."

"A moment, please, Holder Readis," Kami began formally, and she took a deep breath. "My father says that a message has come requesting the Hold to come to Monaco Bay tomorrow morning. My father says the ships will have to be loaded and casting off at the top of the night to reach Monaco by the appointed time."

"All three ships? Hmm, that'll be room enough for everyone?"

Kami nodded, the picture of solemnity. "Yes, sir. Everyone who can come, should, he said. The message said so."

"Very well. Can you take the message round the Hold? Good, thank you, Kami."

Kami slipped out the back door and, through the window, Readis could see her running down the path toward the cotholds.

"The bread, please, Readis, and enough for your mother and Boskoney, too."

It was an odd day. People did what they usually did, but everyone was solemn-faced. Some people were red-eyed and sniffed a lot. Especially when Readis played messenger and gave out the ship assignments, which Unclemi sent for him to deliver. He wondered if Unclemi had told the dolphins. He must have, for when they boarded the *Fair Winds* in the middle of the night, he could see the dorsals crowding the water and the sleek silvery bodies in the starlight.

He couldn't stay awake as long as he wanted to: last night had been tiring and the day had been, too, in the oddest possible way. The dolphins were singing a sad song, too. He curled up in his cover in the prow of the *Fair Winds* and fell asleep to the hiss of water, the dolphin song, and the gentle motion of the ship on a calm sea.

When they arrived in Monaco Bay, there was a great array of ships and small craft, and hundreds and hundreds of dolphins were in the water. In the air, in great fairs, thicker even than those that had swept across the Hold yesterday, the fire-lizards raced back and forth, blotting the sun at times. He was so busy watching their display that at first he didn't notice the ship, all wreathed in black, that was anchored at the pier. The *Fair Winds* was standing far enough out in the bay so that his father had to call his attention to the procession, a small column heading to the dock. Readis was given a chance to use Unclemi's far-viewer.

"I want you to remember this, Readis," his father said, passing him the cylinder. "A great man has died!"

So they watched as the ship unfurled its sails, trimmed in black, and slowly they bellied with the light wind. Majestically it moved from the pier. Unclemi made sail, too, as it passed them by, and the *Fair Winds* followed in its wake, Readis all the time fearful that maybe a dolphin would be hurt, there were so many of them, as they leaped in escort.

What Readis remembered most that day, besides the awful solemnity of that ship and the covered body on its prow, was the dragons in the sky, wing after wing of them in close formation, hanging motionless as the ceremony was conducted. He remembered the terrible keening of the dragons as the Masterharper's body slipped into the water. The hairs on his neck stood up and he could feel the sound down to the heels of both feet. It was far worse than the noise the fire-lizards had made: the dolphins squeeing and clicking only added to the uncanny noise. Had the dolphins known the Masterharper, too? Then all the pods gave one final leap and seemed to disappear. Readis could hold his breath pretty well now, and he had unconsciously held it just as they submerged. But they just didn't come back up, and then he had to take a breath as spots were forming in his eyes. Shielding his eyes, he looked far out to sea and couldn't see a single dorsal fin.

Then he realized that there was only one dragon left in the sky: Ruth, his white hide unmistakable against the blue of sky! He was motionless for so long that Readis began to wonder what had happened to him. Ruth remained, in that vigil, when Unclemi, himself at the wheel of his ship, turned to port and they began their journey homeward. The figure of Ruth dwindled finally—or maybe the white dragon had ended his skyborne post. Readis thought that was the most sad of all he had witnessed today.

The dolphins didn't return until the *Fair Winds* had reached her home waters.

Three days after that funeral, T'lion arrived to take the students to Landing. They weren't taken to the Admin Building as Readis had half expected, but to another building, three over from Admin, where a large crowd of young people had gathered. At the appointed hour, a Master appeared at the main door and, in a clear, carrying voice, announced which rooms were assigned to which class. When the older students had entered the building, he motioned for those remaining outside to approach him.

"Well, now, so you're the ones starting with us this term," he said, letting his gaze range over them. "I am Master Samvel, head of this school, and you will be known as Class Twenty-one, since this is the twenty-first year of the Present Pass. Not very original, I fear, but that designation will identify you to us and you will listen for any messages addressed to the class in general. I shall learn to identify you each by name over the next few days. Meanwhile, I bid you welcome and if you'll all file into room D, we can begin orientation."

Thus began what Readis later found was called the Transition Phase. He was an integral part of it.

10
▼▼▼▼▼▼▼▼▼

Three Turns later, four hundred students were living in dormitories at Landing and pursuing their courses, of which a variety were now offered. When generators were established in other major Holds, additional schools were set up, ranging from primary lessons to retraining. At Harper Hall, Masterharper Sebell inaugurated a totally new course for training apprentices, and musicianship was no longer the dominant concern of the Hall. He was able to implement the new form only because Master Robinton had proposed it to the Masters of the Hall before his death. It had not been acceptable at its initial airing but, afterward, Sebell and Menolly watched, bemused, while the obdurate older Masters insisted on adopting the program. If Menolly's reception of that reversal was bitter, Sebell held on to the advantage and pressed forward, working all the hours of the day to get every phase of Master Robinton's educational plan into operation.

With Fandarel and Oldive insisting, the Smith and Healer Crafts made it compulsory for Masters to attend courses that improved their skills and explained new Craft applications of Aivas's knowledge. After the success of the Red Star mission, Master Fandarel had less trouble getting his Masters to embrace the technology. He was also attempting to produce the radio instrument that Aivas had suggested as a reliable means of communication between distant places. Materials to construct the transistors required were obtainable in quantity on Pern.

Master Oldive was not as fortunate, facing such rebellion from older healers that he concentrated on imparting Aivas's techniques and methods to new and unprejudiced apprentice minds. Although he could prove that healers could now save many from desperate suffering and improve the quality of life for other patients by the discreet use of surgical remedies, Masters in his craft balked at using such methods, to the detriment of patient health and longevity. To Oldive, that was a Craft failure that could not be allowed to continue. Where he could, he introduced new procedures; his instruction seemed to work best with those who had the least training and were desperate to relieve the suffering of their patients. The transition in the Healer Hall was sporadic.

After the initial experiment with the dolphins, Oldive had asked for volunteers to work more closely with the discerning mammals, offering the reciprocal service of removing any bloodfish. Curran had been only too happy to permit the building of a small healer cothold at Fort Sea Hold. A float was rigged at the end of the pier so that patients could be lowered into the water where the dolphins could use their sonar capability on them. There were similar facilities at four other seaside locations: Ista, Igen, Nerat, and Monaco Bay, or rather, the Eastern Weyr.

Aivas had spent much time with Master Oldive and his more receptive Masters and journeymen. Though he had made it clear that Pern did not have certain requisites to bring medicine up to the level the Ancients had practiced, many innovations would improve the Hall. The dolphins were an effective alternative for the Ancients' x-ray machine and other scanning devices, an invaluable exploratory device for healers.

There was one major drawback to the dolphins' ability to perceive abnormalities in the humans they examined: they could not tell the healers exactly what the growth or lump was, nor how to treat it: only that it was inside a body and shouldn't be there. Nevertheless, their sonar readings gave healers more knowledge of the irregularities that could not be seen or palpated.

Master Oldive often had the notion that there had been a great many such devices, which Aivas had not even mentioned to him, and he sighed over those omissions and then went on, as healers had for centuries, making do with what was to hand and had proved helpful.

Once the wind machines had been installed on Fort Hold fireheights, a terminal unit was installed in Oldive's rooms at the Harper Hall, and two more dominated classrooms. Lord Holder Groghe had tried his not insignificant best to get one for Fort Hold, but until the Smithcraft, or the new Computer Craft, could duplicate the components, distribution was restricted to those disseminating information.

The Landing students did not study all day long, as Master Samvel was well aware that youngsters required physical exercise as well as mental. Many old games were annotated in the Aivas files, and some of those Samvel revived: baseball, soccer, and polo, a sport in which Readis was to become quite proficient—as he was in the water sports when they started using the pond below the landing field. Readis suspected that Master Samvel emphasized the water sports in deference to his infirmity, but he thought it made sense that people should learn how to swim when so many long journeys were made on the seas.

Master Samvel also gained permission from Benden Weyr for a half wing of weyrling dragons to take Class 21 to Honshu, to see the incredible artifacts left by the Ancients in the mountain eyrie, not the least of which were the remarkable murals that decorated the walls. They had all seen the devices in action from tapes of that period of Pernese history, but now they could see and touch the machines that the Ancients had left behind. Kami was awestruck by the paintings, while Pardure found the old sled, the big looms, and the finely crafted tools to be of more interest. Readis found the view from the hall to be fascinating—the vista of endless mountains and valleys, a sense of the breadth of the landmass of this southern continent, which was scarcely explored.

F'lessan, rider of bronze Golanth and only son of F'lar and Lessa, had made this place what he called his "weyrhold." As he explained to the students, this unique historical spot should be available to any who wished to visit it—to see the magnificent murals that decorated the main hall walls. He had appointed himself caretaker and spent more of his free time here than at Benden Weyr. The weyrhold had a complement of holders, herding and experimenting with grain crops and vegetables in areas that had once, clearly, been fields, walled by stones set in place centuries before.

"You're Readis, aren't you?" F'lessan asked, joining the boy on the bench placed on the upper terrace, where the best view of the valley could be had. The other students were clambering about the terraces below. "I asked Master Samvel to point you out. I knew your mother." He leaned back against the cliff wall. "She was at Benden Weyr for a while, you know, before hearing dragons got too much for her. K'van, who's now Weyrleader at Southern, was one of the weyrlings in my wing and they were very close before Lessa sent her down to Benden Hold." He gazed out over the view for a few moments. "So, have you decided what to study at Landing?"

"Oh, we're just getting general stuff right now," Readis said. "What Master Samvel calls 'preparatory' courses. There's so much to learn." Sometimes the sheer volume and complexity of the knowledge available at Landing overwhelmed Readis. It was daunting to know how much he didn't know. "Master Samvel says he's learning more all the time himself."

F'lessan grinned down at him. "Samvel's the type of person who'll never stop learning."

"My head aches sometimes," Readis admitted shyly.

"Mine would, too," F'lessan agreed. "I was never a good student. Even Master Robinton gave up on me."

Readis gave him a quick glance of surprise. "You had Master Robinton as a teacher?"

F'lessan's snort was self-deprecating. "I was *in* the room all right but I didn't pay much attention." He grinned. "I was too enamored with being Golanth's rider at the time, I think. Jaxom, Menolly, and Benelek were the real students."

"Master Benelek of the Smithcraft? The one who's keeping the Aivas machinery running?"

"The very one." Then F'lessan cast a look at the awed expression of the boy. "Who knows where some of your study mates may end up? Where you yourself will."

"Oh, I know where I'll end up," Readis said. "I'm to be Paradise River Holder." He flicked a finger at his right leg. "I'm to learn so much that even this won't keep me from being confirmed."

"Your father's a strong, healthy man. You might have to wait a long time to accede. What're you going to do with all that time in between?"

Readis had thought about that. During his initial Turns at Landing, he realized that he had absorbed a great deal of hold management from following his father about and hearing him give orders. Managing the hold would be easy.

"I'd like to be a dolphineer."

"A what? Oh, yes, you've been talking to the creatures, haven't you?"

"There aren't any dolphineers, not like the Ancients had, and the dolphins are very helpful, you know. To the Fishcrafthall and the healers. But we just sort of call them when we want them. We don't do much *for* them apart from prying off a bloodfish now and then . . ." Readis paused, not wanting to appear to belittle the delphinic accomplishments, but he had to be truthful to the dragonrider. "I mean, nothing at all like the great work they did exploring the oceans and coastlines."

"As I understand it, the coastline's always changing. Charts will need to be updated, won't they? Are you studying cartography?"

"Not as much as I'd like. I'm good at the maths but you also need special instruments to do a proper job."

"I understand that Master Fandarel is making those instruments since everyone seems to want a chunk of the Southern Continent." F'lessan chuckled.

"Don't you dragonriders get the first choice?"

"Where'd you hear that?" F'lessan shot the lad an appraising look.

Readis shrugged. "Oh, you hear lots of things at Landing."

"I'll just bet you do." F'lessan snorted. "Have you accessed the tapes on dolphins in the Library?"

"I did that the first term I was here," Readis said, grinning. Then he went through some of the hand signals of the ancient dolphineers, and F'lessan's eyes widened respectfully. "That's how dolphineers gave directions to the dolphins underwater. They still know them. The dolphins, I mean."

"And with you living right on Paradise River and the sea, you must make good use of them."

Readis mumbled a noncommittal answer. This was not the time to confide home problems—nor the person to confide them to.

Oblivious to the boy's hesitation, F'lessan went on. "You might even start up your own crafthall. That's what Benelek did, you know, by learning all he could about Aivas's terminals."

"He did?"

"He did!" Then F'lessan gave Readis a mischievous grin. "Right now, you and all the other students at Landing have a brilliant chance to make sure that Pern *becomes* what the Ancients wanted it to be *before* Thread interrupted their progress." The dragonrider gestured behind him, to the murals. "The sum total of their knowledge and their overview of this planet is available to us. It's up to us, and you, as the next generation, to be sure we pick up the plan where they left off and see that Pern becomes the planet they envisioned. That's what must be done if Pern is to be what it *could* be. D'you see that? That's what Master Robinton wanted. It's what my parents want. But not all the Holders or Mastercraftsmen. They're still hanging back with what's comfortable and familiar." He narrowed his eyes slightly to assess the impact of his words on his audience. "It's going to be difficult, the next twenty-odd Turns, to set in place what Pern will be now that Thread has stopped."

"But it hasn't, has it?"

F'lessan gave him a quick look and grinned. "But it will."

"Were you," Readis began tentatively, "one of the dragonriders who took the engines to the Red Star?"

F'lessan nodded. "Golanth and I."

Readis's jaw dropped in awe.

"All in a day's work for a dragonrider," F'lessan said, dismissing the feat in his usual light manner.

On the top of the weyrhold, Golanth lifted his head and uttered a welcoming bugle.

"Ah, your conveyancers arrive," F'lessan said, standing up, though Readis could see nothing but empty sky in front of them. "Think about what I said, Readis, about the dolphins and about what Pern could be."

Readis nodded, eyes front, waiting ... and was rewarded by the thrilling sight that always made his heart pound faster: the abrupt emergence of a half wing of dragons. They were so beautiful. But not for everyone. Dolphins, now, they weren't so restricted. Anyone could get to know a dolphin. He could be a dolphineer *and* a Holder. Form a new crafthall? That did appeal to Readis, and he turned over that possibility. Of course, his mother would have an attack if he even whispered of his interest in the dolphins around her. She persisted in believing that it was the dolphins who had put his life at risk when it was the other way round. His father might understand, especially now that the dolphins had been shown to be useful in so many ways, guarding the coastline and warning them of bad squalls and good fishing. Certainly mastering another Craft would only show the Lord Holders that Readis, son of Jayge and Aramina, was that much more capable of managing an important Southern Hold like Paradise.

"Thank you, F'lessan," he said.

"For what?" the bronze rider asked, smiling down at the boy.

Suddenly Readis went shy and covered it by waving his arm about to indicate the weyrhold. "For what you just said."

F'lessan grinned and placed his finger beside his nose, indicating secrecy. "Think about it, lad. We dragonriders are, I assure you."

Before Readis could ask him what that cryptic comment meant, F'lessan had walked off to find Master Samvel.

B ack at school, when he had some free time to use one of the keyboards, Readis tried to find out exactly *what* the Ancients had meant Pern to be, before Thread ruined their plans. Eventually, he found the Charter in LAWS, and that gave him a good deal to mull over. He wished he could talk to F'lessan again. By deft questioning, he learned that the son of F'lar and Lessa was considered a competent and much trusted Wingleader but, until he had discovered

Honshu Weyrhold, had not been given to much serious thinking or behavior. That made Readis give more weight to what the bronze rider had said that day.

Of course, the dragons were not mentioned in the Charter, since they hadn't been created at the time the Charter had been composed. Nor in any other file on LAWS or GOVERNMENT or VETERINARY or FARMING. They were listed in BIOGENETICS, though Readis couldn't understand half the words and gave up trying to figure out what the cryptic words in the lab notes meant.

Nevertheless, in twenty Turns or so, Thread would stop falling on Pern and would never come back to rain on the planet. What would dragonriders do then? Surely there had to be something *special*. Readis gave a shudder. Pern without its dragons would be unthinkable. He was awed by the ingenuity that had resulted in dragons. He'd had enough biology to understand the concept of biogenesis even if no one on Pern now could possibly perform it. So what would dragons do when Thread was gone? He fretted over that question for quite a few weeks of that school term. Dragons did so many things that didn't have to do with fighting Thread. They conveyed people, and often these days, materials that would take days to be transferred by cart or ship. Well, the blues and greens did, and occasionally the browns and the younger bronzes before they started flying Thread. For adult dragons to do so was somewhat demeaning. He couldn't imagine a queen lugging things from one Hold or Hall to another.

Dolphins could do quite a few things only they could do, being water creatures. Dragons were of the air. There *had* to be something that only dragons could do.

Readis's distraction had not gone unnoticed. Master Samvel found him staring at a screen displaying the earliest flight of dragons: dragons as small as large runnerbeasts.

"I've been meaning to have a word with you, Readis," Samvel said, sitting down on the next chair. "You've not been paying as close attention in class as you usually do. Are you troubled about something?"

Readis took a deep breath. "Master Samvel, what's going to happen to the dragons?"

Samvel blinked in surprise, and then he smiled and, in a rare gesture, patted Readis on the head. "You are not the only one pondering that question, young Readis."

"Yes, but what can they do when Thread is all gone?"

"This is a huge planet, Readis, and there is much work to be done to settle all the land available to us. Right now the dragonriders are carefully overflying this vast Southern Continent, making as detailed a map as possible. We know only a small part of it, and much of it would be impassable to people on foot or uninhabitable until the Pass ends. Don't you worry about the dragons. Their riders will take care of them, as they've always done. But your concern does you credit. We must never, on Pern, forget what the dragons have done for us for twenty-five hundred Turns."

"How could we forget?" Readis asked, appalled at the very notion of such ingratitude.

Samvel's smile was sad. "We've done it often enough in long Intervals. You concentrate on your studies now, lad, and let the Weyrs worry about themselves. You have your own future to worry about."

That put Readis in mind of F'lessan's advice to him: to learn more about the dolphins. So once again he accessed that information, even though he knew most of it by heart already and had become quite fluent in using the underwater hand signals.

"Underwater" was the relevant word. Though Readis had learned how to hold his breath so he could follow the dolphins on some of their shallower dives, the Ancients had had special breathing equipment that had allowed them to stay underwater for long periods of time. Tanks, smaller but similar in design to those used with flame-throwers, had been strapped to swimmers' backs. They'd had face masks to cover nose and mouth and had breathed proper air from a tube to the tank. The device seemed simple enough to Readis, although how he would acquire one was beyond him. He had a small hoard of marks since his father had paid him the last two seasons for helping with the harvesting, but he doubted that would be sufficient. However, since the tremendous effort from all crafthalls to implement Aivas's plan was a glorious page of history now, some craftsmen might be willing to take such a commission. They might even know how to construct one since they, too, had access to many, more specialized Aivas's files.

So Readis sought Uncle Alemi the next time he was back at Paradise River. He'd brought a diagram of the apparatus with him. In the evening, he turned Delky to the shortcut to the head and, as he'd suspected, he found Alemi and his son Aleki on their way to the pier for their daily talk with the pod.

Readis got through the courtesies as fast as possible and then shoved the drawing at Alemi. "If we had something like this, which the dolphineers used, we'd be able to function better in the dolphins' own environment."

Alemi gave him a startled look and then laughed outright. "You have learned a lot in that school, haven't you, Readis? Kami's nearly as bad with all the terms she throws out to confuse her poor parents. Now, let's see what you have here to perplex an old sailor." He glanced at the drawing as he walked.

"You're not old, Unclemi, and I don't think you'll be the least bit perplexed about an aqua-lung."

"Hmmm. Is that what this contraption is called?"

"That's how I read it."

Alemi wasn't as condescending as many Masters were, but he still liked to tease, and Readis was not in a receptive mood. He was in deadly earnest about this project.

"I looked back over all the tapes showing dolphins and dolphineers. When the partners had to do underwater work, or long-distance swimming, the humans always wore this sort of equipment. And special clothing called wet suits."

"One would need special gear to keep skin from softening too much during long immersions." Alemi examined the drawing closely. "The Ancients had special gear for just about everything, didn't they?"

"More than we'll ever have," Readis replied. "More than we'd ever need. The Charter Preamble states that they formed the Pern Colony to avoid the intense specialization that had stratified Earth culture. They intended to achieve a good standard of living using the lowest possible form of technology needed to supply essential services and a good, rounded lifestyle."

Alemi grinned at Readis. "You're much worse than Kami. Does the Charter really say that?"

Readis nodded, grinning back. At least Alemi wasn't peremptorily dismissing the notion.

"And since this equipment is not beyond our current capabilities—oh, yes, I see the similarities and I know we have this much technology," Alemi added, tapping the mask and the tank with one finger. "It's only a matter of re-creating the elements displayed here. And, since such an order would come better from a Masterfishman, you've come to me to make the request."

Readis nodded enthusiastically now, immensely relieved that Alemi had grasped what Readis hesitated to voice.

Alemi handed the sheet back and sighed deeply. "You know your mother's opinion about dolphins and you, Readis. It wouldn't be right for me to deliberately assist you to further your association with them."

"Oh!" Readis sank into Delky's back and, as she'd been trained to do, she halted. "But you know she's wrong . . ."

"She's your mother, Readis, and my Hold Lady. I'm well aware of the loyalty I owe her. I've not been all that easy in my mind about allowing you to swim with the pod here. Oh, I know you've been doing it, and as long as I didn't actually see you in the water with them, I could pretend I didn't know." Alemi gave a wry grin. "The dolphins don't at all understand your mother's attitude, since Afo warned you about the thorn."

Readis groaned. "But it was *my* fault, not Afo's, or any of the dolphins."

"True. Look, lad, I'm on your side in this even if I can't sail on a dangerous tack. You could—" Alemi paused. "—see what your father says."

"He won't upset mother."

Alemi lifted his hands in a gesture of impotence. "Try him, Readis. He's really easy to approach on matters that improve the Hold, you know. And he never accused the dolphins." Alemi shot the boy a glance. "He knew where the fault lay," he added in a kindly voice. "Afo and Kib are always asking for you. Will you join us?"

Seeing the pod improved Readis's spirits, especially after Kib and Afo did an enthusiastic tail walk when he gave them some of the hand signals he'd learned from the old tapes.

" 'Member! 'Member!" Kib cried, squeeing and blowing with pleasure. "You do good. Very good. Better best. You come under soon?"

"Not today, Kib. But I will, someday," Readis assured the happy dolphin.

"Old old times come back," Afo said, her jaw dropping low as she squeed and chirped.

Readis could not resist giving Alemi an accusing look for failing to fall in with his plan to obtain an underwater breathing device.

It was full dark before the three of them made their way back to the hold proper. When his mother asked him where he'd been so long, he could quite honestly reply that he'd gone to visit Alemi and stayed to play with young Aleki.

Sometime during the night another solution presented itself to Readis. He had experienced a keen sense of betrayal when Alemi refused to help him get an aqua-lung. The device would only make his swimming with the dolphins that much safer. He'd've thought that Alemi would see that, too. However, he had another, stauncher ally in T'lion. When he got back to Landing after this break, he'd leave word that he'd like to speak to T'lion. In addition to his responsibilities as a member of a fighting wing, the bronze rider's duties often brought him to Landing. They hadn't seen that much of each other lately, but theirs was a friendship that could be resumed at any point with no sense of time lapse.

T'lion sought him out one afternoon a sevenday later.

"Sorry to be so long getting to you, Readis, but what with Fall and all . . ." The bronze rider let his sentence dangle.

"That's all right," Readis said, pawing through the sheets that littered the deck in his quarters to find the diagram. "I found this." He shoved it at his friend.

"Ooooh. This is great," T'lion said, his eyes widening as he scanned the sheet. "An aqua-lung? Hey, we could use one of these. No trouble at all. Are you getting one?"

"I'm only a student, T'lion." Then in a rush, he added, "I tried to get Alemi to help but he wouldn't on account of my mother not liking me associating with dolphins and all."

T'lion made a sound in his throat and smiled wryly. "They just won't let you live that down, will they?"

"Evidently not!" Readis couldn't suppress the bitterness. "It'd cost a lot of marks, wouldn't it?"

"Hmmmm. Could. But we're not the only ones who're swimming with dolphins whenever we get the chance. Can I have this?" When Readis eagerly agreed, T'lion folded it carefully and put it in his inside pocket. "D'you have time to come see my pod?"

"Your pod?" Readis said, raising his eyebrows in surprise at the possessive pronoun.

"Well, the pod that answers my bell," T'lion said with a grin. "Coming?"

Readis's answer was to grab up the lined jacket and a swimming clout. He paused only long enough to scrawl a note on the message board at the entrance to his dormitory that he had gone with T'lion. He was old enough now that he didn't have to ask special permission for short absences.

Once on the strand near Eastern Weyr, Readis helped T'lion divest Gadareth of his riding harness. T'lion rang the bell in the Come-in sequence that was less urgent than the Report and gave the dolphins the opportunity to ignore the summons if they chose. They rarely did, but sometimes only one or two answered. By the time the boys had changed into their swimming clouts, the waters of the cove showed half a dozen dolphins leaping and speeding towards shore. Raising himself up on his hind legs, Gadareth opened his wings and threw back his head for a welcoming bugle. The air was immediately full of wild fire-lizards, for they loved nothing better than to play with their large cousins in the water. Flattening his wings right to his back, he walked into the water and began to swim out to meet the dolphins with the fair display above him.

As one of the games dolphins liked best was scrubbing a dragon, they proceeded to "help" the humans wash Gadareth. The boys nearly drowned half a dozen times trying to emulate dolphin acrobatics. The fire-lizards left halfway through the bath to go about their own business.

"We really do . . . need that . . . breathing device," T'lion gasped out to Readis when they took a rest, hanging on to the wing Gadareth had extended for washing. "But you can sure hold your breath a long time when you want to."

"Can't . . . do it . . . too often. Head starts . . . to spin," Readis said. "Other thing . . . we need . . . is a decent . . . ball for them . . . to play with!"

"So they can steal it?" T'lion demanded. "That's what they've done with all the ones I get made for 'em."

"New game? New game?" Boojie asked, head high in the water so all of his smiling face was visible.

"Not today, Booj," T'lion said. "You've worn us out. C'mon, Gadareth, let's go ashore."

Booj swam backward, clapping his flippers and squeeing with delight. "Worn out! Worn out! We play more better."

T'lion and Readis let Gadareth tow them ashore, grasping his tail until they felt the slope of the beach under their feet.

Gadareth found himself a spot on the sand, and a number of fire-lizards returned to find resting places on him while they murmured sleepily to their living perch. T'lion carefully extracted the diagram from his inner pocket and looked at it.

"We've got glass," he said, tapping the face mask, "and we've got material for the straps, and the tanks shouldn't be a problem, nor the hose. Valves look the same as the ones Smithcraft put on flamethrower tanks. It's the rest of the face mask that might be difficult. You got any free marks?"

Readis rolled over on his stomach and propped himself up on his elbows. He grimaced. "If I'd known, I wouldn't have spent so much at the last Landing Gather. But I've maybe three whole Smithcraft marks and some quarters. Now I'm nearly fifteen, Dad pays me for harvesting." He said that with a bit of pride: he'd sweated for those marks.

"Hmmm, well, yes. I've some, too, from a bit of trading I've done."

"Trading?" Readis perked up. Over the Turns he'd heard enough from Temma, Nazer, and his father about trading to be familiar with the Lilcamp family traditions. "What with?"

"Ohh . . ." T'lion shrugged his reluctance to continue. Then, making a quick decision, he went on. "Well, it's like this. Most dragonriders are kind of looking about this continent to see where they'd like to live when the Pass is over. I mean, during Threadfall and all, the Holds and crafthalls tithe to the Weyrs, so we don't have to worry about that. Honestly, we'd rather not be beholden to anyone . . ."

"But Holds and Halls have always tithed to Weyrs . . ." Readis protested, being well versed in Tradition.

T'lion grinned. "Not when there isn't going to *be* more Thread."

"Oh."

"Yes, so we're looking for our own places."

"What F'lessan calls a weyrhold?"

T'lion nodded.

"And you've found one?" Readis asked, excited to learn that the dragonriders were looking so far ahead.

"Oh, I've found several sites I'd like, but we have to put in a bid and then, when it's time, the Weyrleaders will decide who gets what. Right now, we're charting the land to make divisions easier. That's why I've been up at Landing so much, registering what Gaddie and I have overflown."

"Did you find any more ruins? Like F'lessan did?"

T'lion gave a snort. "Ruins, I found. But nothing half so well preserved as Honshu. *That* is really spectacular. In fact, that's the only place that was properly built. The others are all smack dab in wide-open spaces."

Readis mirrored his consternation at such stupidity. The Ancients had known so much: why had they been so silly to build out in the open?

"Of course," T'lion went on in a slightly patronizing tone, "the first few years they didn't have Thread so they didn't build proper."

"Oh, yes, that's right," Readis agreed. "So, where have you seen places?"

"Gaddie wants a lake and there are quite a few and also some wide rivers, which are nearly better than lakes. That big inland sea, the one the Ancients called the Caspian, has some lovely islands. They'd be perfect." He sighed. "But I'd be low on the list for a prime site like that. Another place I like a lot is not far from the old mines that

Master Hamian is working now. Place the Ancients called Karachi. Pretty name, isn't it? They had lots of unusual names. And there's a cliff in the Southern Range which has a fairly decent-sized cave. View is fabulous and the ledge is wide enough for Gad to snooze on." T'lion shot a fond look at his sleeping dragon. "Trouble would be having a weyrmate and family. They'd have to wait on Gaddie to get up or down."

"That would be a disadvantage, but couldn't you make stairs, the way they did at Honshu?"

"I suppose so . . ." T'lion paused, deep in thought. "Rather high up so it'd take a lot of stone carving. Then, too, I'd have to find work somewhere else. At the mines, we could always convey . . ." At Readis's gasp of surprise, he said, "Well, transporting isn't a bad way to make a living for a dragon and his rider. Particularly a big strong bronze like Gaddie. It's a lot less dangerous to hide and health than Threadfighting."

"Yes, I suppose it is. But if you went that far inland, you'd be too far from the sea and the dolphins. They can't swim in fresh water, you know. They don't float well and they get sores."

"Hmmm." T'lion once again retreated into thought.

"Haven't you found any place nice along the shore?"

"Oh, there're coves left, right, and center," T'lion dismissed them. "But you're right. I'd miss Boojie and Natua and Tana. It's a case of wanting what you get, I suppose. Then, too, other teams are searching east of here. I suppose I could ask to switch but the land I've been overflying is magnificent. You wouldn't believe how much space there is!"

"Tell me," Readis urged.

By the time darkness was falling, Readis was relieved to realize that Paradise River Hold had a great many advantages. His parents had been very lucky to be granted hold of it. And it was rather nice to have neighbors farther down the river. There might even be some new ones along the coast, if they could find a decent supply of stone to build their cotholds.

"Why do the Weyrleaders decide who gets what land?" he asked as he changed into his clothes for the trip back to Landing.

"Not just the Weyrleaders, Readis," T'lion said with a grin. "The Lord Holders and the Craftmasters'll have a say, too. But this time, the Weyrs get first choice."

"They do deserve it. If they can hold what they want. The pod warned us just last week of another group trying to land, west of the river."

"Really?"

"Dad sailed out with Alemi and they left. We outnumbered them," Readis said with Hold pride. "One day, we might not," he added ruefully.

"There's a lot of decisions to be made, aren't there?" T'lion said with a sigh.

Gadareth and T'lion brought Readis back to Landing. Seeing the area from a height, buildings lit, and people walking up and down the paths, Readis felt a surge of pride to be part of this place, which had had a glorious past and was now preparing for a future: the future that, in fact, had been planned a long time ago for this planet.

T'lion said he'd find time in the next sevenday to get to the Mastersmithhall in Telgar and he'd let Readis know the outcome.

"You may not have any marks to spend at a Gather for some time to come," he said. "But then, neither will I!"

T'lion was back three days later, looking highly amused as he sauntered into Readis's quarters.

"We're not the only ones," he announced.

"Only ones who what?" Readis asked, half of his mind still on the mathematics he was figuring.

"Who found the aqua-lung and want the Mastersmith to make 'em. And I was right."

"About what?"

"The face mask. There isn't any sort of elastic material that will keep a mask comfortably tight and seal it against a face."

"Oh."

T'lion did not appear to be concerned about that lack. "Seems as if that sort of flexible material is needed for a lot of things the Ancients used. So Master Hamian and one or two of that Hall over in Southern Hold are experimenting."

"Who else wants the aqua-lung?"

"Idarolan, for one. He's really quite an advocate of dolphins. Master Fandarel told me . . ."

"You saw Master Fandarel himself?"

T'lion grinned. "I think I shall miss the courtesies accorded dragonriders." He sighed wistfully. "I did see him but only after I'd talked to half a dozen journeymen and masters. Evidently Idarolan is mad because he's too old to do too much with dolphins—too old and too busy as Masterfishman."

Readis was beset with conflicting emotions: that someone as prestigious as a Craftmaster wanted to be with dolphins and would have more authority than he, Readis, ever could; that someone else might usurp his connection, tenuous as it was, with a pod; and fury at his mother's prejudice, which kept him from openly associating with these marvelous creatures.

"Don't look so bereft, Readis," T'lion said. "It's not the end of the world. Look how many pods we've already contacted—and how many more there are out there. Yours'll be yours. And you already share it with Alemi, don't you? Besides, you're going to be Holder at Paradise River."

"Which is a Sea Hold, too, so the dolphins are important to us. And who knows when, or *if*"—and Readis slapped the knee of his withered leg—"I get to *be* Holder. My father's a healthy man..." F'lessan's words at Honshu came back to him: "What are you going to do in the time between?" Then there was his younger brother, Anskono, with both legs in good working order and growing stronger and taller every year. Readis could be passed over in favor of his unimpaired younger brother.

"Paradise River's a big place, Readis," T'lion went on. "Big enough for you to hold on your own, separate from your parents. Your father's barely touched the heart of it, even with all the folks he's taken in over the last Turns. With a lot of seacoast."

That prospect hadn't occurred to Readis, though it had been standard practice for most northern Lord Holders to establish smaller holds for their sons whenever possible. That was another reason so many northerners looked enviously at all the space available on the Southern Continent: every accessible and workable site in the major northern holds was already long established. Readis knew from conversations at Gathers that Lord Toric had let some younger sons run Holds in Southern, but not every candidate met the high standards that Lord Toric expected or wanted to work under that taskmaster's total authority.

"You could establish a dolphin base of your own and be a dolphineer. Wouldn't hurt."

"No, it wouldn't," Readis agreed absently, thinking

about his mother and cringing a bit at having deceived her, and his father. They'd no idea that he'd spent so much time with the Paradise River pod—unless Alemi had told them.

"And Lord Toric's another one who wants aqua-lungs," T'lion said. "That man!" And he shook his head. "He's not going to let a chance pass him by. He's ordered ten breathers."

"He's going to start a Dolphineer Hall?"

"No," T'lion said with a wry grin. "That would require him to allow others to join." His grin faded. "Not that he'd have the chance with Master Idarolan on the dolphins' side."

Readis gave a sigh of relief.

"Don't worry, Readis," T'lion went on. "I've already put in a good word for you."

"You did?" Readis was torn between relief and the fear that now his mother would learn how he had disobeyed her.

"Never fear. Master Idarolan only asked me how many people were truly interested in dolphins. I said you were because you'd been rescued that time and had learned all the bell peals and hand signals out of gratitude."

Readis wasn't sure that was subtle enough.

"Don't worry, now, Readis. It's all come right. You'll see."

Readis's response was a noncommittal sound deep in his throat. "Thanks anyway, T'lion. Did Master Fandarel have any idea when we might get an aqua-lung?"

"Soon, he hoped, but he couldn't give a time. He's got a whole hall doing nothing but assembling terminals. Do your folks have one yet? No? Well, they should. Fandarel says they have to find the sealer material. If you don't have that, you get water inside the mask and that defeats the purpose. At that, we're lucky because the sea here is so clear. Gets pretty murky in the northern waters. I'll keep you informed, Readis."

"I'd appreciate that, T'lion, and thanks."

"Any time." With a cheerful wave, T'lion left.

11

▼▼▼▼▼▼▼▼▼▼

M*aster Fandarel comes with Master Nicat,* Mnementh
informed both Lessa and F'lar.

"I wonder what the Mastersmith wants," Lessa said,
sharing the report of the new arrivals with R'mart of
Telgar Weyr, G'dened of Ista, and Journeyman Harper
Talmor, who was the Benden Weyrleaders' main assistant
with relocations.

Talmor indicated the council table, spread with maps
and reports that the meeting was discussing.

F'lar shrugged. "Leave it. Not efficient to bundle it all
up, after all," the Weyrleader said, and won smiles for the
Mastersmith's oft-voiced criterion. He and Aivas had had
much in common on the score of "efficiency." Perhaps, of
them all, Master Fandarel missed the voice-address intelligence the most.

"Maybe he has this 'radio' he's been so eager to produce," Lessa said, her smile partly for the many attempts the huge Smith had made to initiate some sort of instant communications system for those who had neither dragon nor fire-lizard. He'd been at it ever since that half-successful attempt at the beginning of the Pass.

"That would account for Master Nicat's appearance," F'lar said. The Masterminer had collaborated with the Mastersmith to find the raw elements, like metals, crystal, and some of the plastics that Aivas had listed as necessary to the production of "electronic" devices.

As large as Benden's Council Room was, Master Fandarel seemed to dwarf its dimensions, as he did the other tall and well-built men in the room. Even the harper was tall, and while R'mart had put on some flesh over the past few Turns, he was certainly not as massively built as the Smith.

Fandarel stood in the doorway, noticed the table strewn with paper, the complement of the meeting, and frowned. "I dislike saying this but you are simply going to have to go more slowly settling people in the South," he said.

"What?" Lessa exclaimed, staring at the Mastersmith. It was the last thing she had expected him to say, and certainly he had never been against the relocations. Her reaction was mirrored by everyone else in the room. Talmor left his hand suspended over the latest Smithcrafthall reports, which had recently been delivered.

"This is the first time we've been asked to slow down," F'lar exclaimed. "And good day to you, Master Fandarel. D'you know how many people complain that we're dragging our heels over settlings?"

"I hear that, too," Fandarel said, nodding his big head and looking as solemn as ever. He had visibly aged since he had helped remove the engines from the three colony ships, and Lessa had noticed that the slow way in which he now moved was due more to the debilities of age than deliberate movements. "But I know it is not the truth and say so. I also hear, and know, that journeymen and women as well as Masters are being offered heavy purses of marks to leave their positions and go south."

"I thought Master Nicat was with you," Lessa said, looking around the big man's figure in the doorway to see if it hid the smaller, rotund figure of the Masterminer.

"Ah," and Master Fandarel's brows drew together as he held up an object, almost lost in his huge hand. "Master Nicat, can you hear me?"

"Of course I can. I'm only at the foot of the stairs." The unmistakable tones of the miner sounded clearly, if reduced, from the instrument, which Fandarel had turned to face the assembled.

"Ah! You've produced the radio!" Lessa cried.

"I have produced an electronic device," Fandarel corrected her. "An improvement on the radios that were mentioned in the history files, and more nearly what the Ancients used to communicate when they were setting up their stakeholds. The old weather satellite that has been giving us accurate predictions is also able to bounce signals, as is the Yokohama. With such hand units as these, we may communicate across long distances—once we've made them a little more efficient."

"Oh, may I try?" Lessa said, slipping to Fandarel's side and holding out her hand for the device. "Oh, it's lightweight." She hefted it, and turned to show the oblong balancing in her hand.

"Press the red button and hold it down to speak. Later you will need to key in the code number you wish to reach but as the only other unit is with Master Nicat, that step is not necessary. Press and speak into this end."

"Master Nicat?" Lessa pressed so hard that her knuckle

turned white and she spoke loudly into the appropriate end.

"There is no need to shout," Nicat said, with some asperity in the small clear manifestation of his voice.

"A whisper will be heard," Fandarel said with an understandable degree of pride.

"Where are you now, Master Nicat?" Lessa asked in a conversational tone.

"Right where I was two minutes ago."

"Remarkable," F'lar said, coming to the side of his weyrmate and taking the device from her. He pressed the button. "May I?"

"Of course," Lessa and Fandarel said in chorus.

"I can hear that, too," Nicat said.

F'lar pressed the red button. "Then join us!"

"Only too happy to since it's raining, you know."

F'lar and Lessa exchanged amused glances. They had been at this meeting for well over an hour now and had had no idea the weather had altered from morning mists to precipitation.

"Master Fandarel, some klah?" Lessa said, getting a fresh mug from the tray and holding up the thermal jug that had been one of the best homey additions to kitchen equipment.

"Please," he said, striding forward and accepting the seat that F'lar suggested.

Nicat arrived, puffing slightly from the climb to the weyr, holding out the damp coat he'd been wearing, which Talmor took from him and hung on a spare chair to dry.

While he was being served a welcome cup and seated, the two devices were passed around the table for everyone to examine.

"Now what's all this about your people being bribed,

Fandarel?" F'lar asked, setting aside the delights of the device for the more important consideration. "That's serious."

"It distresses me, my journeyfolk, and Masters, because it undermines the discipline of my crafthall and the honor and loyalty which has always governed us."

Nicat muttered a "here, here," to that sentiment.

"Who's doing the bribing?" R'mart wanted to know. "Toric?" the Telgar Weyrleader made no bones about his distrust of the southern Holder.

"Not always."

"Oh, then who?" R'mart demanded, surprised.

Fandarel shrugged. "Let them remain nameless, Weyrleader. Our craftsmen and women did not accept the offered bribes and informed me of each occurrence. But I worry about the apprentices who might not have such scruples."

G'dened snorted. "I've heard of bribery in Ista Hold. Lord Warbret's furious. He's also lost some young men and women who're knowledgeable enough about the sea but haven't formally been apprenticed yet. And there it *is* Toric, or his agents, who're promising high marks because Istans would 'understand' the hazards of the Southern Continent since they're already used to tropical conditions." G'dened snorted.

"Not the same at all," F'lar said. "Ista's been settled a long, long time and has no more of the hazards that the Southern Continent has in plenty."

"Exactly, and furthermore—" G'dened began.

"We don't actually have many more sites available right now," Talmor said, looking through his papers. "And it's not just a matter of having trained craftspeople to staff them, Master Fandarel. It's sites that are accessible. So far, we've concentrated on river and oceanside positions so there is at least one means of transportation and contact. Especially when the northern-born have not had a chance to acquire fire-lizards. Of course, that device of yours would be of enormous assistance in that respect." He nodded to the handheld.

"That is the bad news I have for you," Fandarel said with a heavy sigh. "We will need a work force to make the transistors required and to assemble the components. They will have to be trained, and we will need at least one knowledgeable person of journey rank to oversee the work. Master Benelek needs all the young folk he can train for the terminals and cannot give the Hall more time. I have a long list of those who have requested this efficient and effective little device."

Lessa covered her smiling mouth at his use of his favorite words. "Effective" was now always paired with "efficient" in his lexicon. It was ironic that when he finally had achieved a device that satisfied his high standards, he hadn't the people to produce the units.

"As well as the demand for any one of the many projects people have applied for our Craft to fabricate," he added, "I've had to assign Master Terry three assistants to deal with requests alone, and we have given up trying to make efficient and effective deliveries." Fandarel's sigh was more regret than satisfaction at so much business on his books.

"I, too, am overwhelmed, Weyrleaders," Master Nicat put in. "Every mine known to the Craft, and certainly all the new ones from the Ancients' records, are being worked and I've had to ask those older miners who returned to the Hall to do Aivas's work to remain on in supervisory capacities. I can't afford to lose one able-bodied man or those women we have in the Hall. Then"—he threw up his hands—"people started applying to me for stoneworkers. There's not much call for stoneworkers as most holders enlarge their quarters over the winter months. And masonry's not strictly a minercraft skill. But no one else trains men to work stone. And all the dressed stone will have to be shipped south! I ask you, how will that be accomplished?" If he saw R'mart's knowing look or the glances that F'lar and Lessa exchanged, he gave no notice. "One thing Aivas didn't seem to have in those exhaustive files of his was much about improvements in quarrying and masonry." Unexpectedly, a grin spread across Nicat's round face with its fringe of white hair.

"Really? Well, it's almost a relief to find out he wasn't infallible," F'lar remarked at his driest. "*Do* you have men trained for stonework?"

"Actually, we're training some right now," Nicat said, screwing his face up and sighing. "That sculptor fellow, Edwinrus, has a couple of young sons and has taken on a few more likely lads. He's put aside some artistic commissions to give me a hand. I could use half again as many apprentices in that trade and the same number in mining, what with Hamian wanting more and more trained miners down at Karachi. He'll have to take apprentices and train them up as he wants them. I even walked those caves of Laudey's to see if there were any men able-bodied enough for that sort of work."

"Laudey still has people in the caves?" Lessa asked in surprise. "I thought they all got put to work during the special projects."

"Some of those projects have ended, you know," Nicat remarked. "So he got some of the Holdless back, but mainly it's the old and infirm who're in those caves. However, Larad says he could free up some of those prisoners," Nicat continued, "the ones whom he feels have served sufficient time and could be more profitably used elsewhere. At least they're accustomed to stonework."

"In point of fact, it's the dearth of suitable stone that curtails settling in some of the open plains areas," Talmor said, shuffling around his various maps and reports.

"Those areas will just have to wait until after the Pass is over," F'lar said, dismissing that consideration. "Sometimes I wonder why we let ourselves get talked into being responsible for the development of the Southern Continent . . ."

"Because Weyrleaders are the only ones who could be entrusted with such a responsibility," Fandarel bellowed at the same moment Master Nicat rose half out of his chair to say much the same thing. They regarded each other, each taken aback by the other's uncharacteristic vehemence.

G'dened and R'mart grinned.

"With the Harper Hall as *your* consciences," Talmor added in a mild tone, "and the fervent agreement of all the Lord Holders and Mastercraftsmen . . ."

"With the notable exception of Toric," Lessa said, sardonically cocking one eye brow.

"Be that as it may," F'lar went on, with a nod of gratitude to the two Mastercraftsmen, "dragonriders are stretched, too, between Threadfalls all over the world, mapping, and conveying. Shortly, we'll have to open a Weyr in the Honshu area . . ."

"Surely not at Honshu Weyrhold," Fandarel said.

"Not likely," F'lar said with a laugh, glancing at Lessa to forestall a terse comment from her as well. "But we will need stone for a decent Weyrhall for that, as we haven't been able to locate any suitable craters down south."

"You do remember, don't you, your promise to T'bor?" R'mart said, leaning toward F'lar and smiling lopsidedly.

"That he could turn over the Weyrleadership of High Reaches and go back south?" F'lar nodded his head. "When this Pass is over, he can do what he pleases."

"When this Pass is over . . ." Nicat said wistfully on a long sigh.

A respectful silence followed.

"By the bye, Master Fandarel," R'mart said, snagging one of the maps out of the array on the table and sliding it to the smith, "we located that ridge for you, the one which is indicated as a source of iron on the Ancients' spatial map."

"Where?" Instantly alert, Fandarel reached his long arm across the table to retrieve the paper.

"There, in those foothills. We've staked and flagged it to be recognized. Good site, actually, a fine river nearby. You might consider setting up another Hall down there." R'mart was half teasing, knowing how devoted Master Fandarel was to the main crafthall site in Telgar.

"We may indeed have to consider that in due course," Fandarel said, his eyes scanning the map while one huge index finger followed the course of the river. "It wouldn't be fair to have all the main crafthalls in the North. Give some of my good Masters a chance to show their abilities."

"Make it easier to mine and process the ore at the same site," Master Nicat said, rising to peer over Fandarel's shoulder at the map. "See any blackstone?"

"Didn't look for it, Master Nicat, but we can," R'mart replied. "Nice stretch of trees nearby. And a sweet little valley where folks could farm."

"Ah, the possibilities are endless now, are they not?" Nicat said with great satisfaction.

"Did we but have the trained men and women," Fandarel added wistfully.

ANNE MCCAFFREY

"Well," F'lar began, "it is obvious that we can proceed no faster than we are doing in the matter of southern settlements, no matter what accusations are made."

"We shall do our best to counter those," Fandarel said, looking at Nicat, who nodded vigorous accord. "We shall also do our best to indicate that it is a lack of trained personnel that holds the whole process up. I shall so inform my Craft, Masters, journeyfolk, and apprentices." He looked at Master Nicat, who hastily added that he would do likewise.

"When will more of these be available?" F'lar asked, holding up one of the com devices.

"I was thinking of the most efficient way of doing that." Now Fandarel turned to Master Nicat. "Those elderly and infirm at Igen, do they have their wits about them and the use of their fingers?"

Nicat frowned down at his fingertips, splayed out on the stone table. "Aye, I believe they do."

"Good then. That is all that is really needed, sight and ten fingers. We've already put some of our elderlies to work and they are glad of the marks in their hands, I can tell you."

"Besides which, it's an efficient use of available personnel, isn't it?" Lessa commented, managing to keep a straight face, though Talmor took a fit of coughing and R'mart and G'dened looked everywhere except at her or the smith.

"I shall leave this one with you, F'lar, Lessa," Fandarel said, formally bowing to make the presentation. "It will reach me at the Smithcrafthall should you need to speak with me."

"Quite useful, I assure you," Nicat answered. "I don't know how I've managed without it."

F'lar escorted the two Mastercraftsmen out of the Council Room. Then Lessa allowed herself the luxury of a chuckle while the others smiled broadly. When F'lar returned, he was grinning as well, but he rubbed his hands together.

"We'll just wind this meeting up, shall we?"

"Not much more to say, is there?" Talmor said. "And we thought we were busy doing Aivas's bidding!"

"I wonder if he knew just how much he was altering our whole lives," Lessa said, making a sweeping movement with one arm.

"Quite likely he did," R'mart said sardonically, "which is why he quit on us before we could disconnect him, or whatever it is one does with a machine."

"He could at least have stayed around until we were well into the transition," Lessa said, sounding slightly mutinous.

"And bear your reproaches, my dear?" F'lar asked, a mischievous glint in his eyes as he looked at his weyrmate.

Lessa gave a sniff.

"He knew at least one person would make efficient and effective use of the Library," Talmor said, grinning.

"Enough out of you, Harper," Lessa said with mock astringency. "Did you find *anywhere*, R'mart, remotely resembling a Weyr possibility?"

"Not a cave nor a crater we could use among any of those hills," R'mart said with disgust.

"Plenty of stone for Master Nicat, though," G'dened said.

Tamor continued making his notations on the borders of the charts and sighing occasionally.

"Now, here I have no special comments," he said, turning the edge of the map toward R'mart.

"That's because there is nothing special to comment on. More hills, valleys, rivers, rocks."

"Ah, but rocks can be useful," Talmor said, and made the appropriate notation.

"When the Pass is over . . ."

It was an hour or more before the Weyrleaders had finished their discussions of the newly charted lands and the visitors left.

"I'll be so glad when we've got the entire continent mapped out," she said, sighing.

"I doubt we'll have discovered all we need to know about for the time being . . . until we have enough folks to distribute," F'lar said, gathering her slight body to his with one arm as they made their way into Ramoth's weyr. The great gold dragon was asleep, her nostrils twitching a bit and her foreleg claws scrabbling against her stone bed as her dream caused her to open and close them. "Is she hungry?"

"Shouldn't be," Lessa said. "She hunted well earlier this sevenday below Landing. The southern beasts are better-tasting."

"All the fuss is worth the trouble, Lessa," F'lar reminded her. "We shan't disabuse the trust that's been placed in us to dispense the land impartially. And dragonriders will have their own stakes in the Southern Continent. We'll never be beholden to Halls or Holds again."

Lessa knew that he had never forgotten Benden's situation at the end of the Last Interval, when only three holds had tithed to the lone Weyr and dragonriders had been reduced to conditions no small Holder would have endured. It was ironic that, in finding the solution to the recurring problem of Thread, they had also ended the reason for their privileges. Aivas had reassured them on one point: the dragons would not just cease to mate because the orbit of the Red Star had been disrupted. They were as established a species on Pern as the dolphins and would continue to prosper, though perhaps not in the same large numbers. A shallow mating flight would keep the clutches small. It required more control of both queen and bronze but it was a feasible deterrent. Commonly in Intervals, the queens did not rise as often anyway.

"No," Lessa said with a devious smile, her eyes sparkling, "*they* will be beholden to us for the peace and tranquility after this Pass is over!" She liked that.

"We must still wait carefully for the appropriate moment, my heart," he said, but he, too, smiled in anticipation.

"I wager you that it's Toric who provides the excuse," she said. "He's greedy and he's never forgiven us for deceiving him at the true size of the Southern Continent." Her grin was sweetly malicious as she recalled that victory.

"You say that every time the subject comes up, so you're probably right about him," F'lar said equably. 'Still, he's done more to properly site new settlers than anyone else."

"Especially that group that tried to take over his island." Lessa gave a very girlish giggle of amusement. "He'll never let us forget that one. Still, we were right not to interfere."

"Then," F'lar said in a significantly weighted tone. They'd reached the table where they'd been eating a light meal, when Talmor had appeared. He lifted the klah jug and felt it. "Cold. Let's see what's going in the lower cavern. That way we'll be harder to find."

They grinned conspiratorially and, hand in hand, made their way back to the stairs of the weyr and down across the Bowl to the kitchens.

The dolphins gave warning, ringing the bells that were now situated in ten locations on the coasts. They rang the big bell at Tillek Sea Hold early that morning, though Tillek was farther north than the storm's course. But the pod that swam in the great bays also knew that the Masterfishman Idarolan was pod leader for all fish boats and should know what affected his Craft. In appreciation of dolphin help to all seafarers, Master Idarolan had had built a really fine dolphin marina where they could bring the injured and sick animals of the Western Sea.

Idarolan himself answered the bell, well wrapped up against the chill of predawn.

"Bad blow, bad bad *bad* blow," the pod leader told him, waggling her head while her podmates nodded emphatically. The dolphins couldn't measure wind speeds in any gauge comprehensible to humans. They did not have to cope with winds, merely high seas, and then they'd either swim to calmer waters or *through* combers. In fact, they often delighted in the rougher seas as ways of testing their skills. But they did understand the dangers that such storms posed to humans.

"Ships can sink in bad bad bad blow. Blow against rocks." Of which there were many on the less hospitable western coastline.

"Exactly where do you think it will hit?" Idarolan asked. He'd had a harper drawer make up a huge map of

Pern, the seas in the bright primary color the dolphins could recognize as "sea" as opposed to the "dark" land-masses. He lowered this now, close enough for Iggy to nose out the storm's course.

She indicated the vast expanse of water just below the Eastern Current and skidded her nose under Southern Boll, aiming it directly at Southern Weyr and Hold. "Blow big there. First land. Blow all day, all night, all day, all night. Looooong blow. Warm water, much cold air." Iggy shook her head at the unfavorable mixture. "Blow blow blow bad bad bad."

Her podmates squeeed high and loud to stress the dangers.

"We've some ships out . . ." Idarolan ran through the list of those he knew from this port. "Fishing . . ."

"We swim, we see, we tell," Iggy promised. "We warn Iddie pod leader." Iggy loved to say the Masterfishman's name as it was so much like her own.

"I appreciate that very much, Iggy." He held out the first fish from the pail always kept full by the bell, and she rose neatly to accept his offering. Then he flicked out thank-yous into the other waiting mouths. He had good aim and none of those who had accompanied the messenger were slighted.

Master Idarolan trundled back to his warm Hold and started writing messages for fire-lizards to carry. He sighed as he did so for it was likely that the fleet finny friends of the deep would relay the warning far faster than even fire-lizards could be dispatched. His first message went to Lord Toric, for that man would batter his crafthall with complaints if such news was not sent first to him.

There had been rather a lot of storms in the past two Turns, and Master Idarolan had heard whispers that this was due to the alteration of the Red Star's orbit. Master Wansor of the Smithcrafthall, who had made a study of the stars, and one of his own leading Seamasters who had learned the Craft of meteorology from Aivas had ridiculed the possibility, but that hadn't kept it from being repeated, and credited by those without the specialized knowledge to recognize its fallacies. Idarolan had sat in on as many of Aivas's lectures on weather formation, winds, and currents as he could make time for. There were valid reasons for the formation of both calm, clear weather and storms. The weather satellites established by the Ancients still gave back their information but not always were they read a-right. The dolphins were more reliable than instrumentation set at Landing, so far away from the point of the depression. Not for the first time, Idarolan wondered how they'd ever gotten along without dolphins.

Lord Toric was roused from a deep sleep by the chittering of a fire-lizard and the noise his own were making at the arrival of a newcomer. He wasn't best pleased. He had worked late the previous night, going over the recent maps made by his scouts, checking and rechecking the organization of his next move. He had made contact with all those he had felt would be eager to assist in his dramatic move. He'd also sounded out which of the Lord Holders also felt that Benden Weyr should not have the gift of southern lands. Even Lord Groghe had wavered slightly from his loyalty to the Weyrleaders. After all, he had ten sons to place to some advantage. At every Fort Gather over the past three Turns, Toric had been planting suggestions in the boys' ears, intimating that they ought to have the same opportunity as Benelek or Horon. He'd put a flea in the ear of young Kern of Crom, Lord Nessel's third son and Nabol's second son. He'd selected older journeymen, competent and resenting the promotion of others to Mastery above them.

He cursed as he read Idarolan's message about the storm—it meant he'd have to delay the start of his big plan. It could also mean more chance of someone—and his "someone" translated into "dragonrider"—discovering his carefully concealed sites. Or questioning the provision of every one of the Hold's small fishing fleet. So far, the young Weyrleader K'van had accepted the offhanded explanation that Toric was resupplying his southernmost mine sites before the hot season. The sites across the river had not been detected, hidden as they were in dense foliage. The dragonriders had long since surveyed the coast. All that land . . . and his Hold bursting with eager, new, hand-chosen settlers, determined to secure and improve their own holds, looking favorably on him because he had granted their most earnest desires.

He had had to swallow a great many slights and insults from the Benden Weyrleaders, who *thought* they were going to carve up all these lands to their own specifications. Well, they would find opinion against them now. Too many people were aware of the extent of the Southern Continent and were discontented over the dragonriders' claim of first choice. For Turns they had had the best that Pern had to offer. When the Pass was ended and their services were no longer needed, a far different tune would be struck for them to dance to. And he would make sure of that!

He heard the bell that his Fishcraftmen had insisted be installed in the deep harbor. The shipfish may have proved unexpectedly useful in telling fishmen where the schools were running, but he was not at all their advocate.

He resented talking animals: speech was a human attribute. Mammals or not, the creatures were *not* equal to humans, and there was no way he would change his mind on that score. Humans planned ahead: dolphins only cooperated with humans because humans amused them, created "games" for them to play. Life was not a game! The very notion of providing amusement to an animal irritated Toric to the core. And he didn't like their latest "game": patrolling the coastline. He had his own plans for the coastline. He fingered his lips thoughtfully.

They'd seek safety in the Currents during this storm, then, and that might be the best time for him to make his move: before the storm was quite over and the dolphins had returned to their customary waters.

He rose then, pulling on his clothes, ignoring his wife's sleepy murmurs. If he was to push this scheme through on the end of the gale, he had work to do.

When the storm swept down on the southern peninsulas protruding northward in the Southern Sea, its battering winds were the fiercest experienced in most lifetimes. Even longtime fishmen were amazed. Though its eye was well south of Southern Boll and Ista, coastal holds were battered and the seas flooded low-lying lands, crashing up beaches to inundate seaside cotholds and fields that had always been high above ground. Coming as it did during the equinox, its fury was double that of normal storms, battering the lands right up to the hills.

Along the southern coast it uprooted the shallower rooted, flexible trees that generally bowed with wind. The storm rolled gigantic combers as high up the Weyr cliff as the Weyrhall, shredding part of the roof and demolishing many of the little buildings that housed riders. Nothing stood in its way. Especially Toric's plans. The deep harbor, usually a safe enough anchorage, was as storm-tossed as the outer sea, and men struggled to save the ships, many half-laden for their "downriver" journey. Some crew, riding out the storm on their craft, took serious injuries and had to remain there, tended for three long days and nights as best their mates could manage, until the storm finally blew itself away from Southern.

It made good speed, and gathered more, as it headed obliquely south-southeast, blasting toward Paradise River and Cold Hold.

Although the warning served by the dolphin pods was immediately heeded, the exact definition of "bad bad bad" became all too apparent as the weather worsened and the whistling twisting winds pounded the coast. No one had anticipated such a lengthy and ferocious storm.

Paradise River ran high, flooding the line of cotholds and forcing Jayge and his family to the nearest high ground, which was also threatened. The riverside farmlands were inundated, too. With the season's crops all gathered in, at first everyone felt safe enough. But the storehouses were not much more than roofs on posts to keep the sun off material; most of those structures lost their roofs and had their contents blown away. It was too late to try to lash down bales and crates: the wind tossed these indiscriminately as lethal flying objects. Herd- and runnerbeasts who were pasturing in the more open fields were later found lodged in now leafless tree bolls, a strange fruit. It took days to round up those that had fled from the savagery of the storm. Some animals had to be destroyed when they were found with broken legs or wounds that had become infected during the three days in which they had been untended.

At Landing, the storm flag was flown from the mast that had once floated the ancient colors of a forgotten homeworld to the breeze. Somewhat protected by the three slumbering volcanoes and the fact that the storm was blowing itself inland, Landing suffered relatively little damage. Monaco Bay took heavy surf and lost the dolphin float, but not the bell that had clanged for hours in the gale. Eastern Weyr got lashing rain and high winds, but not the punishing blow that had devastated the coastline.

As soon as he could, Readis made a wet journey down to the bay, to ask Alta and Dar to find out if his folks at Paradise River were all right. Kami insisted on coming with him, because a frantic message from Cove Hold told them that Master Robinton's house had been flooded and many of the things that the Harper had valued had been destroyed. She was terribly afraid that Paradise River might also have been devastated. It took a long time for the dolphins to answer the Report sequence: Readis and Kami ended up taking turns at the bell rope.

When Alta finally answered, she told them that while some of the pod had remained on duty in case a ship had been out in the gales, the others had swum to the northern and quieter seas. She said she would sound a message to pass to the Paradise River pod. So Readis and Kami waited until nearly full dark before they received an answer. The blow had been bad bad bad but humans were well, wet and tired.

"Dolphins hurt. You go help?"

"Badly?"

Alta ducked her head under the water and came up. "Don't know. You go."

Further distressed by such unexpected news, Readis thanked Alta and apologized for having no fish to give her.

"Ah, the fish run well and deep," she told him, and then backflipped away.

"*Who* got hurt? *How* badly?" Readis demanded of Kami, who remained silent as they started on the long walk back. "I wish they could be more explicit. Shards! It'll be ages before we find out."

"I'm sure Master Alemi is already helping, Readis," Kami said soothingly.

They were both startled, and Readis cried out with relief, when they heard a dragon's trumpeting above them, the sound almost lost in the still brisk after-storm wind. It was Gadareth and T'lion.

"Could you take us to Paradise River, T'lion?" Readis begged when rider and dragon landed. "There's been dolphin injuries, only Alta couldn't say who or how badly."

T'lion didn't bother to dismount, leaning over to give them a hand up to Gadareth's back.

"That's bad news." T'lion looked concerned and Gadareth turned his head back to show the orange of worry in his eyes. "I was just at Landing and heard you'd walked down here. Look, I'm supposed to report in at Cove Hold. It was badly flooded but I can certainly get you home first. At that, the wind's only just died down enough for dragons to risk flying. Gaddie couldn't lift far enough off the ground to go *between*. That storm was incredible!"

As soon as Gadareth lifted from the roadway, the three were buffeted by the winds—Readis clinging to T'lion, who had his safety straps buckled on , and Kami clutching Readis so hard she hurt his ribs. Dragon flight was usually smooth, but this morning even Gadareth was subjected to unexpected drops in the few moments it took him to reach transfer height.

The winds were not much calmer at Paradise River, and

as Gadareth reentered, all three could see how badly the Hold had fared. Whole swathes of trees were down, the broad-leafed vegetation in shreds, riverbanks deep in mud, and roofs lying everywhere but where they had been built. Readis groaned. Everywhere people were working to clear the storm debris.

Grabbing T'lion's shoulder, Readis shouted in his ear. "Take us to the harbor. The dolphins'll need my help more."

"Oh, Readis, I *must* get home. Just look!" Kami was in tears as she pointed to their once neat hold. The porch roof was awry, mud and storm wrack covered the place, and the chimney had fallen down. The net racks were splinters on the ground, and they could see several nets festooned in high limbs of trees.

"The dolphins first. You won't be far from *your* home there."

Readis also fretted about the fishing ships. Maybe, and surely Alemi would have gone to inspect them as soon as he could, the dolphin injuries had been attended to. That way he could go home to help. His mother might not even realize that he'd gone to the dolphins first.

Gadareth had trouble finding enough clear space to land in, for the pier had been demolished to a few lengths, the dolphin float and the bell gone. With a sinking heart, Readis saw that the two smaller ships had been beached and lay on their sides, masts and rigging gone, hulls broached. The *Fair Winds* was not in much better shape, but he could see figures working on her deck, cutting away the sheets and the splintered mainmast; the second one was still upright even if the rigging had been torn away. The schooner also looked low in the water. Had she sprung a leak, or merely taken on a lot of water?

There were no dorsals visible and that worried Readis even more. How many injuries had there been? And with no bell to summon the dolphins, how was he to call them?

As Gadareth gingerly settled on the beach, pushing splintered tree trunks out of his way to do so, T'lion turned to Readis. "No bell. Gaddie can call them underwater. He's done it before. Haven't you, my fine fellow?" And T'lion affectionately slapped Gadareth's neck.

I call. They come. My bugle is as good as their bell.

When his passengers had dismounted, Readis looked around and shook his head at the devastation. So much to do. Kami was sniffling; she knew that Readis disliked her showing indecision or emotions, but she wanted to cry on seeing the destruction of the smaller boats. Father would be so upset!

Gadareth walked into the water, holding his wings up high at first until he was buoyant. Then he lowered his head in the water. Those watching heard nothing, but they could see the bubbles of his call boiling to the surface. He raised his head, looking out to sea to wait for results. Then T'lion and Readis saw someone on the *Fair Winds* waving vigorously. The ship was too far out for voices to be heard. Gadareth was about to repeat his summons when a single dorsal appeared in the water, speeding toward them. Gadareth extended his head toward the incoming dolphin, but it continued in toward the shore as far as it could before it raised its head. It was Kib, bearing fresh marks on his melon.

"Bad bad bad bad blow. Worse! Two calves hurt. Can you fix?"

"We'll try," Readis replied. "How's the ship?"

"Hole full of water. We help 'Lemi."

"That's good of you with injured calves."

Kib blew water out of his hole. "We help. Our duty."

ANNE MCCAFFREY

"Then we'll help. Our duty," T'lion added. "Bring in the injured. Gaddie's very good at holding."

When the two battered calves were brought it, Readis and T'lion exchanged despairing glances. Both needed stitching to close the gaping wounds. A healer was needed.

"Would your aunt Temma be willing?" T'lion asked Readis. "I think T'gellan will understand me coming here instead of Cove Hold. They'll have lots of help."

From his tone of voice, Readis gathered that T'lion wasn't all that certain of Weyrleader approval of his delay. But they'd need Gadareth to hold the dolphin calves while the stitching was in progress. The dams were alternately squeeing to the humans to help and trying to soothe their offspring. Both dams bore superficial cuts: nothing as bad as the injuries to the lighter and less experienced younglings.

"I'll understand if you don't feel you can stay," Readis said.

"Don't worry about me and T'gellan," T'lion added, coming to a sudden decision. "There're plenty of humans to help other humans, but very few to help dolphins."

"I thought the dolphins just rode out storms," Kami said timorously, her pretty face twisted with conflicting worries.

"They usually can," Readis said.

T'lion shook his head. "That was not any usual sort of storm! Shall I take you to the Hold?"

"*You* go to the Hold, T'lion, and ask Temma to come. She's good at suturing. Had enough practice, Uncle Nazer says. And you go with him, Kami," Readis said, deciding that the girl would fret too much over the conditions of her home to be useful here. "I'll stay with the patients."

"Can you manage?" Kami asked, vacillating again between showing Readis how helpful she could be and worried about not being with her mother in this emergency.

"Sure," Readis said blithely, standing waist deep in water, a wounded dolphin floating on either side of him, surrounded by the dams and the nurse dolphins.

Temma was too busy with human injuries to leave off her duties for dolphins. She said she'd come when she could. T'lion thanked her and asked Gadareth to take him back to Eastern Weyr. They had weathered the three days of storm much better than anywhere else. He'd get Persellan to come.

But Persellan had been collected and taken to Cove Hold.

"Does he need more supplies? How bad was it there?" Mirrim asked, her brows knotted with concern.

"It's bad all along the coast, Mirrim," T'lion said. "I'll just bring what's needed with me," he added and, since Mirrim didn't challenge him further, he entered the healer's hold and helped himself to the items he knew he and Readis would need. There was more than enough and he'd tell Persellan later. He also took the book that was Persellan's treasured compilation from Aivas's medical files. T'lion had watched Persellan work on dolphins often enough to have a good idea of how to proceed, but it would be reassuring to have printed words to refer to.

He didn't think he'd been very long, but the wait must have seemed like Turns to Readis, who called out frantically as Gadareth landed.

"What took you so long? I've had all sorts of trouble keeping the bloodsuckers from attaching themselves to the calves. Temma isn't with you?" Readis's face turned whiter and his expression bordered panic.

"I took what we need from Persellan's hold, and his book," T'lion explained as he stripped off his riding gear and clothes down to his clout. Shivering a bit, for the wind still had traces of storm chill, he waded out, book and sack of supplies held above the rippling surface of the water. "C'mon, Gaddie, we'll need you, too." Gadareth followed him, moving very carefully, one eye on the dorsal fins and heads protruding above the surface.

"What about Temma?" Readis fretted. "I've never sewn up anything. Have you? And I had to stuff Angie's guts back in." Angie was the older of the two injured calves. Cori was younger, just born that spring.

"Ooooo. Wonder if you should've . . ."

"I had to, T'lion," Readis said, his tone a bit strident with anxiety. "Couldn't let any bloodsuckers get attached to her guts. They'd eat her inside out."

"Wait a minute. I'm looking . . ." T'lion riffled through the pages of the book, which he kept well above the water and any splashes. "Oooo! Ugh!" He paused, lowering the book slightly to peer at something. "Ah, here. Human intestines." He bent to peer down at the injured Angie. "Gaddie, hold her for me, will you? C'mon now, Angie, Gaddie won't hurt you."

The calf's squeeing was agonized, but, with her mother and Afo pushing her with their noses, she had no option. Gaddie's talons cradled her.

"Tip her slightly, huh, Gaddie?" And the bronze dragon, head cocked to see for himself, tilted the little body sideways. "Oooo." T'lion shuddered at the raw sight of the cords of visible intestines poking out of the wound.

T'lion tucked the sack on the dragon's upper arm where the angle was just enough to keep it secure but to hand, then tentatively fingered the extruding loops. Referring to the book again, he read with his lips moving, sounding out the more technical words by the syllables. Then he shrugged at the anxious Readis. "Well, the book doesn't give any directions other than 'reinsert the colon in the reverse order of removal.' Hmmm. That's a lot of help."

"I did sort of loop them back in," Readis said. "I've seen runners with their bellies opened. Dad would just put them back in, sew 'em up, and hope. Mostly they lived."

"Then we'll hope dolphins, being mammals like us and runners, will survive, too," T'lion replied, rolling up his sleeves. "All right, start spreading this"—he handed Readis a big pot of numbweed—"around the wound. It seemed to help Boojie, and he didn't squirm when Persellan sewed him up."

Readis liberally slathered on the numbweed.

"I've watched Persellan sewing up dragons often enough, and I helped him with Boojie," T'lion began, taking out a needle and threading it with the fine strong suture that Aivas had suggested to the Healer Hall. "I've even got the hang of how he ties his knots."

"So do it," Readis said impatiently, "before she loses any more blood. That's definitely not good for her."

With a decisive exhalation, T'lion reached for the needle and thread. Numbweed worked really quickly, deadening any flesh, human, dragon, and, he hoped, dolphin.

Doing, he found, was by no means the same as watching. Even getting the sharp needle to penetrate the tough and slippery flesh of the dolphin was different than sewing up clothes or repairing his flying straps. The muscles along Angie's side rippled since he had to jam the needle in her pretty hard. But she wasn't squirming, which would have worried him. The other dolphins were making some sort of soothing noises that, in some mysterious way, seemed to vibrate in the water around his legs. Gaddie, careful to keep the rest of her under the rippling water, held her steady enough so that the jabbing needle didn't go into the wrong places.

"She knows you're helping her," Readis said as he kept up a reassuring rhythm of caresses. That helped his nerves and she seemed to lean into the motions. He also kept checking the reassuring beat of the big heart in her chest. It struck him as significant that dolphins had hearts on the left sides of their bodies, just as humans did.

Cori, the other injured baby, wasn't more than a few months old, and the wound was serious for so young a calf. When T'lion was finishing the last of Angie's stitches, he asked Gaddie to take Cori in hand so that Readis could smear her with numbweed. The baby made odd noises and swished her tail around, but Afo told them that Cori was only relieved to have the pain gone.

"Goodee man goo," she said quite clearly. "Nummmmm weeeed?" she asked.

Readis laughed, as much from relief of the strain as because he was pleased to know the pods were using more words. "Yes, numbweed," he said. "They've learned a lot from you, T'lion." He tried to keep envy out of his voice.

"They didn't learn it from me—I don't think," T'lion said, frowning as he concentrated on tying the last few stitches in the complex knot. "Maybe Persellan used the word when he was doing Boojie. But Afo wasn't at Eastern when we did that. There! That's closed now. Wheeee." T'lion wiped his forehead on his arm, cleaned the needle and returned it to the little case that held Persellan's needles.

"Good mans ... men," Afo said and rubbed against their legs, prodding them gently in their genitals as a mark of extra affection.

"Hey, don't *do* that, Afo," Readis said.

T'lion laughed at his reaction. "Don't forget to thank Gaddie, too, Afo," he said, and Afo responded by blowing a spout of water up against the bronze dragon's chest.

Gadareth rose out of the water, the wave he made swamping the two young men.

"Watch that! I'm soaked, and this water's not so warm today," Readis complained. "I'm also water-riddled." He looked at the shriveled skin on his fingers. "Anyone else need help, Afo?"

"No, t'ank you. We go now, work holes in ships. 'Lemi grateful. Afo grateful, Cori, Angie, Mel grateful and happy."

"Bring the calves back in three days, three sunrises, Afo. So we can take those stitches out."

"Hear you," Afo said as she swam away, ahead of the little group of four, moving off westward and more slowly.

The two friends made their way to the beach, moving wearily after the unaccustomed mental and physical strain.

"I sure hope we did it right," T'lion said, shaking his head. "What we need is a manual on animal treatment. I heard tell that Masterfarmer Andemon finally asked for— Shards!" T'lion stopped, pawing through the sack. "Where did the book go?" His hands came up empty and he looked about frantically, hoping to see the book on the water. He couldn't even remember when he had last seen it, save that he had propped it up on Gaddie's forearm. "Gaddie, where did the book go? Readis, call Afo back. Did we come straight out? How far were we from shore?"

"Don't panic, T'lion," Readis said as he began retracing his steps. "I was in up to my belt . . . which is probably so salt-logged it'll never soften up . . ."

"You're worried about a belt?" T'lion roared. "When I may have lost Persellan's book . . ."

"We were about here, I think," Readis said, and then dove beneath the surface.

"Gaddie, put your head under, too. See if you can see it?"

The waters were still dark from the storm where the sea bottom had been churned up.

I see little, Gadareth responded, though it was obvious from the movement of his neck that he was looking all around. *What do I look for?*

"The book! The book I used. I put it on your arm. You know what the book looked like." Really upset, T'lion framed the size of the book in his hands, although his dragon still had his head underwater and could not have seen him.

Readis surfaced. "It's all stirred up, sand everywhere. Can't see a thing. And Gaddie's been walking about. He might have buried it."

"Buried it?" T'lion's voice broke octaves in his anxiety.

"Easy, T'lion, easy," Readis said, took three deep breaths, and then dove.

T'lion could barely see the holder lad swimming, so murky was the water. He began walking about the area where he thought they had been standing, hoping he might kick it up. But Gaddie couldn't've kicked it. He had been holding up the dolphins, and his hind feet would have been farther out.

"Gaddie, call Afo. Tell her we need her."

Gadareth obligingly bellowed. That his bugle was heard was obvious when two of the seamen working on the *Fair Winds* waved back at them. But not a single dorsal fin came streaking toward them.

"Try underwater, Gaddie. Afo *must* hear you. We need her help."

Afo did not come, though Gadareth called her in air and underwater every time T'lion asked him.

And Readis, who kept diving, going in ever increasing circles out from the spot where they thought the precious book might be, was becoming so hyperventilated and pale under his tan that even T'lion knew he should stop.

"One more dive is all I'll let you take," the dragonrider told his younger friend. "You look awful."

"If only we'd had the mask . . ." And Readis's look was accusing.

"I'm trying, I'm trying," T'lion explained, his voice tense, his mind in a whirl as he thought of how Persellan was going to react to the loss of his invaluable book.

Then Readis took his usual deep inhalation and dove, appearing for that instant more like a dolphin than a boy.

"Lucky last!" Readis shouted as he exploded out of the water. In the hands held high above his head he had the book.

"Don't get it any wetter than it is!" T'lion cried, reaching out in a thankful gesture at sight of the lost object.

But when Readis put the soggy book in his hands, dark runnels of water over their hands told them that considerable damage had been done the contents. T'lion groaned as his trembling fingers flipped open the cover. He flipped it closed immediately, rolling his eyes and groaning again.

"It's ruined. Ruined! Persellan will flay me!"

"It came from Aivas's files, didn't it? Well, then it only needs to be reprinted," Readis said in an effort to relieve his friend's dismay.

"Only?" T'lion repeated. "Do you have any idea of how long someone has to wait to get something *only* reprinted?"

Readis shook his head, determined to supply a remedy. "I'm up there all the time, T'lion. I can recopy what needs to be done directly from the disks." Then he added by way of reparation, "And maybe include some animal treatment stuff at the same time."

"Oh, I dunno," T'lion said, appalled at the damage a moment's inattention had caused.

"Good thing you had it so we'd know how to put her guts back in."

"We won't know until she gets better—and works right—if we did," T'lion replied, shaking his head and staring down at the book, which was still shedding inky drops of water.

"Let's get out of the water, and see if we can't dry out some of the pages in the sun," Readis urged, and they both headed back to the shore. "I mean, we have a duty to dolphins, too, you know."

"Do we?"

Readis gave his friend a startled look. "I think we do. They came with us, didn't they? They didn't have to, but they came to help us with the marine explorations. They've done them, but our responsibility doesn't end there. Does it? Huh? No more than our responsibility to dragonkind will end when Thread stops." He looked a little embarrassed when T'lion turned to give him an odd stare, his jaw dropped in surprise at Readis's vehemence. "That is, when it does," Readis amended. "I mean, we— humans—created the dragons. We owe them, too, you know."

T'lion's slow grin spread across his face. "I wish more of us humans thought the way you did."

Readis ducked his face in embarrassment. "I've known dragons all my life, better than most holder children do. I've scrubbed more." Then he squinted up at the angle of the sun. "Here. Let's prop the book up here so it gets the sun. I'd better dry off, too," he added, noticing the water marks on his hands. "Or Dad will sure know where I've spent time when I should have been back helping him and Mother."

"D'you think the book'll dry out enough?" T'lion said anxiously as he settled the book on a broad leaf so that sand wouldn't damage it further. The inner pages had been sufficiently pressed down so that only the edges showed their immersion. But the ink had blurred some-what, even on the illustrations.

T'lion groaned as they surveyed the ravages. "Persellan's not going to like this."

"I said I'd make good."

"You oughtn't to have to. *I* borrowed the book without permission. You didn't."

"You wouldn't have borrowed it if I hadn't insisted we heal the calves." Readis's chin was at an aggressive angle. "We're in this together."

"You most certainly are," said a new voice, and the two young men swung around to see Jayge and Temma come striding out of the jungle that bordered the cove. "What's all this about dolphins' needing medical assistance? Where have you been? Kami's been back hours and she said she came with you."

Readis sprang to his feet, trying to conceal the water-logged book from his father's sight. "Ah, well, oh!" he floundered.

"I told T'lion I'd come when I could," Temma said, cocking her head and looking from one to the other. Then out to sea. "No dolphins to mend?"

"We did it," Readis said. "I mean, T'lion's watched Persellan and there were bloodsuckers trying to . . . and it was the calves, and they were hurt with awful gashes . . . guts hanging out . . ."

"So you decided that those mammals of yours needed attention sooner than injured humans?" Jayge had crossed his arms over his chest at his most forbidding.

Readis swallowed. He had not often had occasion to suffer his father's disapproval or chastisement, but he knew the pose from those times Jayge had dealt with recalcitrant Hold workers or those whose behavior had not met his standards. Now he raised his chin.

"Yes, sir. They bleed and hurt the same as we do, and there was no one else bothering about *them* and plenty of people, including Aunt Temma, to tend to human hurts. No one was badly hurt, were they?" Readis asked Temma.

"No," Jayge answered. "But you should have found that out first, before you even thought of coming here." He frowned at his son. "You're my son and will be Holder. What sort of an example are you setting"—he waved toward the sea and its denizens—"by coming here first before you knew what help was needed in your *Hold*!"

"When we overflew the Hold, it looked like you had matters in hand. But no one was looking after our dolphins . . ."

"Our dolphins?" Jayge's expression became even more forbidding. "Since when do 'we' own dolphins?"

"The pod—the ones that use these waters—they're ours, in a manner of speaking."

"Sir, the fault was mine," T'lion interrupted, and was waved silent by Jayge.

"Why are you involved in this, T'lion?"

"He's been—" Readis began.

"Dragonriders are able to answer for themselves, Readis."

"But he—"

"I'm liaison for the dolphins in the Eastern Weyr waters, Holder Jayge," T'lion said, stiffening to an erect position. "We heard at Landing that there were injuries in this pod and help was requested. So I . . ."

Jayge frowned. "How would they know at Landing . . ."

Before Readis could capitalize on his father's misunderstanding and absolve himself of his apparent defection by intimating that someone at Landing had given him the orders, T'lion continued. "Actually, sir, we found out at Monaco Bay, not Landing. Readis and Kami were there, hoping to hear word from Paradise River that all was well here."

"So you got a message at Monaco Bay that dolphins at Paradise River were injured?"

"Yes, sir," T'lion replied.

Jayge's frown got darker. "So Master Samvel didn't give you permission to leave, Readis?"

"Master Samvel told me that Readis was down at Monaco," T'lion said, temporizing as he suddenly realized what Readis had been trying to imply.

Jayge shook his head. "Will you boys stop answering for each other? So, you are absent from school as well as derelict in your duty to your Hold, Readis. And you, T'lion, where were you supposed to be when you were busy healing the dolphins?"

"I went down to Monaco Bay when I heard that's where Readis and Kami had gone," he replied.

"I repeat, where were you ordered to go?"

"Cove Hold," T'lion said, "but plenty of folks were helping out there and no one was . . ." He hesitated.

"Helping these dolphins," Jayge finished. "Both of you need to get your priorities in order. I shall expect you to report your afternoon's activities to T'gellan, T'lion. You'd better report to where you should be before the day ends." A Holder could not presume to give a dragonrider, even a young one, direct orders that did not deal with Threadfall, but Jayge was coming close.

"Ah, yes, sir." T'lion hesitated. He needed to take the book back with him, damp as it was, but he also didn't quite like the idea of displaying the damaged thing to anyone.

"Well . . ."

T'lion grimaced. He had to leave, and leave Readis facing an angry father. So, giving a despairing sigh, he reached for the book.

"And what's that sorry-looking mess?" Jayge asked, holding out his hand. When T'lion had reluctantly given it to him, Jayge whistled as he felt the dampness. Turning the first few pages, he then shot angry glances at both son and dragonrider as he realized how valuable it was.

"We know it's been damaged. It fell off Gaddie's arm," T'lion explained. "I needed to know how to restore intestines . . ."

"By using your healer's most valued possession?" Temma asked, incensed when she saw what Jayge was looking through. "He'll not thank you for that."

"I can copy the damaged pages," Readis said quickly. "I've access to the files. I can even add more from the veterinary sections . . ."

"Did you at least have permission to use the manual?" Jayge asked. "Ah, I see not," he added, noting the guilty flush on the dragonrider's face.

"Persellan was nowhere about to ask," T'lion said. "Mirrim saw me and said it was all right."

"To take supplies possibly," Temma put in, "but not such a valuable healer's book."

"I can set it right," Readis insisted.

"That's enough out of you," Jayge said, turning on his son. "You'd better leave, T'lion."

Temma took the dragonrider's arm before he swung past her. "And the dolphins?"

"We sewed them up and they went off with their dams," T'lion said in a muted voice.

"Sewed them up, did you?" Temma looked dubious.

"I've helped Persellan and I can tie the right sort of healer knots to suture securely. That was the critical need, so the bloodfish couldn't enter the wounds."

"The critical need?"

T'lion stiffened, regarding the older woman with an expressionless face. "I did what I could to help and we'll see in three days if what I did was enough."

Temma's expression softened a little. "Happen you did all that was needed. I'd be interested to see."

Without a backward look then, the young dragonrider went to his pile of clothes, dressed, stuffed Persellan's volume in his flying jacket, and clambered aboard Gadareth. The bronze took off westward, away from those silently watching.

Readis couldn't look at his father, but he felt Jayge's suppressed anger in the grip he took on Readis's arm as he pushed him toward his clothing.

"Get your shoes on!" Jayge said. "Let's not have another thorn in your foot."

Readis felt a hard cold feeling in his chest at that harsh remark. His father never referred to his limp, had never before reminded him of the injury or where he had taken it. But then, his father wouldn't know that Readis felt far more comfortable in the sea, where his shriveled leg posed no disadvantage or handicap. The way home was too short for Readis to prepare himself for his mother's condemnation. She'd make sure he never went to the cove again. She would certainly extract a promise from him to have nothing to do with dolphins ever again. It was a promise that Readis could not in conscience give. There was no way now that he would give up the contact. Today's events had proved to him that the dolphins needed to have at least one staunch defendant in every coastline settlement: one committed dolphineer. The word had been hovering in his mind for a long time now and, in that moment, he recognized what he should do and be: a dolphineer.

As badly as Readis thought his mother would react, the actual storm that followed his father's account of his son's various offenses against his Hold and against parental teaching and tolerance, his consorting with dolphins, and his absence from the Landing school, brought such a tirade down on his head that he was unable to speak out in self-defense. Until she ranted that he was without conscience, loyalty, or honor in his devious and unworthy association with shipfish.

"Dolphins, Mother, dolphins," he said. "And I've always kept my promise to you."

She halted in her ranting, her face pale, her eyes huge; if the tear streaks on her cheeks were tormenting him, her injustice had made him speak out.

"You have not!"

"I have, too. I have never been *alone* with the dolphins or in the sea. There has always been someone else with me."

"That isn't at issue . . ."

"But it is. I promised you the day after the dolphins rescued me and Unclemi that I wouldn't go by myself to swim and I never have. Not in ten Turns!"

"But you were a child! How could you remember that?"

"Mother, I remembered. I have obeyed. I have never come to harm from the dolphins . . ."

"But you have neglected your own family and the

Hold's needs at a time when we needed everyone's help, everyone's loyalty . . ."

"The dolphins are part of Paradise River Hold," Readis began, but she slapped his face as hard as she could. He staggered back, rocked from the insecure balance of standing on the toe of one foot.

For a moment there was complete silence in the room. Aramina rarely used physical punishment, and the slaps she had given her children for naughtiness had been admonitory, not punitive. She hadn't even so much as tapped his hand in rebuke since he had started at the Landing school.

"Dolphins . . . are . . . not . . . part of this Hold!" she said fiercely, stringing out the words to emphasize her anger and denial. "I'm sure there is work to which your father can put you now. You will do it and you will never mention those wretched creatures in my presence again. Do you understand?"

"Yes," Readis managed to say. "I understand." He could not at that moment call her "Mother." He turned his head to his father, awaiting orders.

Jayge, whose expressionless face told Readis nothing, beckoned for Readis to follow him.

Fortunately, the Ancients had built all the riverbank holds on stone pillars that elevated the floors four to five steps above ground level. This had provided breezeways under the dwellings for cooling in hot weather, but it also provided protection against occasional flooding. The holders had blessed that precaution when the gale-driven tides had lapped at the top steps, and even flowed onto the porch flooring, right up to the doors, but not over the thresholds. The storehouses had lost their light roofs; there was debris to be removed, and help required to rig some sort of covering for supplies, store crates and canisters to be inspected for damp, clothing to be hung out to dry, dead animals to be butchered. The injured, human and animal, had by then been attended to. Readis was set to help with the skinning and dressing down. That had to be completed by nightfall, and the meat refrigerated.

Nazer had the generator running again, so there was power for lights and cooling. Readis worked alongside other holders, grateful for the fact that no one else knew of his dereliction. Kami had evidently told only his parents that he had returned with her. Readis didn't think he could stand any more reproaches. While he had learned how to compensate for the atrophied muscles in the bad leg—he sat or leaned against some sturdy support whenever possible—he had to work at top speed to dress the carcasses down and, by midnight, the muscles in both legs were jumping with strain and he was exhausted. But nothing would make him take a break until everyone else quit. He had had klah and a fish roll when food was passed round, which had eased his hunger pangs: He'd had nothing since eating at school early that morning.

When the last haunch was prepared for the cooler, Nazer sent everyone to their beds. Readis started off toward his home, and stopped halfway there. He could see that a light had been left burning on the porch but he couldn't—he just couldn't—go back under that roof right now. He veered toward the animal shed. He'd be warm enough under the temporary roof despite the slight chill of the sea breeze. He'd sleep anywhere he laid himself down. And he did.

He was unprepared for being roughly shaken out of a deep sleep.

"So here's where you are!" his sister Aranya said, her expression accusatory. "Father's been searching everywhere for you but Uncle Alemi swore he hadn't seen you. You've got Mother in a terrible state over your shameful—"

"I'll take that from . . . my mother," Readis said, putting his fist in her face and having the satisfaction of seeing his sister stumble backward, frightened, "but I don't have to take it from you, Rannie." Then he decided to take a small revenge on his usually tenderhearted sister. "My leg ached so I couldn't walk another step." And he rubbed both hands down the withered muscles.

"Oh, Readis, Father said Nazer told him you'd stayed on till the bitter end last night. They looked for you there, first. Then Mother was certain you'd gone to those wretched creatures who caused all your problems."

"The dolphins," he said with distinct emphasis on their proper designation, "have caused *me* no problems at all. A wretched thorn did!"

"Well, Mother says you wouldn't have got the thorn in your foot if you—" She broke off when he raised his fist in her direction again. "You'd better come home. I'll tell them where I found you, and that will be that."

It wasn't. His mother was close to hysterical again and his father, reckoning the cost of the storm to the Hold's prosperity, was in a sour mood.

Later Readis would realize how strained everyone had been then, tempers and patience too stretched to allow for any tolerance, but when his mother insisted that he give her his word that he would never again have anything to do with shipfish—and her use of that term as well as the tone of voice she used further inflamed him—then he, too, lost his temper.

"That is a promise I cannot make!"

"You will make it and abide by it," his mother told him, her eyes sparkling with anger, "or you cannot live in this hold!"

"As you will," he said, cold despite the trembling in his guts. He stalked down the hall to his room, where he filled a travel sack with everything he could lay his hands on.

"You promise me, Readis," his mother screamed down the hall at him. "You promise—" She stopped in his doorway. "What do you think you're doing?"

"I'm going, for I cannot promise that, Mother."

"Going to those awful creatures?"

"Now, that's a ridiculous idea," he said scornfully. Though he didn't know it, he sounded so much like his father at that moment that Aramina was stunned; he was able to push past her before she could recover enough to prevent him.

Limping as fast as he could, he made for the kitchen, sending out a piercing whistle for Delky. He'd seen her grazing, as usual, near the house when he and Aranya had left the shed. He saw his wide-eyed sisters and younger brother sitting at the table, an uneaten breakfast proving that they had been listening to the row. As he reached the kitchen door, Delky whinnied a greeting. Although his bad leg nearly collapsed, Readis managed to vault to her back, balancing his duffel before him. He heard his mother, demanding at the top of her voice that he come back inside the house right *now* as he kicked Delky into a canter, putting as much distance between himself and his unyielding parent as possible.

Delky had to dodge fallen trees and piled debris, nearly unseating him several times, but he kept her heading toward the river. The bridge had already been partially restored so that both sides of the riverbank were accessible. There were just enough planks down for Delky, surprised and cautious but obedient to his insistence, to cross without losing a foot in a gap. When he got to the other side, he sent her flying down the sands and on into the scrub vegetation. He slowed her down only when the rough going might injure her, and did not stop until he had reached jungle and would be invisible to anyone searching for him from the air. Then he slipped from Delky's back, his sack under him, and wept in frustration, anger, and heartbreak.

12

▼▼▼▼▼▼▼▼

K 'van strode into the Weyrwoman's quarters with the briefest nod to Ramoth asleep on her couch.

"It's Lord Toric again, Lessa, F'lar," the Southern Weyrleader said, with an angry slap of his riding gloves on his thigh as he came to a halt by the table where they were having an evening glass of wine and studying storm damage reports from the Southern Continent.

Although the youngest Weyrleader now, K'van was as old as F'lar had been when Mnementh had first flown Ramoth, making F'lar Weyrleader. He had attained more height than his adolescence had suggested: his shoulders had broadened, his legs had lengthened, and his eyes were at a level with F'lar's when they were standing. F'lar gestured for K'van to be seated and poured a glass of wine for him.

"You look as if you need it."

"I do," K'van said with a sigh as he dropped into the chair opposite Lessa. "And you will, too."

"So what has Toric done this time?" Lessa asked, amused.

"He hasn't done it yet, but he's about to. Go across the river and settle it with *his* chosen, having prepared a place for them. He's never been the least bit altruistic, so I know he's up to something and I've a hunch what it is." It gave K'van little satisfaction to see how angrily the Weyrleaders reacted to Toric's latest show of arrogance. "We found incontrovertible evidence of substantial shelters in eight different locations—coastal, riverside, and inland. His harbormaster is saying that the ships are being loaded for a downriver supply run, but I doubted that even when he gave me the smooth lie."

Lessa pursed her lips angrily, her eyes sparkling. "Toric's never been satisfied, has he?" she asked rhetorically, and then pounded her fist on the table. "Greedy, that's what he is. And he's got a larger Hold than any of the Ancients ever staked out." She leaned toward F'lar. "We can't let him get away with this, F'lar. We can't!"

"Lessa, we also can't stop him."

"Why not?" she demanded.

"We can't interfere with a Lord Holder." The Weyrleader scowled deeply, for once annoyed to be constrained by that tradition.

"But Toric *isn't* within his Hold if he's across the river, now, is he?" K'van asked, his tenor voice at its mildest. The slight smile on his face was sly. "Oh, I know, he asked us to help him with Denol and that group who tried to take over Ierne Island, but *that* is part of the holding you granted him. This land is all beyond his Hold borders."

"You're sure of that, K'van?" F'lar asked.

"That he's out of his own Hold? Yes, even the eastern bank of the river is not his. Not according to the map I have that outlines Southern Hold, from river to sea, and inclusive of Ierne Island—"

"Which he insisted on having at the time," Lessa said, angry red spots appearing on her tanned cheeks. She had clenched her fists. "And we only gave in to that demand because I wanted Jaxom to have Sharra."

F'lar brushed back the lock that always escaped to cover his eyes at moments like these. "You're right—he's up to something. I have a sudden, totally unworthy thought . . ." F'lar then shook his head and dismissed the thought unspoken with a wave of his hand. "I believe I'd better wait to justify such base suspicions." He grinned at K'van and Lessa. The look in the young Weyrleader's eye suggested he might be entertaining the same notion.

"What suspicions? Of course they'd be base, coming from Toric. But just what?" Lessa demanded.

"Later, love. Tell me, K'van, does he have settlers all lined up and ready to settle?"

K'van nodded. "I had nothing specific to report to you until now, but we kept our eyes open to Toric's doings. Discreetly, of course. Over the past few months there have been more than a normal number of well-laden ships making port at Southern. Each carrying ten to twenty passengers, sometimes family, sometimes singles. You know he's built four coastal cruisers? Yes, well. They're lumberly craft but have shallow draft and good cargo space. At any rate, he's got a lot of people in and about the Hold who haven't gone inland as I'd've thought they would—if they were his new settlers. He's never hidden the fact that he's been recruiting crafters. All perfectly legal, since he hasn't settled all the land he rightfully holds. No reason for a Weyrleader to poke his nose where he's no right to sniff."

K'van grinned, his eyes glinting cynically. The young Weyrleader kept strictly to the Traditions that governed Weyr and Hold, knowing that Toric would rave about any infringement by Weyr or Hold prerogatives. "But when no one moved out, by land or by sea, all I could do was wait until I had something definite to bring to your attention. At the last Gather, there were marks circulating from every northern Hall and Hold and some rumors that Toric's been selling sites. In his own Hold, he has that right but"—K'van lifted his hand—"not across the river!"

"He wouldn't dare!" Indignation and outrage fueled Lessa's anger. "He's got the gall to charge for what settlers should have by right of their own hard work?"

"A neat scheme," F'lar said, sardonically amused. "And I wouldn't doubt if the payment in marks isn't followed by a different sort of payment later on." K'van nodded, and F'lar went on. "When the Council of Holders might need to vote on other business."

Lessa opened her mouth, her dark eyes widening as she began to understand the scale of Toric's plan. "Base isn't a vile enough description of what he plans to do! I knew we were wrong to call a complete halt to new settlings," she said, "in spite of what Fandarel and Nicat said, and in spite of the lack of suitable places. They wouldn't have been half so eager to take up Toric's offer if they could have come to us."

"So, do you have proof of Toric's encroachment on unapportioned lands?" F'lar asked.

"Indeed we have. The storm flattened whole swaths of forestry as wide as a Threadfall, and what do you know? There were five settlements all too visible to my sweep riders. So we went looking to see if there might be a few more, and located another three. All built and ready to be occupied. And then there's Lord Toric's harborful of laden ships . . ." K'van shrugged, not needing to say more.

"*He* didn't lose any ships to the storm?" F'lar asked, a tinge of annoyance in his voice as he nodded at the reports spread out on the table, itemizing storm losses.

K'van grinned. "I know that Master Idarolan passed a dolphin warning on to him as well as to the Weyr so Toric had had time, and the good sense, to batten his shipping down. Toric doesn't leave much to chance."

"Does he know you've overflown these totally illegal sites of his?" Lessa asked, her voice harsh with the anger seething inside her.

"I doubt it," K'van said. "Once they realized what they were seeing, my sweep riders avoided Southern Hold on their way back."

"We can tackle this encroachment several ways," F'lar said, leaning back in his chair, a malicious smile on his lips as he idly twirled the stem of his glass.

"There's only one way—" Lessa began, and he held up his hand.

"Hear me out. We could dismantle those settlements so there'd be no . . . ah . . . accommodations left for these settlers of his when they finally sail forth. They'd be forced to go back to Southern. This is not the season to be without shelter, if that storm is any preview of a rough winter down south. But I would like to show other Lord Holders, who have been courteous enough to bide their time, what sort of trickery Toric has been up to. Making people pay for land they have the right to!"

"He's so certain that we're holding out the best lots for ourselves," Lessa began, giving vent to her outrage. "Just because he wasn't at the Council when the Lords asked the Weyrleaders to officiate, he refuses to believe that we did not want anything to do with land settlements, that we protested about taking on such responsibilities!"

F'lar regarded his diminutive weyrmate with more amusement than choler. "We didn't protest that strongly, love, now did we?"

"Only because it was all too plain what would happen if someone with some claim to impartiality didn't take charge. And it was we who insisted that all Weyrleaders take part, not just Benden, which was the intention of Larad and Asgenar, who proposed the notion. And we also insisted that the Harper Hall keep records of all transactions."

"I know Toric's certain that dragonriders will get preference," K'van began.

"And shouldn't we?" Lessa demanded of the young Weyrleader.

"I certainly feel we should," K'van answered firmly, all too aware of the Weyrwoman's temper and determined not to fall afoul of it, "since it's the last concession we'll expect of Pern. Adrea and I found a place that we feel we'd be very happy in. Found it on my very first mapping sweep."

"Adrea likes it?" Lessa asked, momentarily diverted from her castigation of Toric.

"Oh, yes, we've been down half a dozen times . . . to make sure, and"—K'van grinned—"it looks better every time we see it. It's what we want but I don't think many people would find it so perfect."

"That's what I mean," Lessa went on, gesturing emphatically with one hand as if sweeping Toric's exceptions aside. "Our needs and tastes are very individual and there's so much land out there . . ." She made another expansive gesture. "And he has the unmitigated gall to take marks ..." She was speechless for such presumption. "The man has tried my patience for the last time."

"I do believe you're right, my love," F'lar said, still grinning. "And since he isn't even on his own Hold grounds, I think we have him just where we need him. And where he can do us the favor of becoming a lesson for anyone with similar inclinations. A lesson that will last until the end of this Pass."

"I'm with you there, F'lar." K'van lifted his glass. "Exactly how did you mean to set the lesson?" he asked then. "Mind you, you have Southern Weyr's total cooperation. There have been times when it was all I could do to keep a civil tongue in my head with the great and greedy Lord Toric. And I'm not the only one in the Weyr to find him a bit too high-handed and arrogant."

F'lar's amber eyes were sparkling with such orange lights that for a moment K'van wondered if some of Mnementh's fighting characteristics had transferred to his rider. His slowly widening smile was both sinister and amused. "I think I'll borrow a moment from Benden Weyr's past. How long do you think it will be before the storm damage to Toric's fleet is repaired and he's ready to move out?"

"Oooh, I couldn't say, F'lar, but I can sure find out," K'van said. "How much leeway time do you need—to prepare this lesson of yours?"

F'lar laughed, rising from the table. "No more than I did the first time." He took a roll of maps from those stored in a container and, motioning Lessa and K'van to clear the table, spread it out with a practiced hand. "Now, can you show me the exact locations of each site?"

"Yes, I can." K'van took some notes from his inner pocket. "I checked them out myself against our chart of the area." Referring to his notes from time to time, he used F'lar's stylus to make small *x*'s, all on land east of the river that the Ancient maps called Island River. One was where a river branched off to the old stakehold of Thessaly and a second well east of Drakeslake. There were three in coves along the coast, and three well inland.

"That Toric!" Lessa said in exasperation. "He's—he's grasping, avaricious, covetous, and unrepentantly rapacious! He's like . . . like *Fax*!"

"Is there anyone in any of these sites now?"

"Half a dozen at the most—builders."

"Have they prepared any fields?"

K'van shook his head. "We'd've noticed that a lot sooner, I can assure you."

"Yes, I suppose you would. Is he doing anything at all on his own Hold?"

K'van shook his head again, grinning. "He's had all his crews where they've no right to be." He tapped the encroachments on the map.

Lessa was refilling their glasses when she suddenly looked at F'lar and burst out laughing. The wine began to spill.

"Figured it out, have you?" he said. He took the wineskin from hands shaking with laughter as well as malicious anticipation. "Now, now, Lessa love, that's good Benden red you're pouring. In the memory of our good Robinton, have a care of it."

"Robinton would be howling with laughter over this, F'lar, and you know it," she said.

"Honestly, F'lar, I wouldn't tell anyone. You know how discreet I can be," K'van said, not quite pleading.

F'lar gave him an affectionate slap on the arm. "You'll know. Just be sure we know when Toric's about to move, will you?"

"I can do that. He sets some of his fire-lizards to watch the Weyr Hall and doesn't even realize that two can play the game of See and Say." Reluctantly K'van rose, realizing he wasn't going to get any more out of the two Benden Weyrleaders. Considering how annoyed they had been about Toric's territorial aggressiveness, they were in remarkably good spirits now. "Do let me know when, and how, Southern Weyr may assist you."

"Oh, you'll know," F'lar said, laying a companionable hand on K'van's shoulder as he escorted the young Weyrleader to the weyr's entrance. "In fact, you'll be the first," he added, chuckling at whatever scheme he had in mind.

On the third day after T'lion and Readis had treated the injured dolphins, Jayge, Temma, and Alemi arrived at the anchorage. Alemi had left a dinghy in the water, since there had been no time to replace the float previously used for human and dolphin conferences. Jayge was certain that his son would reappear, if only to see for himself that the two calves were healing properly. The last three days had weighed heavily on Jayge. He wished that Aramina had not been so didactic about issuing that ultimatum to Readis. Although he understood her panic, and certainly agreed with her that Readis had acted disgracefully, he also understood his son well enough to know that forcing the boy to promise against his conscience would make him rebel. The boy was of the right age to resent a mother's restrictions. Jayge earnestly hoped that the three anxious days would be enough for Readis to have made his point and make an honorable return. By this morning, Aramina had been beside herself with remorse at driving her oldest child away. Jayge doubted that she'd renew her demand that Readis stop seeing the dolphins, but he was equally certain she would never cease blaming the creatures for the trouble they'd caused her and hers.

T'gellan had sent an adroit message to Jayge by fire-lizard, asking for confirmation that T'lion had treated injured dolphins at Paradise River. Jayge had succinctly replied that that was true.

Jayge was not surprised to see one dragon in the sky, but he was when a second bronze appeared. One was Gadareth, carrying T'lion, and the other was Monarth, with T'gellan and a passenger. When they landed, the stranger was introduced as Persellan, Eastern's healer. From the moment he dismounted Monarth, the healer did not look at T'lion and addressed all his questions about the dolphins' welfare to the air in front of him—though they were patently meant for T'lion, who answered in humble and subdued tones. Not that Jayge blamed Persellan for his coldness to the young rider. T'lion was lucky to get off with just that when he had borrowed the precious manual without permission and ruined it in the bargain. Well, replacing the damaged portions would be part of Readis's reparation.

"It was made plain, was it not," Persellan was saying in that purse-mouthed pose he adopted when "not addressing" T'lion, "that they should return in three suns?" He was staring straight ahead at the sea.

"It was. Afo understood."

Persellan shielded his eyes, peering out to where the *Fair Winds* rode at anchor. Some of her rigging was restored, and the waterline hole had been repaired with delphinic help; some dolphins were still to be seen, working with crewmen in the water.

"And they knew to come to the beach?"

"Yes."

Alemi suddenly pointed to the west. "There're dorsal fins just clearing the head now. I'd say they were smack on time. Wouldn't you, T'lion? Wasn't this about the time when you and Readis got here? I remember seeing you on the shore."

The Masterfishman was sensitive to more than the rhythms of the sea of his beloved schooner and was doing his best to ease the tension in the air. Now he looked in the opposite direction, down the shoreline, to the spit of land at the eastern end of the cove, and then back over his shoulder at the jungle.

"I'd have thought Readis would be here already," T'gellan said, looking at Jayge for some explanation.

"I expect him to be here" was Jayge's terse reply. He realized then how desperately he was counting on Readis's appearance. Three days was more than long enough to prove his point. It was certainly long enough to throw Aramina into a complete panic of anxieties that Readis had injured himself, had been thrown from Delky, had suffered any number of misfortunes. Worry conflicted with a rising and righteous anger that Readis, who had always been treated with respect, would repay their kindness in this fashion!

The dolphins had escorted the two calves into the shallows by then, and T'lion, who had stripped down to his clout when Alemi spied them approaching, now waded out to meet them, Gadareth following him.

Muttering under his breath, Persellan also discarded his clothing, while T'gellan only removed his boots and rolled up his pants. As Jayge, Temma, and Alemi were already down to the minimum of apparel, they merely kicked off sandals and strode in.

"We come three suns," Afo said, clicking and blowing

water. She bumped into Persellan. "You healer. I hear all about you. Good man. T'ank you."

"You're welcome, I'm sure," Persellan said. "Now which—ah . . ." Angie had swum into the talons that Gadareth had splayed just under the surface.

Jayge was briefly surprised at Gadareth's initiative, but then realized that T'lion had probably mentally asked for his cooperation. Dragons could surprise their riders now and then, but there was no expression at all on T'lion's face as he stood to one side so he wouldn't impede Persellan's examination.

Angie had tilted her sleek little body to expose the stitching. Persellan's hands gently moved across the flesh on either side of the sutured wound.

Now that Jayge saw the wound, he had to admit that Readis had acted properly. No one at the Hold had been so severely wounded: a few broken bones, quite a few gashes from flying debris, muscle strains that numbweed immediately eased. Of course, Temma had also had to decide which herdbeasts would have to be destroyed, but that had been done with a minimum of fuss and no prolonged suffering. Jayge gave an involuntary shudder over the terrific wound the calf had endured.

"A little tight here," Persellan said with asperity, prodding the point. "I think I will release it. There is good healing, and this might soon tear skin." He reached into his sack and pulled out scissors, making the cut and pulling the suture carefully through the skin. He wasn't the only one to hold his breath as the flesh relaxed but did not split. "Hmmm. There is much to be said about saltwater healing." Then he turned to Afo, who was watching him carefully with one bright black eye. "Does she hurt when I touch here?"

"Ask her," Afo said with a soft squee. "Her name is Angie."

"Angie, can you tell me if my fingers hurt you?" Persellan asked, raising his voice. Angie, who had been holding her head out of the water and craning so she could keep one eye on Persellan, let water out of her blowhole.

"Just like a kid not so sure he believes his healer," Temma murmured to Jayge and Alemi, standing beside her.

Persellan poked, gently enough, testing the length of the wound. "How do I ask this? Angie, are you regular?"

Temma cleared her throat, suppressing a chuckle. Then Angie squeeed in a tone that was so clearly "Repeat that, I don't understand" that Temma did give an amused snort.

"Are you eating all right?" Persellan asked.

"I hungry. I eat."

Persellan turned now, in his perplexity even willing to address T'lion. "How do I get across to her that she also has to evacuate what she eats?"

"Her guts work," Afo said in a tone that bordered on disgust with his periphrasis. "Come back sooner if not."

"Well, that's good to know," Persellan murmured. "I think I'll remove a few more sutures to ease her flesh. But she is healing well." That begrudged compliment seemed to release the tension in the taut young bronze rider. "There now, Angie, you come back in three more days and the other stitches can be removed." He turned to Temma, who nodded that she would attend to that.

Angie wriggled free of Gadareth's claws, and obediently the smaller Cori replaced her.

"I think all of these can come out," Persellan said, his voice not half so accusatory now. "It's a jagged enough seam, but I perceive that it was also a jagged wound. Who's this?"

"Cori," T'lion said, almost white with relief.

"Cori. Well, you're a lucky . . . young dolphin," Persellan said, just catching himself before saying "young girl."

He had relaxed enough now that he even smiled as he neatly severed and pulled through each suture. He stroked Cori's side before giving her a farewell scratch under her chin. She squeed and clicked as she swam free, but turned back to him and, looking up in his face, said quite clearly:

"Perslan good man. T'ank you, t'ank you, t'ank you."

Just then, her dam, Mel, pushed herself against T'lion. "Tlon, hand," she said.

"Hand?" T'lion held both up, looking puzzled.

"Hold your hand open under water," Alemi said, having a notion what was to happen.

"My hand?" But the dragonrider had done so and in an instant, Mel dropped something from her mouth into his hand. He held up a smooth oval varicolored shell that glistened in the light. "Oh! It's lovely," he said, and forgot his disgraced state long enough to hold the gift up for the others to see.

"That's one of those bivalve shells," Temma said, impressed. "You don't see many unbroken ones."

"Thank you, Mel, I will treasure it," T'lion said, and Mel's bright eye watched him as he carefully tucked it under his clout waistband.

Then Angie presented herself before Persellan and surprised everyone by lifting herself out of the water high enough to touch her nose to Persellan's lips. "I kiss t'ank you. I clever 'member old t'ank you." At which point she dove down and away as if embarrassed by her actions.

"My word, my word," Persellan said through the fingers of his hand that he had raised in surprise to his lips.

"You're more popular with the dolphins than the weyrchildren, Persellan," T'gellan said with a laugh. "Maybe you ought to let T'lion copy those animal treatment files as well as the ones that got soaked."

"Well, I'm not sure about that, Weyrleader," Persellan replied, but from the expressions fleeting across his face, it could be assumed that he might be reconsidering. He glanced in T'lion's direction, though he didn't quite look at him. "I was far more upset that the boy had borrowed without permission what he knew was invaluable . . ." T'lion looked down at the ripples breaking against his legs, making futile hand motions as Persellan continued. "But, in all honesty, now that I see how well he used the information in the book—despite its damage—I cannot hold the grudge."

Relief and disbelief shining in his eyes, T'lion looked up. "I am sorry, Persellan, but I didn't know what else to do and there was no one to ask . . ." The bronze dragonrider held his hands out to the healer in entreaty.

"Ask the next time," Persellan said, once more stern. "But I think next time we should both be more knowledgeable about the necessary procedures. You did say there was considerable documentation on the treatment of dolphin ailments and injuries?"

"Yes, there is. And D'ram said that I could copy anything you felt you needed . . ."

"Readis was to do the copying," Jayge said.

T'lion, still flushed with absolution, looked anxiously at the Holder. "I thought he'd be here. It's not like him to be absent. Or . . ."

"I was hoping that he would be here, too," Jayge said quietly.

In the sudden silence, T'gellan cleared his throat and started wading out of the water. Alemi, Persellan, and Temma followed him.

"But he went back to the Hold with you," T'lion said, anxiety clouding his eyes. He looked up and down the strand as if he momentarily expected Readis to burst through the thick vegetation.

"He left the Hold the day after and has not been seen since."

"Oh!" T'lion looked anywhere but at Jayge's face.

"You haven't seen him?" Jayge asked, though he knew now that the answer would be negative.

T'lion shook his head. "I've spent every free moment up at Landing. Persellan insisted that since I borrowed the book, I should copy it, not Readis. I thought you'd just made him stay here"—T'lion gestured toward the Hold—"to help clean up."

Jayge shook his head.

"Oh, that's not like Readis, sir," T'lion said earnestly. He opened his mouth to ask another question and closed it without speaking. "If you asked T'gellan, maybe he'd let me and Gaddie sweep-ride?"

Jayge made eye contact and saw the concern in T'lion's eyes. He gave a nod. "I will ask. I would appreciate the help. The last I saw of him he was crossing the bridge and heading west on Delky."

"Oh, if he's on Delky, I'm sure Gadareth and I can find him."

Then they waded out of the water to where the others were drying off and dressing. Jayge asked T'gellan if T'lion could be spared to do an errand.

T'gellan gave Jayge a long look before he flicked his fingers to grant permission. "T'lion has an appointment at Landing for his evening's stint of copying, but he may do your errand until then."

T'lion was so certain that he and Gadareth would find the truant in a short sweep down the coastline that he went off in very good spirits indeed. Readis would be so glad to know that all had ended well; that Persellan had grudgingly approved the suturing and would now learn more about dolphin medicine. The next step would be to get Persellan to let him assist and maybe even work as an apprentice—at least in the dolphin healing. There wasn't a Hall for sea-creature medicine, and Masterfarmer Andemon had made it very plain that he didn't consider them part of his Craft's mandate. But if dolphins could get hurt, they had the right to be healed. He and Readis might be the only two on Pern to consider that imperative, but two were better than none.

How far could he have got, Gaddie? Even on Delky's back? T'lion asked his dragon as they skimmed the treetops— where treetops still existed. This part of the coast had taken a ferocious beating. T'lion thought that should make it easier to find Readis.

When an hour's flight along the coastline failed to turn up any sign of his friend, T'lion had Gadareth turn slightly inland and fly a second search pattern. They coursed back and forth, occasionally landing in a likely clearing to see if there'd been a fire or anything that suggested human presence. They startled a very large furry creature at one point, and only the size of the bronze dragon deterred the beast from charging at T'lion. Instead, it went crashing away from them as fast as it could run.

Darkness came and a weary and discouraged T'lion stopped briefly at Paradise River Hold to inform Jayge that he had had no success in his search.

"I'll ask T'gellan to let me try again tomorrow. He can't have gone too far from here in just three days, sir. He might not have realized it was me and Gaddie, and hidden. I'll try again and we'll call for him. And—" T'lion had the good sense to break off there when Aramina appeared on the porch, hoping for good news. "I couldn't go as far as I should have, perhaps," he added in a self-deprecating tone of voice. Readis's mother had been crying and she looked awful, T'lion thought. "I'll try again tomorrow. I know I'll find him. Don't you worry now. Got to get back to my Weyr before T'gellan flays me." T'lion backed off the porch with that sentence and raced for Gadareth before he could be questioned. He certainly had no answers.

13
▼▼▼▼▼▼▼▼▼

Beljeth, Adrea's queen, forwarded the alert to Ramoth, whose immediate reaction—a stentorian bugle—reverberated around the Bowl of Benden Weyr, startling everyone and bringing the riders out of the Lower Caverns, where they had been eating.

Lessa, K'van says now is the time, said the queen.

"Toric would, wouldn't he?" Lessa said. They had been just about to sit down to a fine late lunch. "Sailing on the dawn tide, is he? I'll *enjoy* giving Toric his just desserts."

F'lar wistfully eyed the meat pie that was steaming on the table, and the assortment of early vegetables that would accompany it, the hot fresh bread and the sweet berries that would have made an excellent meal. With long strides, he collected their riding gear and deposited Lessa's in her arms.

"I knew we should have eaten when the others did," he muttered, breaking off some of the bread and stuffing a hunk in his mouth. Then he grabbed a handful of the berries and crammed them in, too. The juices dribbled down his chin as he went to get Mnementh's harness down from its peg.

Lessa followed his example, and stuck the rest of the bread into a half-closed jacket before she took down Ramoth's harness. The queen was swinging from side to side, her head low, waiting for her rider to slip the harness on.

Does every rider know where he or she is to go? Lessa asked Ramoth as the golden queen shivered the harness down her neck into place. Lessa buckled the straps, then pulled on her gloves.

Yes, and Ramoth dragged out the sibilant vocally as well as telepathically. Her eyes were bright, shot with orange eagerness. *This will be fun. Not like fighting Thread.*

"Just don't get to like it too much, my fine queen," Lessa said. She closed her jacket, wrapped her single braid around her head, and jammed on her riding cap, fastening the chin strap. With a jump to Ramoth's forearm, she deftly snagged the one dangling strap, and pulled herself into place between the last two neck ridges. "I devoutly trust we won't have to do this exercise more than once!" Then she grinned. "Well, this *is* the second time." *Let's go, dear heart.*

Ramoth walked the last few lengths to the ledge of her weyr. Mnementh was above her to the right, F'lar already mounted.

The half-dozen bronze dragons and the other Benden queens who were to take part in this "lesson" were making their way to the rim of the Bowl. Mnementh asked Lessa if everyone involved had been alerted, and Ramoth said that Beljeth had conveyed the message to every other Weyr. Lessa grinned.

F'lar says we should move out now, Mnementh informed the Weyrwoman.

Ramoth gave one more bugle and sprang into the air, spiraling upward, upward above the rim of Bowl, outlined against the farther hills by the late-afternoon sun.

Mnementh flew proudly beside his queen, looking over at her.

Admiring your queen, Mnementh? Lessa asked.

We fly well together was the response, and she grinned as she heard the smugness in the bronze dragon's tone. No other had even come close to catching Ramoth in her mating flights, despite the fact that every bronze, and two very audacious browns, had tried.

As soon as F'lar judged them far enough above the Weyr, Mnementh gave Ramoth the order to go *between*.

This day's maneuver took a little longer than F'lar's capture of Hold ladies the day that the Hold Lords had attempted to storm Benden Weyr. This time, it was the Lord Holders who were being peremptorily required to accompany the Leaders of every Weyr while bronze riders awaited their arrival at each of the fraudulently settled sites. The golden queens would see that the ships that had set sail so blithely from Toric's harbor tacked right back the way they had come.

F'lar and Lessa checked at all eight illegal sites to be sure that each had been inspected by a Lord Holder and Weyrleader, and that the men and women found there were loaded on dragons for transportation back to Southern Hold. The queens who were on ship duty told Ramoth that they'd never had so much fun. The ships had not gone so far from their home port that they would delay the confrontations the Weyrleaders had planned for Toric.

The Lord Holder of Southern heard the shouts and cries of alarm where he sat in his hall, eating a belated morning meal. He had seen the ships leave port and been well satisfied with the sight of their sails billowing with the brisk eastward wind. Without knowing why Toric had asked to know when the weather would be fine for a long sail, Master Idarolan had sent a fire-lizard message that the winds would be propitious today and the weather fair for several days. Toric had even noticed the dolphins who escorted the ships out of the harbor, leaping and plunging in their witless fashion. Then he had come back inside and spent a pleasurable hour figuring out the profit on this enterprise and realizing that it would, as he had hoped, offset the expenses of establishing new Holds on the Seminole peninsula. He disliked resorting to the Ancients' names—they'd had their chance and lost it to Thread—but since Aivas had identified places by what it had in its memory, the old names for the Southern Continent had been seized upon with great enthusiasm as "a link with their heritage." Toric was not of that mind. He had the future to plan for and that was what he'd been doing while everyone else on the planet seemed to be wallowing in ancestral accomplishments and striving to reconstruct all sorts of devices. He was probably one of the few who did not regret the silence of Aivas or the demise of the old Harper—who had been a meddler of the first order.

As Toric had weeded out the "right" sort of settler from the ones who had come, purse in hand, he was reasonably sure he wouldn't have a repetition of the Denol treachery. Those whom he had chosen to stay on Southern would listen and obey him. And he had sufficient knowledge of the ones he had shipped off to know they would have to obey him when the time came. That was all he required of *them*!

Obedience to his orders. Or else. He smiled to himself. Once this Pass was over . . .

His smile died as he became aware that the noise outside his Hold had changed in pitch, rising more often to an angry babble and punctuated with shouts or cries. Not at all the sort of sounds that should go with the event that had been inaugurated this morning. While he was well aware that the residents of the Hold had been complaining for months about the overcrowding by the settlers he'd planted in their quarters, the extra bodies were now gone. His holders should be happy to have regained their privacy now that the ships and their passengers had sailed off.

He was on his feet, annoyed that his contemplation as well as his meal were being interrupted by some stupidity when the Benden Weyrleaders appeared in his doorway.

"What are you two doing here?" he demanded, not at all pleased and hoping that the ships had been well out of sight by the time they had approached his Hold.

"I suggest you come outside and see, Lord Toric of Southern," F'lar said, but his smile was far from amiable, and the Weyrwoman's smile was wider and full of malice.

"Now, see here, Benden . . ."

"No, you see—" Lessa interrupted him, pointing outside. "—there!" She stepped aside so that he had a view of Groghe of Fort, Larad of Telgar, and Asgenar of Lemos waiting in the hall.

"We require your presence outside, Toric," Larad said, his face expressionless.

"The sooner the better," Groghe added. "Being hauled down here when I've more than enough to attend to at Fort, with two generators down . . ."

Toric was nearly apoplectic with fury and barged past

his peers, down the hall, and out of his hold. He came to a sudden halt at the top of the stairs leading down to the huge yard, which was crowded with his holders and their erstwhile guests. Startled, he looked beyond their heads to the harbor and growled to see that the ships he had seen off were back, sails furled and anchors cast overboard. The fact that each had a gold dragon hovering above it suggested the cause of the return.

Glancing now down at the crowded court, Toric became aware that the first few rows of the faces turned on him were the men and women he had planted at his cross-river sites, who should have been at those sites, awaiting the arrival of the settlers, not here, with scared or indignant or nervous expressions on their faces. And certainly not in close proximity to dragonriders and other Lord Holders. He was both surprised and outraged by the fact that *all* the Lord Holders seemed to be present.

"Just what is going on here?" he demanded in a loud and carrying tone, though he was in a fair way toward figuring it out himself.

"I think that should be obvious enough, Toric," F'lar said, taking a position a discreet distance from the enraged Lord Holder. "I wished the Lord Holders to see for themselves that you had illegally initiated settlements outside your own holding."

"What's wrong with that?" Toric demanded, deciding to plow through any objections that could be raised. "The land's lying empty. I've spent months training these men and women"—he gestured broadly—"to deal with any of the hazards found in southern lands."

"The Southern Continent is not yours to parcel out, Toric," Groghe said.

"It's not theirs either," Toric roared, jerking his hand

over his shoulder in the Benden Weyrleaders' direction. "It belongs to anyone strong enough to hold . . ."

"But not someone who already has far more than a just share," Groghe said, his eyes blazing as he took a menacing step toward the much larger Toric. Larad and Asgenar closed in behind him to indicate to Toric that Groghe spoke for them.

Toric sneered down at Groghe. "You never could stomach that, could you, Groghe? That your little Fort Hold would be lost in a corner of mine?"

"That is not the issue, man," Larad said. "It was agreed among us—"

"I never agreed," Toric said with a disparaging snort, determined to embroil them all in an argument and thus turn attention from him.

"You didn't choose to attend the meeting, but its result is binding on all."

"Not on me!"

"Shut your mouth, Toric," F'lar said, and gestured toward the dragons lining the cliff.

"Since when do dragonriders interfere with Hold business?" Toric demanded in a snarl, turning on the dragonrider.

"When the business is not *in* a Hold, Toric," N'ton of Fort Weyr answered, stepping forward from where he had been standing in the front of the crowd.

"Dragonriders have not interfered with *Hold* affairs," cried R'mart of Telgar Weyr. T'gellan of Eastern, G'dened of Ista, and his father, D'ram, formerly that Weyrleader, G'narish of Igen, T'bor of High Reaches, K'van of Southern, and F'lessan of Honshu Weyrhold were ranged beside him. "We have prevented an unfair appropriation of lands not available at this time for colonization by a Lord Holder who hasn't settled a fifth of his own lands."

"You're saving all the best places for yourselves," Toric cried, jeering.

"By no means," N'ton said, and then grinned, turning slightly back to the crowd so the smile could be seen. "But we do want our choice once Threadfall is over."

"But it's *not* over," cried someone deep in the crowd, a cry of frustration, indignation, and anger.

"Twenty-two more Turns," F'lar said, "and you will never again have to tithe to the Weyrs. And we—" He paused; for his tone had become resolute and hard. "—we will finally hold lands we can work and halls of our own!" His words rang with the promise he repeated to them, and to himself. "Of all those who live on Pern, the dragonriders are the only ones who are able to survey the extent of the territory available. At the insistence of the Lord Holders, we undertook that task between Falls, and the Lord Holders can vouch" he said, with a nod to the Lord Holders, standing to one side of the court, "that a significant number of settlements have been started by groups who have the skills and the training to cope with the feral animals, the fevers, and the dangers you all know. You're also very much aware of what happens to people who think it's only a question of picking the next meal off a tree." There was a ripple of bitter agreement for that. "Holdings are being constantly released for settlements for those prepared to prove them. Just as the Ancients did."

"And what gives you dragonriders the right to decide what privileged few go and where?" Toric retorted, again jeering at F'lar. "The Ancients' Charter gave every settler on Pern the right to choose land, to make his own stakehold. I was only insuring that others were allowed their rights."

"And you were not extending your holding, Lord Toric?" Asgenar asked with deceptive mildness.

"Now, why should I do that?"

"And you were not exacting payment for providing the sites?"

"Payment?" Toric managed a very good imitation of total astonishment and dismay.

"Payment!" F'lar said, and gestured to several of the men in the front.

"There were certainly nominal costs involved in building adequate facilities ..." Toric began, until he saw that one of the men coming forward was one of the troublemakers he had wanted *out* of Southern as fast and as far away as possible.

Hosbon was the fourth son of a High Reaches Hold, strongly built and strongly minded that he was going to show his father and others that he ought to have had control of the family Hold. If Toric had been perceptive, he would have seen that what he disliked in that young man were the qualities he prided himself on.

"We could have built our own Holds," Hosbon said. "We've paid and paid ever since we were accepted"—he loaded that word with indignation and repressed anger—"by you as settlers. Paid for everything we've eaten and every tool we've had in our hands. We'd've been better off if we *had* been illegal!" And he cast an angry look at T'bor, the High Reaches Weyrleader, and the Benden Weyrleaders as if they were responsible for the indignities he had suffered.

"You couldn't have built *adequate* shelters," Toric roared back at him. "You have to have *stone* to protect you from Thread!"

"But you *said*," Hosbon responded, waving a fist at

Toric, "that Thread doesn't scour the land down here. We've seen it ourselves . . ."

"And once you cut the leaves and reeds from living bushes, Thread'd go through them as fast as it would your flesh," T'bor said. "I lived down here so I know."

"Oh!" Hosbon subsided briefly.

"The lack of easily accessible quarries is one reason," F'lar said, "why you can't just go where you choose down here—and survive. Lord Toric did you one favor by building in stone."

"My thanks," Toric replied sarcastically.

"Well, we've paid top prices for those stones," Hosbon continued. "Like we've paid for everything else and then more for supplies to take us through the bad season. Shards! We've been here for months. We could have built our own places in that time, and set aside food for the bad season, which is when our good Lord Toric finally lets us go so he can extract the last mark out of us." He snorted.

"Southern's better than High Reaches at any time of the year," T'bor said, "but your point is made."

Grinning, Hosbon turned in T'bor's direction. "I'm not so sure of that, if the storm we had a sevenday ago is a taste of what we'll have to live through. Only, now, do we?" He took an aggressive stance, glaring at F'lar.

"We have a point to make, Hosbon, and you're part of it," F'lar said, but his conciliatory tone and sympathetic expression relaxed the man's pose. "We know where you are, and if you prove your holdings, they will be officially granted you."

"Free and clear?" Hosbon asked, switching his gaze from F'lar to challenge Toric.

"Free and clear," F'lar said, nodding.

A cheer went up from the crowd and the menacing atmosphere cleared.

"Then why'd you drag us all back here?" someone shouted.

"Why did a queen turn my ship back?" one of the captains demanded, pushing his way through. "Is this going to be what happens when the Pass is over? Dragons menacing honest folk?"

"We came to set matters right," F'lar said.

"We have harmed no one," R'mart added, looking at the huddle of workers who had been transported from the distant sites. "Though I imagine we surprised a few."

"The queens are large enough to turn a ship, but you hadn't gone very far from this port to make a return difficult," Lessa said. "And we"—she included the Lord Holders and the Weyrleaders—"have the responsibility of seeing that such a blatant abuse is corrected."

"Dragonriders aren't supposed to interfere with Hold matters," Hosbon said.

"Ah, but that's the crux of the matter," F'lar said, grinning broadly as he pointed at Hosbon. "And let me repeat so that everyone understands the difference. The land you were being settled on is *not* anyone's established Hold . . . Not yet. And certainly not Lord Toric's to dispose."

"That's enough out of you, Weyrleader!" Toric, his patience gone, charged at F'lar.

Immediately Mnementh, sitting above the courtyard on the hold cliff, spread his wings and bugled. Ramoth also spread her wings but barked something at the other angry bronzes and golds, who subsided. The crowd gasped and constricted into a tight knot, as far from the dragons as possible. F'lar had neatly ducked away from Toric's swing and danced out of range, though his hands came up in defensive positions. Larad, Asgenar, and Jaxom, being more agile than the older Lords, closed in on Toric, grabbing his arms and preventing a second charge.

"What we have to say to you now should be discussed in privacy, Toric," Jaxom said, giving his wife's brother a warning squeeze on the arm.

"I have nothing to say to you," Toric said, snarling and struggling to free himself. "Any of you!"

"That makes no difference," Larad said, speaking in a low and cheerful voice. "*We* intend to talk to you or at you, but you would be wise to pay attention." Then he turned his head to catch R'mart's attention. "Let the settlers go on now, R'mart. They'll still reach their destinations in good time."

Then they marched Toric back into his hold. Ramala, Toric's wife, stepped aside, her face expressionless as Larad and Asgenar followed Jaxom's lead to the Hold's main hall. Weyrleaders and the other Lords followed. As they crossed the threshold, Toric tore himself loose and spun around to confront his adversaries.

Groghe, puffing a bit from his exertions, Deckter, Lord of Nabol, Toronas of Benden, and the dour Oterel of Tillek ranged themselves to the fore, while the dragonriders, male and female, made a loose circle behind them.

"You cannot use your absence from a decisive meeting to ignore its decision, Toric," Groghe said. "You had a chance then . . ."

"Ha!" was Toric's sarcastic reply.

"Well, you did. In open Council," Oterel said. "Nothing had been decided . . ."

"Don't give me that," Toric said, dismissing it.

"Well, I hadn't made up my mind," Laudey of Igen said. "Nor had Bargen here and Begamon, no matter what you think. But it was also plain that none of us," he added, gesturing to the other Lords, "could be considered impartial in the matter of distributing lands. And none of us, certainly, had any way of surveying the property."

"The Ancients left all those maps . . ."

"Old ones, and they hadn't the information we needed."

"So you let the dragonriders do it . . ."

"Reporting to the Council, in detail."

"Like the reports you had from Piemur," Corman of Keroon said in a droll tone.

"Which *he* gave to the Masterharper." That also rankled in Toric's mind.

"Reports of lands past your holding, certainly," Groghe said. "We arranged procedures, organized lists of prospective settlers, each with at least Craft journeymen to supply skills. You had the same chance as any of us to establish any safeguard against abuse or foreknowledge of special sites."

"The records have been copied and sets are available," Larad said, "to prove that there have been no special favors accorded dragonriders. They have tended to ask for locations that would not appeal to the rest of us."

"Faugh! You'd say that no matter what."

"Nor have *we*," Groghe went on, "had special considerations for unlanded sons. And daughters. Of course, that wouldn't worry you since you have unused land to provide for your offspring."

Toric merely glowered.

"That's as may be," Toronas of Benden said. "The important consideration is that no one, and I repeat that, no one of us or of the dragonriders can apportion land without the consent of the rest of us. You included. Surely you can accept that as a guideline."

"I think you will have to accept that as a guideline, Toric," R'mart said, "because we"—he gestured to the other weyrleaders—"intend to see that no one oversteps those requisites as you did today."

"Is that what you'll become when you're no longer needed to char Thread? The guardians of order on Pern?" Toric glared at F'lar.

"That is what some of us will certainly be doing," F'lar said, equably, "when, as, and *if*—" He paused significantly. "—such overseeing is needed."

"And who decides the *when, as, and if*, might I ask?"

"You may, and—"

"There will be guidelines for that, too," Larad interrupted.

"Which *we*," Groghe said, "in the Council will decide and refer to the special Gathers that will let everyone, Hold, Hall, and dragonrider, have a vote in the matter. Or will you absent yourself from that meeting as well?"

"The Pass is not over. Are you not interfering before time?" Toric acidly asked F'lar.

"We have not, I repeat, Lord Toric, interfered with *Hold* matters," F'lar said with a slight bow. "We have explained the difference."

"A united show of the difference, I might add," Groghe said, while the other Lord Holders murmured agreement. "You have more than a generous share of the southern lands, Toric. Stick to them and there shall be no further need for disagreements or misunderstandings."

"Don't be so easy on him," Oterel of Tillek said in a harsh voice. "He knew exactly what he was doing. And he now knows exactly what can be done to curtail these incursions of his."

"One Fax in a lifetime is quite enough," Groghe said bluntly.

"You're absolutely correct," Sangel of Boll said with a shudder of dismay. "You won't find *us* permitting that sort of thing to happen again! Not in my lifetime."

Toric gave the elderly and not too effective Lord of Boll

a measuring look, which suggested that he would have found Boll an easy target.

"And you've three, four times as much land as Fax overran," Sangel continued. "Take my advice and be grateful."

Toric snorted contemptuously. "If you have finished handing out today's dos and don'ts?"

"Since you have been gracious enough," Larad said with studied courtesy, "to hear what we had to say, we can leave."

"But you have been *warned*," Laudey of Igen said sternly. "You will voice any complaints in the next Council of Lords and you will abide by the decisions."

"Or?"

"I don't think you want to know," R'mart of Telgar said, with a malicious smile on his face. "I really don't think you want to know." And he turned on his heel and strode out, followed by his Weyrwoman and the other queen and bronze riders.

"*K'van!*" Toric bellowed, and when the young Weyrleader turned in the doorway to face him, Toric raised his fist. "If I see a single one of your riders *anywhere* near this Hold . . ."

"Ah, but you see, you won't, Lord Toric," K'van said with a soft smile. "But then you have been too busy to notice that the Weyr is empty and we have settled in a much more congenial location, heretofore unoccupied."

"With the full consent of the Council of Lord Holders," Larad added. "Good day, Lord Toric of Southern Hold."

14
vvvvvvvvvv

O nce Readis found the seaside caves that he had once seen from the decks of the *Fair Winds*, he chose the one most suitable to his purposes, making it as comfortable as he could. Some of the water and wind-worn openings would be half-flooded with higher tides, but these would also be extremely handy for a Dolphin Hall. This series of caves and hollows were at the base of the rocky slope that led up to the deep gorge and the river shown on the Ancients' charts as the Rubicon. Most of the caves were shallow or accessible only by a treacherous climb over tumbled boulders. There was really only one that could be made into a human living accommodation, with a sea-eroded maw through which he could lead Delky to the space on a wide ledge where he could stable her adequately. Past that point, the ledge led to two interior, water-hollowed chambers, one of them large enough to make a respectably sized hold, and both now high above the full-tide marks.

They'd had to spend their first Threadfall, on their way to these caves, crammed under a barely adequate over-hang, with Delky shivering with fear as Thread hissed just a finger's thickness from her hide.

There was plenty of time, too, for Readis to regret the precipitousness of his departure and bemoan the useful items that he should have packed that would have made his new life considerably easier. But then his exodus had not been planned. He steeled himself against other regrets, like forgoing the studies he had begun to enjoy for the challenge and mental stimulation they had provided. And the tantalizing prospect of things that could be when the Pass was over. He regretted not having access to the wealth of information in the Aivas files—and the chance to copy Persellan's damaged pages, as much for his own information as to make amends to the healer. He worried how T'lion had gotten on with the healer and how he'd been disciplined by his Weyrleader. He worried most about Cori and Angie: had T'lion's stitches held? Were they healing? Who was tending them? How was he going to get in touch with the pod in these waters? And would the dolphins feel the need to tell other humans where he was? He *was* doing this for them, finding sea caves, acces-sible by water: The quieter pools that were flushed out with the tides would be perfect for tending the injured, and the great ledge outside couldn't be better for talking to a whole pod with no crowding. There was deep water beneath the ledge—or as deep as he could dive.

The Great Current was far out, too far to be visible, and that's where the dolphins would swim, riding the west-ward flow. They wouldn't know a human was in this area. And Readis had no bell and no way of obtaining one. If only T'lion were here, Gadareth could attract them with his bugle. No doubt the bronze rider had been restricted to official duties and the Weyr. Readis hoped that T'lion wouldn't be denied access to the dolphins. Surely T'gellan would have understood how important it was . . . His parents hadn't, Readis interrupted himself; why would he think a Weyrleader would care? Except that the dolphins had warned Path's rider about a pregnancy and Mirrim had had a fine son. Was that enough?

Probably not. His parents didn't care to remember that dolphins had rescued him and Alemi from the squall. That had been a long time ago now.

Readis had little time for much reflection: he had to find food, which in this season meant long and sometimes futile searchings, the main growing season being now over. What he could find he had to save, so he hunted until he discovered a supply of clay along a creek and made utensils, which he fire-hardened. It took him several tries to get a mug and a bowl that didn't leak. He knew more theory than he had had a chance to put into practice. He could and did make himself a frond mattress, which gave him comfort at night, and he wove fine grasses into a covering. The tougher ones supplied him with stout rope to secure Delky when he didn't want her straying from the cave. He'd twisted threads from her tail for a fishing line and braided more for a longer line, splicing it to a good length, thanks to those lessons he'd learned from Unclemi. He kept his belt knife honed sharp and hoped the steel blade would last until he could replace it, as the daily honings were visibly narrowing the good blade. He sought the biggest tree nuts and chiseled a hole in the tops so that once he had drunk off the juices, he could store fresh drinking water in them. While the nut juice was considered by many to be very tasty and he knew that

Swacky fermented it for his sevenday night's drinking, he didn't like the almost sickly sweetness of it. Besides fresh fish and shoreline shellfish, he'd find the occasional fowl nest, so he had sufficient protein in his diet. No fire-lizard clutches yet, though he'd searched every sandy cove on his way here. It was really the wrong season for fire-lizards to clutch. He'd never particularly wanted one, but he could have used one now. Delky wasn't that companionable. And, until he made contact with dolphins, he had only himself to talk to.

He was generally too busy to be lonely and too tired not to sleep at night, when doubts would have tended to assail him. If he wanted to communicate with dolphins, he'd have to swim out far enough, and he wasn't so foolish as to venture out that far without the safeguard a vest would provide. Once he had finally located a stand of the fibrous plant from which life vests were made, he spent several days designing and making one.

From small fish bones he fashioned needles and, with clumsy but firm stitches, constructed a passable garment. He gave it a long test the morning he finished it, floating about until the local fishes were comfortable enough with his presence to come nibble his toes. That was brave of them, since he'd already caught so many. But he was as buoyant in the water at the end of the morning as at the beginning, so he felt confident enough in its efficiency. He made sure that Delky had enough fodder and fresh water in her clay pot—though he hadn't been able to make it completely watertight and moisture oozed out slowly—before he donned the vest again.

Today the sea was calm, only wind ripples marring its surface. He might not get another such day in this stormy season. So he tested the ties on his vest one last time and then waded out until he reached the deeper water.

Straight out from the shore he swam with good firm strokes. If his luck was in, he'd get a ride back.

By the time the shoreline was well behind him, he began to have second thoughts. His arms were beginning to tire and his breath was getting ragged. So he stopped swimming and assumed a floating position, letting his head go back until the top of his vest cushioned his neck. He closed his eyes against the glare of the sun, though he could not escape the whiteness of its rays behind his eyelids. His breathing slowly dropped to normal. He had never been afraid of the water and wasn't now. The light waves occasionally splashed over his face, but he only snorted the water out of his nostrils without changing his position. This was very restful, rocking only lightly from time to time. He could almost fall asleep, mesmerized by the watery rhythms. Arms extended, he stopped even a cursory movement of his hands. He'd give himself a good rest before he started off again.

He felt motion in the water beneath him. As he flipped himself perpendicular, his legs encountered something slithery, and he caught sight of the large body aiming at the surface. Then he became aware of the dolphin fins nearby. Abruptly a smiling dolphin face emerged in front of him.

"Save man? No storm. No good far from land?"

"I was looking for you."

"Looking for Cal?" The dolphin squee'ed loudly in surprise and swam past Readis with one bright black eye never leaving his face. "Who you?"

"I'm Readis, Cal."

Abruptly the dolphin came back, stopping in front of him. "Pods looking for Readisssss."

"Are they?"

"All pods looking for Readis," Cal repeated and then flipped into a dive.

Startled, because Readis didn't want to be found, he ducked under the water and hauled hard on Cal's near flipper to prevent her from sounding a message through the water.

"Don't tell the other pods you've found me," he said urgently, his face inches from Cal's bottlenose.

"Don't tell?" The dolphin turned her head so her bright eye was fixed on Readis and her whole expression conveyed an air of total surprise. "You lost. You found."

"I'm not lost. I don't want to be found. By humans."

"You are human. Humans stay together. Live in pods on the land. Only visit dolphins in sea. Not *live* in sea. Dolphins *live* in sea." Cal's response was long for a dolphin and, if the squeaky, pinched tones dolphins used for human speech also conveyed emotions, this time she spoke in shocked amazement.

"I want to live with dolphins, heal dolphins when they're hurt, be a dolphineer!"

Cal's loud squee broke off when she spouted an unusually high fountain of water from her blowhole. "You be dolphineer?" The pinched tone rose to a shrill note. "You be Cal's dolphineer?"

"Well, we've just met. You don't know much about me . . ."

"Dolphineer! Dolphineer!" Cal's response was ecstatic! "Will more mans be dolphineers again? Swim with pods, hunt with pods, go see where coast has changed? New reefs, new channels, new stuff? Visit subsidence and meet the Tillek?"

Cal's brief, earlier submergence must have been sufficient to send for the rest of the pod. Dolphins were homing in on her from all directions, leaping in and out of the water, squeeing and clicking so enthusiastically that Readis came very close to being drowned by their attentions. But he caught a dorsal fin as he was tumbled underwater and hung on until he and—it was Cal he'd got hold of—the dolphin surfaced again. Readis had got a noseful of seawater and had to cling to Cal while he snorted his nasal passages clear and got breathing properly again. Somehow Readis would have to get an aqua-lung. Without it, he was likely to be a liability to any pod, not the helping partner he hoped to be.

"Cal, listen to me," he said, catching hold of both flippers and pulling at first one, then the other to get Cal's attention. "I want to stay here. Don't tell humans."

"Why?" Cal was plainly puzzled, and others poked their heads up to listen to the conversation.

"I want to be alone with the pod. Learn to be a dolphineer."

"No long-feets," another dolphin said. "Dolphineers had long-feets."

"Your name please?" Readis asked, catching one of the speaker's flippers.

"I Delfi."

Then others started squeeing out their names: Tursi, Loki, Sandi, Tini, Rena, Leta, Josi. They poked their faces at him, or walked toward him with flippers extended. He was splashed with the waters of their enthusiasm.

"Hey, hey!" He held up his arms and waved his hands to get them to calm down. "Take it easy. You'll drown me."

"No drown in middle of dolphins!" Delfi cried, and squee'ed as she dropped back into the water.

"Yes, you will. I've no blowhole!"

There was a good deal of clicking and squeeing over

that. The dolphins evidently thought it was very funny. Readis began to feel as if his great idea of being a dolphineer might not be such a childish one. At least the dolphins approved. What did he care if every other human on the planet didn't!

"I have found caves that lead to the sea and the pools that would be perfect places for dolphins to come to talk to me, where dolphins who were sick could come to be healed. I can take off bloodfish, too. And stitch wounds. D'you want to see?"

"See, see," squee'ed the dolphins.

"Give me a ride in?" Readis asked, lifting his right hand in the position to grasp a fin.

"Me!" cried Cal, and squirmed her way through to take up Readis's hand.

There was a bit of splashing and bodies trying to push him away from Cal.

"Hey, wait a bit! You can take turns, swimming me in," Readis shouted, and got a mouthful of water. He couldn't clear his air passage and if not for the vest would have been helpless to remain above the surface.

Almost instantly the scramble ended. Two dolphin bodies supported him until he got his lungs clear, though the seawater he had swallowed nauseated him.

"All right, now, pod, let's take it easy on this poor human. You take turns so I don't tire you out. Huh?"

"Tire? What tire?"

"Ummmm, get weary, lose strength, *exhaust*." Readis made motions of difficulty in swimming. "Like men you rescue, all tired from ship going down."

Scornful fountains rose from blowholes, and two rolled in contempt for the notion.

"Dolphins swim all around Pern and not weary," Cal said, her smile deeper than ever. "Swim you to shore is easy. Easy, easy, easy," Cal said, gently brushing the side of his face with her nose. "We go now. We change. You keep hand up."

And so he was towed to shore, actually at a much reduced speed than he remembered them taking him and Unclemi into shore after the storm. He changed supports, and there was always a new one, waiting for him to switch. He realized that Cal had come back for a second turn by the time the shore loomed above them.

"To starboard . . ." Readis gestured right with his left hand. "To the right."

"Know starboard. Know port. Cal is smart."

"Cal certainly is. Have you been in these caves?"

"Yessss, been in pools here. Good place. Readisss smart to find good place." Her voice echoed in the stone cave, and Delky whinnied in fear.

"It's okay, Delky," Readis called, worried lest she break his vine rope in her panic.

"You have horsss?" Cal asked, carefully raising herself far enough above the water to put an eye on the startled beast.

"Horss?" Readis laughed. "Delky's a runnerbeast. And a weed at that. Easy there, girl. It's all right."

"Looks horsssish," Cal insisted. "Name Delky? Delky, I Cal."

"Runnerbeasts can't talk, Cal."

"Pity. We can talk better now we got you to talk to."

"I think you speak pretty well already, Cal," Readis said, hauling himself out of the water. The vest had held him up all right, but it had rubbed badly underarm and on his shoulders and neck. He'd have to find something to pad it there. Right now the abrasions stung. He also needed a drink. "Stay put, will you, Cal?"

He rose and had to grab at the wall to keep upright. He hadn't realized how tired he was, and his bad leg was not in good working order at all. That was the first time he realized that the dolphins never commented on his wizened leg. At least they didn't seem to care.

Grabbing the nearest of his homemade water bottles, he returned to the pool and found it stuffed full of dolphins.

"Is the entire pod inside?"

"Yes, want to see man's land place," Delfi said, raising her body out of the water to peer about her. "Nice place." And she dropped back.

"Anybody need a bloodfish scraped off?" Readis asked, wanting to reinforce his usefulness. He was tired enough to be grateful that his offer was not taken up.

"We strong pod," Cal said with an understandable pride. "Maybe later. When we swim closer in, where reefs and things make cuts."

"Well, I'm willing to help whenever I can," Readis said.

"Can't be dolphineer to whole pod," Cal said. "Not right. One to one is tradition."

"Until I can find more folks who want to be dolphineers, I guess I'll have to be one for the whole pod."

Readis was surprised to discover that dolphins had a covetous streak in them. But then, dragons and fire-lizards were possessive, one way or another, of the humans they looked to. Runnerbeasts didn't much care who got on their backs, though Readis had always considered Delky to be especially his, since she'd been a gift. The canines responded better to some folks than to others, so maybe it was one of those universal attributes he'd learned of from reading in the Aivas files.

"How people know to be dolphineers if no one knows who you are?" Delfi asked.

If Readis had needed any confirmation of how intelligent dolphins were, that remark certainly clinched it.

"Well now, you have a point, Delfi," he said, settling more comfortably on the ledge, his feet dangling. "Just tell folks that there is now a dolphineer and a dolphin crafthall." Readis wasn't exactly certain how one established a crafthall, but Master Benelek had and so had Master Hamian, when he decided to specialize in the plastic materials that the Ancients had made so much use of. Someone had to start someplace, sometime, and for a good reason. He believed that he had one; the care of the dolphins who had been neglected by humans for so long in their struggle to survive Threadfall. "Was there a dolphin crafthall at Landing?"

"Where the bell rings is where we go. Is not crafthall?" Tursi asked. Readis recognized him by the network of old scrapes on his rostrum. He was very pleased that he was learning to identify the individuals of the pod so quickly.

"I wouldn't qualify then—I've got no bell," Readis said.

"No bell?" "No bell!" "No bell!" The phrase went from dolphin to dolphin.

"That's why I had to swim out to you, I had no bell to ring."

Clicks and hisses, and much blowing out of their holes as they turned from one to another.

"Tomorrow bell," Cal said at the end of this cryptic discussion.

"Sure thing," Readis said amiably, grinning and reaching down to scratch Cal under her chin.

"Give good scritches," she said, dropping her jaw and leaning just hard enough into his hand to get him to increase the pressure. "We get bell." Then she flipped up and over the rest of the pod and started out of the cavern.

ANNE MCCAFFREY

Tursi had lifted his head for similar attentions; but, as abruptly, he pulled away and followed her out, the rest of the pod streaming behind, starting their characteristic leapings only when they were clear of the rock formations.

Readis watched them go, relieved that he had made such a good start and wondering what they were up to. Bells didn't grow on trees, after all. And so far dolphins had shown no real interest in human artifacts. He was also relieved to see them leave because fatigue was settling in on him, and hunger. He checked Delky's water and refilled it, gathered enough dry grass to keep her through the night, and finished the last of the previous day's fish stew before he gratefully laid himself down, dreaming dolphin songs.

Odd sounds roused him at dawn. By now he was accustomed to the various water noises made as the sea flowed in and out of the main cavern, so this unusual thunk, plus Delky's distressed snort, got him out of bed.

His arms were stiff and sore where the vest had rubbed him. He wondered what he could use from his small store of clothing to pad it adequately. He slipped his knife from his belt and peered out into the outer cave. Nothing, and no more sounds. Delky snorted again, but she no longer seemed frightened. He peered around the irregular opening to the outer ledge.

There on the stone was a lump, dripping. There were wet patches, too, suggesting that the lump had been deposited by wet bodies. Readis didn't see a dorsal fin in the cavern, nor could he see one outside. Straightening up and replacing his knife in the sheath, he went to examine the lump. Halfway to it, he realized it was rounded on the top, and he semijumped in his excitement to examine it. The heavy lump *was* indisputably bell-shaped, misshapen by centuries of encrustations. And it had no clapper, only the stout bar across the inside of the dome where a clapper could be hung. First he'd have to clean it up.

"A bell, my own bell," he murmured to himself, and he went to collect the hammer he had made, along with other rocks to use in place of proper chisels. "A dolphin bell makes a proper Dolphin Hall."

While he chipped away the accumulated layers, he kept one eye on the waters leading into the cavern. Dolphins were endlessly curious. Surely they'd come back to see how their offering had been received: to check that he was awake, to see what he did with the bell. He was almost sorry that no single fin cut the water.

He had to take a break to feed and water Delky. By his calculations, there'd be Threadfall sometime today and they'd better stay inside. And not only safe from Thread. He went as far as the patch of root vegetables to pull some to eat later: they were as tasty raw as cooked. He cut enough of the stout grasses to make a rope, broke a branch of a hardwood to make into the clapper arm, and for the actual clapper, picked up several sea-washed, smooth rocks that fit in his palm. He paused long enough by the fish trap to remove two good-sized yellowtails. The trap had been one of his real successes, and he blessed Unclemi for having taught him how to weave them properly.

He stirred up his fire, put his pot on the firestone to heat water, and then returned to the laborious chipping, pausing now and then to rest or work on the clapper. He hadn't that long before he had chipped down to the metal. The lip, once he got all the junk off it, was smooth but dull after its long immersion. He wondered if it would polish up. Was it bronze? Or steel? The Ancients had had good steel. Or maybe it was one of the other alloys they had favored.

It took him most of the day to clear the exterior, and then he had a time getting his tools in to scour the inside. He stopped only briefly when he heard Delky's fearful squeal and saw her swinging as far inside the cavern as possible. Outside, the gray rain of Threadfall hissed against the surface of the water. He saw fish heads protruding to eat of the skybourne bounty, but not a single dolphin. He checked Delky's tether, but it was firm, and she wasn't likely to bolt out of safety no matter how scared she was. Then he returned to his work. He was constantly scraping his knuckles, and they got bloody and sore from the knocking. He couldn't quite get the stuff at the very top of the bell but managed to clear the hanging bar so he could attach the grass thong to hold the clapper. So, by the light of his fire, he wove grasses about the roundest of the stones he'd picked up and attached it to the hanger. He had trouble getting the grasses over the bar, partly because the light from the fire had died down so much that he couldn't really see. Finally, when he realized he hadn't eaten, he put his work aside, determined to finish that night and have a proper dolphin bell to ring the next morning, but by the time he had grilled a yellowfish, chewing on a root vegetable while it cooked, and eaten it, he could barely keep his eyes open. His scraped and bruised knuckles hurt, his shoulder muscles were knotted from the laborious chip-chipping, and he never even made it to his bed, curling up by the remains of his fire and falling instantly asleep.

He woke with a start, but that was more from the discomfort of his chilly position on cold stone than from an external sound. His bad leg was very stiff and spasmed, knocking against the bell. It gave a soft *bong* that delighted him. He picked up the clapper arm and very softly tapped the rock against the rim of the bell. Not quite a perfect sound, but indisputably a bell ring! Would the dolphins have heard that muted sound? He needed a belfry, too, and a long rope that would dangle in the water for them to pull.

Quickly, he stoked up the fire, gutted and filleted the second yellowtail, and put it on the cooking rock. Then he picked up the bell and the clapper. His fingers were slightly swollen from the previous day's exertions, and it took him quite a time—he nearly lost his temper twice—to get the grass around the hanging bar and secure the clapper arm. And then the bell pull.

He made himself eat the fish—it was tastier hot than cold—before he rose, hand on the clapper, and carried the bell to the water ledge. There was a protrusion near the entrance to the cavern. He put the bell down and returned to his supplies for more of the rope he had twisted. At last he hung the bell, wincing every time it issued a small complaint in the process. Delky kept one wide, white eye on him, not quite sure what he was doing. He hoped she wouldn't panic when he rang the bell.

The sun was only just up in the east, he noted, so the pod would have finished its morning feed. He couldn't have timed it better if he'd tried.

Taking a deep breath, he grabbed the pull rope and listened critically to the sound that reverberated through the cave.

"Not bad," he said as the still slightly sour *bong* echoed in his ears. Then he rang the Come-in sequence. Not that a Report to celebrate the hanging of the bell wouldn't be appropriate, but Report was urgent: Come-in gave them an option.

As if they'd been waiting just outside the cave for the slightest bell sound, sleek gray bodies glistened under the pool water and heads lifted right under him.

"Bell ring! Ring bell!" "We come!" "We come!" "Reporrit!" "Reporrit!"

"No report, you silly fish faces," Readis said, laughing with relief and delight. "I only rang Come in."

"We come in!" "We come in!"

Then the bell rope was yanked out of his grasp and enthusiastically pulled as a dolphin discovered it hanging down in the water.

"Hey, hey," Readis cried, grabbing for the clapper. The ringing was like thunder all around him in the confines of the cavern. He should probably place it outside or he'd be deafened. Delky was rearing and kicking, screaming with panic. "Easy, there, now. Easy!" He meant the advice for both runner and dolphin. He was also none too sure that the grasses would hold under such ardent manipulations.

Then he knelt down at the side and delivered scratches on all the chins that were presented. "Where did you find that bell? I couldn't believe it when I saw it yesterday morning. It took all day to clean it up."

"Bell long lost," Cal said. "Long, long, long."

Readis grinned at the delphinic repetitions. He really must teach them "good, better, best," though Cal's pod spoke very well: much better than even the Paradise River ones.

"Did you find it on the sea bottom?"

"We find. We bring. You fix. You ring." Loki said. He identified her by the splotch on the side of her melon.

"Loki! You're a poet! Did you know that?" Readis exclaimed.

"Yes. I poet, I know it. See?"

Readis howled so with laughter that he lost his balance and sprawled on the ledge, repeating her words while dolphins faces regarded him in their constant amusement and clicked and squee'ed.

"You have bell now. Need long-feet, mask, tank so you can swim far with pod!"

That sobered Readis almost instantly. "That would cost more marks than I have ..." And Readis suddenly realized that such marks as he did have were back in his dormitory room. Or, if Master Samvel had taken his long absence as a withdrawal from the school, maybe his belongings had been returned home. Either way, the marks were out of his reach, as was the aqua-lung. "And I don't have any to buy an aqua-lung, even if one could be made."

"No thing left over?" Cal asked.

"If you mean diving stuff from the Ancients' time, no, they didn't last the way the bell did. Where did you find it?"

"Where storm sink Dunkirk ships," Cal said as if the event had taken place recently and not nearly twenty-five hundred Turns before.

"And you know where that was?"

"Still find man things when bad storm turn over," Cal said, and Readis was astonished.

"How *could* you remember something that happened so long, long, long ago?" he asked, absently scratching her chin again.

"The Tillek. She holds history in her head."

"Now, don't tell me there's a dolphin who's twenty-five hundred Turns old."

"No, not tell what isn't true. But she knows from *her* Tillek."

"Oh, you've sort of a Harper Hall?"

"We have the Tillek," Cal repeated firmly. "You must have lung to go see the Tillek. You must go see the Tillek."

"I'd love to. When I'm able." Readis sighed. "If I ever am."

"If you be dolphineer, you meet the Tillek." Once again Cal spoke so definitively that Readis gave a wistful chuckle.

"I be dolphineer, already. I have bell, I have cave, I have you! Did you eat well yesterday on Thread?"

"Eat good, good, good," squee'ed some of the other pod members. "Too bad, bad, bad, men don't eat."

"Well, that's the way it is, fellas," Readis said. "And I'd better eat," he added as his stomach rumbled.

A large rainbow fish was flipped to the ledge, and instinctively he grabbed it by the gills before it could wriggle off. A second one followed the first, and then a large leaf, two beautiful shell fragments, and a barnacle-encrusted object.

"You eat, then we swim. Much to show you."

"I've no long-feet, no lung. And my . . ." He had started to mention the abrasions the vest had made and how loath he was to put it back on and risk opening those barely healed scrapes.

"You dolphineer. Your pod swim you safe," Tursi said with such authority that Readis could only laugh.

He took care of Delky while the rainbow cooked. After his breakfast, he collected more wood for his fire, and banked the coals with wet seaweed. He also lavished scratches and pattings on the waiting pod. Occasionally one of them would pull the bell, just to hear it ring. Finally, Delky had become so accustomed to the sound that she didn't so much as twitch an ear when it rang.

The "much" the dolphins had to show him had to do with the coastline up to the mouth of the deep gorge of what the Ancients had called the Rubicon River. It required him to swim with the pod long but thrilling hours. When he needed to drink they seemed to know where little brooks and freshettes drained into the sea. They provided him with fish whenever he needed, they also kept up their gifts of items that attracted them. Almost every morning there were offerings. He'd removed only four bloodfish, so he felt he hadn't earned any special gifts, but he remained grateful for anything. Once they brought him a "man thing," a plastic crate with one side knocked in, but the color was as bright, when he cleaned off the clinging mud, as the day it had been made. They told him there were more where that came from. Over the next few weeks, he acquired seven, three of which were filled now with "treasures."

Winter storms had set in, so he also had days when it was inadvisable for him to swim with the pod. The sea would lash waves into floods over the ledge and he'd have to bring Delky inside with him. The wind found all kinds of crevices to howl into, so that he often had to stuff his ears with plugs he made from fibrous plants. Invariably, if he went to the ledge at low tide, there'd be a fish left high and relatively dry, for him to eat. Occasionally branches with the tougher-stemmed fruits clinging to them would be added as special treats. It amazed him that the dolphins knew what humans could eat.

During the first of those storms, he padded the rough spots of the vest. He wore it as a "man thing"—his excuse to them—but there were many occasions when the vest kept him from being half drowned by the enthusiastic aquabatics of his companions. They began to learn how to swim with him, not over or under or impeding his movements. They could not quite understand why he had to spend time out of the water because his skin began to shrivel and slough off. He learned to qualify such matters as "man" things as opposed to "dolphin" or "sea and marine" things. He also tried experimenting with wood to carve the best approximation of "long-feet" he could; he tied these to his feet with a mixed grass and tail-hair rope. But the devices were too cumbrous and either twisted off—as he couldn't carve a 'pocket' for his feet without breaking off a piece of wood—or banged into dolphin bodies. They never complained, but he could see the darker marks on their skin, which he knew he had caused with his wooden water shoes.

His days were so full now of sea work that he almost considered turning Delky loose. It wasn't fair to keep her standing in the cave. Declining to go with the pod one day, he used all the rope he had made to cordon off a pen for her, not far from the cave but with enough grass and shelter from the sun for her old hide and by one of the many brooks so she'd have water. As he kept a calendar on his cave wall to mark off Thread days, he could always keep her in when she might be in danger from Fall. That way, he didn't feel as bad about confining her. With no other runners to lure her away, Delky was content with these arrangements.

He was therefore horrified to return late one evening to find evidence of a bloody struggle, bushes knocked over and trees scarred with kick-marks and no sign whatever of Delky. Searching the little paddock to discover what had attacked her, he finally found clear paw prints and knew his old friend had fallen victim to one of the huge cats. He blamed himself, and was disconsolate for days after Delky's removal. The size of the paw prints dissuaded him from going after the beast with only a belt knife to defend himself. His father had always rounded up all the men in the Hold to go after the big marauders. He missed her for more practical reasons later on, when mourning turned to regret: he had no more of her long strong tail hairs to braid into rope.

He also had very few clothes left. It was apparent that the dolphins had not informed people of his whereabouts. There were moments, despite his full and exciting life with the pod, when he could almost wish they had disobeyed him. But then Cal or Tursi or Loki the Poet would do or say something and make him so glad that he was a part of their lives that his mood would swing up again.

The worst of the storm season passed, and he could gather some of the green shoots that supplied nutrients he didn't get from fish or what root vegetables remained in his immediate environs. He really ought to start a garden in the glade where he'd kept Delky, he thought. Her manure would be good fertilizer. He knew what to plant and where to get the starts, and took some time off from the pod to organize his garden. That's when he came across Delky's tail. He almost didn't bring it back with him. The urge to bury it as a tribute to its former owner was great, but common sense overcame sentiment and he made a bundle of the long hairs and stuffed them in the pack he had with him.

On his way back he heard the bell, heard the Report sequence, and broke into as fast a run as he dared with the precious starts and sprouting plants he had gathered. Constant swimming had improved the muscles in his bad leg so that he could achieve a respectable speed, but he was breathless by the time he reached his cavern.

There was only one dolphin, pulling the bell, and that surprised him. It was also the largest dolphin he had ever seen. That should have warned him.

"I'm here, I'm here," he blurted out, breathless, prop-ping his pack against the inner wall before approaching the pool. "Is someone hurt? Where's Cal? Tursi?"

"They come when I call," the dolphin said, rearing her splendid head up, her flippers out of water.

"Are you hurt? Do you have a bloodfish?"

"Yes, I come to you to remove bloodfish," she said. "It cannot be scraped off." She turned on her side and eased slowly by him until he saw the bloodfish, precariously near her sex organs.

"Good thing I honed my knife, then," he said, and slipped into the water. "Over here. And what's your name, please?" he asked as he took three good strokes to where an underwater protuberance gave him a place to stand while he ministered to dolphin needs. "I like to know the name of my patients," he added jovially in what he had decided was his "healering" mode.

"I was called Theresa," she said, gargling her words slightly as she remained heeled over to place herself close to him.

"That's a very fine name. One of the originals, isn't it?" he asked. "I'm Readis."

"Your name is known. You call yourself the dolphineer."

"You speak really well, Theresa," Readis went on, his fingers, now deft at this task, assessing the depth of the bloodfish's sucker. Often now he could get the whole thing out without severing the head first. If he punctured the thin skull at just the right point, the sucker released. He found the spot on the bloated body and inserted the thin knifepoint, and with a deft flip of the point, the bloodfish came off. With a flip of his wrist, Readis sent the parasite flying to the wall. It slipped down on a trail of blood until it lay, after two final convulsions before it expired, gape-mouthed. "I'm always glad to get rid of those vicious things for you." He looked down at the minute hole and shoved water hard against her flank to rinse the puncture. "There, that should close shortly."

"Thank you, that was well done, dolphin healer."

"Oh, I'm not a healer by any means, though I can do small repairs now," Readis said, washing his knife blade before returning it to its sheath. And he'd need a new one soon, as the salt water was rotting the leather. Whatever had the Ancient dolphineers used? More of their versatile plastics?

"I had heard of major healings?" She eased herself back so that she could focus her eye on him.

He smiled down at her, accustomed to such dolphin maneuverings. She was one big mother. And old, judging by the scars on her melon, though all looked long healed. Could she be full of calf? Near to birthing? None of his pod were carrying young. He very much wanted to be present during a birth. It was such a magical moment, especially in the sea.

"Don't I wish I was able for major stuff," Readis said, leaning back against the side of the pool, still supported underwater by the wide protuberance. "Maybe I could get more training . . . but I'd need to have more people working with me as dolphineers before I could take time off."

"You are not the only dolphineer," she startled him by saying.

"I'm not?" He jerked bolt upright, the sudden movement whooshing water over her eye. She blinked.

"There are dolphineers at Eastern Weyr, at Monaco Bay"—she was the only dolphin he had heard pronounce it correctly—"Paradise River, Southern, Ista, Tillek, Fort, Nerat Bay . . ."

"There are?" His heart sank within him. He would not

be the first new dolphineer. The new Hall he had so proudly thought he might found was a dream dying in a single, casual sentence. Others had preempted his grand idea. He might as well go home now and take whatever punishment his father decreed for him. He probably wouldn't be able to go back to school, so he'd lost that opportunity, too. He might even have lost the best chance to secure Paradise River. But he would have to make it very plain to his mother that he must swim with dolphins. He couldn't give that up now. He was nearly eighteen now, he realized suddenly, if he'd counted days correctly. He was old enough to go off on his own in any case. Maybe, maybe, he could just come back here. He already had the makings of a small hold. And if he could prove enough land around him, under the terms of the Ancients' Charter, he could own that. And he'd have Cal and Tursi to swim with, he could listen to Loki's poems, and . . .

"Come, swim with me, Readis," Theresa said in the very gentlest tone he had ever heard a dolphin use.

"I'm sorry, Theresa, I don't feel much like swimming right now." For all he was nearly eighteen now and thus considered a man, a sob caught in his throat and he turned his face from the dolphin's knowing eye.

He was knocked off his perch by a deft swipe of her rostrum. He was coughing as he bobbed up, and she was facing the cavern entrance.

"Come, Readis, swim with me."

"I need my vest." He extended one arm toward the ledge, meaning to climb back up.

"No vest is needed if you swim with Theresa," he was told, and he was nudged away from the side of the pool.

"I didn't mean to offend you . . ."

"None taken," she replied.

He caught her dorsal fin with his right hand. Her tow

was deceptively smooth, but the speed with which he passed out of the cavern told him she was fast. Just outside the cave, they were joined by others, and Cal poked her head up on the other side of him, grinning.

"You help her?" Cal asked.

"She had a wicked bloodfish, yes, and I removed it."

He was being pulled with such speed that he had more water in his mouth than words and gestured that he couldn't speak. Then he saw that the entire pod was there, ranged on either side of Theresa. Some were in advance, leaping and diving as if they escorted a ship. Behind him, others were dipping in and out, but more sedately than usual, not displaying the more athletic maneuvers. He spotted Loki and she rolled her head at him before dipping her nose under again.

Theresa just kept swimming, heading directly toward the Great Western Current. He'd been out to it several times with the pod, and been caught up in the incredible current, fearless only because he had been in the company of dolphins.

They were nearly upon the ships before he realized that her bulk had kept him from seeing them bearing down on them.

Two ships, one of them Master Idarolan's *Dawn Sisters*, and the other, Alemi's *Fair Winds*.

"Oh, no, Theresa." He dropped his hand and was immediately upheld by Cal on his left.

"Take hold, Readis," Theresa said, screwing her head around so that he could not deny hearing her words. "You will come with me."

"She speak, you obey!" Cal said, squeeing emphatically.

That was when Readis had the first suspicion. Later he realized how stupid he had been. Just then more pods could be seen, leaping and diving, plunging and cavorting, all heading toward the ships, which had furled their sails and seemed to be standing still. Sea anchors out, he thought in his bemusement. As they neared, and Theresa was closing the distance with incredible speed, he could see that each ship had a longboat in the water beside it, and that there were dolphins clustered all around. He'd never heard that dolphins had Gathers, but that's the word that came to mind. According to what Kib and Afo had suggested, the only time dolphin pods met was in the Northwest at the Great Subsidence for . . .

"You're the Tillek, Theresa!" he shouted. He lost his grip, and swallowed a mouthful of water that had him gasping for breath and grasping for the nearest solid form. Which happened to be the Tillek, Theresa, and that made him reach for any other form, for to grab at *her* seemed tantamount to sacrilege.

"Hold me, Dolphineer," he was commanded, and his hand was flung up and landed against the dorsal fin, which he obediently clutched.

"I shouldn't—" he gasped. "It's not right. You're the Tillek."

Loud squees and clickings of approval answered him, and then they were so close to the longboats that he could hear the welcoming shouts. The Tillek swam him up to Master Idarolan's ship, and slowed to come to a complete stop, her flippers holding her steady with deft subtle movements, by the *Dawn Sisters'* longboat. Looking up, he saw his father, smiling, his mother, unsmiling but somehow looking proud, Alemi, and Kami, of all people, and she looked as if she was about to weep. Beyond her were T'gellan, the Benden Weyrleader, D'ram, T'lion, looking excessively pleased, a dour-looking man he didn't know, Master Samvel, Master Menolly, and Master Sebell. His father and Alemi held out their hands to him.

"Grab hold, Readis," Jayge called. Too surprised to disobey, he held up his arms and was hauled aboard. His mother herself handed him a big towel, even as she ran critical eyes up and down his tanned body as if she hadn't expected to find him in such good and healthy condition.

"Thanks, Mother," he mumbled, and didn't know what else to do because there was the Tillek herself raised up from the water to be part of whatever was about to transpire in the boat. For this had the feeling of more than the recapture of a recalcitrant truant.

"Well, Readis, lad," Master Idarolan said, planting his hands on his hips and grinning at him. "Led us a fine and merry chase you have, lad."

"I just wanted to help the dolphins," Readis said, speaking to his father despite the press of other important people around him. "No one else was."

Jayge took Readis's arm and pressed it affectionately, his expression wistful. "We know that now, son. And I honor you for what you did that day, despite what I said, and felt, at the time."

"I should never have said what I did," Aramina murmured right beside him, and there were tears in her eyes when he looked around at her.

"Ahem, we can't keep the Tillek waiting, friends," Master Idarolan said. "We are come at her request, Readis," he added.

"At her ..." Readis looked from the Fishmaster to the looming shape of the Tillek.

"She wishes you to be the Dolphineer," Master Idarolan said. "We've never had a Dolphin Hall on Pern ... never realized we *should* have had one all these years. But, well, she's been very understanding."

"The Thread caused many problems for humans," the Tillek said in a tone that suggested she really couldn't understand quite why. Beyond her, Readis could see the masses and masses of dolphin bodies. Why, every pod on Pern must be here! "We are grateful to men for many things. For history, for knowing what we are, and for giving us the tongue to speak. For speech is what raises the human—and us—above the animals and fish of land and sea."

"And you, Theresa the Tillek," Masterharper Sebell said, "are obviously my counterpart among dolphins."

"I do not play music makers. But I sing the songs of old so that the young do not forget the past and the old Earth and how men and women swim with us in these new seas."

"Close your mouth, Readis," his father murmured softly.

"But he said—she said—a Dolphin Hall?"

"A Dolphin Hall," Master Idarolan repeated.

"A Dolphincrafthall," said F'lar of Benden, "and I speak for all the Weyrleaders . . ."

"And I, Oterel of Tillek Hold, speak for the Lord Holders . . ." said the gaunt man Readis didn't know, and then he smiled and didn't look half as forbidding.

"And I for the Harper Hall," Sebell said, "that the new Hall is needed and is herewith situated at the sea caverns of . . . what will you call your place, Readis?"

"Huh? I don't know. I don't know anything . . ."

"Kahrain is the name we dolphins know of that place from the Ancients," the Tillek said.

"Kahrain Hold it will be then," Readis said, wondering if a man's heart could burst from his chest. "But I really don't have *much* of a Hold there right now, only the caves and the pools where I can do healing. And I'd need to learn much more healing to be a *good* dolphineer . . ."

"That has been promised you," the Tillek said, and

ducked down into the water, rising again to blow out of her hole.

"Why? Why me? You said there were other dolphineers . . ." Readis said, almost accusing her of gentle treachery.

"There are!" T'lion said, bursting with the news. "Because Gaddie wants to help, too, and T'gellan has given his permission for me to spend my free time with you and the dolphins. I've copied another set of medical stuff for you, too, Readis . . ."

Readis began to shiver suddenly, though the sun was warm and the breeze mild.

"He is cold and needs hot food," the Tillek said. "We will retire and return when he has been cared for." She either did not hear or did not care to acknowledge the outraged "Well, I never" from Aramina, for she went on: "You swim strong and well, Dolphineer Readis. You will be Tillek and Thea to all in your hold." Then she disappeared below the side of the longboat. Stunned by all that had just happened, Readis stared at the space she had been occupying until he saw her long body gracefully arch out of and then back in the water, many dolphins following her away from the ships.

Readis was then bundled up the rope ladder and into Master Idarolan's cabin, and given hot soup and hot klah and made much of by his mother, attentions that he endured out of gratitude for the day and for her forgiveness. His father handed him a new shirt and muttered something about other things that had been brought along that he would possibly need. Then, with Aramina still anxiously hovering over him, he was ushered back out to the deck. There everyone else on this extraordinary voyage had wineglasses, which were being topped up by Master Idarolan's seamen.

"Now, lad, I've some cargo destined for your new Hold," Master Idarolan said, handing Readis a full glass. "I know the Tillek wants to talk to you further . . ."

"I think I'd like to talk to *you* first," Readis said, including his father and mother with a glance in their direction. "I didn't know anyone knew where I was."

"We have for the past three sevendays," Jayge said, laying an arm across his son's shoulders. When he saw Readis glance suspiciously toward the sea, he added, "No, the dolphins didn't tell on you."

"I've been on daily sweeps trying to find you, and then I saw the seaside caves and I figured that they were so perfect for you and dolphins, you had to be there," T'lion said, looking very pleased with himself. "Only, what with one thing and another, Gaddie and I didn't get a chance to check the place out. Made yourself right comfortable, didn't you?"

"I got by fine," Readis said, a remark calculated to take the anxious expression off his mother's face and, at the same time, prove to his father that he'd coped well.

"Then," Master Idarolan said, beaming at all impartially, "I was approached by no less than the Tillek herself. The dolphins at Paradise River were upset when you didn't return."

"I got questioned by the Eastern pod," T'lion put in. "And so did Master Persellan—who forgave me, by the way!"

"That's a relief," Readis said.

"And the Tillek asked me when would dolphineers come back to the sea to work with her pods," Idarolan went on. "So naturally I informed Lord Oterel . . ." He gestured to the Lord Holder.

"And I asked T'bor of High Reaches and he . . ." Oterel said, turning to the Masterharper.

"Didn't know anything about dolphin pods, and while I knew a little from Menolly here," Sebell said, "I conferred with Alemi, who told me of your disappearance, Readis, and why. I also spoke to . . ."

"Us," Lessa said, picking up the tale in her turn, "and I remembered something that Master Robinton had told me about these creatures." She turned to D'ram.

"And I remembered all the tapes which Aivas had shown of the early days when there were dolphineers," the old Weyrleader said, and then shrugged. "So the Tillek went to Paradise River and spoke to your parents."

"She asked us," Jayge said, looking slightly embarrassed while Aramina ducked her head and nervously twitched the hem of her tunic, one of her Gather tunics, Readis now noticed, "if we objected to your becoming a dolphineer."

Readis waited.

"It is an honor to be asked," his mother said softly, hesitantly, before raising her head to look him straight in the eye. "I was once asked to accept an honor—" She shot Lessa a quick glance. "—and could not. I cannot stand in your way, Readis."

"Thank you, Mother," he murmured, his throat blocked with the surge of relief and happiness.

"You're in for a lot more training before you can become a Craftmaster, young Readis," Master Idarolan said, "but you've made a fine start. Ahemm . . ." He cleared his throat. "However, the Tillek plans to instruct you herself, which is why she has come all the way down from her natural habitat."

"She will?" Readis closed his mouth as soon as he realized that it had dropped open in surprise.

"She has insisted," Sebell said with a wry grin. "She is

the living repository of all delphinic history, tradition, and knowledge."

"She speaks the best of any dolphin I've ever heard," Readis said.

"She claims it's because she has had to repeat the Words and the History every spring to all the new dolphins wishing to take the Test. I gather that's swimming across the Great Subsidence whirlpool."

Readis nodded and then asked softly, "I wouldn't have to do that, would I? I mean, I'm a good enough swimmer but . . ."

Sebell wasn't the only one to chuckle. "She'll set her own test, and you should know that you've already passed the critical entrance examination."

"I did?"

"You did. That's why she brought you to us."

"You'd have all just gone home?" Readis was astonished.

"No, we'd've gone in and brought you back home, lad," Alemi said, "and no blame."

"Oh!"

"Listen!" Menolly said, holding up one hand. "Listen!"

"To what?" Idarolan asked, but now Sebell held up his hand, too, and they fell silent. Even the sailors in the rigging and on deck stopped what they were doing, as the odd but melodious sound reached their ears.

"Music, but where is it coming from?" Sebell said, glancing around the ship.

"I've heard that before," Aramina murmured to Jayge, and leaned close to him. "Only it's not—quite—the same."

"It's not so lonely a sound," Menolly said as she swung slowly to face the sea. That's when those on deck saw the wedge of leaping dolphins coming alongside. Suddenly

Menolly jumped back in surprise as a loud squee was clearly heard.

"The big one's back, Master," one of the seamen in the rigging said, pointing. He, too, involuntarily flinched away as the Tillek reared high from the sea.

"Readis," she said plainly before she fell back into the water.

"Coming," he said, and started toward the rail. Then he paused, startled by his own compliance, and not sure he could just leave the eminent company on the *Dawn Sisters'* deck. "Do I just go?"

"When your Master calls, lad, you go," Idarolan said, grinning, and giving him an encouraging push on his way.

"We'll drop the supplies off at your caves," Alemi shouted after him.

"Listen well, learn hard," Sebell added.

"We're proud of you, son," his father said just as Readis arched himself in a dive over the railing and into the sea, carefully aiming at the space left free for him by the dolphins waiting there.

EPILOGUE

▼▼▼▼▼▼▼▼▼▼▼▼▼▼▼▼▼▼▼▼▼▼▼▼

T he dragonriders stayed a while longer, talking about this unusual meeting between humans and dolphins and eating the small repast that Master Idarolan had had prepared.

"Sometimes, I feel that we are rushing forward at unbelievable speeds," Menolly remarked, "with hardly time to catch our breaths. So much has happened!"

Sebell nodded. "And not enough time to make songs out of most of it." He gave his wife a droll smile and ducked as she playfully swatted at him.

"The song . . ." Aramina said, leaning toward Menolly. "The song we heard. Where did you hear it?"

"At night, near the sea, I must admit. And . . ." Menolly paused, frowning. "At Paradise River when I was there harpering the children. You've heard it?"

"Yes," Aramina said in a sad, wistful tone. "I always

thought it was a dream, but I wasn't always asleep when I heard it."

"When you think how long the dolphins have waited for us to acknowledge them again, it would make any creature sad," Sebell said, slipping a reassuring arm about his wife.

"Dragons don't sing, so I knew it wasn't them, but Ramoth has complained about 'lonely' sounds impinging on her sleep," Lessa said. Then, with a brisk twist of her shoulders, she smiled at Aramina. "Now we all know, don't we, that the dolphins of Pern are part of our future. I like to think, one of the better parts of our future when this Pass is over."

"When this Pass is over!" Master Idarolan said loudly, raising his glass.

And the others drained their glasses to that toast!

ABOUT THE AUTHOR

ANNE MCCAFFREY shuttles between her home in Ireland and the United States, where she picks up awards and honors and greets her myriad fans. She is one of the field's most popular authors.